the

SCORE

BETH BOLDEN

CHAPTER 1

Carter Maxwell was out of control.

The tsunami of rage rising inside him was familiar enough he could recognize it easily, but recognizing meant jack shit, because feeling it didn't mean that he could actually fucking control it.

They'd lost.

The scoreboard felt permanently etched into his eyelids. Even when he closed his eyes, like he was doing right now, he could still see it.

The Condors had lost to the Piranhas by two touchdowns.

It didn't matter that he'd scored one of the few touchdowns the Condors had managed over the course of the game.

Carter had wanted this game for himself; yeah, of course he had, but the truth was, he'd wanted it so much more for Micah—and for the whole team.

Proving that they'd left that shit from last year behind once and for all.

But you didn't, that voice inside him, with its nasty, sly tone, reminded him. *You can't ever leave it behind. You're never leaving anything behind. You're carrying it with you forever.*

Fuck.

Carter's fists clenched, and he tried to relax them by degrees, but they wouldn't unclench.

He'd need to get up from this bench soon.

He could feel eyes on him. So many fucking eyes. Not just in the Condors' stadium, but everywhere, the cameras trained on him.

No doubt all the media were saying their usual bullshit.

Carter Maxwell's lost it again.

Carter Maxwell doesn't have it. Maybe he never did.

Carter Maxwell's gonna find himself on a new team next year.

You know how many teams Carter Maxwell has been on? The most in the NFL in his short tenure.

Nobody wants him.

Nobody can handle him.

He can't even handle himself.

It wouldn't bother him so much if it weren't all true.

He felt a body drop down next to him, but Carter didn't open his eyes. Didn't trust himself if he did.

And wasn't that the whole fucking problem?

He didn't trust himself.

How was anyone else supposed to trust him—how were *Riley* and his teammates supposed to trust him if he couldn't even believe enough to trust himself?

"You alright?"

Carter didn't know who he'd expected the person to be.

But Grant Green—known as Mr. G to his team since he'd bought the Condors in the offseason—was the *last* person he'd expected to come sit down next to him.

Carter braced himself. This was not going to be good. He could already feel it.

But instead of starting in on the inevitable lecture of *hold your temper, control your rage, if you can't, I'm gonna have to let you go or trade you again*—Mr. G said, "You alright, Carter?"

His tone was deceptively casual. Like Carter hadn't broken two tablets, destroyed countless pieces of equipment, and raged across the Condors' sideline and the locker room during halftime. Like *none* of that had happened.

Carter opened one eye.

Mr. G's expression was just as mild as his tone.

There wasn't even a hint of judgment in his gaze. Concern, yes, but judgment, no. Like what he worried about first and foremost wasn't the football team he'd spent nearly a billion dollars on, but Carter himself.

That, unfortunately, was not Carter's experience with the NFL so far.

"You alive in there?" Mr. G asked again, this time with a hint of a smile turning his lips up.

"Uh, yeah, I...I'm okay," Carter said cautiously.

He didn't know if it was true.

Now or in the future.

The coping mechanisms—he wasn't stupid enough to even call them that, because screwing your way across a city was hardly therapist approved—he'd been using forever weren't working so well anymore.

He knew it.

But he didn't know what else to do about it.

"You sure?" Mr. G asked.

Carter sighed. "No." He leaned over, resting his elbows on his knees.

Mr. G patted him on the back. "You want to do something about it?" The question was offered again without judgment and without pressure. Like it was actually Carter's choice. Like Mr. G would support him either way.

Carter didn't know what to say. Of course he wanted to change. Of course he didn't like being this way.

He didn't *enjoy* it.

Okay, well, that was partially a lie. He might not enjoy the problem, but he'd sure enjoyed the Band-Aid he slapped across it—the sex. If he didn't appreciate it, if he didn't get what he did out of it, it wouldn't work as well as it did.

Carter froze.

Maybe that was why it was no longer quite as effective as it had been.

Was he getting *tired* of sex?

God, that sounded fucking awful—and it made up Carter's mind for him.

"Yeah," he admitted. "Yeah, I *would* like to do something about it."

"I know you've talked to Mitchell a few times."

"You know Alec?" Alec Mitchell was one of the most renowned professional agents in the NFL. He managed a lot of very famous players—most of them queer, not particularly surprising since he was queer himself. And he'd famously turned around Chase Riley's career—another wide receiver with temper problems. Had helped him get control of himself.

At the time when that had happened, Carter had been a rookie, and full of disdain for someone who wanted to be controlled and boring versus a constant party.

But now he could see the appeal.

Mr. G nodded. "Known Alec for a while. He said you two went back and forth a few times a month or two ago, but it never went anywhere."

Carter felt *that* judgment—but as censure went it was astonishingly mild.

"As the owner aren't you supposed to *not* want us to have decent representation who'll milk you for every freaking dime?" Carter joked weakly.

Mr. G rolled his eyes. "I want you to have someone who'll fight for you and be in your corner. Who'll put you first. I do my best, but in the end, I gotta put the *team* first."

"You gonna do that now?" Carter wanted to swallow the question back down but it escaped before he could.

"You mean, am I going to trade you or drop you?" Mr. G paused. "No. This team is better with you on it than off it. And it seems to me like those other teams gave up on you way too quick. I'm stubborn. I'm not going to do that."

"Oh." Carter didn't quite know what to say to that. He *knew* he was good. But so many times his positives had been outweighed by all his negatives.

"But seriously, call Alec back. Get some help, Carter." Mr. G gave him another gentle slap on the back and then stood.

You need it, Carter heard Mr. G's unspoken admonition, but for once, it didn't sting even though he knew it was the truth.

Maybe because he was finally going to do something about it.

Two weeks later

Ian Parker sat across from Alec Mitchell, managing to keep his expression neutral as Alec settled into his chair, even though what he wanted, more than anything else in the fucking world, was to *be* Alec Mitchell.

He'd known him for several years now, because his mom, who was a therapist frequently working with NFL players and other athletes, had taken on a few of Alec's clients.

He and Alec weren't friends. Barely acquaintances. But Ian had still tried his best over the last six months to convince Alec just how serious he was about following in his footsteps and becoming an agent himself.

"Thanks for coming here, Ian," Alec said, shooting him a friendly smile. Alec was a friendly sort of person—until he wasn't. He was a wolf in sheep's clothing. A wolf who devoured both anyone who stood in his way *and* anyone who deserved it.

He'd gone up against so many heavy hitters in the NFL and he'd won every single fight.

It was the power Alec wore easily, like one of his famous three-piece suits, flawlessly tailored to his long, lanky body, and the comfortable, easy way he wielded it.

That was what Ian wanted—not power for power's sake, but the power to help others.

"Of course," Ian said. He did not say anytime Alec beckoned he was going to come running. Considering how smart and dialed in Alec was, *and* how many times Ian had subtly and not-so-subtly hinted at his future career aspirations, there was no way he didn't already know exactly what Ian wanted.

"I hear you're interested in becoming an agent," Alec said and Ian's heart rate accelerated.

Was this it? He'd been trying forever, hoping that Alec might give him a chance—or a job—and teach him how to *be* him.

He'd hoped that this might be what this summons was about, but he hadn't been sure.

"Yes," Ian said, nodding emphatically.

"You didn't go to law school," Alec observed. *He* had. Ian knew everything about Alec Mitchell. His history. All the fights. All the wins.

"I took some law classes." A *lot* of law classes, in fact.

"And certainly you know how to manage people," Alec said mildly.

An understatement. For the last five years Ian had been working as a sober companion. In the glittery shitstorm that was Los Angeles, he never had to look very far to find his next client. They didn't all stay sober, but it wasn't because Ian wasn't fully committed to helping them.

He was very good at his job, but that didn't mean he wanted to keep doing it.

"You could say that," Ian said, trying to match Alec's casual tone, and not quite making it there. Nobody could blame him; he wanted this chance too fucking badly.

"That's the biggest part of this job," Alec observed, leaning back in his chair. "The managing."

"I've heard that," Ian said cautiously.

"I've got this new client," Alec said. He stood, and began to pace behind his chair, worry creasing his face. "I'm not sure what to do with him."

"What to *do* with him?" Ian didn't understand and wasn't going to pretend even to get a job he wanted *very* much.

Be honest with him, he's too smart to not spot prevarication a million miles away, his mother had told him a hundred times. And while his mother drove him crazy half the time, he couldn't argue with her assessment of Alec Mitchell.

He was way too sharp for Ian to bother pretending anything.

Alec sighed. Rested his elbows against the back of his chair. "He's not got an addiction, per se, but I think he could use someone like you."

Ian hesitated. He didn't want to be hired as a sober companion; he wanted Alec to hire him to be an agent, to *teach* him how to be an agent. "You want Ian Parker the sober companion," he said.

"Yes, and no," Alec said, smiling now. "I want you to be his companion, yes. I want you to help him curb some of his worst tendencies, which are to indulge in booze and sex and parties, all to avoid and poorly attempt to control his temper. But I know you want more than that. So I thought we'd help each other. You help *him*, which will undoubtedly help me, and then I'll help you. You want to be an agent? I'll make that happen."

"You'll teach me? Hire me?"

"Yes," Alec said firmly.

Ian considered this. "Why can't you do this yourself?" he asked.

Was the situation so bad Alec couldn't do it himself and that meant it was a fool's errand for Ian too?

"He's on the east coast, and my husband would kill me if I spent the next few months in South Carolina," Alec said wryly.

Alec was married to a player himself: Spencer Evans, who was one of the best defensive ends of the last few decades. He'd finally won a Super Bowl last season with the Los Angeles Riptide, after Alec had succeeded in convincing the Stars, Spencer's old—and homophobic—team to trade him.

It was Alec's masterful handling of that situation that had convinced Ian he wanted to be an agent. He'd been interested before that, but after, Ian was one hundred percent convinced not only that he could be a great agent, but that he wanted to be a great agent just like Alec was.

Someone who fought for the people who belonged to him, with every weapon he could find. Even weapons that weren't weapons at all.

"It's Carter Maxwell, isn't it?"

Ian kept a very close eye on what not only Alec was doing, but the NFL in general. At first it had been easy, because his mother was a therapist to a number of players. And then, he'd done it because he'd realized if he was ever going to get what he wanted, being informed was the bare minimum requirement. He—and everyone else—had heard about Carter Maxwell's problems, and also when he'd started trying to deal with them by signing with Alec two weeks ago.

Alec nodded.

"I thought I could handle the situation from here," Alec said, "but if the last two weeks are any indication, that's not realistic. I need someone on the ground. Living in his house. Monitoring him. Helping him walk the right path. You're the perfect choice."

Carter Maxwell.

He was infamous for being traded more times than seasons he'd been in the NFL.

Infamous for his temper. For his voracious and unapologetic sexual appetite.

And for his gorgeous face.

"Well, not *perfect*," Alec added apologetically. "I guess the perfect choice would probably be someone who was asexual."

Ian had been out for a number of years—and no doubt that was one of the things Alec had discovered when he'd done his research on Ian.

Because there was no question that Alec had done his research.

"Carter's going to hit on me." Ian said it matter-of-factly.

Alec raised a flawlessly groomed dark eyebrow. He always looked this way—in those immaculate tailored suits, presenting an irreproachable front. Ian had dressed carefully this morning with that in mind. He didn't own suits, but he'd worn a fitted polo and a pair of slacks. He'd even cleaned and polished his best pair of loafers, and slipped into them this morning hoping they'd give him the confidence he couldn't quite own *yet*.

"Carter hit on *me*," Alec said.

Honestly, Ian couldn't really blame the guy. Alec was easily forty, but he was still attractive, with his chiseled bone structure, otherworldly light blue eyes, and the dark hair, swept back from that gorgeous face.

Of course, he was famously *married*, too.

But that didn't stop some guys.

Ian wouldn't have ever done it, because he wanted Alec to *hire* him, not fuck him.

But that would hardly stop Carter Maxwell.

From what Ian had heard, *nothing* stopped Carter Maxwell.

Not even the threat of Spencer Evans, one of the greatest defensive players in the NFL, pounding his face in for daring to hit on his husband.

"Noted," Ian said. Like he was taking the job. Which...of course he was taking the job.

"You'd be perfect if you were straight, too—though I wouldn't put it past Carter to turn a straight guy not-so-straight," Alec said wryly, "but otherwise, you're exactly the kind of person that I trust to handle Carter."

"He needs to be handled?"

It was kind of a stupid question.

"You didn't see the meltdown a few weeks ago? Against the Piranhas?"

Oh right. Yes, Ian *had* seen it, and he recalled the details. It had been major news. Or not so much major news as just another day at the office for Carter. But the sports media had covered it relentlessly, and then, a few days after, when Carter had dropped his agent and hired Alec instead.

The media had breathlessly wondered if Alec was going to be able to rein Carter in the way he'd done with Chase Riley.

Apparently the answer to that question was: *not quite as easily as he'd hoped.*

"Yeah, I saw it."

"He *wants* to be better. Came to me, because he thought I might be able to help him. I do think I can." Alec hesitated. "But I need someone *there* to do a lot of that day-to-day work."

"And that someone is going to be me."

"You're the best option I've got. Can you do it? Moira said you were between clients."

He was, because he'd been hesitating to take another one. He didn't particularly feel compelled to start the process over, so for the last few months, he'd been dithering, turning down perfectly good actresses and rock stars, who'd all heard great things about his work.

But he hadn't been motivated to help them, and the one thing he'd discovered after five years as a sober companion was it wasn't easy and he had to *want* to do it. Had to feel called to the work.

The only question was if he was willing—and *wanting*—to help Carter the way he clearly needed help. Obviously Ian was interested first and foremost because of the deal Alec had offered, but he knew there needed to be more.

"I can do it," Ian said.

"I thought you might be able to fit me in," Alec said, his smile turning warmer, more genuine. He morphed from the shark negotiating for every single inch into the man underneath, glad that Ian was joining the team.

"Tell me everything," Ian said.

Alec looked surprised.

"Do you think I ever go into a situation not knowing every detail? Or *wanting* to know every detail?" Ian challenged. "I can't say I always get what I need, but you're smart. You know Carter. You know what I need."

"Currently, we have a list of behavioral guidelines that I've asked him to follow." Alec slid a piece of paper across the desk.

Ian looked down at the list.

None of the bullet pointed items were a surprise.

No sex.

No more than 4 people invited to current residence.

No clubs.

No social media.

Curfew: 12 a.m. (unless as part of a team-sanctioned or sponsored event).

"And it's not going well, with all these restrictions?" Ian questioned.

Alec's sigh was heavy. Full of resignation.

"He told me last night when we talked that he thought they were more *guidelines*, not *rules*."

"So he's not following them."

Alec shrugged. "Half-heartedly, maybe. He's also going to therapy, with the hopes that he can learn some better coping mechanisms to control his temper."

"That sounds like a good start," Ian said. He already could guess who the therapist was, even though Alec hadn't necessarily specified.

She would do a good job with Carter. Moira Rogers was a consummate professional and had learned how to reach deep down in these emotionally stunted players and figure out how to help them get in touch with all the things professional athletics had told them weren't important.

"It *is* a good start. But last night, he didn't get in until after two a.m. And I'm pretty sure rule number one got blown to hell."

"How do you know?" Ian wondered if Carter Maxwell was an oversharer too, and that was another thing he'd need to learn to deal with. Honestly, though, he wasn't particularly worried about resisting Carter Maxwell's advances. Sure, the guy was hot. Sure, the guy was built. But he'd been hit on by half of Hollywood, and Ian had exceptional self-control. He wasn't controlled by his dick; *he* controlled *it*.

"How do I know?" Alec chuckled. "He *told* me. He had sex with not just one, but *three* people last night."

Three people. *Jesus.*

"And," Alec added, "he was *very* sorry, but he clearly did not regret it."

"Oh. Well. I guess it's good he's not in a habit of hiding things?" That was a start. Ian had had a few clients over the years who'd believed the sober agreement they'd signed meant that as long as *he* didn't find out about what they were doing, they were good.

But that was not the way it worked.

"He's definitely transparent," Alec admitted.

"Does he know you're hiring me?"

"I told him I was working on an altered plan." Alec paused. "We'll fly out tomorrow, together. Meet with the Condors' owner and the head coach. When I say you're going wherever Carter goes, I mean, *you're going wherever Carter goes*. We're not taking any more chances."

"I can do that." He often had similar arrangements with his sober clients, though the idea was when they were in recovery, they returned to their regular lives carefully, and not all at once. Unlike Carter, who, halfway through the season, had no choice but to continue to play football.

Ian had a feeling that to be successful at this particular task, he was going to have to throw out a lot of his standard practices and adapt on the fly. This was not going to be easy. In fact, he already had a feeling Carter was going to be his hardest client to date.

"We'll fly on my private jet. I'll have my assistant forward the itinerary," Alec said.

Was it any surprise Ian wanted to be him? The man had a freaking private jet, and he'd gotten it by being *freaking awesome*.

"How long should I prepare to be there for?"

Alec shrugged one shoulder. "Two months. At least. Maybe more. Maybe through the whole season."

"He needs that much help?"

"Listen, I know a lot of this might seem like an overreaction. Believe me, I wish it was. But he needs *hands-on* help. And after he figures his shit out, I don't trust him not to backslide right back to where he was."

"Right." Ian got it. Once, he'd spent eight months with a very famous actress. She still sent him a Christmas card every year. *And* even more importantly, she was still sober.

Major change took time.

"I know this goes without saying but..." Alec inhaled sharply, like he couldn't quite believe what he was saying. "You can't have sex with him. You absolutely cannot have sex with him."

Ian stared at the man in front of him.

"I know," he said slowly. "I don't sleep with my other clients, either. *Ever.*"

"No offense, but your other clients aren't Carter Maxwell. The man's slippery as hell. Charming as all get-out. Friendly and sweet, like the most adorable puppy dog you've ever seen, and so you let down your guard. Begin to trust him. And then he cranks the sexual magnetism up to eleven, and it's...well, nobody could blame you for being tempted. The man could tempt a saint. A whole *bunch* of saints, in fact."

Ian raised an eyebrow.

"Not *me*, obviously," Alec said. He flushed. "I'm *very* happily married, which you know. I just...I've heard stories. A lot of stories."

"Believe me," Ian said, emphasizing each and every word, "me wanting to sleep with Carter Maxwell is *not* going to be a problem."

Alec did not look reassured, but what else could he do? He'd warned Ian, and Ian knew his own limits and his own self-control, both of which were substantial. Plus, he had no intention of fucking this up, because this was the chance he'd been gunning for, since he'd known he wanted to be an agent.

"I sure fucking hope not," Alec said.

Chapter 2

Ian had spent the last twenty-four hours stuffing his brain full of every single detail about Carter Maxwell that was available publicly—and not so publicly, either.

He'd grilled Alec nearly the whole flight about Carter's history and his personal impressions.

He'd stopped just short of reaching out to Moira and asking for her session notes—mostly because he knew she wouldn't share them. Alec had told him that he'd start forwarding on Moira's progress reports, but Ian already knew those contained the bare minimum.

Still, despite all the footage he'd watched and the information he'd read and heard, he was not prepared for the presence of Carter Maxwell when the man himself walked into the conference room in the Condors' facility.

Grant Green, the owner of the team, was already seated next to Alec, casually chatting with him about some of Alec's other clients.

Next to Carter was a man Ian recognized as Jonathan Kelley, the head coach of the Condors.

And then there was Carter himself.

Their eyes met, and Ian hated that he felt a jolt. Wanted to deny that he felt a jolt. But the jolt was undeniable, surging from his toes up to his stomach and then practically blowing the top of his head right off.

Carter was hot, *yeah*. Ian had expected that. He'd tried to immunize himself to the hotness by looking at about a hundred pictures of the guy.

But pictures and video didn't do his size or his body or his magnetism justice.

In person, they all fused together into one lethal combination.

Ian swallowed his reaction down, all too aware that Alec was watching him closely.

Monitoring him to make sure he could handle himself, and goddamn it, he *could*.

Then Carter smiled, and Ian realized just what Carter's superpower was. He turned those warm golden-brown eyes on you—sincere and inviting—and you wanted to be his friend.

You wanted him to trust you. You wanted him to laugh with you. You wanted him to have everything he wanted.

Including *you*, if it came to that.

And Ian had a feeling it nearly always did.

"Carter," Alec said in measured tones, "good to see you."

Carter grinned, wild and easy and carefree. *Holy fuck*, that was a potent look. "Alec, here to chastise me in person." He did not sound even remotely disappointed or ashamed about this. "I must be pretty damn special."

"You know you are," Alec said, sounding a little testier. He turned to Ian. "This is Ian Parker. Ian is my associate, and he's going to be my representative here."

Ian only had a moment before Carter turned that megawatt smile on him. It was like being blasted with a furnace. "Representative? That seems pretty official."

"It is. It's as official as it gets," Alec emphasized. "Ian's been a sober companion for five years, and while sobriety isn't necessarily our aim here, I think his unique skill set is going to be a good match for your...your issues."

"There's definitely types of sobriety happening here. Sexual sobriety, for one," Ian said. He kept his voice ice cold. It took effort, but the effort would be worth it, because if he didn't, all of Carter's heat was going to melt his control like it was nothing.

"Oh, man, you're already killing me," Carter said, shooting him an impossibly brighter, more adorable slightly lopsided grin. "*Sexual sobriety*. God, shoot me now."

"You've been the recipient of *plenty* of shooting. More than any one person needs," Alec said sternly.

"Truth," Carter teased. "Well, it's nice to meet you, Ian, even if you sound like every party pooper I've ever met."

So he'd noticed. Well, good. Maybe the icy reserve he'd put up would keep Carter at arm's length, at a place where Ian could actually help him.

If he got too close...well, they just weren't going there. They *couldn't*.

Ian knew better.

"Yes, that's me, and don't expect that to change," Ian said, rising, and extending a hand. Carter shook it. His grip was firm and warm. A big hand, for sure. Warm and big and capable. He shook it briskly and then let go.

Carter looked him over appraisingly. "You think Ian's equal to the task?"

"He comes highly, highly recommended," Alec said. Ian noticed he didn't say *who* had made the recommendation. Alright, so Alec wasn't going to be divulging Ian's uniquely personal connection to Carter's therapist. It made sense, because Ian typically didn't and their last names were different, not necessarily for this reason, but it did come in handy.

Ian expected he would tell Carter himself, in a few days, when they were a little more used to each other.

"We trust Alec's assessment of the situation," Grant Green spoke up.

"Alec's brilliant, that's why," Carter said.

They did agree on that, at least.

"If I'm so brilliant, then you should listen to me more," Alec stressed.

"Yeah, I probably should."

"I'm assuming," Alec said, turning to the owner and the head coach, like Carter hadn't even spoken, "it won't be a problem to give Ian unlimited access to this facility."

"Is that necessary?" Coach Kelley asked skeptically.

"Yes," Alec and Ian said together.

He hadn't been one hundred percent sure before meeting Carter that Alec wasn't slightly exaggerating the need to keep Carter shadowed at all times. But now, after meeting him, Ian began to understand why Alec's prior efforts had failed.

According to Alec, Carter had made it clear he wanted to change. But it was hard to see it now, and even harder to believe it.

He seemed not exactly unrepentant but...unbothered.

Like he was just gliding along, wherever life took him, no worries or cares affecting him deeply. But Ian knew better, and knew there had to be subterranean shit going on that he was burying—until he couldn't anymore, and it came exploding out of him.

Basically, Carter said he wanted to enact change, but he wasn't particularly invested in doing it when everything seemed fine—which was most of the time.

The temptation to misbehave would be strong.

"Alright," Coach Kelley said with a shrug. "You've got my cooperation. Whatever's best for Carter, we'll do."

"Ditto. You just let me know what you need," Grant said, glancing over in Ian's direction.

"Access," Ian said steadily, "and cooperation."

Carter made a face, but even now he didn't seem particularly bothered.

"Done," Grant said. He stood, and so did Coach Kelley. "Carter, you've got practice in an hour. So better grab some lunch—and get acquainted with your new shadow."

"Yes," Alec agreed. "I'll let you know exactly what we'll need." He stood. The glance he shot in Ian's direction was easy to decipher. He wasn't to let Carter out of his sight, from this moment on.

"And, Carter," Alec said as he gathered his suit jacket and leather laptop bag, "remember the rules."

"I know the rules," Carter said.

"*Do you?*" Alec questioned mildly as he headed towards the doorway. "No sex. *No sex.*"

"Why do you keep repeating that one rule?" Carter complained. He flopped down in the chair opposite Ian. He waved in his direction. "I can control myself."

"You have to *choose* to control yourself," Alec reminded him.

"Then you shouldn't have given me *him*," Carter teased.

Alec made a face and shot Ian another look masquerading as a reminder that he needed to be *hands off*, which he did not need, thank you very much.

He had this.

"Don't you want to know what I meant by that?" Carter drawled, the corner of his mouth quirking up the moment Alec and the rest of the room left.

"No," Ian said.

Carter looked slightly surprised. "No?"

"No."

Carter hadn't known what to expect when Alec had told him two days ago that he was coming up with a new plan.

He certainly had not expected the "new plan" to be this guy.

Ian Parker.

When Alec had introduced him as his new "sober companion," Carter had been surprised. Surely Alec knew better than to put him with someone he was practically *duty bound* to seduce, even if he wasn't supposed to be even thinking about sex these days.

Of course, it wasn't like that had ever stopped him—and it definitely did not stop him now. Especially not when Ian was so goddamn cute.

And he was. It was undeniable. It was all that curly reddish-brown hair and then there were the freckles scattered over the tan bridge of his nose—Carter was a sucker for freckles—paired with that steely, icy look in his green eyes. That look should've frozen Carter right down to the bone.

Normally any hint of frigidity would've turned Carter right off.

Even the *thought* that this guy wasn't willing and pliant and all-too-ready to get down and dirty would've made him a no go.

It would certainly be better for both of them if Ian's look worked the way he'd clearly meant it to. Better, too, for Carter, if he wasn't intrigued despite all his semi-good intentions.

But the frozen wall of his stare didn't turn Carter off at all.

Instead, it made him want to melt it all down. See what lay behind it.

"No," Ian said firmly. Resolutely.

He apparently didn't want to know what Carter had meant when he said, *then you shouldn't have given me him.*

The insinuation being that he found Ian Parker attractive.

Most people—okay, *all* people, at least *all* the people Carter had ever met—wanted to know if he found them attractive.

It was a natural reaction.

And luckily for them, Carter didn't typically have a type.

He liked everyone, and it was usually easy to find something attractive in everyone.

It wasn't even going to be a hardship to find Ian Parker attractive. Honestly, that had already happened.

But Ian Parker did not care one way or the other—or else he was annoyingly good at pretending he didn't—and that pricked Carter in the back of his mind. Waved a red flag he never should've acknowledged.

"No?" Carter questioned. Because apparently he couldn't leave well enough alone.

"No."

Normally, if someone *did* brush him off, he got over it and moved on. He wasn't egotistical enough to keep barking up trees where he wasn't wanted, and even people who presented a challenge had never particularly enticed him before.

But Ian was different. Already he was different.

"I know you're going to hit on me," Ian continued coolly, "but that's not going to work out so good for you because I'm not interested, so you might as well get it out of your system now."

Well.

Well.

"How do you know it's not going to work out and you're not interested if I haven't done it yet?"

Ian regarded him steadily. Didn't say anything.

"Are you not interested in guys?" Carter asked. That would make sense.

But Ian shook his head—then immediately looked like he regretted it.

Carter felt a spike of relief he had absolutely no business feeling. Okay, so Ian *did* like guys, but he didn't like Carter.

He could work with that.

"All I'm saying," Carter said, because he could never shut up even when he should, "is that maybe you've been hit on by other guys before, but you've never been hit on by *me*."

Ian crossed his arms over his chest. Like that would be enough to fend Carter off. "I already knew that," he said dryly.

Newsflash to Ian Parker. Carter was damn good at this.

You're not supposed to be good at this. Not with him.

But Carter ignored that voice, which unfortunately sounded *very* much like Alec's. Basically, if Ian expected Carter to hit on him, who was he to turn down the opportunity?

He leaned in, angling his body in the way that had never failed him once. "I'm just saying, you gotta at least give me a chance."

Ian looked skeptical. "I do?"

"You said I was gonna do it, so I'd better do it." He flashed Ian one of his grins—the ones that never failed to melt the clothing off any person in his vicinity.

"Alec told me you were going to," Ian said in a measured voice. Those standoffish eyes and his crossed arms hadn't changed.

Was this how it was going to be all the time now? For the next few months was he gonna be lugging this gigantic block of ice around?

No. No way.

"You can relax and stop bracing for the worst." *Or my best.* "I'm not going to do it now."

He *wanted* to, but he also wanted to melt that icy reserve of Ian's, and Carter could tell it was gonna take a hell of a lot more than just a few enticing smiles and a semi-shitty pick up line.

If he wanted to seduce Ian—*and you're not supposed to*, Inner Alec reminded him insistently—he'd have to make a study of the guy first. Even better, if he was going to be following him around as Carter's personal minder, he had nothing but time.

"You're not?"

"Don't sound so disappointed," Carter teased.

"I'm not," Ian said. But he was frowning. "I just expected…"

But he didn't say, which should have been the end of it, but Carter knew he had a streak of insatiable curiosity which was now piqued. Well—it had been piqued before this. Now it was aroused.

"Expected what?" Carter asked. "Expected that I'd sexually harass you at every opportunity? Leer at you? Not waste a moment trying to convince you if you came to my bed you wouldn't only *not* regret it, you'd have the best goddamn time of your life?"

Ian raised an eyebrow.

"It's true," Carter said, not bragging because it wasn't an over-inflated ego talking. He'd heard it enough times *and* he'd certainly done everything in his power to make sure that the people who did share his bed were never left wanting.

"Doesn't matter," Ian said. He pointed to the list sitting on the table between them. "See rule number one? *No sex.*"

"I don't know why Alec had to make that the first rule," Carter complained.

"Probably so you couldn't avoid it," Ian pointed out in a tone as dry as the desert.

"How do you know Alec then?" Because clearly Ian wouldn't have said that if he didn't know Alec. Carter had only known Alec personally for a couple of weeks now—before, it had merely been by reputation—but he could already tell this was the kind of crafty, manipulative bullshit Alec was brilliant at.

But so was Carter, and since nobody ever expected it out of Carter, he was even better at it, because it always came as a surprise.

"He's a professional acquaintance," Ian said.

And that was all. Nothing else.

Carter couldn't help just a little mild exasperation. "Listen, dude, if we're going to be close for the next few months, you gotta loosen up a little."

"How do you know I'm not plenty loose?"

"Seriously?" Carter couldn't help the disbelieving look he shot in Ian's direction. "*Seriously?*"

Ian softened a little at that, actually smiling for the first time since Carter had come into the conference room. "Fair," he acknowledged.

"I told you." Carter grinned. "You can fucking relax, okay? I'm not going to hit on you." He paused for dramatic effect. "*Yet.*"

"It's the *yet* that worries me," Ian grumbled, but he had relaxed a fraction.

"Worried you're not gonna be able to resist?"

Ian shot him a look. "No," he said. "Worried you're going to embarrass yourself."

Carter threw his head back and laughed. "Oh, sweetheart, trust me, that's not something you should be worrying about. You think

I haven't gotten shot down before and kept on coming? Half this team has shot me down."

Ian looked genuinely astonished, and for the first time, Carter caught a glimpse behind that wall of ice.

Not a lot, just a glimpse.

But just a glimpse was enough.

"What, you thought you were the first person to tell me to fuck off?" Carter grinned.

"No," Ian protested, shifting uncomfortably in his chair.

But clearly, he had.

"You don't know me as well as you think you do," Carter pointed out. "I don't care what Alec's told you, but you gotta learn me for yourself."

"That's a good point." Ian looked both surprised *and* thoughtful now. Like he hadn't expected Carter to call him on all his rotten assumptions.

Carter stood. "And there's no time like the present to get started. Let's go grab some lunch."

"Wait a sec," Ian said, standing too, but reaching out and casually catching Carter's arm. "I know this is going to be awkward, me being around all the time. I just wanted to acknowledge that, first off."

"Is it?" Carter really hadn't thought much about it; honestly, he'd been too busy trying to figure out how to get around rule number one.

"Well, yeah, in my experience it is. Most people who run into us together are going to want an explanation. Your friends. The players here. The coaches. The staff. Anyone you meet."

"And what? I shouldn't tell them why you're really around?"

"I'm…" Ian hesitated again. "I know what my previous clients and I would do. We'd discuss ahead of time what role I'd be playing. Often, since I was in LA, they were well known, so it was easy to pass me off as a personal assistant or a friend. But here—"

"Nobody's gonna have a personal assistant around them all the time," Carter said. "Especially not me."

Ian looked surprised again.

"What," Carter retorted, "I'm not an idiot, okay."

The frost in Ian's expression melted a little more. "Sorry, I didn't mean to imply that you were."

"You wouldn't be the first," Carter said wryly. "Why can't we just tell people what you really are?"

"You'd be okay with that?"

Carter realized with a jolt that the person who was really worried about this wasn't *him*, the way Ian was concerned about, but Ian himself.

Wasn't that interesting?

"It's hardly like people don't know my reputation," Carter said.

"Oh. Alright. Well, that's your choice."

"We can just say you're my what…companion?"

"If that's the word you want to use," Ian said.

But as they walked out of the conference room, Carter couldn't shake the feeling that *Ian* was the one who was preoccupied with not only what to call himself, but maybe even what kind of position he'd be occupying in Carter's life.

As they walked down the hall, and Carter pushed the down elevator button, to take it to the lower level and the team cafeteria, Ian turned to him and said, "Well, you getting shut down by half the team is pretty good news for rule number one."

Carter rolled his eyes. "Not when I could go to the Pirate's Booty or any other bar or restaurant or coffee shop in the city and find someone to pick up in point five seconds."

"Modest, much?"

"Listen, you wanted honesty, that's the honest truth right there." Carter had sex because it was easy, *yes*, and it also helped stem the tide of his temper. Maybe if sex had been harder for him to come by, he'd have found something else to use.

But sex *was* easy, for him, so sex it was.

Or at least it *had* been sex.

Carter mournfully poured one out for all the great sex he wasn't going to be having in the next few months.

"Maybe that's the key," Ian said as the elevator dinged open. He settled against the back wall, crossing his arms over his chest again.

He wasn't nearly as tall as Carter—or as broad—but then he didn't need to be because he wasn't a professional athlete. But he was no slouch either, Carter thought, as he glanced over at him, head to toe. His biceps and chest in his tight polo were clearly defined, and his thighs in those slim-cut slacks? He loved the way Ian looked in them, but Carter wished they were a little tighter so he could see a little more of his incredible legs.

"What's the key?" Carter asked, realizing half a second too late Ian was staring at him just as intently as Carter was staring at *him*.

Okay.

Maybe not quite as intently.

"Seriously?" Ian retorted.

"What? You're not exactly hard on the eyes. I said I wasn't going to hit on you yet. That doesn't mean I can't at least look and *enjoy* looking. If Alec didn't want me to, he should've sent..." Carter struggled with what to say. He found a whole swath of people attractive. Who *could* Alec have sent? "Maybe someone old."

"Older?" Ian questioned, like he was also curious who Carter wouldn't have been tempted to hit on.

"No, *old*," Carter said. "Like eighty plus. Someone who smelled like mothballs. Who looks down their nose at me, like my grandmother did, sometimes."

Ian shocked him then. He threw his head back and laughed and laughed. When their eyes met again, right before the elevator reached the ground floor, the ice in his gaze had melted another fraction.

"You are *not* what I expected," Ian confessed as they walked out of the elevator.

"People say that all the time, and I don't know why," Carter said. Except that wasn't quite true. He knew why. It was because everyone who met him underestimated him because of his reputation.

He pushed open the door to the cafeteria and gestured towards the food. "You can grab something to eat over there. Whatever you want."

"It's on the house?" Ian asked, and Carter nodded. "One of the perks Mr. G brought back, when he bought the team. Old owners made us pay for every goddamn thing."

"That sucks," Ian said.

It had. It had not been a particularly good time last year, and there'd been a point, right after he'd been traded—an NFL-high fourth time—when Carter had begun to wonder, late at night, in the back of his mind when it wouldn't quiet, if maybe this treatment was all he deserved.

But he couldn't quite believe it, if only because he *knew* Deacon and Jem and Beckett didn't.

They'd never done anything worth being treated like shit over. But Carter?

He'd done plenty.

"Well, it's better now." Carter pointed to a table where Riley and Landry sat already. "After you grab lunch, we'll sit over there. You gotta start fitting in."

"I don't need to fit in," Ian grumbled under his breath, but he was already heading over to where the food was set out. Carter followed, and even though he was hungry, he didn't head over to where he normally did. Instead, he watched as Ian picked up a bowl and began to load it with lettuce and toppings from the salad bar.

Carter patted him on the shoulder. "Don't worry," he said, "you'd be hot no matter what."

Ian nearly dropped the tongs he was using to transfer chunks of grilled chicken to the top of his bowl.

"What?" he said.

Carter grinned and then leaned down, letting his mouth get close enough to murmur into Ian's ear but not technically graze it. "If you want to eat rabbit food, then you should eat rabbit food. But just so you know, I like people. Just people. Doesn't matter what your eye color is or your size, or if you had hair down to your ass, I'd still want to get into your pants. It's those freckles. I'd like to kiss every single one. And I mean *every* single one."

Ian's jaw dropped.

Frankly, Carter thought as he headed over to the sandwich station, he'd *told* him he was gonna hit on him, so he shouldn't have been all that surprised.

"Doesn't matter what your eye color is or your size, or if you had hair down to your ass, I'd still want to get into your pants. It's those freckles. I'd like to kiss every single one. And I mean *every* single one." Carter's seductive purr echoed through Ian's head, somehow breaking through even the clanging warning bells.

Ian's fingers froze on the tongs he was currently holding.

It was stupid. It was so fucking stupid.

Alec had warned him. *Carter himself* had warned him. Had practically promised that he'd be hitting on him, later.

Well, apparently this was later.

It had been what...less than ten minutes?

Ian shouldn't be surprised it was happening, and he wasn't necessarily. No, the surprise was the painful jolt of satisfaction.

And, even worse, just how much he'd *liked* it.

He'd told himself he wouldn't, that not enjoying being just one of many people Carter hit on daily would make it easier.

But then Carter had pulled out something so painfully specific to *him*, that Ian knew it wasn't just a practiced line.

It was *him* that Carter wanted.

And goddamn it, Ian wished he didn't, but he'd felt it, too.

Okay, maybe his initial plan was not going to work as well as he thought.

Ian watched with narrowed eyes as Carter sauntered off, looking very smugly pleased with himself.

His mother would tell him if one method of self-control wasn't going to work, there were always others to try.

So maybe Ian couldn't rely on *not* liking it when Carter flirted with him. Instead, he needed to turn that *like* into something else.

As he finished making his salad, Ian purposefully let his mind wander in between the bowls of sunflower seeds and croutons.

Purposefully let himself think of what might've happened after Carter dished out a line like that, if he *wasn't* duty-bound and Alec-bound not to sleep with him.

If he'd let himself blink slow, long sweeps of his lashes, right back at Carter.

If he'd dished it right back.

Yeah, he'd say, *show me how you'd get into my pants.*

He wouldn't protest if Carter slid a hand, one of those big capable hands, right down his back and let it rest right along the curve of his ass.

Wouldn't do anything other than gasp if Carter dug his fingertips in and *squeezed*.

Carter's low chuckle as he gasped.

Wouldn't even budge if Carter leaned in and found one of his freckles, right on the side of his neck, and pressed his lips there.

Kissed his way down the column of his neck, using his freckles as a roadmap, lips skirting down his collarbone, tugging down his shirt, and lingering on his pectoral muscle.

"Hey, you okay there?"

The deep voice jerked him right out of the fantasy—the fantasy he'd meant to cut off *on his own.*

Ian had meant to indulge in only a little of the fiction, instead of the reality. He'd never meant to let himself go so deep.

He glanced behind him, and there was a big man, tall and broad, with the widest shoulders he'd ever seen, and dark hair falling into his even darker eyes.

With a jolt, Ian realized he *knew* that guy. Had seen him on his television at least a dozen times, every time he pulled his helmet off.

It shouldn't have been a surprise. After all, he'd spent the last five years in Hollywood, going from rock stars who filled stadiums to actresses who commanded millions for their performances. He was used to celebrity.

Ian had even met some of the players his mother worked with. Heath. Chase. Spencer.

"You're Deacon Harris," Ian said, hating how starstruck he felt.

He'd had a Deacon Harris poster on his wall, from his rookie season.

He'd *jacked off* to that poster more than he wanted to admit.

God, how embarrassing was this? What if Carter found out? He'd never let him forget it. But then, Ian reminded himself there was no reason why Carter *would* find out, unless he told him, and Ian was definitely not that stupid.

"Yeah," Deacon said with a smile. "And you are?"

"Oh, God, sorry." Ian flushed. Hated, for the millionth time, how easily he blushed. Held out his hand, and Deacon shook it. "Ian Parker. I'm with—"

But he didn't get the rest of the sentence out, because Carter was suddenly right there, a knowing expression on his face as he glanced over at Ian's glowing cheeks. Goddamn it. "He's with me," Carter said enthusiastically. *Proudly.*

Deacon raised an eyebrow. "He's *with* you? You bringin' your hookups around for practices now, Carter?"

Ian's cheeks flamed even redder.

It was bad enough he'd been caught out fantasizing about his new client—but by the guy he *used* to fantasize about, when he was fourteen, skinny and awkward, without a chance in hell of actually kissing a guy?

Worse. So much worse.

"I'm working with Carter's new agent, and helping him as his companion," Ian said, trying to muster some kind of dignity.

"Ah, well, good to meet you." Deacon nodded at him and headed off towards the exit doors.

"*Well*, that wasn't so bad, right?" Carter said as they headed over to the table he'd indicated earlier. "'Course I didn't turn bright fucking red the first time I ever met Deacon Harris, so maybe a little better for me than you."

"Thanks," Ian said dryly.

It was really too much to hope that Carter hadn't noticed.

"I thought you did this for really famous clients, way more famous than me. Way more famous than say...*Deacon Harris.*" Carter waggled his eyebrows. "You said you weren't interested in me, but maybe he's more your type. Tall, dark, and handsome? Could pin you to the wall without breaking a sweat?" He looked Ian up and down, and Ian prayed he was not trying to size up if *he* could do it, too.

Frankly, yes, Deacon was big, but Carter wasn't exactly *small*.

"If that's what does it for you, I think I could manage," Carter continued, because apparently Ian was not red enough yet—what the fuck had happened to his frozen reserve? It was gone, lost, *melted* right away.

Shit.

Could he blame Deacon for that? No, not entirely. Carter had started it and then Ian himself had practically finished it right off, by letting his mind wander in a direction he'd been so sure he could control—and then couldn't at all.

"What does it for who?" Riley asked curiously.

Landry shot him a look. "You really want to ask that?"

"Sorry," Riley said, shooting both Ian and Carter a lopsided grin. "I *should* know better. You must be Carter's new minder. I'm Riley, and this is Landry."

"I'm Ian," Ian offered, shaking both of their hands. He recognized them both, of course. And at least, *thank God*, he'd never jerked off to either of them, or had posters of them on his wall.

Or fantasized about them, when he was supposed to be immune to their sex appeal.

"Is Carter here behaving himself?" Landry asked as they sat.

"It's been..." Ian checked his watch. "Half an hour. Hard to misbehave in that kind of timeframe."

"You've clearly never met me before," Carter said cheerfully, no shame whatsoever.

No, he had not.

"And," Carter added, turning towards him. "You didn't answer my question."

So much for changing the subject.

"What does it for who?" Riley repeated with a smile.

"Yep." Carter was staring at him. Ian could feel it even though he was keeping his eyes on his salad.

"It's...I'm good, thanks," Ian said in a strangled voice.

"So, Ian, is this something you do for a living?" Landry asked, obviously taking pity on him. Ian would take it. He would take *all* of it.

"Being a companion? Well, actually, normally I work as a sober companion," Ian said. "Not quite the same thing, but this is a favor I'm doing for Alec, as he's a friend and a, well...professional acquaintance."

"A sober companion? That's fascinating," Landry said, sounding like he actually meant it.

"Yep. I'm meant to offer support and help with reintegration into regular life, after time in rehab. I'm based in California, and usually work with high-profile clients, so Alec thought this would be a good fit."

"Is it so far?" Riley asked.

"Yeah, I think so," Ian said. "I *hope* so. And if I'm not the right fit for Carter, then we'll find someone who is."

"See?" Carter clapped him on the back. "He's a good guy!"

Riley nodded.

Ian could tell from the way both of them were eyeing him that they were close to Carter, and were sizing him up to make sure he would in fact be good for Carter.

Ian hadn't been laboring under any delusions that this would be an easy job. He'd known it wouldn't be, but even thirty short minutes after meeting Carter, he'd already been forced to revise his opinion.

This wasn't going to be a tough job; it was going to be practically fucking impossible.

But he was still going to pull it off, because this wasn't just about someone else's sobriety. This was about his own future. A future he wanted so badly he could even resist a man practically nobody else resisted.

What had Carter said though? Half his team had turned him down?

Maybe the secret was spending more time with the guy. Maybe with time, they could settle into a friendly sort of truce. Maybe Carter only looked good at first.

Ian glanced over at him.

No way.

Carter was never going to *not* look good.

Physical attraction, you can handle that, no sweat.

Okay, there might be a little sweating going on, but Ian could handle that too.

Chapter 3

ALEC HAD SENT HIM a text, saying he'd sent Ian's bags along to Carter's house, dropping them off.

That meant Carter drove them both back to his house, after practice had ended.

"So," Carter said, breaking the silence that had fallen between them, after they'd met up outside the locker room.

Ian had been slightly apprehensive that Carter would somehow find an excuse to drag him into the locker room while he got naked.

But thankfully, he'd not said a word when Ian had told him where they'd meet up.

Besides, it wasn't like practice hadn't had its own share of difficulties.

Ian had forced himself to stop counting the number of times Carter had yanked up his practice jersey to wipe the sweat off his face.

He'd told himself that Carter wasn't doing it because of him. But even if Carter wasn't doing it on purpose, the flash of chiseled abs and firm stomach had affected him nonetheless.

You'll get used to it, he kept telling himself.

But Ian honestly wasn't sure he would.

Could you ever become immune to a guy like Carter Maxwell?

That was a question he wasn't sure he wanted to hear the answer to.

"So," Ian repeated right back.

Carter shot him a look. In the dusk falling over Charleston, his face was a mask of shadows and light, somehow even more beautiful than it had been in the full daylight of the conference room.

"Was it what you expected?" Carter asked. "Practice and meeting the guys? I know you were worried."

"I wasn't *worried*, I wanted to make sure you wouldn't feel awkward about it," Ian retorted. God, he didn't want Carter to be concerned for him. He needed him to stay the surface-level guy. The guy who hit on him without a thought and then moved on.

"I hate to break it to you, but awkwardness isn't usually something I deal with."

Ian had begun to figure that out.

He was good at melting into the background, into shadows, being there while *not* being there. Even pretty good at dealing with that inherent awkwardness of being around someone all the time, even when they didn't really *want* him to be. But Carter had been so different, from the beginning. He'd not complained once about Ian's existence in his life. Not pushed back on the time they'd be spending together. In fact, he'd told everyone they met exactly who Ian was, without even a hint of shame or embarrassment.

That had never happened before.

That's because this isn't like any job you've had up til now.

That *was* true, but it was more than that. Even as Ian wanted to deny it, he knew the difference was Carter himself.

"Where do you live? Downtown?" Ian asked, changing the subject as Carter took an exit off the freeway, leading not, like he'd expected, to downtown, but away from it.

"No," Carter said. Flashed him one of those inscrutable, unbearably charming grins.

"Just no?"

"Hey, you did that first. *No. No, I'm not interested in knowing why Alec shouldn't have given me to Carter.*"

"Alec didn't *give* me to you," Ian retorted.

"You're right." Carter paused, shooting him that look again. The look that so far had never failed to spike Ian's heart rate, no matter how much he fought against it. "He *gifted* you to me."

"I'm not a gift." Ian was annoyed. He *was* annoyed.

And yet...

"I think you secretly like it," Carter proclaimed.

If he let himself, he might—but Ian already knew he couldn't.

"Are you going to tell me about your house or not?"

And Carter did, and he didn't, all at the same time.

"After I was traded here last year," he said, "I considered just renting. After all, who knew if I was staying? I hadn't stayed anywhere else. But then...Deacon said something to me. Like, you're the person you want to be. The person you make yourself. So I bought the house I wanted, like if I did, maybe it would mean I could stay."

Damn it.

Carter Maxwell wasn't a thoughtless asshole. Ian had *known* it, of course, because Alec wouldn't take on a project he had no hope of succeeding at, but hearing the vulnerability hiding in Carter's words meant that Ian wouldn't be forgetting it anytime soon.

"You wanted to stay here, even last year?" Ian asked.

In for a penny, in for a pound.

"Were things great last year? Not really. But...yeah. Yeah, I did."

Ian could hear the ring of truth in Carter's voice, as he pulled them off the main thoroughfare, down a side road.

They were still driving, surprisingly.

Carter did not live anywhere like where he'd expected.

He'd also thought Carter would say he'd wanted out of Charleston as soon as he'd been traded there.

"You look surprised," Carter said.

"I just heard things. Like it was shit here last year."

"So you thought I'd want to get out as soon as I could? Normally, yeah, but..." Carter shrugged. "I had a feeling my chances were numbered. And I liked some of the guys. And as wretched a person as Tom Taylor was, he could throw a decent ball."

Ian considered this, but before he could say anything, could think of not only what he could say, what he *should* say, Carter kept going.

"You probably think that makes me an asshole. Thinking of myself. Tolerating that guy, just 'cause he was a good quarterback. Just like everyone else who let his shit slide, over the years." Carter sounded unexpectedly bitter.

"Actually, I think it makes you a realist, who knew you couldn't succeed by yourself. Your job is to catch the ball. Score touchdowns. You can't do that alone." Ian said it slowly, and realized, as each word came out, that he meant every single one.

"Thanks, man," Carter said, reaching over to pat him on the leg.

It was a brief touch, but Ian ground his teeth at the sensation that rocketed through him.

Didn't let himself consider what it would feel like if Carter's touch wasn't brief or casual.

"So you bought a house."

"Yeah, a place I really *liked*, not that everyone else thought I'd like."

The sun was nearly done sinking over the far edge of the horizon when Carter pulled onto what was undeniably a country road and then, a minute later, turned down a long curved drive lined with trees.

The big farmhouse sat by itself, shaded by more trees, with a circular drive that deposited them right in front of a big garage, painted yellow with white trim, to match the house.

"It's really nice, Carter," Ian said honestly.

The house had a huge wraparound porch, white shutters framing big picture windows on each side. It was relaxing and inviting and unlike anything he'd ever expected Carter to own.

But by his own admission, this was what Carter *really* wanted. It was an undeniable glimpse into the man who Carter was, underneath all the false fronts and the easy, affable, charming attitude he tried to pretend was all that existed.

Ian took note, and because he'd been doing this long enough, he knew better than to not pay attention to this tiny, impossibly valuable glimpse into Carter's real self.

For professional reasons.

"Thanks." Carter's voice was full of pride. He hit the button to open the far garage door, only one of four, and he pulled his SUV in slowly. Down the row there were several other expensive-looking vehicles.

After Carter led him in through the main door into the kitchen, there was Ian's luggage, piled just where Alec had said it would be.

Carter took in the bags piled next to his big kitchen table, the burnished wood expanse gleaming in the light over the white ceramic farmhouse sink. "You stayin' forever?" he teased.

Yeah, there were a lot of bags. Four of them, in fact, and Carter didn't even know how neatly and carefully they'd been packed.

He definitely did not need to know those bags were basically all of Ian's life.

Typically, he moved from job to job. When there *was* an in-between, he stayed in his mother's guest house, but it was rarely for more than a few days. At the beginning, he'd had his own place, a small apartment he could keep some stuff at, but as one year had stretched into two, and he'd settled into the role of sober companion more fully, he'd begun to realize he didn't need it, and he was just paying for an empty space he never visited.

After that, he'd let go of it, gotten rid of the cheap furniture he'd acquired, and started traveling around from client to client with everything he owned in those four bags currently sitting in Carter's kitchen.

"Wasn't planning on it," Ian said lightly. He didn't want to go into the fact this was *everything* he owned, because that often made the people he worked for uncomfortable. Of course, the people he worked for frequently owned multiple homes, and so much stuff that four bags wouldn't have a hope and a dream of containing it all.

"How long *are* you planning on staying?" Carter asked. No judgment, only curiosity.

"However long Alec thinks I need to," Ian said. He also had no intention of divulging the deal he and Alec had made. Carter didn't need to know that, to Ian, he was the means to an end that Ian wanted very, very much.

The chance to stop being so transitory, to settle down, not just with a few clients long-term, but maybe to have a place of his own again.

A life of his own, not one dedicated entirely to others.

He'd learned so much as a sober companion, not just about people in general, and his clients specifically, but about *himself*. The one thing Ian knew above all others was he no longer wanted to spend just a few months fighting for someone. He wanted to form a much longer-term relationship with his clients. Like the kind Alec enjoyed.

It was time, as his mother liked to say.

"Sounds good to me." Carter flashed him a bashful grin. Ironically, because he'd never imagined Carter was *bashful* about anything. "Won't exactly be a hardship to have you around."

Ian rolled his eyes. "What if Alec *had* sent someone…what did you say? *Someone really old and dried up?*"

"I'm sure I'd find something I liked about them," Carter said casually. Like he had no idea what kind of a gift it was that he consistently found the best in everyone.

Sure, he was down on himself because of his temper problem, and the shit he used to deal with it, but deep down, Carter was a miracle that way.

That's why he's different.

Maybe why he was so irresistible, not just as someone people wanted to hook up with, but why everyone on the team gravitated towards him. He was genuine with everyone. There wasn't an ounce of artifice to Carter Maxwell, and *that* was actually his secret power—and the secret power that Ian had never, in a million years, anticipated.

The secret power that was going to make Carter Maxwell just that much tougher for Ian to resist, because the interest glowing in his honey-brown eyes *was* legit.

Carter might feel that way about lots of people, maybe even everyone he met, but he meant it *right now* for Ian and Ian alone.

"You're not what I expected," Ian admitted.

Carter smiled. "I didn't know what to expect, but I gotta say, I like Alec's taste."

Ian ignored the lick of heat that went up his spine, and instead focused on the professional interpretation of Carter's words.

"He's a good man. He'll make smart choices for you, fight for you. I'm glad you signed with him." And that was the other problem, wasn't it? Ian was wired to give a shit about his clients. To *want* them to succeed—though not necessarily to just plain fucking *want* them—and he already was invested in Carter's future success. Not necessarily his sobriety, but he wanted him to be happy. Well-adjusted. To find the balance he clearly needed in his life.

Carter leaned against the counter. "Yeah. I hope so. You want something to eat? Dinner?"

Ian realized with a surprised glance at his watch that it *was* past dinner time. He'd been so absorbed in Carter that he hadn't even noticed himself get hungry.

"You cook?" Ian asked, before he could snatch the question back.

"No, not really," Carter admitted. "But a personal chef delivers ready-to-eat meals once a week, so I've got some of those. And on nights I'm not into those, even though I'm pretty much out of every delivery zone, they'll make an exception if I ask real, real nice."

Ian raised an eyebrow. "You just *ask* and they'll deliver all the way out here?"

"I'm not sleeping with the pizza delivery guy," Carter said with an eye roll. "I *promise*."

"I'm not asking you if you're sleeping with him," Ian retorted, even though yeah, he'd wondered. Because once Carter turned that sweet, warm, *interested* gaze on someone, he had a feeling it was hard to turn him down.

Whatever *he* wanted, *you* wanted.

"Yeah, you were, and it's alright. I know it's rule one, and that's why you're so interested in my sleeping habits," Carter teased.

"Or *no*-sleeping habits," Ian said before he could stop himself.

"True." Carter grinned. "Trust me, if I got you into bed, there wouldn't be much sleeping."

"That's not happening," Ian said automatically.

But he could already imagine it.

Could practically taste the sweet saltiness of Carter's skin as he dug his teeth into his shoulder, bracing himself for the inevitable onslaught of pleasure Carter could give a man.

Ian had watched videos of him dancing in the end zone, celebrations after touchdowns, and the man's hips were so fluid, he'd fuck like an absolute maniac. He'd make Ian moan louder than he ever had before. He might even make him scream.

But you're never gonna get a chance to find out.

"So, what did you want?" Carter leaned in and leered a little.

And *oh God*, did Ian want.

"For dinner, man," Carter teased with another one of those irre-sistible looks. "Just for a sec, it looked like you really wanted some-thing else."

"No, no, of course not," Ian stuttered. Which...that was a dead fucking giveaway, and Carter wasn't stupid enough to miss it. And he didn't, if his knowing expression was any indication. "Dinner. Right."

"Dinner," Carter said slyly. "You thought about what you want to eat tonight?"

You. Alive.

Ian nodded. "Any of your pre-made meals, those are fine. I'm not picky. I'll put in a grocery order, and pick it up tomorrow on our way home from practice. Unlike you, I *can* cook."

"You've got a car here, too. I told Alec you could borrow any of mine. Keys are by the door over there," Carter said, gesturing to a line of hooks, with keys hanging from each one.

"Oh, wow, thanks." He'd expected to be more centrally located to downtown, so he'd anticipated using ride share or cabs to get around when he needed to run errands—but being all the way out here, having access to one of Carter's cars *would* make things a lot easier.

It wasn't the first time one of his clients had made a vehicle avail-able to him, but it *was* the first time it had been done so casually, so easily.

But then that was just who Carter was.

"I trust you, you know," Carter said, turning and heading over to the fridge.

"You do?" Ian was surprised, because Carter didn't *know* him.

"Alec trusts you, and I trust Alec," Carter said, his head buried in the fridge. "You want parmesan chicken or teriyaki salmon?"

"The salmon," Ian said.

"Anything to drink?" Carter asked.

Ian wasn't surprised, because again, Carter was uniquely Carter, but *not once* had any of Ian's clients asked him what he wanted to eat or drink. They'd never once considered serving him, because he was there *for them*.

But Carter didn't see him that way.

"You got any Diet Coke?" Ian asked.

Carter shot him a look. "What did I *just* tell you at lunch?"

Ian remembered. The memory alone made him hot and cold all over.

Hot because he still could hear Carter's silky soft voice sliding over his nerves like velvet. Cold because he couldn't let Carter get to him.

"I like it, okay? Chemicals and carcinogens and all. Don't give me a lecture, because I don't need it. My mom's always emailing me articles about how it's gonna kill me someday. Maybe it will, but I'll die happy."

"It is gonna kill you, you know," Carter said, but when he closed the fridge he had two cans of Diet Coke in his hands.

Ian shot him a look, and Carter flushed. "Okay, I like it too. We've already established I've got no self-control when it comes to things I like."

"I wouldn't say that," Ian said, taking one of the cans from him and popping it open. That first trickle of artificial sweetness down his throat was like nothing else.

"Well, *everyone* else would," Carter retorted.

Ian knew it but he wondered if anyone else had taken the time to dig deep into Carter and really know him.

He hadn't even gotten that far, and he could already see a different Carter lurking right there, under the surface.

His mother would find it, too, because it was her job to look.

"I'm not everyone else," Ian said softly.

"While these heat up, I'll help you take your bags upstairs," Carter suggested, and if Ian didn't know any better, he'd think he was changing the subject.

Also, it was a given that it was totally fucking unheard of for one of his clients to help him schlep his bags to where he'd be staying—but Carter picked up three of them, easy as nothing, his muscles bunching under his T-shirt.

Ian wanted to say that he didn't watch Carter's gorgeous legs and ass as he followed him up the stairs, but he'd be lying.

It's alright, looking isn't touching. You can look til you're crazy with it, but you just can't take it any further.

Once they were up the stairs, Carter led him down a long hallway, walls lined with photos—Carter in different uniforms over the years, Carter eating a huge slice of watermelon with that easy grin peeking over the pink fruit, Carter next to an older lady, with an equally bright smile—and then through the door to a large suite of rooms. The bedroom was big and airy, with a large window and a low-slung window seat, light-green pillows tossed across a darker green cushion.

"Bathroom's through there, and there's the closet," Carter said, gesturing towards two doors on the other side of the room.

"Looks great," Ian said, meaning it. He'd been relegated to much less. Basements. Sweltering attics. Tiny houses on the far reaches of the property. Some of his clients were awesome, but a lot of them were still unpacking the shame they felt that Ian was required at all, and they wanted him as far away, and as out of sight, as possible.

But not Carter.

"I'm just down the other way, past the stairs," Carter said, shooting him a knowing look. "Feel free to come by anytime."

There was no need to worry about that. He'd be staying far, *far* away from Carter's bedroom.

"There's a gym downstairs in the basement," Carter added. "If you want to use it, anytime, you're welcome to it."

"Did I see a swimming pool in the back?" Ian thought he'd glimpsed the corner of something that might be one. Admittedly, he'd gotten *very* spoiled, staying at all these Hollywood estates over the years, because almost every single one had a swimming pool, and swimming was, *by far*, his favorite way to exercise.

Carter looked him up and down, his lazy glance sending trails of heat up and down Ian's body.

Carter was hardly the first guy to find him attractive, or to find his body appealing, but somehow it was like he was sixteen and a virgin all over again when Carter did it.

Sadly, he could totally imagine Carter saying something like, *well, you were, until you had sex with me. 'Cause sex with me is special.*

It probably was, and yet Ian was going to have to live without experiencing it.

"You're a swimmer, huh? I can see it."

"Do you have one or not?" Ian asked, testily. He kept telling himself this would get easier. *It's been less than twenty-four hours,* he reminded himself.

"Yep," Carter said. Flashed him a knowing grin. "And it's all yours, baby."

"I'm not your baby," Ian retorted automatically.

"Not yet." Carter leered as they headed back down the stairs.

"Not ever," Ian corrected.

Carter had hoped that even though nothing was supposed to happen, he'd at least get to see Ian wet and mostly naked tonight—in the swimming pool, *duh*—but instead, after they ate, Ian said he was worn out from the early morning flight and went upstairs, saying he was going to unpack and then fall asleep.

Leaving Carter bored and on his own.

He put a movie on, but it didn't hold his attention, just as he'd worried it wouldn't.

Normally, this was the time of night when he'd be tempted to go back out again. When the prickles on the back of his neck became more insistent, and harder to resist.

He glanced over at his phone, and considered, for a few seconds, pulling up one of the hookup apps he'd installed, but then he remembered that one of Alec's first executive decisions had been to delete them.

He *could* always reinstall them.

But Carter had a feeling that while Ian said he was going to bed and going to sleep, he'd be a light sleeper. Would he realize if he snuck out? And could you even sneak out of your own freaking house?

The truth was, Carter didn't *want* to know the answer to that question, but he was afraid he'd be discovering it anyway.

He reached for his phone, but instead of reinstalling the apps Alec had insisted he delete, he hit his agent's phone number.

"Carter?" Alec answered, only sounding slightly harried. "Everything okay?"

Alec had made him promise, as his second executive action, that if he ever felt tempted to do something he shouldn't, something that went against the rules, he could call him.

Carter had a feeling Alec hadn't meant *every* single time, because if he had, they'd never be off the phone, especially not since he'd brought Ian here to his house. But Alec didn't really want to know just how appealing he found his new "minder."

"Everything's fine," Carter said.

"Ian's settling in okay?"

He could hear Alec switching ears, mumbling something to someone in the background.

"Ian's fine. *Really* fine if you get my drift," Carter teased.

Alec sighed heavily. "I was afraid of that. Probably not my smartest move, sending someone even remotely appealing into the lion's den, but he's got a good head on his shoulders. And don't you dare make it any harder on him, okay?"

"Would I do that?"

"Yes. Yes, you absolutely would." Alec sounded resigned to this inevitability. "But he's *good* at this, if you'd let him be instead of constantly trying to seduce the guy."

"I'm *not*, though." Despite every molecule in his body screaming at him to do it, and do it now, he'd barely even tried. The sparks that kept lighting up between them were hardly Carter's fault. He had a feeling they'd exist, no matter what he did or said.

"Okay," Alec soothed. Like he really believed him. "So if everything's alright, why are you calling?"

Carter felt a pulse of guilt. Alec had been working hard for him, already. He knew he wasn't the easiest client to have, but Alec *had* taken him on, eyes wide open.

"Sorry," he mumbled.

"You don't need to apologize," Alec said kindly.

"Yes, he does," a voice inserted itself into the conversation. Deep and rough and amused.

Carter recognized that voice. It belonged to Alec's husband, the massive defensive end, Spencer Evans.

"Oh, am I interrupting something?" Carter asked innocently. But his mind was already racing. He could barely help the thought of them together—they were *both* really fucking hot, and the one time he'd met Spencer, at their house, electricity had practically crackled between him and Alec.

Carter had always imagined that marriage would destroy that energy completely, but he'd definitely been sure that the moment he'd left, Spencer would be pinning Alec to the nearest flat surface.

It was only too bad he hadn't been able to witness it for himself.

Still, even the thought he *had* interrupted Alec and Spencer's sex life distracted him enough from the prickles.

"No," Alec said firmly. "Nothing whatsoever."

"Aw, no fair. You're not even gonna give me any details?" Carter teased.

"You think you're awfully cute, don't you, Maxwell?" Spencer asked. Making it clear *he* didn't think Carter was very cute at all.

He was probably the only person on Earth who didn't think so. Unfair.

He'd had half a thought when he'd first met Alec that maybe he could seduce the two of them into a threesome, but it had become very clear, very early that was not going to happen. Unfortunately.

"Yeah, actually. And lots of other people do, too."

"Let's hope that's all they're doing," Alec said. "Just *thinking* you're cute."

"It is. I told you, I'd tell you if anything happened. Besides, your guy keeps trying to freeze me out."

Ian was, but not as well as he probably *thought* he was.

"I told you, for the millionth time, Ian's in charge of your behavior. The rules. Which...need I remind you what rule number one is?" Alec asked archly.

"No," Carter said glumly.

The rules were practically emblazoned on his brain at this point, Alec had pointed them out so many times.

"Good."

"You're bored, aren't you?" Alec asked, before Carter could even say it.

And that, right here, was why Carter was glad he'd hired him. He didn't even *have* to say it, because Alec already knew the worst of him.

"Yeah," Carter admitted.

"Well, go to sleep then," Alec said. He paused. "It's pretty late there."

"That's just so…boring and responsible."

"Exactly," Alec emphasized.

"Ugh." He could already see his life stretching out in front of him—all boring shit and nothing fun. Why did he want to do this again?

Oh right. To prevent that sinking, horrible feeling that always hit him after he was out of control.

"You should talk about this with Moira tomorrow," Alec said.

"How do you know I have a therapy appointment tomorrow?" But Carter already knew why. Alec was Alec. He knew everything.

"Because Alec knows everything," Spencer chimed in again.

Carter laughed, because apparently that *was* a thing.

"This is exactly the kind of thing you should be discussing with her," Alec said, ignoring his husband's interruption.

"I'll think about it," Carter said.

"Good, you should," Alec replied. "Honestly, though, Carter…go to bed. *Alone.*"

Carter grinned at the addition. "Fine, fine, I'll do it, if it makes you happy."

"It makes me *relieved,*" Alec said.

"Me too," Spencer added and Carter laughed.

But, in the end, he *did* go to bed.

Alone.

Didn't even hesitate as he hit the landing off the stairs, and though he glanced down the hallway towards where Ian's room was, he thought Alec would be very proud that he was only a *little* bit tempted to wander down there instead.

CHAPTER 4

"I hear you have a new visitor with you," Moira said, her voice loud and clear and certain over the laptop.

Carter had grabbed an empty room after practice, locking the door behind him as he'd settled down to talk to his therapist. It wasn't that he didn't trust his teammates—or that he wouldn't even admit to them that he was currently in therapy. After all, he'd admitted to them exactly why Ian was around, hadn't he?

But this was different.

In the last session, Moira had started to ask pointed questions about his childhood, and it wasn't that he didn't want to answer—okay, he *didn't*, Carter could at least admit that—but more than that, he didn't want anyone else to hear her questions or his answers.

He'd had four sessions already with Moira Rogers, the therapist Alec had put him in touch with—who apparently had made something of a second career of counseling NFL players in need.

He liked her, but that wasn't a surprise because Carter liked just about everyone. But he'd been surprised at how much, even when he hadn't even been remotely tempted to hit on her.

They'd begun to tentatively discuss how he felt during his out-of-control episodes (unsurprisingly, out of control), and how he felt after (absolutely shitty), and she'd begun to suggest some coping mechanisms he could rely on instead of all the now-banned activities he *had* been using.

But it was still early. She'd said specifically that this was going to take time, *and* that she wanted him to remember that he was *worth* the time it was going to take. Which was something Carter hadn't really considered before.

"Yeah, his name's Ian, and I guess he's there to make sure I behave," Carter said, leaning back in his chair, crossing his arms behind his head.

"You guess?" Moira asked archly. On her side of the screen, he could see bright sunlight spilling over onto the corner of the desk.

He didn't know where she lived, but if he had to guess, it was in California, just like Alec.

"Okay, I *know*," Carter said, rolling his eyes. Even though it was only their fifth session, he already knew Moira liked him to be certain about whatever he said.

"So, he's there to make sure you behave yourself. How do you feel about that?"

"I feel..." Carter took a deep breath. "I wish he didn't make me want to immediately break the rules."

Moira's eyebrow skated upwards. "Did you tell Alec that?"

"Yeah, and he told me it was good practice to control myself. I'm sure he's *right*, but it's annoying, having him right there and not doing anything about it. Alec also said he was good at his job, so I guess that's another motivation for me to keep my dick in my pants."

So far, it had seemed difficult to fluster Moira Rogers. After all, she'd been through the first real test already—when he'd broken down and picked up three guys at the Pirate's Booty after the Condors' second loss in three weeks. That had been almost a week ago now, but he still remembered *distinctly* the disappointment and the jolt of surprise on her face as he'd told her all about the very pleasurable night of debauchery he'd enjoyed with them.

He'd called Alec that night, not even bothering to hide what had happened, and after that, Alec had changed gears and hired Ian to "mind" him.

"What about the fact that he's Alec's employee? Someone he's paying to be with you?" Moira asked. "Isn't that motivation, too?"

She'd extracted a promise out of him in their first session that he'd always be honest, though Carter had made sure to tell her honesty wasn't his problem.

He'd gladly say everything he ever did, even right after he did it.

It was the *deciding to do it* in the first place that was the issue.

"Well, yeah, I don't want to make the guy uncomfortable," Carter said. He wasn't a *creep*. "But I think he likes it. He keeps trying to hide his smiles when I hit on him."

"And that's a problem for you?"

"It..." Carter hesitated. "It worries me. I don't want my behavior resting on his self-control. Not when it comes to me."

"Carter," Moira retorted lightly, "we talked about the ego statements."

She'd been very clear that there was no room for them here. Especially when she'd neatly and succinctly informed him that he was probably overcompensating for something else when he used them.

But this, this was not overcompensation. And it was definitely not ego.

"Trust me, this isn't like that. I...I know what I'm doing."

"We've established that, Carter," Moira said dryly.

"I'm just saying, I know Alec trusts this guy so *I* trust this guy, but what if he...what if I break him down? Without meaning to?"

She raised that eyebrow again and Carter felt a pulse of shame. "Okay," he corrected before she could force him to. "Fair. I would totally mean to. He's sort of irresistible."

"Carter, you don't know him. He's not irresistible. The only reason you want him is because you're not supposed to. Because you know he's off-limits."

"Not true," Carter argued staunchly. "If you saw him, you'd understand. He's got this peach of an ass...he's a *swimmer*, that's totally why, I wish I could—"

"Carter," Moira interrupted sharply, "what did we also say about oversharing?"

He shrugged. "That you didn't like it. But you didn't say I *couldn't*."

"New rule," she said, and for the first time since they'd started meeting, he heard a hint of temper in her voice. "No oversharing, no matter how irresistible you find...well, you find your new minder."

"*Fine*," Carter said with a resigned sigh. He didn't like it. If he couldn't talk about how much he was struggling with the desire to seduce Ian, how could he continue to try to be the straight-and-narrow person Alec wanted him to be? That *he* wanted himself to be?

She must've guessed at his frustration, because her expression softened. "We *can* talk about this—in fact, I think we should. But

I'd just ask you to keep your comments and opinions on his...ir-resistibility to a minimum. Can you do that?"

Could he do that? Sure, Carter supposed he was capable of anything he set his mind to. It was more of a matter of his mind deciding the outcome was worth the effort.

"Sure," Carter said.

"So, let's unpack this. Alec has sent Ian to spend time with you and make sure you follow the rules. Could it be that his very existence makes you want to break them?"

He opened his mouth to answer, but Moira held up a hand before he could. "Not your first instinctual answer," she said firmly, "but I want you to think about it first. Really think about it. He's practically a red flag in human form, Carter. It would make sense for you to want to take the person Alec has sent to make sure you follow the rules and use him to break them. Especially if you find him...appealing."

"I'm not *mad* he's here." Carter wanted to make that clear up front. "I'm not upset that Alec sent him, and I don't want to use him to make a point, either. I just...he's reserved and a little cold, like he thinks he *needs* to be, around me, and..." Carter grinned. "To use *your* word, I find that appealing."

"But," Moira said, flipping through the pad she'd been making notes on since their first session, "last week we talked about lim-its and hard lines, and you talked about how you've never crossed one. Never ever even been interested in doing it. If someone tells you to stop, you will. To quote you, 'it turns you off.'"

Carter considered this. Why wasn't Ian's icy wall of reserve a turn-off? He didn't know. Because like Moira claimed, he *had* said exactly that, and he'd meant it.

"I think because..." Carter took a deep breath. It was actually tough to talk about this, because it only reminded him of what he wasn't going to have. What he *probably* wasn't going to have, he pointed out to himself. "Because, deep down, I think he *is* interested. I want to melt that ice and figure out what's underneath it. If we met in a different situation, like if we were both out at a bar, and we met, I wonder if he'd want the exact same thing I do."

"Ah," Moira said.

Then changed the subject. Annoyingly. Carter wanted to talk about Ian some more.

"Last session," she said, "you told me that when you were eleven, your grandmother died."

"Doc, I'd much rather talk about Ian than that," Carter admitted.

"I know." Moira smiled softly. "I told you that this wouldn't always be comfortable. That you wouldn't always like it."

"Well, I don't."

"Tell me about your grandmother."

What was there to say about his grandmother? Whenever Carter thought about her, there was a deep, pervasive sense of loss and pain. And regret. Like why couldn't she be here now, to see what he'd made of himself? Sure, okay, not *all* of it was good, but maybe if she had been there, and hadn't left him so young, he wouldn't have struggled so much.

Or maybe he'd have been just as fucked-up as he was now.

"She left me," Carter finally said and he heard the reluctance and the pain in his voice.

This was why he didn't talk about it.

"I'm sure she didn't want to, Carter," Moira said gently. "You spent a lot of time with her?"

"A lot of time. She liked having me around unlike…" He trailed off. This right here was why he was talking to Moira. Why he *needed* to talk to Moira. He wasn't dumb enough not to know that. But that still didn't mean he wanted to do it.

He'd spent a lifetime not talking about it, and while that hadn't necessarily served him well, he'd preferred it that way.

"Unlike?" Moira unsurprisingly prompted.

"Unlike my parents."

"They didn't want you around?"

Carter grimaced. "Do we have to do this?"

"Yes," Moira said.

"No, they didn't, okay? I don't know why. Maybe they shouldn't have had kids. But I was always being told I was too loud, too noisy, getting into too much shit, calling them on their shitty parenting. They didn't like it. I was…" *God*, it was hard to admit this. "I wasn't what they wanted. They wanted an easy kid, I guess, and I wasn't *easy*. And they were preoccupied with their careers and their own lives. I was…I got in the way."

An understatement.

Some days, some weeks, some *years*, it had felt like they'd barely remembered he even existed. And then he'd become a famous football player, and *then* they'd become interested in their son.

"That doesn't mean the fault's yours, Carter," Moira pointed out. "They probably *shouldn't* have had kids."

"And, can you fucking believe this? I wanted them to have another one," he said, before he could stop himself. "So it wouldn't be *only* me, you know? Even though I knew it would be misery for that kid, too. But maybe less, for both of us together." *And because I'd have had someone. Instead of just...me. Just me.*

"And you feel guilty about that? Even though it didn't happen?"

"Of course I fucking feel guilty about it," Carter said. "I was willing to condemn that kid, my little brother or sister, to a lifetime of that shitty kind of pain—the kind of pain I *knew* about already—just so I wouldn't feel so goddamn alone."

"Carter." Moira leaned forward on the screen, voice so gentle. "That's a perfectly legitimate reaction for a kid to have. To think maybe your life wouldn't be so hard if there was someone else to share it with."

Carter didn't say anything. He'd held that guilt inside him since he'd first had the thought. Yeah, he *had* been young. But he'd also not really believed he'd ever been young. He'd had to work so hard, way too hard, for a young kid, to get his parents' attention. The only times he'd ever felt like he could relax and just *be* had been with Enid, and then he'd lost her.

Was it any wonder he was so fucked-up now?

"I want you to spend the next few days thinking about it—even though I know you don't like that," Moira instructed, her firm tone making it clear he didn't have a choice. "And then when we meet Thursday, we'll talk about it some more."

"Shit, we can't do Thursday. We've got a game that day this week." Carter had the sudden hope that maybe he could get away with *not* thinking about this or talking about it, but Moira just nodded. "Friday, then," she said.

"Ugh, doc, *really*," Carter complained.

But Moira didn't budge. "Friday, same time as our Thursday meeting. And during the game, I want you to use some of the techniques we've talked about, if you need them. And we'll discuss the efficacy of those, too."

"Fine," Carter said with a resigned sigh. "*Fine.*"

A small smile quirked her lips up. "Not comfortable or easy, remember? That's what makes it worthwhile."

"I'll try to remember that," Carter said.

He shut down his laptop, shoved it in his bag, and walked out to his car to head home.

There were still plenty of cars in the lot—no doubt there were a lot of players and staff putting in extra time because of the early game this week—but Coach had pulled him aside and said he didn't want him to over-practice.

But Carter didn't need Coach to say the truth for him to *know* the truth—he was trying to keep him steady and calm and isolated so he wouldn't fuck up the rest of the team. He didn't *want* to, he really did not, but Carter worried that he might.

So he'd gone along with it and now, he tucked that little flare of guilt away, next to all his other guilts.

This late in the evening, traffic was basically nonexistent, and he made good time, pulling into the driveway of his house a little over fifteen minutes later. The one time his parents had come here, they'd made sure to point out what a haul it was from the Condors' practice facility. Carter hadn't said anything back, but he'd thought, *fuck you, I like it that way.*

And he did.

His bad habits, and all his prior coping mechanisms, rarely intruded here. This was his haven, his sanctuary.

At first, when he walked into the house, he didn't see Ian anywhere. He considered texting him, even though he'd seen that the car Ian had taken to the facility, so he could run errands on the way home, was back in its normal spot in the garage, and the keys were hanging on their hook.

But then he spotted the lights on out back, and knew Ian had gone for a swim like he'd said he might.

Don't go out there, don't go out there, don't even think about going out there, a voice that sounded suspiciously like Alec's yelled at him, but he didn't listen.

Instead, he pushed the door open and didn't say a word—okay, *couldn't* say a word—as Ian lifted himself out of the pool.

And goddamn.

Carter had told Moira earlier that Ian's long, lithe body, and his absolute fucking peach of an ass were because he was a swimmer.

And God, now he was seeing the evidence of that in spades.

Carter had seen a *lot* of naked bodies in his life—and not just because he'd personally taken their clothes off, either; after all he'd grown up a three-sport athlete—but Ian's was something special.

From the top of his curly red hair, plastered to his skull, to the spray of freckles across the bridge of his nose and his cheeks, iridescent in the dim lighting of the pool, to the gleaming wet tan skin of his slim but defined biceps and triceps, to the water snaking down his collarbone and lower still, down his toned chest and even more toned abs, to the tight bright blue swimsuit that cupped his dick in all the best ways. Carter's gaze snagged there, before coming to a rest on his incredible thighs—thick and corded with muscle, engorged from his workout. Then there was that ass.

Please don't turn around, please don't turn around.

Carter didn't need any more motivation to want to touch Ian. He already had plenty, fuck you very much.

If Alec had seen this guy naked, Carter knew he'd have never sent him.

Or he'd have sent him in about fifteen layers of clothes, with orders to never take them off.

Because Carter's attraction to Ian wasn't because he was attracted to just about everyone, in one way or another, or because Ian was forbidden fruit and therefore automatically more appealing.

Nope. Ian was appealing because he was hot as fuck and Carter wanted to do dirty, dirty things to him. As soon as fucking possible.

But you can't. You won't. Doesn't matter what you want, it's not happening.

Ian reached for the towel, and Carter nearly cried that he was covering up all that gorgeous skin.

"Are you freaking serious?" he ground out and Ian's gaze snapped up and caught his own.

Ian's watch beeped at him and he finally let himself slow down, rubbery legs still kicking absently as he reached for the edge of the pool.

Dusk had long ago fallen, and Carter's patio, edged in dim atmospheric lighting, meant that he didn't realize he wasn't alone until he was out of the pool and was just beginning to reach for the towel.

"Are you freaking serious?"

Ian jolted, wiping his face on his towel as Carter emerged from the shadows by the back door.

"Am I—" Ian stopped. Both his words and his steps.

"Yeah," Carter said, his voice rough and full of gravel, eyes raking across Ian's mostly naked, wet body.

And okay, he'd *known* this was a potential problem. He had. But he'd also thought he was alone, and Carter probably wouldn't come home for a while yet, because this week the Condors were playing early, on Thursday night, and also he'd mentioned he had a therapy appointment. He'd thought he had at least another half an hour to finish his workout, take a shower, and become fully clothed before Carter returned.

Instead, he'd come home earlier than expected, and discovered Ian in the worst possible situation—and only wearing the admittedly skimpy swimsuit briefs he liked to swim in.

He'd already acknowledged as he'd changed into them an hour earlier that he'd *need* to get something else, because he couldn't always guarantee Carter would be out of the house. He certainly wasn't going to give either of them any more reason to be tempted.

And being mostly naked and totally wet?

Definitely reason to be tempted.

Carter waved at him. "It's not that I can't control myself—I sure as fuck intend to—but *goddamn it.*"

"I'm..." Ian nearly apologized but then stopped himself. Instead, he wrapped the towel around his waist but it was already too late.

Way too late.

"I should get another swimsuit," he said instead. Because that was the problem. Not his own self-control, or his lack of interest in *being* self-controlled right now because of the way Carter was staring at him like he could eat him up. Nope—the problem was definitely how little this particular suit covered.

Ian usually liked it that way because it gave him way less drag in the water.

But he'd take the drag, and his much slower times, if it meant he wouldn't be tempted by the look currently on Carter's face.

Carter snorted. "You should get another *body*," he said. "And while you're at it, another smile. Another personality, too. Just..." He waved in Ian's general direction. "Goddamn it."

It was impossible not to smile. Because Ian *was* pleased. Pleased and touched, at how appealing Carter found him, even though Carter had already explained that wasn't unusual.

But surely, he didn't spark like this with just anyone?

Because Ian knew they were sparking, something fierce.

Why?

Because *he* didn't spark with just anyone.

If he was smart, he'd go shower and change and then go to the airport right now. Tell Alec that this was a Bad Idea, capital B, capital I.

But that wasn't necessarily true, either.

Him helping Carter was a good idea, because Carter needed the help, and Ian was uniquely positioned to offer the exact kind he required.

"You keep saying that," Ian teased.

Maybe he could make light of the situation, and they could laugh about it, and Carter's expression would stop lighting him up inside.

"I keep saying that," Carter said, beginning to pace. Far enough away that he couldn't reach over and touch. Which, definitely better for both of them. "I keep saying that because it's fucking true."

"I'll get another swimsuit." Ian couldn't help the semi-apologetic tone this time around. It just slipped out. He hadn't *meant* to make things harder on Carter. He hadn't really thought he could.

Carter shot him a look. His honey-brown eyes were dark and intense, and Ian realized with a jolt he hadn't considered that Carter could be more than good-natured and laid-back.

Those attitudes weren't exactly *easy* to dismiss because Carter was still charming as fuck, but that unexpectedly dark desperate intensity was another thing altogether.

Please don't do this to me, he wanted to say. *I don't want to leave. I want to stay for Alec—and for you, and for myself, too.*

"Okay, maybe a whole wetsuit," Ian joked weakly.

"A *baggy* wetsuit," Carter said. He let out a short, unamused laugh and collapsed on the seat of one of the pool chairs.

Ian didn't get closer to him until he'd wrapped his whole body in the towel. The good news was it was a pretty big towel, and he wasn't a particularly large person.

"How was therapy?" he asked casually, taking a seat opposite Carter on the next lounger over.

When Carter glanced back up at him, that dark had almost entirely faded away. "Not bad," he said. "She didn't give me any suggestions on how to resist you. Especially not when I come home and you're mostly naked."

"You talked about me with her?" Ian wet his lips, suddenly uncomfortable—though probably not nearly as uncomfortable as Moira had likely been.

"Well, *yeah*," Carter said, like it was a silly question.

He hadn't really intended to confess this particular truth so quickly, because he usually found it was better if his clients didn't know right away that he and their therapist were related. But that subterfuge was not going to work here. Not if Carter insisted on bringing him into his therapy sessions.

"You really shouldn't," Ian said.

"Why the fuck not?" Carter's handsome face creased with confusion. "Am I not supposed to talk about 'tough situations' with her? And the one with you—"

But Ian interrupted him before he could finish.

Because Carter's appeal wasn't just in his undeniably attractive package—the handsome face, the warm eyes, the gorgeous hair, and the *hot* body, big and lean, with muscles in all the right places—but in how interested he was in *you*.

Ian did *not* need to hear how tough resisting his apparent appeal was for Carter. Especially right now.

"Because she's my mother," Ian said frankly.

Carter's expression was shocked. "She's...she's your *mother*?"

"She kept her last name. I took my dad's," Ian said. "We don't usually tell people we're related, mostly because it doesn't usually matter, or come up, honestly, but this time, clearly it could be an issue, and I didn't want to make you uncomfortable."

"Or her," Carter said. He didn't look upset. More amused.

Ian's eyebrows skidded upwards. His mother, with all her experience, rarely seemed awkward *or* uncomfortable. "What did you say?"

Carter waved his question away. "Doesn't matter," he said. "But I'm glad you told me, though not because of what you think."

"What do I think?"

"That I wouldn't say anything to her about you because she's your mother." Carter grinned. "You must think I'm total shit at compartmentalizing."

"I..." Ian suddenly wasn't sure *what* he thought of Carter's ability to compartmentalize.

"She's my therapist first. And if I need her to help me out here, to stop me from..." Carter waved in his direction. Thankfully, *blessedly*, not going into details about what he wanted to do to Ian. "Then I'm gonna use her. No matter how weird it is."

"Oh. Okay." That wasn't what he'd expected Carter to say. He'd expected him to be weirded out and regretful. Not...accepting. Not...determined to keep talking about Ian.

Sorry, Mom, I tried.

"Aren't you going to ask why I *was* glad you told me?" Carter asked archly.

"You seem really disappointed that I don't pick up on any of your not-very-subtle attempts to charm me," Ian said, and this time it was him who was grinning.

It was *fun* to tease Carter like this.

To not be what he expected.

There was the fear this was all a slippery slope to losing his self-control, but they had to forge some kind of relationship outside of Carter lusting and Ian enjoying being lusted after.

"I am," Carter complained. "I don't dish out these lines to entertain myself. You *really* don't want to know?"

"Maybe I *shouldn't* want to know," Ian reminded him.

"Good point," Carter said, but he still looked disappointed.

"So there's a game in two days, yeah?" Ian asked, changing the subject to something that was a little safer, considering they were out here in Carter's backyard, with all that mood lighting—emphasis on the *mood*—and he was still practically naked under this towel.

"Yeah, it's early this week. Thursday games kind of suck," Carter said. "But at least we get to skip staying at a hotel the night before, even when we're playing at home."

"Oh yeah, you can?"

Ian was surprised. Every team he'd ever heard was forced to spend the night before every game in the hotel—either at home, or on the road.

"Coach thinks we can control ourselves well enough, as long as we show up to the stadium early on Thursday."

"Can you?"

"Can I what?" Carter wanted to know.

"Control yourself."

Carter rolled his eyes. "I'm fine. Perfectly fucking fine. Gonna go upstairs and jerk off, sure, but I'm not going to accost you where you sit."

"That...that wasn't exactly what I meant," Ian said. Swallowed hard. Wanted, more than he should, to ask just what Carter would be thinking about when he got himself off. *Who* he might be thinking about.

But he didn't.

"You, I'm definitely going to be thinking about you," Carter said, then grinned that carefree, light, wild grin. That fucking irresistible grin. "See what I did there? I didn't *ask* if you wanted to know, I just said it."

"I realize that," Ian said dryly. "What *I* meant was, how are you feeling about the game? About your temper?"

"It's...it's fine. But then it usually is. Until it isn't."

"What if you lose again?"

Carter reached over and smacked a hand over Ian's lips.

Ian froze.

"Don't say that shit," Carter insisted, and then he, too, froze. Like he'd just realized what he'd done. Where his hand currently was.

He removed it slowly. "Sorry," he said, and actually sounded contrite. "No matter what it seems like, I don't usually touch people who don't want me to."

Ian tried to clear his suddenly very dry throat. The truth was he did want Carter to touch him, but that was undeniably the *slipperiest* slope.

"It's alright," he said. "Sorry I said something that upset you. I don't want to...worry you? Make you paranoid?"

"It's not that. We just don't do that. We don't think about how we might lose, before we ever step on the field." The glance he shot Ian was thoughtful. "We're a superstitious bunch, I guess."

"Or a smart one," Ian argued. "There's a lot of studies on self-actualization. Books written about visualizing what you want, until it's within your grasp."

"Really? So it's not just superstitious bullshit?"

Ian shook his head.

"Huh." Carter leaned back. "That's really neat."

"I can get some books for you, if you're interested," Ian suggested, though he was ninety-nine percent sure Carter would blow off the idea. This was Carter Maxwell—what was Ian doing, suggesting he *read*?

"Yeah, I would be," Carter said, standing up. He didn't offer a hand to Ian, but Ian had a feeling he'd wanted to.

Yeah, definitely easier if they didn't touch.

"Thanks," Carter said as they walked into the house. Ian detoured into the kitchen, grabbing a bottle of water from the fridge and downing it in a couple of swallows.

"Of course," Ian said. "It's a fascinating subject."

"For getting the books, yeah, but more than that." Carter hesitated. "For asking if I wanted to read a book."

"Surely people don't assume you don't read," Ian said, even though *yeah*, he'd had that thought, same as all those assholes who thought Carter Maxwell was just a pair of awesome biceps and some killer abs. Nothing going on upstairs.

But it was already becoming clear that wasn't the case.

Carter didn't need any more ways to be appealing, but the truth was the brain nobody thought he had appealed to Ian, too.

"They think I *can* read, but that I do it? Yeah, not so much." Carter shrugged. "I guess I get their assumption."

"I don't," Ian argued.

The corner of Carter's mouth kicked up. "Well, thanks for that. For not assuming the worst of me."

"Anytime," Ian said. He tossed the plastic bottle into the recycle bin, next to the trash.

As dangerous as the patio had been, this dark kitchen felt equally as treacherous. Especially with Carter being so undeniably earnest and intelligent.

"I should grab a shower and head to bed. Early morning tomorrow."

Carter nodded. "Same," he said.

As Ian headed up the stairs—*alone*, thank God—he realized that it was actually tougher to deal with the fact that Carter *hadn't* made some over-the-top comment about joining him in the shower or in his bed. That he'd only looked at Ian with that warm, appreciative honey-brown gaze as he'd said goodnight.

That shouldn't have made Carter tougher to resist.

But it did.

CHAPTER 5

"You good?" Deacon stopped in front of where Carter was currently stretching, getting warmed up for the game that was starting shortly.

"I'm solid," Carter told him.

Deacon didn't look entirely convinced, and Carter decided he couldn't blame him.

"If you start to lose it..." He trailed off, then pointed to his chest. He was already in his jersey, the bright orange contrasting with the white outline of his number. "Come and talk to me, okay?"

"You're gonna be on the field, Harris," Carter reminded him, refraining from rolling his eyes. He wasn't going to lose it. Okay, maybe he had two weeks ago against the Piranhas. But he hadn't last week, when they'd lost. Of course, instead of losing it, he'd headed right out to the club and picked up not just one guy, but *three*, and spent the night doing all the stuff explicitly forbidden by Alec's rule one. But he hadn't lost it *during the game.*

"Then go to Riley. Or Landry. Or Coach K." Deacon's expression softened. "We're on your side, Maxwell."

"I don't know why everyone thinks you're such a tough guy," Carter teased.

Deacon shot him a look that illustrated exactly why.

"Or," Deacon said, like he hadn't even spoken, "talk to Jem. He's gonna be on the sideline." His frown deepened, like just the thought of his partner-in-crime on the sideline instead of on the field hurt.

And Carter assumed it must.

"I didn't know he'd be here today," Carter said. After Jem had been injured in the Piranhas game, he hadn't seen him on the sideline. But then, he hadn't been looking for him, either.

He'd been too focused on not totally losing his shit.

"He wasn't in the Bengals game, but he was against the Bills," Deacon said. "He's not traveling, but yeah, he's here for us. Here for *you*, Carter."

"Thanks," Carter said. "Ian's here, too."

Deacon looked thoughtful as he crossed his arms over his chest and Carter switched positions, leaning into the burn of it as he stretched out his hamstrings. "How's that going?" he asked casually.

Like that wasn't a fucking loaded question.

Deacon probably didn't even know just how loaded it was.

"Fine," Carter said. "He keeps an eye on me, like he's supposed to, so I'm a good little boy."

Deacon raised an eyebrow.

"Okay, *good* is probably stretching it," Carter admitted.

"You're not *bad*, Carter," Deacon reminded him.

"But if you're asking if I've managed to seduce him yet, *no*. He's apparently built of the same stuff as the rest of you and won't budge."

But even after coming home the other night and catching Ian just out of the pool, completely, utterly irresistible, Carter had tried *not* to seduce the guy. It was his first time trying not to do something he really, *really* wanted to do and it turned out it wasn't easy. But while it might not have been nearly as straightforward as he'd hoped, the opposite was also true. Being around Ian, just talking to him was as easy as breathing.

After he'd gone upstairs, and put his hand on his cock, dragging out the pleasure until he was overwhelmed with it, he decided that maybe it didn't matter what would've happened if they'd met under different circumstances. Because they hadn't.

They'd met under *these* circumstances, and no matter how frustrating they were, Carter was finally acknowledging that they weren't going to change.

Instead, he was trying to enjoy Ian's presence for what it was—supportive and accepting. The guy didn't make shitty assumptions about him. He was thoughtful and thought-provoking.

And, okay, if Carter thought about him in that blue Speedo as he jerked off, that was only natural. Anyone red-blooded would be *way* into that. He wasn't a freaking monk.

"Come on, Carter, you might talk a big game with us, but you wouldn't *actually* sleep with any of us." Micah had come up next to Deacon and was grinning down at him now.

"Hey, I might've slept with you *and* your husband if you'd been smart enough to see what a unique, once-in-a-lifetime opportunity that was," Carter teased.

But Micah was probably right.

He hit on them more out of habit than desire.

Frankly, even though he enjoyed having sex—that much was hard to deny—how long had it been since he'd *really* wanted someone?

He had sex with people because they were easy to pick up, or they picked *him* up, and since he usually wasn't super picky about partners, he often went along with it.

He couldn't remember the last time he'd burned for someone the way he did for Ian, and did nothing about it.

Or *couldn't* do anything about it.

"Your problem is that it's all too easy for you." Micah's husband and fellow defensive player, Beckett West, had joined them now.

"I thought this was pregame warmups, not beat-up-Carter's-ego time," Carter complained.

Beck rolled his eyes. "Your ego's plenty fine."

"Completely intact," Deacon agreed. "Especially if, like you say, Ian keeps shooting you down."

"How is that supposed to keep my ego in one piece?" Carter complained. Landry held out a hand and helped him up from the turf.

"Because that's a guy who wants you but doesn't do anything about it. Not because he's not interested, but because it's better for both of you if he doesn't," Deacon said with finality.

And like, Carter decided, he knew exactly what he was talking about.

Carter opened his mouth to bring up Mr. G, the Condors' owner who was no doubt the personal experience Deacon had with this situation, but Deacon held up a hand. "Don't," Deacon warned.

And yeah, okay, Deacon *could* be a scary motherfucker, when it came down to it, so Carter didn't.

He much preferred having the guy on his side.

Instead, he asked the other question. "How do you know what Ian wants?"

Deacon shot him a look. "Didn't we just establish that your ego doesn't need any additional assistance?"

"Well, yeah, but you said it and now I'm curious."

"It's kinda hard to miss," Landry said apologetically. Like he was actually *sorry* he was saying it, and on cue Deacon glared at him.

"What?" Landry added defensively. "*It is.* It's like when Micah showed up two months back, and whenever he and Beck were in the same room, the air *crackled*."

"Now you sound like you write romance novels," Deacon complained.

"You mean, those romance novels *you* read?" Riley asked with a raised eyebrow.

"I..." Deacon spluttered.

"See? Big softy underneath," Carter teased.

"Yeah, yeah," Deacon said, but he was grinning.

"Maybe it's just that I want *him*, and I can't have him," Carter theorized.

This time it was Riley who risked Deacon's wrath. "Yeah, that doesn't happen if it's one-sided," he said. "Trust me on this one."

"Ah, okay."

"Carter—you are the *master* at picking up people. How do you not know this?" Landry asked.

How could Carter explain?

"It's different," he just said. "With Ian, it's just different."

"You mean, instead of thinking you *should* pick him up, you actually *want* to," Deacon said sagely.

Carter would say this for Deacon—he was not an idiot.

"Sure, maybe," Carter said breezily. He was not about to admit the truth. Not to his friends. Not to anyone.

It was bad enough that he'd finally found someone he really, truly wanted, and he couldn't have him.

The group broke up after that, Deacon heading deeper onto the field to meet up with some other defensive players, and Carter jogging back over to the sideline to grab his water bottle.

"You good?" Riley said, joining him.

"Ugh, I wish people would stop asking me that," Carter said to his quarterback.

But Riley just shrugged. "You've been a little...high-strung lately."

"That's a nice way of putting it, but then you're a nice guy."

Riley was. There was no denying it.

"So are you," Riley said loyally.

"You just don't want me to fuck up another game," Carter said.

"Listen—" Riley caught his arm before he could turn away, and Carter tried to pull away, but the truth was Riley was strong as hell. "Listen," he repeated. "You're a monster out there. Every single game. Win or lose. You always bring it. Never once have I thought, I'm gonna make this happen, but Carter won't be with me. I know you will be. Every step, every down, every series."

Riley's eyes were intent on his. Serious.

"Against the Piranhas—"

But Riley didn't let him finish his sentence. "Yeah, we lost that one," he agreed. "But it wasn't because you had a meltdown. We want you to deal with this, because you're *you*, not because you're the number one receiver for the Condors. Or because you're Carter Maxwell."

"Oh. Huh." Carter had not anticipated this. He was used, on every team he'd ever been on, to being seen first and foremost as a player. A guy who could get them yards and touchdowns. And then when the cons began to outweigh even his extraordinary performance on the field, the teams always cut bait—and then traded him to another team that thought, delusionally, that they could handle the infamous Carter Maxwell.

It was downright fucking weird to be seen as a *person*.

Good, yeah, but still weird.

"I just wanted to say that," Riley said.

"Well, thanks," Carter said self-consciously.

He wasn't used to anyone giving a shit about him, and now it felt like the list was overflowing with names.

Mr. G.

Coach Kelley.

Deacon and Riley and Landry and even Micah and Beck.

Alec.

And now, Ian.

Because it was undeniable he did. He'd told him the truth last night, even though he hadn't wanted to. Even though there was no denying it had made Ian feel awkward as hell—he'd still done it, because he hadn't wanted Carter to feel betrayed by the truth. And wasn't that a fucking trip?

Ian had been tangentially connected to football through his mother for years now. He'd gone to plenty of Riptide games at her invitation and then Heath's, after they'd become friends. But he'd never once been invited to stand on the sideline and practically be on top of the action.

Of course, back then, he'd been lucky that he'd never actually been seriously attracted to a player before—and he'd never been forced to see them up close and personal in their uniform, sweat dampening their hair as they tugged their helmet off.

Okay. Not *they*. *He*.

Ian's brain fogged.

Carter shook out his hair, then reached up to tug it into a bun.

"Hey," he said, grinning over at Ian. "Imagine seeing you here."

"Hey," Ian said, trying very hard to look like he belonged—and not like he wanted to drag Carter by those tight-as-hell-pants back through the tunnel.

It was mid-way through the second quarter, and the Condors were up two touchdowns—one of which Carter had scored from more than forty yards out—and the defense was holding its own, even without Jem on the field.

"Looking sharp out there," Ian said, because it was true, *and it was true*. Carter was not only making the Texans' corners look like they were standing still, but he looked damn good doing it.

Especially when he jogged back to the sideline, took his helmet off, and shook his hair out like he was starring in a fucking shampoo commercial.

"Thanks. Feels good too," Carter said, shooting him a wide grin. "We knew their secondary was weak, but I didn't know how just how weak til now."

It wasn't like Ian *wanted* the game to go badly. He didn't. But it was hardly a good test of Carter's control when he was currently running circles around the Texans' defense, and the Condors were seemingly scoring at will.

The crowd roared, and Ian glanced around Carter's big figure to see that Beck had jumped a route and snagged the ball right out of the air, and was now running along the sideline, trying to turn his interception into a touchdown, making the Condors' two score lead a *three* score lead.

Micah met him in the end zone and they jumped up together, celebrating Beck's pick-six.

Next to him, Carter whooped, and the whole Condors sideline was rocking with positive energy, as the half drew to a close.

Coach K had pulled him aside before the game and said he wasn't against Ian coming into the locker room during halftime, but only if he felt Carter needed it. "Otherwise," Coach K had said, "I'd prefer to keep halftime to only our team."

Coach K had been nothing but supportive of Carter, and as Ian watched the team begin to stream into the locker room, Carter's smile bigger than just about anyone else's, Ian decided it wasn't necessary.

He'd stay out here, do some stretches, maybe a little bit of a jog. Enjoy the halftime show. Pretend that Carter wasn't in the locker room, stripping off his jersey or pushing a hand through his sweaty but gorgeous hair, like he didn't know just how fucking stunning he was.

But he knew.

Carter was like one of those dangerous but enticing murderous plants that seduced bugs with their bright but innocuous-looking colors. He pretended he wasn't deadly, but the whole time he was watching and waiting for the perfect time to pounce.

The problem wasn't with the pouncing—it was just how badly Ian wanted to be pounced on.

"You staying out here?" Ian glanced up and Mr. G, the Condors' owner, was standing in front of him, smiling in that kind, welcoming way he had.

Speaking of someone who looked nothing like who he was underneath...the Condors' owner had that in *spades*.

He was literally a billionaire. One of the most powerful businessmen in the world. And he looked like just any other guy on the street, not like the owner of a professional football team—and that wasn't just his age, but even what he wore.

His polo was crisp white, with the Condors red-and-orange logo embroidered just over his heart, and with it, he'd thrown on jeans and sneakers.

"Yeah, I thought I would," Ian said, not wanting to bring up what Coach K had asked of him. He was used to being welcomed—but only so far. None of this was a surprise, and Ian thought he'd gotten pretty damn good at being there when he was needed and distancing himself when he wasn't.

"Carter's playing great," Mr. G said, tucking his hands into his pockets, observing the field.

"Carter plays great, no matter what," Ian said.

Mr. G shot him a knowing glance. "You've studied how Carter plays?"

"Considering how integral football is to him, and how it seems to trigger his temper, *yeah*," Ian retorted.

"Alec said you were good at this, and it wasn't like I didn't believe him, but so far, I'm impressed," Mr. G said.

"Thanks," Ian said dryly. Would the owner be so impressed if he knew just how hard it was for him to encourage Carter to keep his hands to himself? Or how much he wanted Carter to lose that particular battle?

"You know you *could* go to the locker room, if you wanted," Mr. G said mildly.

"I know," Ian said. But he also got why Coach K didn't want him there. He'd be a distraction—not just to Carter, but to the rest of the team, who needed to keep their focus tight on the second half of the game.

"We all appreciate what you're doing for Carter."

"Carter's doing it for himself," Ian said. "I'm just here to help him. That's all."

"Well, we still appreciate it," Mr. G said with a crooked smile.

"What do we appreciate?" Jem appeared next to them, a white bandage wrapping his left arm peeping out from under the collar of his shirt.

"How Ian here is helping Carter out," Mr. G said.

"Oh yeah, totally," Jem agreed.

Mr. G excused himself, saying he was going to drop into the locker room quickly before halftime ended.

"How are *you* doing?" Ian asked, turning to Jem. He hadn't been in Charleston before Jem's injury, but he knew the guy by reputation, and of course he'd seen him a few times in passing at the practice facility, even sharing a table with him at lunch once or twice. "Or are you really sick of people asking you that?"

Jem winced. "A little yeah, but you haven't asked before so you get a free pass. Honestly, it's okay. Healing fine, according to the doctors. Be awhile yet before I can start physical therapy. But ugh, it's not looking good for me rejoining the team this season." He sounded disappointed, but Ian could also detect a hint of something else in his voice...was it relief? Was it bitterness? Since he didn't know Jem very well yet, it was hard to identify but it was there nonetheless.

"That sucks," Ian said.

"Yeah, Deacon's not happy about it." Ian noticed that Jem didn't say *he* was unhappy about it. But clearly this was a difficult situation he was still coming to terms with.

Ian understood; when he'd first considered doing something else other than being a sober companion, he'd been torn. Was he just temporarily burned out? Did he really want to leave the work that had come to define him? And he hadn't even been working at doing that job for half his life, like Jem and so many other football players. They'd devoted so much fucking time to playing football, Ian couldn't even imagine the difficulty they'd have deciding if it was time to call it quits.

His mother had ended up coaching a number of players through that transition, including Heath Harris.

Maybe he'd slip her number to Jem, just so he'd have someone to talk to, if he needed it.

But before he could consider it, the players began to stream back onto the field, including Carter, whose gaze locked onto him and then lit up. He jogged over, hair swinging like he was back in that stupid hair commercial, bright eyes framed by the black swatches of eyeblack.

"Where were you?" Carter asked, sounding like he'd actually looked for Ian and been disappointed that he hadn't been able to find him.

"I hung out here instead," Ian said.

Carter made a face. "I *missed* you," he murmured, leaning in closer. Maybe he should've smelled like every gym Ian had ever been in—but instead, all Ian could smell was sweet and clean and *Carter*.

"Uh, thanks?" Ian said, stammering a little. He wasn't used to clients telling him they missed him when he wasn't around.

"What if I did something bad in the locker room?" Carter teased.

"Were you gonna?" Ian asked archly, raising an eyebrow.

Carter shrugged.

"You seemed like you were doing well, so I didn't want to distract you, not when you had a second half to plan for," Ian said.

"I was good. More distracted that you weren't there," Carter murmured, a mischievous glint in his eyes.

"Carter," Ian said sternly.

But it wasn't Carter's fault he was practically irresistible.

He wasn't even doing anything in particular to be that way, and yet he still *was*.

"Carter," Riley called out as he jogged past them. "Come on, let's go."

Carter flashed him one last devastating grin. "Don't go anywhere," he said.

Ian had no intention of letting him out of his sight.

CHAPTER 6

YET, WHEN THE GAME was over, the Condors winning by fourteen, it seemed like Carter had forgotten about his admonition entirely.

When the field began to clear, Ian finally made his way into the tunnel, intending to hang around outside the locker room until Carter finished showering and changing. He was *not* stupid enough to go in there, not with any chance he might see Carter naked, but to his surprise, Carter was nowhere to be found.

He waited for ten minutes. Then twenty. Then thirty.

Then, a bad feeling mounting inside him, ducked his head inside to find the room basically empty.

Definitely no Carter.

He headed upstairs and in the distance saw Landry and Riley chatting with Micah and Beck as they headed towards the player parking lot.

"Hey," he said, running a little to catch up with their group.

"Hey, Ian," Riley said, shooting him a smile.

"Great win," Ian said. "Have you guys seen Carter?"

"What, he didn't take you with him?" Micah frowned. "I thought you were supposed to go everywhere with him. Especially the Pirate's Booty."

"The *what*?" Ian exclaimed. That did not sound good. That did not sound good at all.

"It's this bar we go to after games, sometimes. Victory party, like tonight, or sometimes as a consolation for a hard loss," Riley explained. "Carter told us that you knew he was going."

"I did *not* know he was going," Ian said, in a hard voice. The Pirate's Booty was definitely against at least one rule, but more than that, Carter had betrayed his trust by giving him the slip.

Especially after all that charming bullshit after halftime about not letting him out of his sight.

"Uh-oh," Beck said. "Carter's in trouble, isn't he?"

"Oh yeah," Ian said. He was almost looking forward to yelling at the guy. Being angry with him was a hell of a lot easier to deal with than wanting him.

"Excellent," Landry said, rubbing his hands together. He turned to Riley. "And you didn't want to go tonight! But now look at the fireworks we're gonna get to witness!"

Riley shot his boyfriend a look. "You shouldn't be so excited about this."

"Oh, he should," Ian said.

Micah looked surprised. "He's really not supposed to go to the Pirate's Booty?"

"I believe the term Alec used was *no clubs*, but I think we can count the Pirate's Booty."

"You can *definitely* count the Pirate's Booty," Beck agreed.

"I can't believe he wasn't supposed to go to the victory party," Riley said, shaking his head. "He doesn't get into *too* much trouble at those, because the rest of us are there, keeping an eye on him."

"I can't say I wouldn't have let him go," Ian said in a hard voice, "but he didn't *ask*. And definitely not without me."

"Well, can we give you a ride?" Micah asked.

Ian debated this for a second. Carter hadn't taken his transportation—they'd come to the game separately, because Carter had needed to be there way earlier, and Ian had assumed he couldn't get into any trouble at a team meeting.

But now that he thought about it, maybe Carter had planned this the whole damn time.

"Yeah, actually, that would be great," Ian said. After he dragged Carter out by his ear, he'd take an Uber back here and get the car.

Micah looked delighted. "We like you, you know," he said.

"Thanks?"

"You were *worried* about him being around," Beck said to his husband. "Not even a week ago!"

But Micah just shrugged at Ian's confused glance. "Carter's not that easy to resist, especially when he's supposed to be resisting himself. I was worried Ian here would get caught in the crossfire. But you're tough, man. Made of steel."

"Gotta be in this line of work," Ian said.

He would not admit to any of them how dangerously tempted he'd been.

The drive to the Pirate's Booty was short, and after Micah parked his Mercedes SUV, they all climbed out, heading into the nondescript brick building, the doorman waving them in with barely a second glance.

Ian hadn't known what to expect from a place called the Pirate's Booty, but it wasn't a lush paradise. Real palm trees were grouped in the corners, and an entire brick wall inside was trellised with creeping vines. A large wooden bar stretched across the room, shining dully in the dim light. He could hear the pulse of music close by.

"It's gonna be weird to be celebrating and it's not Disco Night," Landry said as they approached the bar.

"Hey, 90s is good too," Beck said.

And 90s Night it was, because Ian could recognize Britney now, cooing about hitting her one more time.

"Kieran!" Riley exclaimed as he leaned over the bar and did a complicated handshake with the bartender—a blond man in his thirties with a knowing grin.

"Great win today, Riley," Kieran said. He turned to Ian. "Who's this?" he asked as his hands began to make drinks.

They must be regulars here, Ian considered, as nobody had actually *ordered* a drink.

"Ian. He's Carter's minder."

"Carter's here already," Kieran said. "Gave him a Mermaid's Asshole because he demanded one." He shook his head. "Gonna regret that later."

"Kieran here has a superpower," Landry explained. "He knows what drink you should have."

Ian raised an eyebrow. "And Carter wasn't supposed to have a Mermaid's Asshole?" *That* was a drink name. Sounded just like something Carter would demand when he was in party mode.

"He just likes it cause it's sparkly. I put that edible glitter in that one, and he likes the way it shines," Kieran said. "But he should be drinking a Paloma tonight." He shot Ian a look, poured something into a glass and then set it on a coaster on the bar in front of him.

"What's this?" Ian asked skeptically. He hadn't intended to drink tonight.

He'd *intended* to collect Carter and head back to his place.

Maybe then he'd have a glass of wine. Or two. Just to numb the swirl of desire and frustration and anger inside him.

"Soda and a squeeze of orange." Kieran's eyes were otherworldly—warm and gray and they seemed to see right through him.

"You didn't know I wasn't drinking," Ian said slowly.

"Yeah, I did," Kieran said matter-of-factly.

"Told you, it's his superpower," Landry said, picking up his own drink.

Ian took a sip and nodded. It *didn't* have booze in it. Apparently this guy was really that good.

"Thanks," he said. "What do I owe you?"

"Without booze, it's on the house," Kieran said, shooting him a brief smile before he turned away to start more drinks.

"I gotta go find Carter," Ian said, and glanced down the hallway where the bulk of the noise and light was emanating from.

"You want any help?" Riley asked, sipping something bright orange.

Ian shook his head. "I've got this. No need to drag anyone else into it." He turned, heading towards the sound, and was surprised when the narrow corridor dumped him out in a massive open courtyard, full of dancers writhing along to the sick beat of old-school Marky Mark and the Funky Bunch.

It was easy to spot Carter—he was taller than almost anyone else here, the strobe lights catching on the antique gold streaks of his hair—but harder to get to him.

Ian slid and wiggled between dancers, taking the rest of the song to finally end up behind Carter.

He tapped him on the shoulder, and Carter turned, a wide smile on his face that only wavered for a moment when he realized who had touched him.

"Ian," he yelled brightly. "You're here!"

Ian regarded him steadily. "So are you," he retorted.

Carter took a deep breath, like he was gearing up to explain, only there were two problems with that. *One*—Carter was a smart guy and knew, no matter what he tried to pretend, that there wasn't a good excuse for not only ditching Ian, but coming here at all. And *two*—no matter what excuse Carter came up with, there was no way Ian was going to be able to hear it here, in the middle of the dance floor.

So, instead of staying put and only hearing every fourth word, Ian wrapped a hand around Carter's forearm, ignoring the thrill of how strong he felt, how smooth his skin was over all that muscle.

He tugged Carter out of the group, telling himself that it wasn't a turn-on at all that Carter went as easily as anything, just with a little tug from Ian.

"Where are we going?" Carter asked, but he didn't seem particularly concerned with their destination.

Ian wasn't sure, but he found at the dark edges of the courtyard, there were little nooks, quieter and with considerably fewer distractions.

He pulled Carter into one and immediately let go of his arm.

Of course, no matter how quickly he let go, he'd still remember how Carter had felt. Ian flexed his hand.

"I thought you didn't want to *do* this," Carter said, grinning down at him. Then he took a step closer and Ian thrust a flat palm against his chest, stopping him in place.

"We're *not* doing this, whatever *this* is," Ian said forcibly. "We're going home."

"What? Seriously?" Carter had the nerve to look both shocked and disappointed by this pronouncement.

"What's rule three?" Ian demanded, crossing his arms over his chest.

"Rule...three..." Carter trailed off, then immediately brightened. "No sex! And that's probably the only time I've ever said that with enthusiasm and probably the only time I ever will."

Ian sighed. "That's rule one. And you *know* that's rule one."

"Oh."

"Rule three," Ian emphasized, "is *no clubs*."

"The Pirate's Booty isn't a club; it's a bar!" Carter argued.

Ian rolled his eyes. "If you didn't think the Pirate's Booty was off-limits, why did you ditch me?"

"I didn't *ditch* you."

"Strangely, I was there, by myself, waiting for you to finish in the locker room, and by the time I realized you weren't coming out, you were gone. That's ditching me, Carter."

"I thought you'd say no if I asked and I've *never* missed a victory party at the Booty," Carter said, absolutely deploying his full lower lip to its maximum pouting potential. It shouldn't have been sexy at all, but Ian had to force his mind not to consider what nibbling on that lip would feel like.

Way too good, Ian's subconscious supplied as the answer. *Even better than in your fantasies.*

"Plus," Carter continued, "how could I miss 90s Night?"

"By missing it?" Ian retorted. "Come on, we're going home."

Those warm eyes of Carter's hardened a little. "But we're *already here*. And I haven't done anything crazy or stupid. I've had one drink and been dancing to the freaking Spice Girls. You can't do anything crazy or stupid to the Spice Girls."

"I had a roommate in college who'd have proved your theory wrong in a second," Ian said, trying not to smile.

"What if I had *asked*? Would you have let me come and not been all hardcore about it?" Carter wheedled.

Ian considered this and didn't like the answer.

He was not normally a pushover, but in all honesty, the Pirate's Booty didn't seem *that* threatening. Not if he was here to supervise, anyway. And the idea was to give Carter opportunities to test his limits without breaking the rules.

"Your curfew is at midnight, remember?" Ian asked.

"Which rule number is that?" Carter asked, his eyes lighting up, like he knew Ian was on the verge of giving in.

"Does it matter?" Ian asked.

"It sure mattered when I couldn't remember *rule three*," Carter retorted.

"Five. I didn't think you cared about any of the rules except one."

"You get told not to have sex and end up near someone you *desperately* want to have sex with, then tell me what *you're* thinking of all the goddamn time," Carter said.

Ian's heartbeat accelerated.

It was not fair.

"I'm just a convenient target."

"Trust me," Carter said, giving his body a head-to-toe sweep with that honey gaze of his—and suddenly it wasn't just warm, it was fucking scorching. "That is not why."

Ian dragged his uncooperative brain back to the subject at hand. Then checked his watch. "Your curfew is an hour and fifteen minutes from now. You can stay that long."

"Awesome!" Carter's face broke into a wide grin and he put his hand up for what Ian assumed was a high-five. But he'd already touched the guy enough tonight. "You gonna dance with me?"

"No," Ian said and then leaned against the pillar supporting the second floor surrounding the courtyard. "But you can dance, if you want."

Carter didn't look pleased about this.

"Hey, you wanted to be here, so be here," Ian said, waving his hand at the crowd. "Just..."

"Don't pick anyone up?" Carter laughed and it was humorless. "Trust me, that's not going to be an issue."

And then before he could even explain what that meant—with or without Ian asking for specifics—he was turning and walking back towards the crowd on the dance floor.

"You're sulking," Riley said, reaching up on his tiptoes to deposit his pronouncement right into Carter's ear.

Riley was one of his favorite dance partners, quick on his feet with hips that did not quit, and he'd finally gotten him away from Landry.

They'd danced through a Mariah Carey song, then Robyn, and now NSYNC, and Carter knew he should've been fucking thrilled because this playlist was *lit*, but all he could see, even when he shut his eyes or turned away from where he'd left Ian, was *Ian*. Just fucking standing there. Arms crossed over his chest. His tight T-shirt pulled taut against his pecs and his abs. His red curls glinting under the flashing lights, his eyes cool and remote.

Like Carter wasn't out here, giving the music all he could, grinding against Riley like his life depended on it. So well, in fact, that it seemed like any moment Landry was probably going to come over here and yell at him.

But would Ian?

Of fucking course not.

"Is this about your minder?" Riley asked again, even though Carter had refused to rise to his bait.

"He's just standing over there, like a fucking statue. Having *no* fun."

"Well, bring him over so we can dance with him," Riley suggested.

Carter made a face.

"He didn't want to dance. He just wants to stand there and *watch* me."

Riley's expression turned speculative. "Is that why you keep trying to grab my ass?"

"No, of course not. I'm trying to grab your ass because it's *fantastic*," Carter lied.

"Trying to make him jealous, huh?" Riley laughed. "One of your most solid plays, for sure."

"It's not working." And yep, right there, Carter could hear the sulkiness in his voice. Just like Riley had said, he was totally sulking. Over *Ian*.

God, how embarrassing was that.

"Go over and ask him again," Riley suggested.

"And get shot down again? I know y'all think my ego is infinite, but it's not."

Riley punched him in the arm. Hard. Carter winced and rubbed the spot, glaring a little at his quarterback as he did it.

"Please," Riley said, "you've been dying to go over there practically from the moment you left."

It was true.

"What if he says no again?"

"Tell him he knows how to blend in, and he's standing out right now," Riley said.

Carter looked at him skeptically.

"A sober companion's whole job is to blend in, so you don't know why they're really there. Right now? He looks like a combo of a hot bodyguard and a stalker."

"He's looking at me?"

Riley shot him a look. "He's fucking *staring* at you, Carter. Go over there and *talk to him*. Here, a slow song's just starting. I'd better get back to Landry before he decides he should murder you in a jealous rage. And *you*, you're going to go get Ian and convince him to dance with you."

"You want me to *slow dance* with him?" Carter wasn't sure *one*, that was possible, and *two*, that was a good idea.

But Riley just nodded and turned away to look for Landry.

New Kids on the Block were crooning about how they weren't the kind of guy who could take a broken heart as Carter walked over to where Ian was still leaning against the wall.

Observing, but not participating.

Was that what he'd been doing, since becoming a sober companion? Always only standing back, never allowing himself to get into the thick of things?

Carter thought that might be a pretty damn lonely way to live.

That was what finally convinced him to go over there and try again—not just for himself, but for *Ian*.

"You look like you're having a terrible time," Carter said as he approached.

Ian shot him a look. Cold enough it should've given him frostbite.

"Why do you care?" Ian retorted. "You wanted to be here, so we're here. *My* feelings aren't the ones we care about."

"You could at least relax some. Enjoy yourself. Stop looking like a cross between a hot bodyguard and a stalker."

Carter gave Riley all the extra points because Ian's jaw dropped at his comparison.

"I do not look like that," he argued.

"I know how you could *not* look like that," Carter said, holding out a hand. "Dance with me."

Ian looked at his outstretched hand like it was dipped in poison. "Not a good idea," he said.

"It's one slow song, Parker. I promise, I've not managed to seduce anyone in three minutes yet. So I think you're safe."

Ian still did not look convinced.

"We'll dance like we're in middle school, even, with enough room for the holy spirit between us," Carter teased. "Unless you're so into me, you can't even resist for a whole three minute New Kids on the Block song?"

He'd known that would be the thing that broke Ian's good intentions and sure enough, Ian gave in.

"Fine. *Fine.*" Ian slapped his hand into Carter's and let himself be dragged over to the dance floor.

Carter did a little flourish, spinning Ian around and tucking a hand into the curve of his waist. Ian's hand went to his shoulder, resting so carefully there it was like he was barely touching him—except he was.

They began to move together awkwardly and then easier and finally easier still, Carter finding the rhythm and Ian matching it. It wasn't easy, but Carter ignored how goddamn good he felt. Ignored how Ian sucked in a breath as Carter's fingers stroked the fabric of Ian's shirt. Not the skin. Just the fabric. He was *behaving himself.*

Carter told himself that this was how he'd have danced with his grandmother.

But that wasn't exactly true, was it?

"I was too young for this one," Ian said stiltedly. Like talking during the slow dance would be enough to invalidate its inherent slow-ness.

Or just how fucking romantic it was.

Carter could see Riley tucked into Landry's shoulder, the two of them swaying like they belonged together.

"Me too, though my grandmother was a huge New Kids on the Block fan," Carter said.

Ian's eyebrow quirked up. "She was?"

"Yeah." Carter must be going insane from the total lack of sexual release. He'd talked about her, albeit briefly, with Moira the other day, and now he was volunteering info about her to Ian.

"Do you think the number of times they sang *girl*, convinced anyone they were totally straight?" Ian asked.

Carter laughed. This right here was why it was worth working so goddamn hard to get Ian to relax. Because he was wickedly funny when he did. "Probably."

His hand tightened around Ian's waist, and somehow they ended up a lot closer together. Was that him? Had he done that? Or had Ian?

Maybe both of them. Gravitating together like they were...

Carter shook his head, trying to clear it. The saccharine sweet nature of the song was getting to him, that was all. He wanted to *fuck* Ian, not laugh with him and hold him and see the ice melt out of those gray-green eyes.

"You're a good dancer," Ian said.

Carter smiled, as they swayed together. "So are you. Which begs the question, why were you hiding over there, pretending you didn't want to join in?"

"Because I'm not supposed to," Ian said, a hint of a frown crossing over his face before it smoothed out.

"Says who? Alec? I doubt he'd say that."

"No, Alec wouldn't." But Ian didn't elaborate.

"So the reason you didn't dance with me wasn't because you didn't want to," Carter said. "You didn't dance with me because you decided you weren't *allowed* to."

Ian shrugged, but there was no denying it. "I'm dancing with you now, aren't I?"

"Yeah, yeah you are." Carter couldn't help his smile. He tugged him a little closer, and Ian shot him a hot look, but he didn't pull back.

There was no denying it—Ian's body felt so fucking *right* pressed against Carter's. Maybe because there hadn't been any pressing whatsoever in at least a week, but he had a feeling it was a lot more than that. Ian *fit* him. When Ian tipped his head back, he was just the perfect height for Carter to lean down and...

Yeah, that would be a really great way to end this song.

A great way to end the dance, too.

But still, Carter didn't kiss Ian.

Because you're not supposed to, his brain reminded him. But it was more than that. The reasons why were tangled up together, too complicated to untangle, even if Carter wanted to.

Ian, who had been determinedly staring over Carter's right shoulder, into the distance, and not meeting his eyes, shifted, and his gaze caught on Carter's face.

"Come on," Carter coaxed, "isn't this nice?"

"I'd be able to relax more," Ian admitted, "if I wasn't worried I'd give you an inch, and you'd take a mile."

Carter knew what kind of shit people said about him, and he usually found it hard to get offended because so much of it was actually true.

But hearing Ian say that sucked.

"Do you really think I'd seduce you, even if you didn't want to be seduced?" Carter *did not* want Ian to think he wouldn't be respectful of boundaries, no matter how much he disliked what they represented.

Ian chuckled. "Not necessarily. After all, you tried to seduce your teammates, and that didn't work."

"It didn't work, not because I'm not incredibly charming and attractive and fucking amazing in bed—" But Carter didn't get the rest of it out, because Ian interrupted him.

"And modest too," Ian inserted, eyebrows raised.

"Who needs modesty?" Carter teased.

"Apparently not you," Ian said, but he was smiling now.

"Exactly," Carter said. "But I couldn't seduce them, not because I'm *me*, but because they were already in love. Can't seduce someone in love."

"They're all in love?" Ian sounded very skeptical.

New Kids were wrapping up their song, and it suddenly seemed very important that Carter convince him of this. "Well, they don't all know it," Carter said seriously. "But yes."

"I was pretty sure Deacon told me the other day he was single."

Jealousy blasted through Carter.

Fucking *jealousy*.

There was no other way to identify it, as much as Carter absolutely loathed feeling that way.

"Why are you and Deacon talking about how single he is?" Carter asked, trying to sound like he didn't give a shit. He *did not* give a shit.

But if he wasn't allowed to touch Ian, he sure as hell was not going to stand by and watch as someone else did it.

He loved Deacon—from the moment Carter had shown up in the middle of the clusterfuck that had been the last season, he'd been there for him, and a good friend—but he was damned if he was going to watch as Ian and Deacon hooked up.

Ian whacked him on the arm. "Don't sound so jealous," he said.

"I'm not, I'm *not*," Carter argued, but he didn't sound very convincing, and Ian didn't *look* very convinced.

"I was making a comment about how your whole team seemed to have paired off," Ian said. "And Deacon said *he* hadn't. Neither had Jem. And you haven't, clearly."

"Clearly." Riley would've told him he was sulking again, and he wouldn't have been wrong *again*.

Good thing Riley was over there, dancing with Landry.

"You can calm down now," Ian said matter-of-factly.

"I'm calm." But he didn't *feel* calm. He felt like grabbing Ian by the hair and dragging him off to the nearest dark corner and convincing him with his mouth and hands just how much Ian didn't want to hook up with Deacon. That *Carter* was who he really wanted.

Ian shot him a look, just as the song thankfully came to an end.

Because yes, okay, Riley had been right. It had been fun. Ian didn't look like a bodyguard or a stalker any longer. But it looked like they were *together*.

And Carter, despite that he'd never wanted more than sex in his life, thought he might actually like that.

Especially if it meant that Deacon kept his hands off.

"I'm going to get a drink," Ian said. "Do you want anything?"

He'd convinced Kieran to give him a Mermaid's Asshole earlier, but now it sat uneasily at the base of his stomach.

"Whatever Kieran thinks I should have," Carter said.

Ian nodded and took off, putting enough distance between them that Carter wouldn't be tempted to grab him right back.

And that was the problem, wasn't it? He was beyond tempted.

"Thought you weren't drinking," Riley asked as Kieran added a shot of vodka to his soda and slid it back across the bar with a knowing smile.

Ian was in no mood to quibble about what he'd said before Carter had put his hands all over him—and he'd done the same to Carter.

"I wasn't, not until..." Ian trailed off. He didn't really want to tell Carter's friend just how hard he was finding this assignment.

Of course, if it was only hard, he'd have called Alec days ago and quit. Instead, it was both unbelievably difficult and also one of the easiest assignments he'd ever had.

A conundrum Ian hadn't figured out how to reconcile yet.

"You guys are cute together," Riley said, raising his own glass and clinking the side of it against Ian's.

"We're not supposed to be," Ian reminded him. "I'm here to make sure Carter doesn't break the rules."

"And how's that going?" Riley asked, raising an eyebrow. "Didn't he run off tonight, without you?"

"Yeah," Ian admitted. They were definitely going to talk about that—but he already knew it would be useless to do it here. Which was why he'd given Carter his time, and then either tonight or tomorrow, they'd have a discussion about why Carter had felt the need to break the rules, even though the Condors had been ahead the entire game, had won by a healthy margin, and had done it with Carter as an integral part of their on-field strategy.

But right now, Ian thought, checking his watch and noting there was still twenty minutes left before Carter's curfew, he was going to enjoy his drink and try to forget how it felt to slow dance with Carter Maxwell to New Kids on the Block.

His fifteen-year-old self would be doing fist pumps in the air right now.

"Well, good luck with him," Riley said, grinning. He turned away, two drinks in his hands, no doubt to find Landry.

"Can I get you anything else?" Kieran asked, wiping his hands on a towel. He had an easy, welcoming smile that made Ian immediately feel included. It was a great skill for a bartender to have—and then there was his superpower.

"What did you want to give Carter before? When he insisted on the Mermaid's Asshole?" Ian asked.

Kieran looked surprised. "You're gonna bring him a drink?"

He was. It was very stupid, but there it was. Still, Carter was a big guy, and they'd been there for a while, and it wasn't like even two drinks would be enough to get him wasted. They were out, celebrating. It was totally reasonable. Even Alec would've thought so.

"I know what he likes," Kieran said, and began pouring different bottles into a shaker he'd filled with ice.

"What is that?" Ian asked, leaning over the bar so he could get a better look.

"Paloma, but I'm adding a little blue curacao into the bottom for visual interest," Kieran said, drizzling the bright blue liquid into a glass. "And maybe since I'm feeling magnanimous, I'll add some more of that glitter he's so into."

"Kind of you," Ian said, grinning, because of course Carter was into glittery drinks.

It had been so much easier to dismiss the guy when Ian had assumed he was some ridiculously hot, totally ripped, charming-but-brainless idiot who hit on everything that moved. But Carter wasn't like that at all. He was sweet and quirky. He had a sense of humor—and even more than that, he could laugh at himself. He had *depths*, and Ian was stupid enough to want to dive into them.

"Kind of *you* to bring him a drink," Kieran said, shooting Ian a lopsided grin as he finished pouring Carter's drink with a flourish.

"All part of the service," Ian said. Which was not true at all. In fact, the opposite was true, and after this, they were a hundred percent going back to Carter's house.

Before Carter could convince him to stay. Or to have another drink. Or God forbid, to slow dance with him again.

Ian paid for their drinks—Kieran shooting him a knowing look when he insisted that he didn't want to just put them on Carter's running tab—and headed back to the dance floor.

Carter was where he'd left him.

But he wasn't alone.

Ian wasn't proud, but he gulped down half his vodka-and-soda when he saw the very cute guy currently putting the moves on Carter.

The game tonight had been a test, but this was the *real* test.

Would Ian be forced to intervene when Carter tried to pick this guy up—or when this guy tried to pick Carter up?

"Oh, Ian, you're back," Carter said, shooting Ian a bright—and *grateful*—smile. "And with my drink. Oh, *oh*, Kieran gave me the glitter, too! You must've asked him to do it."

Before Ian could react, Carter had taken the drink from his hand and then with his other, wrapped it around Ian's waist and tugged him close.

Not just close.

Ian was practically fucking plastered against Carter's big warm body. He tensed.

Not because he hated it.

Actually, the opposite.

"I told you, my guy is the *most* thoughtful."

My guy.

Ian's brain short-circuited.

That was his only explanation for why he didn't immediately pull away or ask Carter what the fuck he was thinking.

The other guy was short and cute, with flawlessly styled blond hair, a probably fake tan, and the kind of build that meant he spent just enough time in the gym to give him decent tone.

Ian didn't know the guy so he shouldn't have disliked him, but it was the determined slant to his blue eyes that pissed Ian off. Like it didn't matter if Carter had called Ian *his guy*, he was going to go home with Carter anyway.

Ian tucked a hand around Carter's waist. Ignored his pulse fluttering at how solid and perfect Carter felt as his fingers spread out and he just let himself stroke, possessively.

"Yeah," Ian agreed, gazing up at Carter's face and letting the dazzled way he'd felt about Carter reveal itself for the first time, "I really *am* the best, aren't I?"

"I wouldn't have settled for anything less." Carter looked charmed and amused *and* adoring. Ian hadn't thought he was this good of an actor, but he was really pulling it off. Looking like a man who hadn't wanted to be caught by love but was anyway, and instead of being unhappy about it, was discovering how great it was.

It's just an act; it doesn't mean anything.

The guy in front of them frowned. Seeing for the first time that this might not be so easy? Possibly.

"You're really together?" His eyebrows skidded up.

"Yep," Carter announced proudly.

"Are you freaking kidding me?" The guy looked pissed off now. "I *came here* just for you."

"I'm definitely flattered, but unfortunately, Ian here's captured me. Completely."

"Utterly," Ian agreed, his gaze drifting back towards Carter's.

The guy turned and marched off without even so much as a *goodbye* or a *have a nice life*.

"Well, that worked like a charm," Carter said, grinning delighted-ly. "I wasn't sure you'd be into that."

Ian let go of Carter reluctantly. The moment had passed. He shouldn't feel so bad it was over. He should be *relieved*.

"He was just...so proprietary, like just because you were here and so was he, it was a given that you'd go home with him," Ian grumbled.

"I hate to break it to you, but before all this, I probably would've."

Ian shot him a look.

"What? It's not my fault it was *easy*." Carter paused. "And it did what it was supposed to do."

Ian didn't say anything. Didn't quite trust himself to say something that wasn't cutting or rude. *You have to keep living with the guy after this*, he reminded himself. And the thing was, he had no issue with people enjoying their sexuality or indulging in one-night stands. But in Carter's case...it was more than that, wasn't it?

It felt kind of sad...and lonely.

"Not like I didn't enjoy them, and they definitely enjoyed *me*," Carter continued, but the defensive note in his voice was new.

Ian didn't know what to say.

Normally, that meant he should absolutely keep his mouth shut. He'd developed a good reputation in Los Angeles and had been referred among the celebrity set because he had that ability. He didn't judge. He didn't offer criticisms. He just supported within the terms of his contract.

But Carter had already wiggled around so many of his other good intentions it wasn't particularly surprising that he managed to get around this one, too.

"Don't you ever want to just...wait and have sex with someone you're attracted to?" Ian asked softly.

Carter stared at him. "Do you know you're the first freaking person who's ever asked me that question?"

Ian wasn't surprised. After all, so many looked at Carter and got stuck on the surface. And who could blame them? It was an undeniably beguiling surface.

If he hadn't been forced to look closer, he might've gotten stuck there, too.

"I'm not surprised," Ian admitted.

Carter took a sip of his drink, looking thoughtful. "To answer your question, I'm not sure."

"Maybe that's something you should talk about with your therapist."

Carter shot him a look. "You mean, *your mother*?"

"Okay, that's fair," Ian said with a shrug. "But yeah. You're deliberately not giving yourself a chance to find someone you can really connect with. Maybe the sex is more about that than it is managing your emotions."

"You're too smart for your own good," Carter teased.

Ian finished his drink. "I've heard that before."

"A lot, I bet."

"My ex, who got tired of me having to prioritize clients during our relationship, but really hated it when I 'shrink-ed' him."

"Sounds like he had shit he wanted to hide," Carter said sagely.

And hadn't that been the fucking truth?

"I mean...don't we all?" Ian admitted. "Come on, it's just about your curfew. We should be getting out of here."

"Aw. You're not gonna let that go, are you?"

Ian shot him a look. "I already let the 'no bars and no clubs' rule go. I'm not gonna let you get away with everything, just because you asked me to slow dance and then used me to get rid of a guy trying to pick you up."

"And here I thought we were finally getting somewhere," Carter said, slinging an arm around his shoulders as they headed for the exit. But this touch of Carter's didn't feel more than just friendly.

The same kind of touchy-feely he'd be with any of his teammates.

Ian couldn't count all his ex-clients as friends. Only a handful of them had ever become close enough for their professional arrangement to morph into friendship.

He certainly had not intended Carter to end up on that list. In fact, it would be a lot easier if he didn't.

But Ian had a feeling it hadn't been up to him, at all.

Carter had decided they were friends, so they were friends.

Chapter 7

"Iꜰ ʏᴏᴜ ᴛʜᴏᴜɢʜᴛ ᴡᴇ weren't going to talk about you dodging me yesterday, think again," Ian said as Carter walked into the kitchen the next morning.

"Not even going to give me a chance to have my caffeine first?" Carter asked. He walked to the fridge and pulled out a can of Diet Coke identical to the one sitting by Ian's laptop on the kitchen table.

"Go ahead. You can drink. I can talk."

Carter made a face. "Do we have to?"

"Yeah, we do. Honesty and transparency are, in my opinion, the only way to do something like this. You ditched me. Didn't even ask if I thought it was a good idea that you go."

"But," Carter said, deploying his most charming grin, "you *did* think it was a good idea, in the end." He pulled one of the premade breakfast meals out of the fridge, but Ian gestured towards a plate, wrapped in plastic, on the edge of the island.

"I made eggs and some turkey sausage. Saved some for you, if you were interested," Ian pointed out.

It wasn't technically in his job description to cook for Carter, but he'd been cooking for himself, hadn't he? And weren't they friends?

Of course, friends didn't spend half the night tossing and turning, arousal and desire persistently sticking around despite the fact he'd told himself a thousand times that nothing they'd done at the Pirate's Booty had changed anything.

But deep down, Ian knew that was a lie.

"Thanks, that's nice of you," Carter said. He picked up the plate and headed towards the microwave.

"I was already cooking," Ian said defensively. Like being nice was a problem, even though that definitely was *not* the problem.

Carter stuck two halves of a whole wheat bagel into the toaster and then leaned against the countertop, watching Ian with a knowing gaze that made him feel even more defensive.

Like he knew what Ian was thinking

Like he knew what Ian wanted.

Have this conversation, because you need to, and then you can escape to your room.

He'd managed to keep himself from jerking off since showing up at Carter's house, but his self-control in that department was running awfully thin these days.

Maybe it was time to break down.

He could get in the shower…a nice hot shower…imagine Carter joining him.

How good would Carter look wet?

Way too fucking good.

Ian dragged his thoughts back to sanity.

"I didn't think going to the Pirate's Booty was a *bad* idea. There's a difference," Ian said, changing the subject back to the one that mattered.

"Okay," Carter said. Not even patronizingly, which Ian was pretty sure he at least partially deserved.

Ian sighed. This was going just about as shitty as he'd feared it would.

"Listen," he said. "It's easy enough to do the right thing when things are going well. You guys won yesterday. The Condors were ahead the whole game. You scored two touchdowns. You ran fucking circles around the defensive guys trying to cover you. You weren't going to have a problem with your temper yesterday."

"Probably not," Carter agreed.

"But that doesn't mean you can't just drop the shit that's helping you. You never know when it's gonna get hard. When push comes to shove. And if you're used to just letting the good practices go, then when you need them, you might not have them. They might not work."

Carter didn't say anything, just considered this argument.

It was a damn good argument.

It was one Ian knew his mother would've made. Would undoubtedly make herself when she and Carter met next—if Carter told her about the rule he'd broken, anyway.

"So if I'd asked you if we could go to the Pirate's Booty, you'd have said yes?" Carter finally asked.

"I'd have considered the circumstances and the environment and probably said yes, with restrictions."

"Kinda like you did when you showed up."

Ian nodded.

"Hmmm. Okay."

"You're not in the same position as my regular clients," Ian pointed out. "This isn't an all-or-nothing thing."

"But Alec made those rules—"

"Not saying you should break them," Ian interrupted. The last thing he needed Carter deciding was the first rule was no longer valid, and pouncing.

He *thought* he might be able to push him away, but he didn't want to rely on his weakening self-control.

While Alec might not freak out about them going to the Pirate's Booty last night, there was no way he'd be okay with Carter breaking that particular rule, especially with *him*.

It wasn't just that Alec was tough, or had expectations of Ian staying professional, Ian knew this was a test.

Could Ian give his word and stick to it?

If Ian couldn't, then Alec wouldn't want to hire him. Couldn't trust him, not the way he needed to.

"So you're saying *you're* allowed to decide when I can break the rules," Carter stated, still looking puzzled.

"Within reason, yeah," Ian said.

That was not his agreement with Alec, but Alec had also hired him because he knew how to do this. And hard and fast was not going to be a way to manage Carter. That much was becoming rapidly obvious.

"So the next time I want to break a rule, I just ask you?" Carter was smiling now, like he knew something Ian didn't.

"Yes," Ian said cautiously. Not sure what trap he was about to fall into but sure there had to be one, just about to snap closed right above his head.

There'd been a time when he'd been convinced and utterly sure that Carter Maxwell was just a stupid football player.

Ha.

"Then, I could do this?" Carter pushed off from the counter and prowled closer. *Way* closer. Until he was practically on top of Ian, who froze.

"Do what?" Ian wasn't proud of how his voice stuttered.

"This," Carter said, and leaned down, his lips not-quite grazing Ian's neck. "You wanna go upstairs?" he murmured, breath warm against Ian's ear.

Ian shivered.

He knew—he *knew*—the only way to deal with this sudden surge of desire, so thick and hot and *right*, was to cut it off before it could even begin, but instead of telling Carter to back off, that *no*, he did not want to go upstairs, he said, "And do what?"

Carter chuckled, clearly delighted. "Why don't you tell me what you'd like to do?"

Ian opened his mouth to say everything he'd thought of earlier. The hot shower, the cool tile walls. Carter pinning him there, kissing his neck, then his chest, mouth lingering on his nipples, until he was panting with need, and then sinking lower, and lower still.

But he snapped his teeth shut again.

They could not do this.

He could not do this.

He'd given his word, and the very last thing he wanted—even more than he wanted Carter—was to have to call up Alec and tell him the truth.

I couldn't do it. I couldn't resist. I thought I could, and I'm sorry.

"Stop it," he barked out, his own sudden spike of frustration and temper biting into the air.

Carter, to his credit, immediately stopped. Took a few steps back and held his hands up. "Sorry," he mumbled. "I shouldn't have done that."

"No, you shouldn't have," Ian said, but then instantly felt bad, because the guilt lingering in Carter's eyes was working on him in unpleasant ways. There was no denying he'd *liked it*. He'd practically *encouraged it*. How could he put all the blame on Carter when he'd been just as into it?

When he'd let Carter play-act with him as a happy couple yesterday?

When he'd agreed to dance with him?

"We can't do this," Ian reminded both of them, softer this time. "I can't say it doesn't appeal to me." He hadn't wanted Carter to know the truth about his weakening self-control *or* the deal he'd made with Alec, but maybe if Carter knew, it would help. "It does. *You* do. And not for all the reasons you think, so keep your ego in check. But I need to do this job. Not just for you, but for me."

Carter was so sharp, he immediately picked up on what Ian wasn't quite saying. "What do you mean?" he asked as he went to grab his food.

"I mean, I don't want to be a sober companion anymore, and Alec's agreed to hire and train me to be an agent if I complete this job."

"You mean, if you watch me for him," Carter said, cutting through all of Ian's vague, politely worded phrases.

"Yes."

After all, hadn't Ian *just said* this would be easier if they were transparent with each other?

"So let me get this straight." Carter put the plate down on the table, next to his Diet Coke, and sat. "My therapist is your mother. And Alec didn't just hire you because you're good at this, but he had to bribe you to come out here and watch me by offering to make you an agent, just like him?"

Maybe Ian needed to start taking his own goddamn advice.

"Yes," Ian repeated, wincing a little.

"Hmmm," Carter said noncommittally.

"I wanted to tell you," Ian said, which was not technically true. He hadn't wanted to tell Carter—but he couldn't rely on his own self-control much longer. Carter was a good man. He seemed to have some affection for Ian, and Ian was desperately betting on Carter at least attempting to do the right thing.

Carter shot him a look. "I'm not sure I buy that."

"Okay, fine, I was hoping to appeal to your good intentions."

"I have those?" Carter asked, raising an eyebrow as he munched on a bagel half.

"You do," Ian emphasized. "You absolutely do."

"Huh." Carter didn't seem *mad*, exactly, but he was definitely perturbed about something. "Why don't you want to be a sober companion anymore?"

It was hard to know where to start. "I don't dislike the work. I *like* helping people, but it's...it's fleeting. I'm with someone all the time, for a few months, and then I never see them again. That gets old. And you know how you came over last night and complained that I was on the sideline and wouldn't join in?"

Carter nodded.

"Well, that's another reason. I'm *supposed* to do that. I just feel like...it's time for me to be the leading man in my own life, you know?"

"And you think being an agent would do that? You really want to be like Alec?"

"Yeah, yeah I do, and I have for a while," Ian said, and that was as honest as he could be.

Carter tilted his head to the side. Still hadn't taken his eyes off Ian, even as he continued to plow through his breakfast. "I think you'd be good at it," he finally said. "Being Alec."

"Thanks," Ian said.

"And you'd look damn hot in those slick suits he wears all the time," Carter said.

Ian couldn't help the laugh that escaped him. Carter was going to Carter. It was inevitable.

But now that he knew the truth, it felt like some of the pressure for Ian to hold himself apart was gone. He couldn't *relax*, not exactly, but he could stop being so vigilant.

"Thanks," Ian repeated, still chuckling.

Carter finished his breakfast and then leaned back in the chair. "You didn't protest last night."

"When you pretended like I was your boyfriend?"

"Yeah."

"It was..." *It was hot, and I loved it. For a second, I wanted it to be true.* "It was expedient."

"Like...easy?"

When Ian nodded, Carter's forehead crinkled in confusion.

So Ian explained. "Easy like, you didn't have to tell the guy you weren't interested. And I'd guess that, before the last few weeks, you'd have been the opposite."

"Yeah." Carter didn't sound too enthused over the prospect.

Ian didn't know why he kept picking at this, but he couldn't seem to stop himself. "He was attractive. Clearly interested in you."

Carter sighed. "You're probably right. But now I look at someone like that, a guy like that, and I just want..." He trailed off, looking suddenly awkward and uncomfortable.

Ian had a feeling he knew what Carter had been about to admit to.

"I told you, I thought you were just going through the motions," Ian said.

"Yeah, maybe I was."

"It's different when...when you've got chemistry with someone. When it's more than just physical attraction, when it's more than just one night." Ian was currently marching right into a minefield. Why didn't he turn around and run back to safety?

Because yeah, this shit was hard. Hard to admit to. Hard to deal with. But also a valuable lesson for Carter.

Ian just wished it hadn't been with *him* that Carter had discovered a deeper, hotter attraction.

"You sayin' you *like* me?" Carter teased, his smile brightening the whole room.

"I'm not saying anything like that," Ian grumbled.

But he was.

You like Carter and he likes you. Likes likes you.

Apparently between this conversation and the slow dance yesterday, they were back in junior high. All he'd have to do to complete the picture was send Carter a note written in glittery gel pen. *Do you like me? Check yes or no.*

"Well, good talk," Carter said. "For a talk, anyway." He grinned again. "I gotta go get ready for my meeting with your mom."

Ian must've looked surprised because now Carter looked apologetic again as he stood and stretched. His T-shirt rode up, giving Ian a very quick and yet very distracting glimpse of his abs.

"Is that okay to say?" Carter asked, looking actually concerned that he'd stepped wrong.

"Absolutely," Ian said. "I told you she was my mother, didn't I?"

"I think you were trying to save me the embarrassment of finding out later," Carter said. "Or maybe her the embarrassment of what I was saying about you. Not sure that's gonna work."

"Me either," Ian said, smiling at the thought of his very put-together mother dealing with all of Carter's X-rated thoughts.

It wasn't like he didn't *want* to hear them.

Or that he didn't have plenty of his own, about Carter.

He heard Carter shut himself into the office just off the living room, and to give him additional privacy—and because he couldn't seem to help himself any longer—Ian headed upstairs, with the shower his destination.

He turned the water on hot and stripped off his T-shirt and shorts he'd started sleeping in, because the last thing either he or Carter needed was a middle-of-the-night emergency and there he was, dressed only in his briefs.

Ian had resolutely *not* asked Carter what he slept in—but if he had to guess, it was nothing.

Normally, he'd push that thought away as soon as he had it, but with the bathroom fogging up with steam, he let himself go there.

Let himself drift into the fantasy.

His cock was already hardening as he stepped into the shower, letting the glass door close behind him.

Leaned his overheated body against the cool tile and trailed his hand down his chest. Tweaked his left nipple, groaned a little under his breath and then did it again.

He couldn't remember ever being this horny. In general. Or for one specific person. Not even his last boyfriend had been able to work him up this quickly.

The first brush of fingers against stomach had his hips thrusting, eager for his touch.

No.

Not his touch.

It was Carter touching him.

Carter leaning over him, Carter capturing his mouth with his own, not with the smooth, knowing seduction he'd no doubt perfected, but a rough desperation that Ian craved.

Carter would push him back against the tile, and his hands would be calloused but sure, as they skated down his chest, right to where Ian wanted them so badly.

His hard cock, bobbing in front of him.

There was no question if Carter would tease—he would, and then he'd give as good as he could, sinking to his knees, mouth hot and wet around him. As greedy to give it to Ian as Ian was to take it.

Ian's hand was wet around his cock, as he hissed through the pleasure, trying to prolong it, but knowing it was impossible to last. Not when he was thinking about Carter.

Carter on his knees.

Carter bending over him.

Carter kissing him.

Carter's lips on his mouth, neck, his chest, his cock.

Carter's arm pushing him back against the wall as he took everything Ian needed to give him.

Ian's orgasm tingled at the base of his spine, and he finally gave himself over to it, stroking himself in rough, needy motions as he came.

When it was finally over, he slumped against the tile, and even though he'd just come his brains out, he didn't feel entirely satisfied.

His imagination was earnest and creative and malleable, but the Carter in his mind wasn't *quite* the same as Carter in real life.

You're never going to have the real-life Carter, he reminded himself as he washed off, then scrubbed his hair. Wallowing, a little, in the hot water and in the annoying inevitability that he'd never get what he truly desired.

He was just about toweled off when a loud knock on the bathroom door made him jump.

"What?" he barked.

Don't ask if you can come in, please God, don't ask if you can come in.

Ian was feeling particularly weak right now, and if Carter asked—because he *would* ask, there was no question about him just barging in—he might be tempted to say yes.

"I need to talk to you." Carter's voice was muffled through the door but even with the heavy wood in the way, Ian could hear the panic in Carter's voice.

Screw the emergency in the middle of the night.

Apparently there was an emergency right now.

Ian didn't think, he just reached over and yanked the door open. Not necessarily *forgetting* that he was only wearing a towel and his eyes were probably warmer and sleepier than they normally were. He probably looked very satisfied.

Oh well.

There was no question about it.

Carter stared at Ian, and *knew* he'd just had an orgasm.

Warm and flushed, sleepy-eyed Ian with all that ice gone from his gaze, was fucking incredible.

Carter's grip on his phone tightened. "I...uh..."

He'd knocked on this door for a reason. Nearly interrupted Ian's jerkoff session for what had to be a *very* good reason, but fuck if he remembered what it was right now.

"What is it?" Ian's gaze sharpened, and the impatience in his voice punctured the hazy arousal swimming through Carter.

Less than an hour earlier, Ian had informed him that it was different when you had chemistry with someone. Carter knew it had to be true, because he'd never felt this fierce kind of wanting ever before in his life, and he wasn't prepared to deal with it at all.

Maybe, like Moira said, his life before this had both been *too* easy and also *too* hard, and in all the wrong ways.

They'd been on their therapy call when his phone had kept ringing and ringing and then he'd finally gone to just turn it off and realized it was Alec.

And he was frantic.

Carter snapped his fingers. "I know what it was now."

"Well, are you gonna tell me what it is?" Ian asked impatiently, holding his towel around his waist with a white-knuckled grip. Like Carter might fight him for it.

"Remember that guy from last night?" Carter was aware of how ominous he sounded. *Alec* had sounded ominous, and frankly, Alec was not the kind of person who panicked.

"Of course I do," Ian said.

"Well...you'd better get dressed. Get dressed and come downstairs. Alec wants us to Facetime him when you're decent."

Ian made a face but nodded and then shut the door on Carter.

Carter considered hanging out in the bedroom, maybe hoping to catch a peek of Ian-in-only-a-towel on the move, but he'd promised himself just this morning that he wouldn't push himself on Ian anymore. Not after Ian had told him the truth about his motivations for taking this job.

If Ian wanted to be an agent, then Carter wasn't going to do anything to fuck it up.

Carter sighed as he headed down the stairs. Well, any more than he already had.

Five minutes later—Ian's hair was still wet but beginning to dry in dark auburn waves—Ian appeared in the kitchen but didn't say a word and didn't take a seat at the table next to Carter. He just crossed his arms over his T-shirt-clad chest and motioned to Carter, who dialed Alec.

Alec's face, handsome and full of doom energy, appeared on the screen almost immediately.

"Oh good, Ian's there, too," Alec said.

"Apparently I was requested specifically," Ian said, shooting Carter a heated look.

Carter hadn't just gotten himself off, like Ian clearly had, and he was horny enough even Ian's annoyance did it for him.

"We have a situation," Alec said. "That guy you two ran into last night at the Pirate's Booty—and don't think we won't be talking about *that*, too—he's apparently somewhat of a local social media celebrity."

"Apparently?"

"He posted something last night about how Carter Maxwell is now officially, and I quote, *off the market.*" Alec's stare was intense, and Carter couldn't help himself. Between Alec's anger and how much he wanted Ian, he kept squirming in his chair.

"I can explain," Ian said, chiming in, much to Carter's surprise. He'd expected to have to answer for all of it—sneaking out to the Pirate's Booty, then pretending Ian was his boyfriend so he wouldn't have to turn that guy down—but instead, Ian was explaining how he'd allowed Carter to go to the bar, under "his supervision."

"And then," Ian continued, "it was just easier to pretend to be Carter's boyfriend than to explain my real presence at his side and also it helped smooth over Carter's rejection."

Alec did not look particularly relieved though. "To be honest, from the video, it didn't seem like it stung this guy any less."

"He clearly has a very high opinion of himself," Ian said with a sniff.

Carter realized now that Ian *had* actually been jealous. Not of Riley or his fabulous ass, but of *that* guy.

Nameless, vaguely attractive guy, who'd just assumed because they were both in the same physical space, that was all it would take to hook up with Carter. Before, that was true, but everything had changed now.

Carter had news for him: he knew something of what he'd been missing before, and he was never going to settle for vague interest again.

Not when he knew how intensely he could burn for someone like Ian.

Okay. Not *someone* like Ian. Ian himself.

"Well, regardless of that guy's ego," Alec said, "we have a problem on our hands now. The rumor mill is fast and swift, and Charleston isn't that big of a town. It seems that whether you confirm it or not, there's an understanding that you're off the market."

Carter didn't know what to say. Wasn't that a *good* thing? Shouldn't Alec look relieved?

"Worse things could have happened," Ian pointed out carefully.

Score one for Carter cause Ian *agreed* with him!

"True," Alec said thoughtfully. "But if we go with this, that means it's on you two to continue to act like a couple in public." Alec's gaze pinned itself to Ian. "That's a lot to ask of you, Ian."

Ian didn't answer right away and Carter found himself consumed by the silence. Did that mean Ian agreed? That he thought Alec was right? That it *was* a lot for Ian to even temporarily hitch his ride to Carter's?

God, it would suck if he did truly believe that.

"It's actually not so terrible," Ian finally replied with a wry tone.

"No?" Alec's dark eyebrows rose and he looked more concerned than worried now.

"No," Ian repeated firmly.

"I'll add," Alec said dryly, "that it wasn't *only* this guy's story that went viral, but also some shaky video of you two in the club, slow dancing like your thirteen-year-old lives depended on it. So, I'll ask again, is it a lot to ask of you, Ian?"

"I notice you haven't asked *me*," Carter said petulantly.

Alec shot him a look. "You know I get notes from your sessions from Moira, right? I know you're into him." He jabbed a thumb towards Ian. "You've probably been waiting for this opportunity, and now you're gonna pounce on him any chance you get. Need I remind *both* of you of the first rule?"

"You're being unfair to Carter," Ian said quietly but firmly. "He's held up his end of our bargain. He's not broken any of the rules. He's not even been too difficult about them."

Alec seemed to relax at that news.

And Carter couldn't deny, there was currently a party going on in his pants—and perhaps in a few other places, too—at how vehemently Ian had just defended him.

I was hoping to appeal to your good intentions, Ian had said earlier. He'd believed Carter had them, and not only that—he'd go toe-to-toe with Alec over that belief.

Carter didn't know how much he'd needed Ian to have that kind of confidence in him, until he had, unequivocally.

"Okay then," Alec said. "So, let me ask you again, Ian: is it too much for you to act like Carter's boyfriend *in public*?"

"Why are you emphasizing that last bit?" Carter complained, though he knew why.

Alec shot him a hard look. "You know exactly why," he said. "Though I supposed if you wanted Ian to be your boyfriend in private, I wouldn't argue with that."

Ian's eyes widened. Carter noticed because he was looking—couldn't *stop* looking.

"Without sex, of course," Alec added blandly. "I will repeat, this is *not* an invitation to break the first rule."

"In public is plenty fine," Ian said in a firm tone. "Right, Carter?"

Carter didn't agree with that at all. In public was *not* enough. Which should've told him everything he needed to know, because he'd never, not once, even been vaguely interested in committing to a relationship.

But Ian wasn't like anyone else.

He couldn't imagine just spending one night with him. Or even more than one night. He wanted the nights, and he wanted the days, too. He wanted to laugh with him and drink Diet Coke with him and watch him as he came out of the pool every single damn time. And the next time Ian's eyes got sleepy and sweet like that—he wanted to be the reason why.

"Right," Carter said weakly. What else *could* he say, especially after Ian had made it very clear that he was only interested in pretending to be a couple in public?

"Alright, that's settled then. Though…" Alec hesitated, breaking into a grin. "You need help learning how to be a boyfriend, Carter?"

"Of course not," he scoffed, though he *hadn't* ever been one before. But didn't he spend enough time with happy couples to know how that shit worked?

He'd be fine.

"I'm sure Carter can figure it out," Ian said dryly.

Alec's smile didn't dim. "I'm sure he can. And if you need help, I'm only a call away," he said.

A minute later, Carter disconnected the phone, and couldn't help the glance over at Ian.

"You could've told him to fuck off," Carter said. Though why he'd reminded Ian of that, when he'd—*nearly*—gotten everything he'd wanted, he didn't know. Apparently, when he got down to it, he had a real and unexpectedly masochistic streak. He didn't *want* Ian to change his mind.

But he also really, *really* wanted Ian to be in *this* the way Carter was.

Not because it was convenient or because Alec had asked him to, but because he wanted it, too.

Ian walked over to the fridge. Pulled out another can of Diet Coke. "It's that kind of morning," he said wryly as he popped the top.

"A two Diet Coke morning?" Carter asked, raising an eyebrow. *Don't bring up that he totally jacked off in the shower, don't bring up that he totally jacked off in the shower.* "Why?"

"You know why," Ian said. "And yes, I absolutely could've told Alec to fuck off. But it seemed imprudent to do that to the man paying my salary."

Carter was speechless. Silent.

"That's why you said you'd do it?" he asked before he could snatch the words back. He rarely regretted anything that came out of his mouth, but he really regretted those.

Ian didn't say anything at first. Just leaned over the counter, toying with the tab on the Diet Coke can, and looked at everything except Carter.

"Maybe that's what I wanted *Alec* to believe," he finally admitted.

Carter laughed. "Oh, I *do* like you."

Ian's grin was smug. Smug *and* adorable. Two things Carter hadn't known could exist in the same space, and yet *did*, with Ian Parker.

"Obviously," Ian said, the corners of his lips tilting up, even more smugly, if that was possible, "the feeling's mutual."

"Or else you would've told Alec to fuck off," Carter guessed. And yep, he was completely fucking thrilled, from top to bottom.

Ian shrugged one shoulder. Didn't answer. But maybe he didn't have to because Carter was beginning to figure out that this wasn't *just* him.

Ian was in this, too.

Chapter 8

"Okay, I lied. I love having Thursday night games," Carter announced that night.

"Why?" Ian asked.

"More time off after a game," Carter said with a grin.

But after that, Ian returned to his book like Carter hadn't even spoken.

Silence. Not something Carter liked. Or *wanted*.

Earlier, Ian had made dinner—or rather, they'd made dinner *together*, Ian throwing together a salad and a marinade for some chicken, Carter wrangling the grill outside to cook it. He'd even managed not to burn it or leave it raw in spots. Ian had been pleased—*proud*, even.

It had been a quiet day after their call with Alec.

Nothing had changed. *Nothing is supposed to change*, Carter reminded himself. *We're only faking it in public.*

He'd reminded himself of that through his workout. He'd pushed himself harder on the weights and the treadmill—harder anyway, than he usually did on a day off—but while Ian might be okay getting off all by his lonesome, Carter was used to more. On top of that, he wasn't used to wanting someone as much as he wanted Ian.

Hitting the treadmill at a prolonged sprint until his muscles were screaming and he was dripping sweat hadn't really changed the intensity of his desire, but Carter thought when he finished that maybe he was too tired to act on it.

He'd been too tired, anyway, to do much more than let the cool water pour over his head in the shower and then later he'd napped through the afternoon on the couch, though he'd put a movie on.

Now, they were sitting out on the back patio, letting dinner digest. Carter was watching the stars emerge in the darkening sky, and Ian was reading.

Carter had asked what it was, but Ian had only shot him an opaque look and said, "A book."

Like *that* helped him figure the guy out.

He hadn't known exactly what to expect when Ian had agreed to pretend to be his boyfriend in public, but it wasn't Ian retreating again, putting that wall back up.

Maybe it was the good kind of space. Maybe it was self-preservation.

But whichever it was, Carter was tired of it.

He wanted to get close, and he wanted Ian to want him too.

Then suddenly, it occurred to him.

If they went out somewhere, *anywhere*, Ian couldn't freeze him out anymore.

He'd have to lower those walls, and let Carter back in.

"We should go out," Carter said, breaking the silence that had fallen between them.

Ian looked over his tablet at Carter. "We should?"

"Yeah," Carter said. *So you can't lock me out, anymore. I know what you're doing and it's not gonna work. Not with me.*

"Anywhere in particular?"

"Uh, ah, no?" Carter hadn't gotten that far. Just somewhere with people, where he'd get to touch Ian and Ian wouldn't have a choice but to touch him in return.

Ian raised an eyebrow, and Carter tried not to flush. Had Ian figured out his deep, dark secret plan?

But instead of calling him out on it, Ian yawned and stretched, his T-shirt riding up his stomach, and he was tan and smooth there, with just the barest hint of a happy trail of auburn hair down to the waistband of his cut-off jean shorts.

Carter's mouth watered.

If you can convince him to go out, you can touch him there.

Carter would've done way more for way less.

Of course, he wouldn't get to taste. He wouldn't get more than just a few tantalizingly barely-more-than-platonic touches. But that was better than nothing, right?

"Alright," Ian said cautiously. "I could go for something cold. An ice cream cone?"

"There's a frozen custard place just down the street," Carter said, eagerly.

He'd do *a lot* to watch Ian lick an ice cream cone. Just the thought of it, never mind the reality, would be enough to power his fantasies for *days*. *Weeks*, even.

"Sounds good."

Carter grabbed keys and they took the convertible, the hot, muggy air feeling less oppressive with the top down, wind rushing by their ears.

He pulled into the place, which, *thank God*, was totally packed.

Of course...it made perfect sense it would be. Friday night, and still warm enough in early November.

Carter parked the car in the last available spot, all the way at the end, and he and Ian walked down towards the little shack and its crowd of people in front.

He knew the moment he was recognized. It had been happening to Carter for so long it was barely worth a second thought, but Ian tensed next to him.

Carter nudged his hip with his own. "You alright?" he asked under his breath as people started murmuring as they passed, pointing and whispering at their appearance. "Thought you worked in LA with a bunch of celebrities."

"I did, *I do*," Ian said. "But in LA practically everyone's famous, and so nobody notices or cares."

"Ah." Ian's nerves made more sense to Carter now; in Charleston, the biggest celebrities were the Condors players. They didn't have any other major sports teams—the Condors were it—and they got a fairly significant amount of attention wherever they went.

Especially Carter. Probably because he was both famous *and* notorious.

But he'd been grabbing attention wherever he went even as far back as high school, in the small town outside Atlanta where he'd grown up.

"It's fine. I'll just…" Ian hesitated and then cautiously hooked a few fingers around the waistband of Carter's shorts. Not tugging or pulling, just holding it there, the barest brush of his fingertips against Carter's back.

He shivered.

He'd had *orgies*, and they'd affected him less than three of Ian's fingers touching his skin.

You got it bad.

He had *something* bad, though he still wasn't sure it was more than just pure old-fashioned lust. And if it was actually more than that, what the hell he should do about it.

"This okay?" Ian asked.

Carter's nod was possibly more vehement than he'd intended.

Ian chuckled under his breath. "Don't get *too* excited now."

"Too late." That was probably way too honest, but it was the truth.

But Ian didn't pull his hand away. In fact, it felt like he tucked himself more insistently into Carter's side as they approached the line in front of the custard stand. People parted in front of them like he was a superhero—an *actual* hero, not just a freaking football player who was freakishly good at catching a ball.

It was easy to sling an arm around Ian's shoulders and tug him in even closer. He stopped, right at the back of the line, eyeing everyone in front of them, who were looking right back at them.

"We're good," Carter said, raising his voice. He could wait in a line. If it looked like he couldn't, if he was that fucking spoiled, then Ian might think less of him.

In another time *might* he have taken advantage of the group's unspoken offer to let him go straight to the register? He was pleading the fifth.

"So, what's good here?" Ian asked. Not moving away even an iota from where he was tucked into Carter's side.

"Uh." Carter wasn't sure he'd ever actually *been* here. He'd just driven past about a thousand times, and nearly every time he'd thought, *oh, that place looks cool. Might be fun to bring someone here.*

But he never brought his hookups back to his house. That was his sanctuary and he didn't want that to change, *ever.*

But the place did in fact look very cool. Even more so up close. Strings of lights crisscrossed the gravel patio, hung over old, worn wooden tables and benches, covered in a dozen or so years of teenage scribbles and graffiti. A community kind of place.

"You've never been here, have you?" Ian's dimple emerged his smile was so wide.

"Guilty as charged."

"Why not? It's cute. Close by your house, and everything."

For a split second, Carter considered lying. But hadn't he promised to be honest? Not just to Ian, but to himself?

"Never wanted to stop by myself and uh...never had anyone else I wanted to bring here."

Ian's eyes, leaf green and luminous, gazed up at his.

God, he was so gorgeous. Carter wanted to nibble on every one of those freckles and then on his plush pink bottom lip.

But he had a feeling that even though they were playing being a couple in public, that would be crossing about a hundred lines.

Besides, the first time he was lucky enough to kiss Ian—the first time Ian made it clear he *welcomed* Carter's kiss—he didn't want either of them to be pretending a goddamned thing.

"I'm the first, huh?" Ian sounded pleased by that.

You are; for so many more reasons than you realize.

"Yeah," Carter said.

There was that dimple again as Ian smiled.

"Awesome," Ian said, and sounded like he meant it. "Well, what are you gonna get?"

Carter hadn't even looked at the menu. Hadn't even glanced at it. It was too hard to even take his eyes off Ian, especially now that they were touching. *Allowed* to be touching, even.

He tore his gaze off Ian's face. *Don't be creepy. You know how to do this.*

But did he?

Carter suddenly wasn't sure.

"Maybe a milkshake."

Ian considered this. "I bet you're a chocolate guy."

"Wrong," Carter announced triumphantly. "Totally wrong."

"Seriously? How could you *not* be a chocolate guy? I thought you were awesome. Awesome people are chocolate people."

"I *am* awesome, and chocolate's fine and good, but have you ever had a strawberry shake? Strawberry's where it's at."

Ian shook his head. "You're so weird. I'm gonna pretend you didn't just tell me strawberry's where it's at."

"It's alright, I'll learn to live with your strawberry prejudice," Carter said in a pseudo-mournful tone. "You *do* still like Diet Coke, so I won't be dumping you anytime soon."

"Thanks, I think?" Ian hadn't stopped smiling, and his fingers curled more firmly, more insistently, into the back of Carter's shorts. Like he didn't want to let go.

It wasn't like he'd become immune to the tiny, minute brushes of Ian's fingertips against his skin—after all, each one felt like an earthquake—but he'd become more used to the way they shook him to the core.

Carter definitely was *not* thinking about what Ian's touch would feel like anywhere else.

If he did, he wasn't entirely sure he could keep this PG.

"You're Carter Maxwell, aren't you?" Carter looked over and there was a girl in front of them who was wearing cut-off shorts and a very interested expression, tossing her blonde hair to the side as she directed the question towards Carter. Like Ian wasn't even there, and they weren't practically—okay, *almost*—breathing each other's air.

Anyone smarter or perhaps more intuitive would've realized Carter only had eyes for one person and it was the guy next to him, but she had her *I'm very interested and very determined* expression on.

Carter recognized it, because he'd seen variations of it for years, and for all those years, it had been easier to just go along with it.

But not today.

Not anymore.

"Guilty as charged," he said.

"I thought so. Nobody else has hair like you, even *me*." She tossed hers again, for emphasis, like somehow Carter had missed that she probably paid her colorist way too much money.

Carter did not mention that his was *almost* entirely natural.

"You come here often?" she asked next, when Carter didn't engage further.

He'd felt Ian tense next to him. This was their first test.

Well, *second*. First when they actually knew what the fuck they were doing—though, Carter could argue the jury was still out on that.

"Nope," Ian said it before Carter could, his tone cheerful and yet completely, utterly dismissive.

She frowned for a split-second before her expression smoothed out again. "And you're here together?"

Carter wasn't going to let Ian answer this one. "Yes," he said, firmly and clearly. So there could be zero confusion.

"Really?" She managed to be both cool and skeptical at the same time.

Was she freaking kidding? Carter was only stopping himself from wrapping his whole self around Ian like an octopus because they were in public—though it wasn't like that had stopped him ever before—and he didn't know how Ian felt about PDA.

"Really," Carter said. "Really *really really*."

Ian elbowed him a little, but Carter was annoyed and not afraid to show it. He didn't have to deal with this shit. Okay, maybe a month ago, he'd have gone along with whatever she wanted to do, but that was before he'd begun to realize how predatory some of these people seemed. He hadn't ever seen it before but now he did, and he couldn't unsee it.

It wasn't like he went to their beds unwilling—he'd always been willing—but sex had become a tool for him.

And now, it was something he wanted, desperately, entirely, with his whole being.

Before Ian, he hadn't even realized there was a difference, but there was no denying it now.

"I just didn't realize you had a boyfriend," the girl said, snapping her gum insistently.

"Yes," Carter said.

Maybe if she continued to be unconvinced, he could provide a hands-on demonstration.

"And just..." She hesitated. "It's just...surprising."

"Oh?" Ian didn't sound amused.

"Yeah," she said. "See you guys around." She turned and walked away, which...Carter could admit he was both happy she was gone, and also a little bit disappointed.

He'd been looking forward to providing a lot of practical evidence on the subject.

"I think I'm going to get a dipped cone," Ian said like she hadn't ever existed.

"Chocolate dipped?" Carter asked.

Ian shot him a look so hot around the edges it nearly singed him.

He wanted to call that girl back and say, *hey, do you see it now? You see the way he looks at me? And the way I look at him? We want to do dirty, dirty things to each other.*

They weren't allowed to, of course, but that didn't change the base desire.

"Yep. And you're gonna get a strawberry shake."

"That's the plan," Carter said. He wanted to bring up what that girl had said. But he didn't know how. He didn't even know exactly what she'd meant.

But it was clear from the tense line of Ian's shoulders as they approached the order window that he'd guessed and he hadn't liked it at all.

They gave their orders to the friendly guy on the other side of the humidity-fogged plexiglass, and a few minutes later, had settled down at a table on the far side of the lot.

Carter was doing his best to ogle Ian eating his cone, pale yellow vanilla custard underneath the chocolate shell dripping onto his hand, while not looking like that was exactly what he was doing.

God, what he wouldn't give to have Ian lick *him* that way.

He had an agile pink tongue, slipping effortlessly between those even pinker lips, and *Jesus*, Carter's shorts were tighter than they had been only a few minutes earlier.

Ian shot him another one of those hot looks.

Not of the *let's get naked variety and I'll lick you instead of this cone* variety, but instead, *stop weaving fantasies about me in your head, please.*

Maybe a good time to change the subject.

"What do you think that girl meant?" Carter asked.

Ian sighed. "Seriously, Carter?"

"What?"

It hadn't been a particularly stellar change of subject, but he was working with not very much blood in his brain right now, thank you very much.

"You know what she meant," Ian said, sounding like he very much wanted to stop talking about this.

Which made no fucking sense.

Why would Ian be pissed off that Carter's reputation had preceded him so far in advance nobody actually believed he could settle down with *one* person and one person only?

If anyone should be pissed off at that, it was definitely Carter.

"Actually, no," Carter said, puzzled.

"She thought it was ridiculous we were together because you're *you*, and well...I'm *me*," Ian said.

"What? Like..." Carter couldn't even believe it.

"Like you're a solid ten plus, and I'm, *at best*, a five or six," Ian said with exaggerated patience, his voice wry.

Carter was fucking boggled.

He had half a mind to set his milkshake down with an emphatic thump and find her again. Demand that she stand there and just listen to why that was absolutely fucking insane and also ridiculous. Was she blind? How could she look at Ian and not think *he* was the one slumming it, by spending time with Carter, willingly?

Okay. Not willingly. But he *had* willingly agreed to do this fake boyfriend thing in public.

"You look very surprised," Ian said.

Well, no shit.

No fucking shit.

Ian laughed, and Carter realized he'd said that out loud.

"It's not shit," Ian insisted. "It's facts."

"If you're digging for compliments..." Carter trailed off.

"Absolutely fucking not. I said it, didn't I? I'm stating *facts*. Fact: Carter, you are seriously gorgeous, and don't try to argue with me on this one, because you're not stupid and even if people didn't tell you all the time, your mirror would."

"Right, I know that," Carter said impatiently. "That's not the part that has me so pissed off."

"Oh?" Ian raised an eyebrow.

God, he was so fucking flawless.

Carter wanted to worship him like they were in a temple and Ian was an idol.

But he wasn't hard, cold marble. He was flesh and blood—so warm, Carter couldn't help but reach over and just touch, curl his fingers around Ian's forearm.

"I can't believe I even have to say this." But clearly he did. "You're *stunning*."

"Thanks," Ian said dryly. He went back to his ice cream cone, and Carter realized he didn't believe him.

He believed that stupid, judgey, probably insecure woman.

Not him.

And wow, that was totally not going to work for Carter.

"No," Carter said.

"No?" Ian licked his cone.

Carter leaned forward. "You know how you're licking that cone?"

Ian looked at him, confused. "Yes?"

There was no way to do this but to *do* it.

Carter braced himself and let loose.

"I want to lick you the way you're licking that cone. I want to start at your toes, which...don't think I haven't noticed that you're always fucking barefoot in my house, and they're really, really cute toes. Not cute like I have a foot fetish cute, though I've done that, and I'll be totally honest. Didn't do it for me. But your toes? Totally edible. And your calves? God, they're a work of art. Slender and muscular and I'd love to nibble my way up them. And your thighs? Jesus fucking Christ. I'd do unholy things to your thighs. I saw this tendon in them the other night—you know the one I'm talking about, when you pranced around in that swimsuit and I wanted to fucking *rip* it off you—and I thought, wow, that would look really, really great with my teeth marks on it. Not a lot, just a little. Just enough for me to see and then to fade. I'd be gentle. Well, not *gentle*, but I'd make it so good for you. And I know *you* know what's next. But..." Carter hesitated, feeling his lips curl into a grin.

"I'm not gonna give you the satisfaction of talking about your cock. I haven't been lucky enough to see it yet, but I know it's gorgeous, just like the rest of you, and that I'd want to put my mouth all over it. I'd want to tease you, just a little, until you're crying for it, until you're begging me to give you more. Give you exactly what you want, and I'd do it. Anything you wanted. But since I haven't been lucky enough to put my eyes on it yet, let's stick to what I *have* seen. Your hipbones, *God*, those are fucking carved by a master, and you've got freckles, all over your abs, I saw them in the moonlight, and I'd taste every single fucking one. Up farther, I know your nipples get hard when you're horny. I saw it the other night." Carter hesitated. "I'm seeing it now," he said. "They're hard right against your shirt, and you know what it makes me want to do? Lick them. Bite them. Spend so long tormenting you with them, you'd be crying out for more. They're just so pink and perfect. And speaking of pink and perfect, your fucking lips. I want them against mine. I want them around my cock. I want them so badly I'm dying for it. But you know what's even more perfect than your lips?" Ian shook his head wordlessly.

"Your eyes. They're stunning. Even when you're icing me out, they're beautiful, but right now? When they're melting for me, and they get all soft and gooey and warm? And I know you feel this, same as I do. God, there's nothing I want more than to just stare at them. All day. All night. As long as you'd let me."

Carter took a deep breath.

Ian said nothing. Just sat there, jaw dropped.

His ice cream fell off the cone with a slushy, wet plop and still, neither of them moved.

Ian's eyes were molten now. Not just warm, but *hot*.

"So that," Carter said, even though clearly more words were unnecessary, "is why I think that woman was full of bullshit. Why I think I'm lucky you're willing to even give me the time of day."

"I…" Ian's voice came out strangled.

He looked about five seconds away from launching himself across the table, ice cream be damned, and devouring Carter.

Carter could push him. It wouldn't even be hard.

But for the first time in so long Carter couldn't even remember when it had last happened, he didn't immediately latch onto the idea and do it, everything else be damned.

Instead, he leaned back. Put some air and distance between them. It was hard, one of the hardest things he'd ever done, because he did want. He wanted so badly he was aching with it, but this had to be something Ian wanted, too.

And then there was the little issue of the first rule.

Breaking it might mean Ian was fired, and before, that absolutely would've sucked. No question. But now that Carter knew just how much was riding on Ian *not* giving in?

Well.

Carter wasn't proud of a lot of things, but he wasn't going to be the one to ruin Ian's dream of being an agent. If Ian chose to take the step, it was going to be him doing it, with his eyes wide open.

"I guess...I guess I was wrong," Ian finally said.

"Guess you were." Carter knew how smug he sounded.

Ian shot him a crooked smile. "From now on, I'm gonna have to take you everywhere I go, as my very own hype man."

"Clearly I wouldn't be upset about that," Carter said wryly.

"You didn't say anything about my hair," Ian teased, grabbing some napkins to start wiping up some of the melted ice cream from the table. But his own hand, with its streaks of semidried custard?

He licked those off. One at a time. Slowly. Deliberately. Daring Carter to say a word.

And Carter was *Carter*, so what was he supposed to do?

"You know your hair's stunning. Unusual and beautiful. Like a flame in the night, and all that metaphorical shit," Carter said, waving his hands in the air. "You *know* that."

"Yeah," Ian admitted with a suddenly sheepish grin. "But I *didn't* know the rest of that."

"Now you do, and that's all that matters," Carter said.

Ian's gaze was speculative on him. "I guess you did warn me you'd hit on me. I just didn't expect...*that*."

"In my defense, I've never told anyone anything like what I just told you." Maybe he shouldn't be admitting to that, but now that he'd unstopped his tongue, he didn't know how to quiet it.

"Nobody?" Ian looked shocked. Even more so than when Carter had been telling him, in probably way too explicit detail, what he'd like to do to him.

"Not a goddamn soul."

"But—" Ian took a deep breath. Let it out. "You've had a *lot* of sex, with a *lot* of people."

Yeah, he had. Carter didn't know why Ian was so different, only that he was.

He only knew that they hadn't known each other very long, but still, somehow, he was the stars dotting the sky overhead, and Carter couldn't take a real breath in the morning until he saw him, sitting at his kitchen table and fucking *shining*.

"If you say again it's only because we haven't slept together yet, and I'm not used to not having my way with anyone I want, I'm gonna get up and leave you here. You can get a ride home with that mean blonde girl."

Ian smiled. "Then I won't. 'Cause I sure don't want to spend any more time with her than I already have."

"Poor her," Carter teased. "You want another cone?"

"No, no, I'm good. I...I've had plenty."

Carter sucked down some of his milkshake. It had melted, too, and wasn't nearly as thick as it had been, but it still cooled this throat.

Maybe not his thoughts, but he'd take what he could get.

CHAPTER 9

IAN WANTED TO PRETEND that nothing between him and Carter had changed.

Not after he'd agreed, with Alec as their witness, to pretend to be Carter's boyfriend in public.

Not after Carter had told him, in more words than Ian thought anyone had ever used on him, exactly why he wanted him. Exactly *how* he wanted him.

Yeah, there was still a part of him that wondered why. Was it just because Carter was not allowed to have him?

Because he'd tried his damnedest to keep himself apart?

Ian didn't know.

He tried to tell himself in his strong moments it was just curiosity. In his weak ones, he knew that wasn't only why.

Three days had passed since the custard incident, as Ian was thinking of it.

They'd gone out twice more since then. Once to dinner, not to some romantic candlelight-and-white-tablecloths place, but to a building Ian would charitably call a shack, all the way at the coast. They'd eaten peel-and-eat shrimp by the bucketful, shared a few beers, and they'd both been too messy to even dream about touching, though Carter had before they'd sat—just the brush of his fingertips against the small of his back—when the hostess, in her cutoffs and cowboy boots, had cooed over just how cute they were and led them to their table overlooking the water.

The other time just to the grocery store, and Carter had been in fine form, teasing and joking, a hundred tiny touches between them that by themselves shouldn't feel like anything, but all together built up to a blaze of lust that both frightened him and warmed him from his toes to the top of his head, and so deep, in a place Ian wasn't sure anyone had ever touched before.

What were they doing?

Why was he still trying to pretend this was just another job?

There weren't answers to those questions, or to any of his others.

Today, Carter returned to work, and Ian had dutifully come along with him.

He'd already decided he didn't need a front row seat to Carter being all sweaty and glorious, so he'd asked if he could keep an eye on him from the offices upstairs. Coach K had arranged a spot for him, and he pulled out his laptop now.

Yesterday, Alec had sent an email with several contract case studies attached, and at any other time, Ian would've taken that as an excellent sign of both Alec's good faith and his belief that Ian could get the job done.

But after spending half the night jerking off to the memory of Carter's rough growl, telling him exactly how he wanted him, and tossing and turning in bed when even *that* didn't make a dent, it was hard to feel the same kind of confidence Alec did.

The same professional faith.

Still, he opened the emails and began reading, glancing up every once in a while to watch Coach K putting the players through their paces.

It would be a late evening for Carter—with a few meetings keeping him after practice—and he'd offered for Ian to head home by himself, but even though some space had seemed like a very good idea, Ian had declined to take a separate car.

Why?

Yet another question Ian didn't know the answer to.

So he was stuck here for the rest of the day, and well into the evening.

Might as well get some work done, while he was at it. And after that, maybe he'd take advantage of Coach K's invite to use the gym. He preferred the pool, but he wasn't naive enough to think that was a good idea right now.

He needed to keep *all* his clothes on, especially if there was even a chance of seeing Carter.

His phone rang, and Ian flinched, just for a second, before he glanced over at it and realized it was his mother—not Alec, calling to tell him he'd learned all his deepest, dirtiest secrets and didn't think he'd be able to do this after all.

"Mom," he answered, putting the phone on speaker.

"Just calling to see how everything's going," she said.

Such bullshit.

You'd think for such an intuitive and perceptive woman, she'd be a better liar.

"Everything's fine." Ian told himself to leave it, but she'd called for a reason and he wasn't going to fucking wait around for the other shoe to drop. "Why do you think it wouldn't be?"

Moira Rogers sighed.

"You know I had a call with Carter yesterday."

Yeah, he wasn't proud that when Carter had ducked out to take it, he'd locked himself in the bathroom and spent the next ten minutes trying to assuage the lust that was no longer satisfied with only his hand. He'd had more orgasms in the last three days than he'd had in weeks, and yet every time Carter looked at him, he was burning for him all over again.

"Yeah," Ian said hesitantly. Even though, yes, he often worked with his mother's clients, she rarely called him like this.

"He seems...edgy."

Yeah, Mom, it's not just him.

"What an official-sounding diagnosis," he teased. Deflecting from the real problem.

"Ian," she chided him. "I'm worried, and you should be worried too."

"He's not doing anything, Mom."

"Except obsessing over you."

There it was. Ian flushed, glad they weren't on video so she couldn't see.

"I'm surprised he's willing to share that. He knows we're related."

"I only wish that would stop him," she mused.

Of course it wouldn't, because this was Carter.

He could only hope that Carter hadn't treated his mother to the same speech he'd given Ian.

"Nothing's happened. Nothing is going to happen," Ian reassured her. Trying to convince himself, all at the same time.

Maybe when he finally left. Maybe he'd come back for a long weekend. Or after the season ended, Carter would fly out to California, to LA, and they'd finally fuck.

Or maybe by then, it wouldn't feel the same. Maybe without giving this thing between them space and oxygen, it would just die off.

You're stupider than shit if you really believe that.

Okay. He believed that it wouldn't be that way for him, but for Carter? Absolutely.

He'd find someone else to fixate on, and Ian would be long forgotten, a fond memory of a time when he'd needed help and Ian had given it.

"I'm worried," Moira repeated, and it was evident in her voice that was true.

"What, do you really think I can't resist Carter Maxwell?" He was annoyed. Annoyed that she believed that. Annoyed that it was possibly true.

"I don't know." Now she sounded reluctant.

"You must hate that, not knowing," Ian retorted, because it was easier to deflect than to deal with the problem. Even if she guessed exactly what he was doing.

"It's not that I hate it, Ian, it's that I'm not sure it's...controllable. We're trying to give Carter a framework to bring control to his own life, to control his emotions—but you're a distraction."

"If it wasn't me, it would be someone else," Ian said, and *God*, that hurt. But what else was he supposed to believe?

No matter how many times Carter insisted that this thing grow-ing uncontrollably between them wasn't because Ian was forbidden, Ian couldn't quite bring himself to believe it. Because it was the likeliest explanation.

"Yes," Moira said cautiously, but that was the worst of it—she didn't even sound convinced.

"Like I said," she finally continued, into the uncomfortable si-lence, "he's on edge. Was on edge yesterday. Surely you can sense that."

Ian had, but he'd assumed it was just the same edginess he was feeling himself—unfulfilled lust that had nowhere else to go.

"Yes, but it's under control."

"*Your* control, Ian," she reminded him.

"And that's the point of me being here: I'm here to remind him until he can remind himself," Ian said. He didn't need to tell her why, but maybe it would be a good reminder for both of them.

If Carter was truly struggling, he hadn't said so.

He hadn't told Ian explicitly.

But hasn't he? What else do you think all that touching was? That long speech he made the other night?

"Talk to him," Moira said firmly. "And if we need to do an emer-gency session, I trust that you'll tell me."

"I'll get him to talk to me," Ian promised.

No matter how fucking hard it will be.

"And," Moira added, "if *you* need someone to talk to, I'm here."

"Mom," Ian said, rolling his eyes. Yes, she was his mother. No, she had never been his therapist. But it wasn't like that had ever stopped her from trying; after all, it was as natural to her as breathing.

"I'm just saying," she said lightly. "This isn't a normal job. For so many reasons."

"Trust me, Mom, I'm aware."

"Well. I *do* trust you, Ian. You know that, right? You're good at this. And despite everything, you're good for him. I do think he's making real progress. A big part of that is you."

Guilt stabbed him low in the belly.

If he'd needed more reminders of why he should be keeping his hands to himself, this was it right here.

Not just because of the professional opportunities Alec could give him.

This was Carter's *whole fucking life*.

And Ian cared about him and wanted better for him.

His mother couldn't have reminded him any better why he was here. Why he needed to stay strong.

"Thanks, Mom," he said dryly, but he meant it, too.

Thank you for reminding me of what I was losing sight of.

"You'll be fine, Ian," she said, and he agreed with her.

"Love you too, Mom," he teased and she chuckled.

He hung up the call and glanced back out towards the field, then froze.

Panic lanced through him.

From all the way up here, he couldn't hear a word Carter was saying, but he didn't need to.

The anger and frustration were evident in every line of his body, the tenseness of his shoulders and thighs and even the way he shielded his eyes from the sun.

"Shit," Ian said, and leaving everything where it sat, hustled his way down the hall, picking the stairs over the elevator, and a minute later, was jogging onto the field.

Carter was yelling. At Riley.

Landry was hovering behind Riley, looking about five seconds away from deciding he didn't give a shit how much he liked Carter, he *loved* his boyfriend. The other wide receiver—Ian couldn't place his name right at this second, with all the panic surging through him—was there, too.

"I was open, asshole, I *told you* I was open, and you threw it to fucking Nick. *Nick.*"

When he'd shown up to practice today, Carter had known he was riding close to the edge.

The last few days with Ian had been so good—and so frustrating.

The biggest problem was Carter knew he was used to just taking what he wanted. In this case, that was Ian. But instead of just taking, he'd *thought* about it first, and unfortunately all that thought meant that while he still wanted the guy as badly as he had at the beginning, or maybe *more*, he'd abstained for good reasons. So many fucking good reasons.

But just because good reasons existed, it didn't make any of this any easier.

Still, he'd come to practice, thinking he could keep himself under control. Hadn't he mostly kept his hands off Ian? Even when that was the last thing he wanted? Yeah, he had. Moira had given him lots of coping mechanisms. Things he could do, things he could remind himself, when his whole-self threatened to go off the rails.

But today, when Riley had looked right at him and he was fucking *open*, as open as he'd ever get, and then thrown the ball to the other side, to Nick, he'd lost it. None of this dealing with his frustration in a cool, reasonable manner, like Moira kept telling him how to do.

Nope.

He went right off the cliff.

"I was open, asshole, I *told you* I was open, and you threw it to fucking Nick. *Nick.*"

Riley's face was carefully blank. Calm. He was so fucking calm.

Carter was *not* calm.

"The point of the exercise wasn't that you were open, Carter," Riley said in a careful voice.

He knew what they were all doing.

Contain the beast. Don't give it fuel. Don't let it get out.

But instead of it having its intended effect, Carter was only *more* pissed off that Riley was treating him like that. Like nothing Carter did or said could affect him. So instead of calming the fuck down, too, he pushed.

"You really want to throw the ball to *Nick*," Carter yelled, throwing his arms up. "Do you think he's gonna win you games? Really?"

"Hey," Nick said, his slightly annoyed voice sending a lick of temper up Carter's spine.

Carter was honest about his own abilities. Nick should be honest about his.

He was *never* going to be a fucking number one wideout.

Never.

Not with Carter Maxwell on this team. Not even *without* Carter Maxwell on this team.

Nick was just second tier material.

He kicked a helmet. Then threw himself onto the sideline bench, temper heating up his body in a way the workout hadn't.

"Carter, seriously, dude, it's fine," Landry said, with more of that exaggerated patience that just ratcheted Carter's temper up a few degrees.

He looked up at Landry and realized, probably a minute too late, that Landry wasn't alone.

Ian was standing next to him, arms crossed over his chest, sun glinting in the copper highlights of his curls, looking so goddamn good if Carter hadn't been in such a snit, he'd have really considered crawling over to him.

Crawling and *begging*.

Put me out of my goddamn misery, he'd plead. Stop this. Before we both lose our minds and ourselves to whatever the fuck this is.

"Carter, do you remember the breathing exercises Moira taught you?"

Oh, he remembered them alright. But did he want to use them? No fucking way.

He sneered. "Yeah, sure."

Ian shot him a hard look.

Was that supposed to make him any less edgy? Any less desperate? Hardly.

"I was open, *goddamn it*," Carter repeated. "And I was open the time before that, and the time before that, and the goddamn time before that."

"We know," Landry said. "We were all there. We saw."

Carter launched himself upright again and started pacing back and forth, because sitting still was suddenly intolerable. "Then why the fuck didn't your *boyfriend* throw me the ball?"

Landry's *boyfriend*, the starting quarterback for the Charleston Condors, regarded him stonily.

"Really, are you gonna do that shit now?" Riley asked in a bored voice.

Was he?

Carter didn't know *what* he was going to do. He was gonna do something, though. Something that made everyone pay him some fucking attention!

"No," Ian spoke up, "he's not."

He didn't shoot a glare in Ian's direction, but maybe he should've. This was all his fault, wasn't it? He'd shown up and been so fucking irresistible that Carter hadn't been able to help wanting him.

"Come on," Ian said, reaching out and taking his arm. For once, Carter didn't ignore the sparks inside when they touched—instead he leaned into them, into Ian.

Let his grip on Carter's arm pull them closer together.

God, he looked so damn good like this, in the sunlight. All those colors in his hair, his skin glowing, eyes light as he shaded them with his other hand.

Carter wanted to dive into him and never surface for air.

"Carter," Ian murmured in a low voice as his body collided against Carter's.

"I got this," he said. And yeah, miraculously, he *was* a bit calmer. Just feeling them touch in half a dozen places: Ian's chest against his own, their thighs brushing, Ian's fingers wrapped around his forearm.

"Do you?" Ian questioned as he gazed up at him.

"Now I do," Carter admitted.

Ian tore his eyes away from Carter's, which...that didn't feel great. But then Ian announced, raising his voice, "Just give us a minute, guys, alright? Can you live without him for a few?"

"Yeah," Riley said, nodding. "He's no good to us like this anyway."

And well, *that* stung. More, probably, because it was true.

Carter was afraid Ian would let go, but he did the opposite. He gripped Carter's arm with a surprising amount of strength and then practically dragged him closer to the tunnel that led to the locker room and then through it.

The building was quiet and cool—all the players and coaching staff already out on the turf, but that wasn't enough for Ian apparently, because he kept on dragging him until he found an even quieter hallway, the only sound the air conditioning whirring away and his own heavy breathing.

"What the hell was that?" Ian let go of him and went way too far away, leaning back against the opposite wall, crossing his arms over his chest again.

Like that would really keep Carter from touching him again. Touching him all he wanted to.

Carter didn't answer.

"Seriously?" Ian finally asked. "You're seriously gonna freeze *me* out now?"

"It's *your* fault." Carter knew how sullen he sounded.

He was fucking pouting.

Mommy, I didn't get the toy I wanted, and it's not fair!

Ian raised an eyebrow. Didn't say anything else. Didn't need to.

"Fine, I'm sorry. I lost it. I...I should have told you—or Moira, or even Alec, I guess—that I was...I wasn't as okay as I wanted to be."

"Do you want to be okay?" Ian asked.

"What kind of question is that? Of course I do." Now that he was calming down, the blood not rushing through his ears, his reactions more reasoned and less quicksilver, he *did* want to be okay. In the moment, he never did. He always wanted to fucking wallow in his anger. In his emotions.

But after...always regret.

So much fucking regret.

"Then we need to catch this shit before it gets bad. Mom—" Ian hesitated, then corrected himself. "Moira, she called me earlier. Said you were tense. I thought maybe you were, but I thought it was..." Ian stopped in the middle of his sentence again. Like he didn't want to call attention to what he'd *really* thought it was. "But I didn't realize just how tense." He sounded guilty, like he was embarrassed he'd missed it.

Carter lost the pretty damn quick argument with his self-control and pushed off from the wall and prowled closer to Ian again. He was beautiful outside, in the sunlight, but somehow he looked just as good in here, in this drab, sparse hallway, with freaking fluorescent lights above him.

Ian's attractiveness defied facts, because Carter had never looked at anyone under a fluorescent bulb and thought, *oh man, I gotta get me some of that.*

Not until now.

"What are you doing?" Ian asked, forehead creasing in concern.

"You wanna know why I was so tense? Why I didn't want to talk about it?"

Ian nodded, but he looked very hesitant. Like he wasn't sure he'd like the answer.

"Because I'm looking at you under this ugly-ass light, that's not flattering to a single person on fucking earth, and you're still the person I want more than anyone else. How messed up is that?"

Ian chuckled self-consciously. "So you're saying if I just keep myself bathed in fluorescent light, I'll be safe?"

"Apparently not anymore," Carter grumbled. "What I mean is that *this, this* fucking thing between us, it's what's got me so tense."

"Well," Ian said with consideration. "Maybe it's a good test."

"You're not gonna just leave, now that I've admitted that?"

"No way. You don't get off that easy," Ian said with a quick grin.

"Believe me, if you were involved, I *could* get off that easy," Carter mumbled under his breath.

"As I'm sure Moira told you, recovery isn't a straight line, Carter. No—we'll use this. You feel like you can go back to practice?"

"Yeah. 'Course, that's not what I *want* to do," Carter said.

Ian shot him a crooked smile. "Not what I want to do either, but it's the right thing to do. And apologize to Riley, too, while you're at it. That was kinda a low blow. He's way more than just Landry's boyfriend. He's your starting quarterback."

"I was already planning on it," Carter said. He hadn't meant to drag Riley—or his relationship with Landry—into any of this, and he felt guilty, nausea blooming low in his belly at the thought that he might've burnt that bridge, or at the very least scorched it a little, with his words.

He'd make it right.

He *needed* to make it right.

"You're a good guy, Carter," Ian said, closing the rest of the distance between them. He put a hand on Carter's shoulder. *Playing with fire*, Carter thought about reminding him, but he wasn't stupid. If Ian wanted to touch him, he wasn't ever going to stop him. "I know it's hard to see it, sometimes, but this team gives a shit about you. They're willing to work with you."

"What about you?" Carter asked before he could stop himself.

Ian's green gaze was clear as a pond. Not cold, almost never anymore. Like Carter kept him so warm the ice was impossible to keep around. "What about me?"

It felt so easy to put a hand on Ian's waist. He felt the muscles tense under his touch, but he didn't move. Didn't even lean in the way he desperately wanted to. "Do you give a shit about me?"

Ian's lips curved into a wry smile. "Do you think I'd still be here, fighting for you, if I didn't?"

"But your job with Alec—"

Carter didn't get the rest of it out before Ian stopped him. "Yeah, there's that, of course, but no, I'm here for *you*, Carter."

He heard the words even though Ian didn't say them. *Why else do you think I'm still fighting this irresistible pull between us?*

"You're kinda great," Carter said. *No kinda about it.*

"Thanks," Ian said and then stepped away. Carter felt the loss of him immediately. "Now go out there and make me proud."

When he returned to practice, Carter didn't take the time to apologize to Riley right then—instead, he gave his quarterback a quick nod—and got back to work. He figured that Riley would appreciate that more.

He endured Riley throwing to Nick two, three, then five times more, only tossing one long ball in Carter's direction, which he caught and took for a touchdown, thank you very much.

But then after practice ended and they'd both showered, Carter approached where Riley was putting stuff away in his locker, getting ready to go to another one of his interminable meetings.

Nobody worked harder on this team than Riley Flynn. And it felt extra super bad that he'd been shitty to him, especially when Riley was shouldering all that burden, day after day, week after week.

He needed people to support him, not teammates—and Carter hoped, *friends*—to tear him down.

"Hey," Carter said quietly.

Riley turned and smiled at him. "Hey, Carter, you doin' okay?"

Like he was actually worried about him. Like he *mattered*, even after everything he'd done to screw up. After the shitty comment he'd made earlier.

"I'm good. Solid. But I wanted to apologize..." He trailed off. Still waiting for Riley to tell him to fuck off.

"Yeah?" Riley said.

"I'm sorry I let it out on you like that. You didn't deserve it. You were prepping us the way we needed to be for the game."

"Nick isn't as good as you are. Not even close." Riley pitched his voice lower, even though Carter had already noticed most of the team had already left. Including Nick. "You know that. He needs the work, Carter. I know you can get by a double team most of the time, but what if they try to triple team you? The whole offense can't rest on you. Nick's got to pull his weight. We need him to keep the opposing defenses honest."

"Right." Carter wiped his damp palms on his shorts. "I know that."

The worst part was that he did.

Riley's expression softened. "Of course you do, but a reminder every now again isn't a bad thing. I know you want the ball. God knows, I wanna give it to you."

That meant something. Mended something inside Carter that he hadn't even realized might be broken.

"Yeah, it's..."

But Riley didn't let him finish. "What else is going on, Carter?"

"What else?"

"You came in today on a freaking tear. Like if you played hard enough, if you scored enough touchdowns on that poor second team defense, you'd be able to handle whatever it was."

Carter didn't like admitting it—it was easy enough to *think* it or to say it to Ian. The *easiest*, actually, which was kind of terrifying now that he thought about it. But saying it out loud to someone else, even a friend like Riley, was hard.

"And then," Riley added with a lopsided grin. "I didn't throw you the ball."

"It's Ian," Carter said in a rush, before he could chicken out.

"Oh?" Riley went back to his locker, his voice carefully casual. "What about him? Is it not working out having him there at your place?"

"Don't pretend you didn't see us at the Pirate's Booty, dancing. Don't pretend you didn't *encourage* us to do that."

"You sound like you're complaining."

"I'm *not*. I just...I want more. I want *him*."

"And you can't have him?" Riley actually had the nerve to phrase it like a question. Like there was actually a scenario in which it was allowed.

Carter was tempted to yell at him again, even though he wasn't feeling that same sickly surge of anger that usually accompanied the desire to yell.

This was different.

"Of course I can't. He's off-limits. *Everyone's* off-limits, but especially him."

"Why do I have a feeling that the *everyone* bothers you less than the *him*?" Riley asked.

"It does," Carter admitted.

And wasn't that the most fucked-up part of this?

If he was allowed to have sex with someone else, he *still* wouldn't do it because it wouldn't scratch the very specific itch Ian had given him.

"That's new," Riley said. He pulled his tablet out of his locker and then slung an arm around Carter's waist. "Must be tough to adjust to that."

"It's not easy," Carter admitted.

He and Riley walked towards the door to the locker room. "I remember," he said, "when I realized that it might not be *just* me crushing on Landry. That he might feel the same. It was the scariest thing in the whole fucking world. I'd carried my feelings by myself for so long, I didn't even know how to deal with the possibility that he might return them."

"Really?" That was confusing to Carter. Why would it be scary?

"It's scary because it means everything's changing. Your world is shifting underneath your feet. And it's shifting in a big way for you, Carter."

"I don't know…" Carter blustered, but Riley stopped in the middle of the hallway and gave him a hard look.

"Carter. It's shifting. There's no denying it. You're trying to deal with your anger, not just give in to it. You're changing your lifestyle. Probably dealing with some of the underlying shit to deal with the real problem and not just the symptoms. And then here comes this guy who for the first time, you actually *like*, not just lust after."

"I don't know," Carter repeated dubiously. He was *definitely* interested in getting Ian into bed.

"Come on, Carter, you *like* him. You light up whenever he's around. Even today. You were pissed as hell, but you *paused* when he showed up. Like he made you think when you couldn't really think." Riley punched him lightly in the arm. "Don't try to lie to me, even if you're gonna lie to yourself."

"Fine," Carter grumbled. "I…he's nice to have around. *Real* nice to have around."

"See, there, that wasn't so hard," Riley teased.

"That doesn't help me, though," Carter argued. "He's still fuck-ing off-limits."

"Is he, though?"

"Riley," Carter yelped.

Riley threw his hands up. "Just saying. You could always ask Alec to make an exception."

"And face his disappointment that I couldn't do this?" *And possibly ruin Ian's chances at working for him?* "Not likely."

"Just saying, it's an option," Riley said lightly. "I gotta get to this meeting. But—" He paused and then to Carter's surprise, tugged him into a tight hug. "You're good, yeah? You didn't have to apologize, but I'm glad you did. And you're forgiven, of course."

"Thanks," Carter said when Riley released him.

"You're one of us, Carter," Riley reiterated. "You don't get to ditch us that easily."

Riley's words glowed, warm and comforting in him, as he approached the car, which Ian was leaning against.

"Hey," Ian said as he unlocked it and they both climbed in. "I watched the rest of the practice. Seemed like it went well."

"Yeah, it did," Carter said.

"That touchdown." Ian shot him a fierce grin. "I bet it felt good."

It had felt good. Damn good.

But somehow not as good as sitting side by side with Ian, pulling out of the parking lot on the way to his house.

Damn it. Riley might be right after all.

"Yeah," Carter said.

He'd never *liked* anyone. Not the way he liked Ian.

And yep, Riley was right again. It was scary as fuck.

"You're quiet," Ian said as Carter pulled off the freeway. "You're sure you're alright?"

"Yeah," Carter repeated again. Didn't know what else to say. Maybe he was feeling the shake of that suddenly unsteady foundation more than he'd imagined. "I thought I'd call Moira when I got home, actually."

"That's a great idea." Ian glowed with how much of a great idea he thought it was. "You're doing good, Carter, seriously. Identifying when you need help is a major step."

Of course, was Moira going to say the same thing when he called up, sounding thirteen in a way he'd never sounded even back then, and said he *liked* her son?

Carter wasn't sure.

But he didn't know what else to do about it.

Chapter 10

Ian knew he was taking a risk, but it had been an unexpectedly warm day for November in Charleston, and Carter wasn't due back for at least another hour, so he'd hopped into the pool.

After Carter's meltdown two days ago, he'd kept a much closer eye on him. Hadn't missed a single practice until now. But Alec had called, wanting him to sit in on a meeting where he was going over a contract with a player about to graduate from college and declare for the draft. It was such a great opportunity, Ian hadn't wanted to say no.

Besides, Carter had added with a lopsided smile when Ian had brought it up, "There's lots of people around to watch me."

He was right, *and* it was just one evening practice, so Ian had ducked out early and returned home.

The call had gone well, the player committing to signing on Alec's dotted line, and now Ian pulled on the big, baggy swim trunks he'd bought instead of his normal sleek briefs—just because he wasn't expecting Carter home yet didn't mean he was going to be stupid about it.

Before, when they'd been merely swamped in mutual lust, Carter catching Ian mostly naked, just out of the pool, had been bad.

But now, Ian could recognize them edging towards a bigger kind of disaster. He enjoyed Carter's company more than he ever had with any of his other clients, and with every day that passed, they were drawn closer and closer into each other's orbit.

If Carter caught him now, Ian wasn't confident how it would end.

Ian walked out onto the patio, dropping his towel on the chair, and after pausing for a second, the glimmer of the water calling to him like a siren, he dove in.

He'd intended to get a good hard workout in, maybe work off some of the tension bubbling just under his skin before Carter came home.

But he only ended up making a dozen or so halfhearted laps before finally settling in the deep end, arms stretched over the concrete edge of the pool, floating there with his head tipped back, relaxing.

He knew he should get out and be showered and changed before Carter came home, but this felt so nice, cool water lapping against his overheated skin, he didn't want to move.

Surely, it wouldn't be the end of the world if Carter *did* return and he was still in the pool. It wouldn't be a total catastrophe, Ian reasoned.

Whether it was overconfidence or laziness, he wasn't sure, but he didn't move an inch, even when he heard the patio door open and Carter's footsteps as he walked across the concrete.

"Didn't expect to see you out here," Carter said and there was something uneasy in his voice that had Ian's eyes snapping open.

Carter was sitting closer than he'd expected, on the edge of the lounge chair closest to him. His elbows were on his knees and he looked tired.

The thing Ian had learned, spending the last two weeks with the guy, was that he had a nearly inexhaustible supply of energy. Carter Maxwell was a freaking energizer bunny. And yet, here he was, shadows under his eyes, lines bracketing his mouth.

Don't look at his mouth.

The thought was automatic and yet completely fucking ineffective these days.

Ian looked anyway.

"Yeah," Ian said. "It was pretty warm today. Thought I could use some decompression time after that call."

Even tired, Carter Maxwell might've been the most attractive man he'd ever seen—and not just because of his body or his hair or his eyes, or the unique-but-somehow-totally-perfect arrangement of his features.

It was his kindness and his humor. The way he seemed genuinely interested in other people. Carter Maxwell was like stardust, and when he sprinkled some of it on you, you glowed because *he* glowed.

No wonder he'd never had a problem finding people who wanted to bask in that glow, even if it was just for a little while.

"Did it not go okay?" Carter asked. Clearly, something was up with him, and instead of talking about it, he was asking *Ian* if he was okay.

"Oh, it was fine. Just...really technical. A lot of legalese." Admittedly, he was still trying to understand all of it. But he'd get there.

"Ah."

"Did something happen at practice?" Ian asked hesitantly when Carter didn't volunteer anything else, just sat there, staring at the ground quietly, like even speaking was too much.

"Yeah." Carter met his gaze. "Micah picked one off me. And then I dropped the next pass. Just...not a great practice."

Carter didn't seem particularly angry. Just worn out.

"You seem alright, though?" Ian questioned carefully.

"I'm not angry if that's what you're asking. Too tired to be angry," Carter admitted. "I did way, way too many sprints after practice. Trying to...work out some of that tension."

"You wanna try something else?"

It was a terrible, very bad, completely catastrophic idea.

But he was going to suggest it anyway.

Carter needed better decompression than just running himself into the ground, until he was too exhausted to care about anything anymore. Until he lost his inherent Carter-ness.

"I don't know? Does it mean I have to move?" Carter cracked a smile.

"Yeah, kinda. But I think it'll really help." *Maybe it'll help you relax, but it's not gonna help either of us with all this sexual tension.*

"I trust you, so yeah," Carter said, and he wasn't so tired he couldn't shoot Ian a grateful smile.

"Get in," Ian said, gesturing to the pool.

Carter raised an eyebrow. "That's your good idea?"

"Swimming's the easiest kind of moving, and the water feels great, and it just sort of...lets *me* get out of my own head."

Carter looked down at his body. "Just...get in?"

"Yeah. Just strip down," Ian said, trying to sound casual, even though surely he was going to burn in some kind of hellfire later for even uttering those words in relation to Carter Maxwell, "and get in."

The twinkle was back in Carter's eyes as he stood. Pulled off his shirt with zero ceremony, and Ian looked everywhere but at his chest. His arms. His abs. All the inherently lickable parts of Carter that were now on full display.

He was *really* going to regret this, wasn't he?

Well, if he was up all night trying to come hard enough that he wouldn't want Carter anymore, then that was probably inevitable anyway.

He heard Carter's shorts hit the ground and he got a glimpse of *thighs-dick-omg-thighs* covered in tight black boxer briefs before he hit the water with a huge splash.

A second later he rose out of the water, shaking out his hair like he was a cover girl on the *Sports Illustrated* swimsuit edition.

"That *does* feel good," Carter announced a minute later as he slowly kicked around the pool.

"Yeah, it does." Ian hadn't missed that he'd kept a good distance between them.

A smart choice.

At least one of them was still being smart.

"You know, I don't know why I had this pool put in and then I never use it," Carter observed as he took the wall, kitty corner to Ian's position, and stretched out his own arms on either side, groaning a little as he settled back.

"If I had a place with a pool, I'd use it all the time. Though I guess that would mean I'd need *a place*," Ian said.

"You should get a place," Carter said lazily.

"It's not a bad life." Ian didn't know why he felt compelled to defend his decisions *or* his life. He'd never felt that before, but there was something about Carter's expression that forced it out of him.

"Yeah, except you're leaving it," Carter pointed out.

"True. I guess I'll have to find a place when I go back to LA." *Stop. Do not pass Go. Do not collect two hundred dollars.* He'd assiduously avoided even *thinking* about leaving Charleston.

But it was an undeniable fact: someday, probably in a few weeks or even a few months, he'd move on.

He always had to move on.

Didn't matter if he wanted to stay here in this pool with Carter, forever.

That wasn't realistic. Or even something currently on offer.

Carter would get better, and then he'd inevitably want his own life back. His own space uncluttered with people who reminded him of every one of his low points.

"Make sure it's one with a pool," Carter said, not even flinching the way Ian had internally.

Maybe he just wasn't putting two and two together.

Or maybe Carter didn't care about the possibility of Ian leaving in the same way Ian did.

"You swim a lot as a kid?" Carter asked, before Ian could figure out something noncommittal and safe to say that wasn't: *I'm sorry, but I'm stuck on that, and stuck on you, and I don't know what the fuck to do about it.*

"Yeah, swim lessons every summer. And we lived by the beach. So lots of time out there. I was practically half-fish."

"I was just thinking why did we stop playing in the water, the way we did as kids?" Carter's voice was full of regret. "We go to the pool, but we don't do it to get in the water. We do it to party. To drink. To show off how hot our six-pack looks. Or I guess, you go the other way. You swim to work out. But we don't freaking *play* anymore."

"I think we can do anything we want to," Ian said slowly.

"Yeah?"

"I don't see why not."

"Then you wouldn't argue if I did this?" Carter grinned at him with that undeniable mischievous energy. He was clearly feeling better and Ian told himself that made all this painful torture worth it.

Carter pushed off the wall, then swam closer and even though Ian's brain was yelling at him, *danger, danger, danger*, he didn't move away.

Then, to his surprise, Carter closed his eyes and then yelled out "Marco!"

Ian laughed, the sound startled out of him.

He'd expected a lot of things out of Carter, but not this.

Carter's arms were long and they reached out in the direction where he'd initially been leaning against the edge of the pool, but Ian moved quickly, ducking away and kicking as swiftly and silently under the water as he could.

"Polo!" Ian called back after he'd already dodged out of the way of Carter's grip.

The key here, he realized as Carter yelled "Marco!" again, and he responded, carefully keeping himself a good six feet away from the other guy, was to not get caught.

Getting caught would mean...well, it *could* mean a lot of things, and Ian wanted to actually enjoy this game.

Carter was fast on land, and he was fast in the water too. But instead of moving quickly and as silently as Ian was, he blustered around, splashing a lot and making a lot of waves and noise.

Even though Ian was smaller and as a result much more agile, he wasn't a professional athlete. Not like Carter. Not someone who'd made it his life work to run the best routes, to get inside people's heads and figure out what they were going to do before they did it.

For a while it did feel like Carter was just playing around, and then after shooting a sharp toothy grin in Ian's direction, he went after him in earnest, pushing hard, constantly calling out, "Marco," and barely even seeming to listen to Ian's increasingly weak, "Polo!"s.

Then, all of a sudden, Ian's back hit the pool wall—and he only saw Carter's grin widen before he was caged in by his hands landing on either side of his shoulders.

He'd totally boxed him in *on purpose*, and Ian discovered, deep down, that he wasn't even particularly sad he'd been caught.

Carter's eyes opened.

Every fleck of gold in them felt molten as he stared directly at Ian.

"Marco," Carter murmured. Low and gruff.

Ian swallowed hard as a droplet of water meandered along Carter's cheek and dropped down on his shoulder.

His eyes followed it lower as it dripped off his collarbone and finally into the water below.

Carter's knee brushed his and neither of them moved.

Ian wasn't sure Carter was even breathing.

He sure as fuck wasn't.

"You caught me," Ian said in a low voice. He heard the yearning in it, and in between every word, how much, deep down, he'd *wanted* to be caught.

Carter tipped his head against Ian's. But didn't move any closer.

It was already too close. Ian could practically taste Carter's breath. It would be so easy to just close the gap between them. Kiss him, the way he'd been dreaming about doing, for two weeks now.

"What are we doing?" Carter asked, the question tumbling out rough and desperate.

That was simple enough. "Playing with fire," Ian replied truthfully.

He tucked a knee around Carter's and felt their lower bodies brush together. Felt the brief, but indelible impact of Carter's torso and thighs against his own.

Ian had never been harder in his whole fucking life and based even on that very slight contact, he was sure it wasn't just him.

"I didn't do this for..." Carter cleared his throat. "For this."

He didn't say what *this* was, but it wasn't tough to fill in the blank.

To touch you. To feel you. To break you down, until kissing feels like the most natural thing in the world.

"I guess I could admire your six-pack next," Ian tried teasing, but the sparks in Carter's eyes glowed hot.

"I'm *trying* to be good, but you make it hard."

"Hard? Tell me more." Ian was still trying to brush this whole thing off as a joke. Unsuccessfully.

But the more he tried, the deeper the crease in Carter's forehead became.

"Ian," Carter said seriously. "I *mean* it. What are we doing?"

Like Ian had any freaking clue.

He'd been trying to avoid looking right *at* Carter, instead letting his gaze hover over his shoulder. His gorgeous curved-with-muscle shoulder.

Like that was really any fucking better.

"Trying to do the right thing," Ian said slowly.

But Carter just shook his head. "If it's the right thing, why does it feel so wrong to keep pulling away from you?"

Not questions Ian wanted to touch with a ten-foot pole. Suddenly he was desperate to get out of this pool, to get as far from the irresistible temptation Carter provided as he could.

"I...I don't know." He lied. Ian was not proud of it. But what was he supposed to say?

It's cause I'm increasingly into you, and you're right there with me, and it's not just sex, anymore, though the sex would be undeniably fantastic.

"How about this?" Carter smiled, and this time, it was full of the devil, and the angel was nowhere in sight. "If you don't want me to touch you. Touch you and kiss you and make you moan and then scream, you'd better get out of this pool. *Now.*"

Ian's fingers trembled.

His whole fucking body shook.

But when Carter lifted his arm, he was swimming on shaky legs to the ladder. Climbing up it, he didn't dare look back because what if Carter was right there? Watching him? Chasing after him?

The way his body steamed from the inside out, there was no denying Carter was half a step behind him as he took off for the patio, not bothering to even grab his towel.

He tracked wet footprints into the kitchen and then took the stairs two at a time, finally falling into his bedroom and shutting the door behind him.

He fell against the wood with a sharp thud, and with shaky hands already had his wet, baggy swim trunks down around his ankles, his fingers curling around his rock hard cock.

Letting out an uneven groan, he pressed himself farther back against the door.

And then between one breath and the next, he heard it.

Carter's footsteps. Inexorably moving closer. Not passing his room by, but stopping in front of it.

Ian wasn't even fucking breathing and his hand stilled on his cock, no matter how much it was crying out for *something*.

Was Carter going to come in here? Was he going to barge right in?

The answer to Ian's question was *no*—but also, *yes*.

He felt a weight settle against the other side of the closed door. Heard something hit the floor with a wet plop. Those were his boxer briefs. The thought surged, hot and undeniable, through Ian's brain.

Then next, Carter's audible groan.

Ian gasped. Loudly.

So loudly Carter couldn't have possibly missed it.

"Yeah," Carter said, pitching his voice so there was no question now—he *wanted* Ian to hear. "Come on. Touch yourself. I wanna hear it. If I can't do it. If I *can't*, then at least let me fucking hear it."

"Ahhhh." Ian couldn't even form words. It was just all gibberish as he moved his hand again, the pleasure shooting through him in a dizzying rush.

"Fuck, I want you bad," Carter growled against the door. "I wanna *see* you."

Ian groaned again at the thought. Of what Carter might look like when he was crazed with lust like this. How he'd look. How he'd sound. How he'd *feel*.

The door thumped between them, straining between two bodies straining for something else entirely. Heard the undeniable slick sound as he took his cock in his hand.

Squeezing his eyes shut, he tried not to come just from that sound alone.

"Come on, baby, let me hear you," Carter coaxed again.

The more Carter talked—and it turned out he was a *talker* during sex, even sex of the solo variety—the surer Ian was he wasn't going to last.

The way he kept up a litany of pleading, begging, increasingly insistent orders as Ian pumped his cock with frantic movements.

Let me hear you.

Let me hear you moan.

Let me hear you fucking scream.

I want that to be my *hand. My mouth. My cock.*

Make you feel so good.

Make you never want anyone else.

Then he heard it, Carter's low, stuttering breath. The way he gasped, and he knew Carter had gone right over the edge.

Ian's brain completely shorted out, and he jerked, coming over his hand in endless spurts as his mind fixated on what Carter had just said.

What he'd implied.

Maybe after this he *would* never want anyone else.

That was both the hottest thing on the whole fucking planet. And also the most terrifying.

Chapter 11

"You've been avoiding me," Carter said after they'd gotten into the car to head to the practice facility, where they'd catch a bus to the airport and then fly to New Orleans for the tenth game of the season.

Ian couldn't take Carter's pronouncement seriously. "I can't avoid you. We're literally living in the same house and it's my job to go wherever you go."

"Yeah, I *know*, which is why it's even crazier that you're trying to avoid me."

"I'm—"

But Carter didn't let Ian lie to him again.

"No, don't do that shit again. Tell me whatever you want to say, but don't act like nothing's changed."

The morning after, Carter had come downstairs, and Ian had been there, at the kitchen table, the same as he had been for the last two weeks, but he'd barely glanced up from his laptop.

Carter hadn't been surprised; he'd been expecting that or even Ian lecturing him about how they couldn't do that again. But Ian hadn't done that. Hadn't once mentioned that they'd maybe not *broken* the first rule, but skirted right up to the edge.

He was tired of not talking about it. He wanted to talk about it. He wanted to do it again, damnit.

He'd had threesomes, foursomes, and even an orgy or two. But the hottest sex he'd ever experienced had been against his guest bedroom door, and it seemed if Ian had anything to say—or *not* say—about it, they'd never do it again.

Go fucking figure.

After that, Ian had made sure they were barely ever in the same room. If they were, he was on his phone or distracted.

The ice Carter had totally melted from his gaze was back in spades.

Carter didn't know which was worse: that fucking ice wall or the metaphorical and physical arm's length Ian kept between them.

Like, before, even at the beginning, Ian had still been friendly. They'd still talked.

But now, they'd barely had a conversation in two days.

Ian didn't answer for a long time. They were almost halfway to the practice facility when he finally said, "I know everything's changed. I should have called up Alec right after it happened and told him I couldn't do this anymore."

"You might as well," Carter muttered. Yeah, Ian had been physically present the last few days, but that was all.

"Listen," Ian said, and he sounded a lot more heated. Carter's hands tightened on the wheel. "*Listen*. This is how I am with *all* my other clients. A little more involved, maybe, but from the beginning, with you, it's been more. I told myself it was because it wasn't a typical job for me. You didn't really need a sober companion. I told myself you needed a friend who gave a shit about you and watched out for you, was aware when you were skirting too close to the edge, and helped you off it, but now I wonder..." Ian took a deep breath. "Was I lying to myself the whole goddamn time?"

"I don't know, were you?"

Ian sighed.

Carter was furious and also, impossibly, felt guilty. He'd pushed them, even though he really hadn't meant to. He'd just wanted to *play*, the way they did all the time as kids. And maybe if they didn't have all this sexual tension between them, it could've been that. Instead, it had morphed into something else so fast he hadn't even realized it was happening until he'd caught Ian.

And after that?

Well, shit had gotten out of hand.

He could admit that.

"I'm sorry," Carter said. "I'm really sorry if I made you uncomfortable."

He pulled into the players' parking lot and shut off the engine, but neither of them moved.

"You didn't make me—" Ian stopped abruptly. "Well, you *did*, but it's not your fault that we're like this together. I guess it's not just that I'm forbidden. 'Cause I'm feeling it too."

It wasn't the first time Ian had admitted it, but when Carter glanced over at him, Ian looked like he was...well, softening.

Maybe this was just inevitable.

Like the sun rising in the east, and the moon in the sky at night. And Carter scoring touchdowns.

"What are we going to do about it?" Carter asked. He'd asked a version of this question that night in the pool, but Ian had never answered. Not satisfactorily anyway.

"I don't know," Ian admitted.

That wasn't much better.

Carter made a face.

"I know," Ian said, and he was laughing. Covering his face and honest to God, *laughing*. "We are so fucked."

"I keep hoping so," Carter teased, because he couldn't help himself.

Ian elbowed him. "No," he said firmly. "*No*. I know that happened—"

It shouldn't have been annoying Carter that Ian kept obliquely referencing what they'd done, but it was.

"You can at least *say* it," Carter interrupted him.

Ian raised an eyebrow. "You sure that's a good idea?"

Honestly, Carter wasn't sure of anything right now. He'd never expected to feel this way. While *yes*, he undeniably wanted a redo of what had happened that night—hopefully with both of them on the same side of the door—he wanted to just *talk* to Ian again. To laugh with him. To feel comfortable around him again and not worry when Ian was going to just announce this was over.

That was really the root of it: he didn't want it to be over. Whatever this was, he didn't want it to end.

And *that* fucked him up.

"Okay, fine," Ian answered his own question. "After we...after we mutually got off together. But separately. *Separately.*"

"You repeating that for my benefit or yours?" Carter asked.

"For both of us," Ian said firmly. "And it's not like you didn't know I was...or that I didn't know *you* were."

It was so cute watching Ian flush and try to talk his way around what had happened. *I got you off. I told you to get yourself off and you did it. Everything I said. While thinking about me.*

"Maybe you're repeating it for Alec's benefit," Carter said.

"Maybe," Ian retorted darkly. "But it's not like he's ever going to find out what happened, because he's *not*."

Carter didn't know how he felt about keeping it a secret. If Ian didn't believe there was anything worth telling Alec about...

Shut up, Carter told himself firmly. *It doesn't mean anything.*

"Okay," Carter said. He gestured towards the building. "We'd better get in there. We've got a plane to catch."

"Right. Right." Ian seemed flustered still.

So it made perfect sense to fluster him a little further. Carter unlocked his seat belt and before Ian could react or protest, he hugged him.

Oh yeah, this is so much better.

But he didn't put up any kind of fight at all. Instead, Ian sank into him like he was butter and Carter was white hot.

"I'm sorry again," Carter murmured into his shoulder. Because he *had* pushed. Yeah, Ian had seemed one hundred and ten percent into it and he'd not come close to saying anything like *no*, but this *was* Ian's job. A job Ian needed to succeed at so he could become something he wanted. Something, Carter had decided, he'd be really good at.

He felt Ian tense, and then he let go.

"Yeah, me too," Ian said, but his eyes didn't quite meet Carter's.

"Hey, I wanted to show you this thing I saw the other night," Deacon said, flagging Carter down as he climbed onto the plane and looked down the narrow aisle towards where Ian had taken a seat nearly at the back of the plane.

"Yeah?"

"Yeah," Deacon said. "You can get back to your...well, whatever it is you're calling him these days, in a minute. But I wanted to show you this first."

"I'm calling him my..." Carter hesitated. Minder felt wrong. Companion was weird as hell and had a bunch of connotations he didn't like. Chaperone was just a fucking joke. What *was* Ian anyway? His celibacy coach?

Yeah, that was maybe even worse than chaperone, because while *yes* he was technically celibate, Ian made him not want to be so badly he could taste it.

"I can see you still haven't figured out exactly what he is," Deacon teased as Carter sat next to him.

"He's a friend, how about we start there," Carter said, stowing his bag under the seat in front of him and stretching out his legs.

"A friend?"

"I thought there was something you wanted to show me," Carter reminded him.

He didn't really want to talk about this with Deacon—or with anyone, really. Because how on earth was he supposed to make sense of the jumble of feelings swirling around inside him? If he couldn't even explain it to himself, how could he possibly explain it to someone else?

Deacon gave him a hard look. A searching look.

"I can't say I'm not worried about you. But it's not the same now. You're..." Deacon hesitated. "You like him, don't you?"

"I thought that was obvious," Carter grumbled.

"I mean, you're *crazy* about him," Deacon corrected gently. "You want to not only take him to bed, you want to spend time with him. You keep glancing back there, over your shoulder, every five seconds, like somehow he'll have evaporated. Newsflash, Maxwell. We're on a plane."

"I know we're on a plane. I might be an idiot, but I know that," Carter said.

"You're not an idiot." Deacon shook his head. "You're really smart, which is why you're not even looking at this, because if you did, you'd see it as plainly as the rest of us do."

"Did you have anything you actually wanted to show me, or am I just here to admit to you that things have gotten...complicated?"

Deacon chuckled. "No, not just that," he said, pulling a tablet out of his bag. He pulled up some video and handed it to Carter. "I was watching some film last night, and saw that, and thought, *huh*, might come in handy for you."

Carter pressed play and watched as the Saints' defense ran a pattern against the Vegas Raiders, when they'd played two weeks ago.

He liked to think he was just as good of a receiver—if not better—than the Raiders' leading wideout, Davante Adams.

The video played once, and then he played it again. And then a third time. "Yeah, Adams should've just blown right past that guy. He was hesitating."

"Can't believe he didn't see it," Deacon said, taking the tablet back.

"And why did *you* see it? Why are you watching defensive film of the team we're playing?"

"Uh, well, Jem actually sent it to me. He's bored as fuck. Watching a lot of games, lot of film, these days."

"It sucks what happened to him."

"Yeah," Deacon said, looking like he wanted to say more, but then he clammed up, instead.

Carter had discovered last year that Deacon wasn't always the most vocal guy in the locker room, but when he had something to say, he said it. This reticence was unlike him.

"You ever going to tell me what's going on?" Carter asked. If Deacon could do it, then so could he. "You and Mr. G finally fucking?"

Deacon flushed bright red. "*No,*" he said emphatically. "And that's not...that's not happening."

"Sure it's not," Carter grinned.

"I just..." Deacon hesitated. "You can't tell anyone this."

"You're telling me I need to keep a secret? You know who you're talking to, right?" Carter was used to relying on his self-deprecating routine, but the problem with Deacon was he was *also* crazy sharp and had always seen right through it.

"Don't start being stupid now," Deacon drawled. "You can keep shit locked tighter than a drum if you want to. It's a matter of wanting to. And this, you're gonna want to tell people, but you can't. Not til I...well, til I figure out how."

Carter realized, with a dawning sense of dread, exactly what Deacon was trying and failing to say.

"You have one year left on your contract. A contract you've not tried to renegotiate or extend, no matter how tight you are with the owner, and how much he'd want to keep you around. You're done. You're quitting."

"Retiring," Deacon corrected with a quiet, resigned smile. "Yeah, I am."

"This is *terrible*." Carter wanted to cry. "I don't know how to be here without you." The words came out in a tumble before he could stop them. "Last year…"

"But last year was last year, and now's different," Deacon reminded him gently. "There's other guys around, guys you can count on. Guys who can watch your back. It's not just me and Jem anymore."

Carter swallowed hard. "Is Jem retiring, too?"

But Deacon just shrugged. "Not sure. We haven't talked about it."

"You mean, you haven't told him what *you're* doing, and that's why you're extra bummed he got hurt and won't play again this year, because this was your last chance to play together."

Deacon's gaze was sad but resigned. "Yeah," he said.

"You need to tell him."

"I was going to, right after the Piranhas game, but then he got hurt, and how was I supposed to tell him then? He's already so frustrated and pissed off. Now I gotta say, *Jem, you're my best friend and now we're not gonna play together again.*"

"Is he gonna stop being your best friend?"

Deacon shot him a look. "Hell no."

"Then, you *tell* him," Carter repeated with more emphasis this time.

"I guess." Deacon rubbed his jaw.

"No, you gotta do it. If he finds out you told me before you told *him*..." Carter trailed off, feeling suddenly very shaken at the thought.

"He's not going to, because you're not going to tell him," Deacon reminded him.

"Right. Right. Okay." Carter took a deep breath. "God this sucks. You and then Jem, probably."

"Probably? You don't think he'll play next year?"

"I was having a meltdown during the Piranhas game, I'm not *stupid*, as you like to say," Carter reminded him.

"Right, of course not. Well, wow. I can't believe I told you. I guess I needed to tell..." Deacon stopped in his tracks. "No, that's not true." He slung an arm around Carter's shoulders, tugged him in. "You're not just anyone. You're Carter. And you've been a good friend."

Carter raised an eyebrow.

"Okay," Deacon corrected, "you *are* a good friend."

"Damn straight," Carter said with a nod. "Which means you're not allowed to be a stranger, okay?"

Deacon nodded. "Okay."

The Saints, even after the retirement of Drew Brees and the departure of Sean Payton, were still fighting hard to be relevant and as the Condors discovered in this game—they weren't going to go quietly into the night.

Carter collapsed onto the bench, breathing hard after yet another drive where they'd come up just short, settling for sending Ethan out to kick a field goal.

God, he wanted a touchdown.

Wanted it so badly he could practically fucking taste it.

Riley clearly felt the same, because he dropped down next to Carter, Landry on his other side, and said in a serious, focused voice, "Come on, guys, let's look at these last few plays."

"We need to start making some more third downs," Landry said. He sounded as frustrated as Carter felt.

But Carter hadn't lost it yet.

Wasn't going to lose it.

He wasn't stupid enough to think they could've won the Piranhas game even if he hadn't melted down, but it sure as fuck hadn't helped.

He wasn't going to let his temper take over now and doom them, when they were *very* much in this game.

"This was why we worked with Nick this week," Riley said, gesturing to where the other receiver was standing by Landry's shoulder. "You're getting double-teamed to death, Carter."

He was. Every play it felt like he had to wade through coverage two or three players deep to even get into the flat.

"I can get loose," he insisted. "I can shake them loose."

The corner of Riley's mouth curled up into a smile. "I'm actually thinking maybe not."

"What?" Carter demanded flatly. "Of course I can, I can handle those assholes in my sleep—"

But Riley put a hand on Carter's knee. "No," he said reassuringly. "Can you? Of course you can. Eventually you'd break them down, but I have another idea in mind. Coach Rufus made an observation when I was jogging off the field. He said that every play, the defense is checking where you're at, Carter. Every single damn play."

"Well, of course. That's 'cause I'm Carter Maxwell."

Landry rolled his eyes. "No ego at all."

"Is it ego if it's true?" Carter wondered.

"We're not here to be the sidekicks in the Carter Maxwell show," Nick grumbled.

"I don't know," Carter said with a lazy grin, "you make pretty good ones."

"Carter," Riley exclaimed and smacked him in the arm. "We need to talk about this. *Seriously*."

"I can be serious," Carter said.

"They're watching you *every* play. Every play they're arranging their defense based on where you're gonna be and what you're gonna do." Riley glanced over at Carter, then met Landry and Nick's gazes, too. He seemed excited and galvanized—but Carter wasn't because he had a feeling he knew where Riley was going with this.

And he didn't like it. At all.

In some ways—okay, in every way that mattered—it *was* the Carter Maxwell show, and this would be putting someone else front and center.

Nick Johnson, specifically.

Ugh.

He only had a moment to come to grips with the fact that if someone was going to be winning this game, it would not be him. God, that fucking sucked.

But, a voice inside him that sounded exactly like Ian observed, *does it matter if you get a W? Isn't that all that matters? The team?*

It had never been that way before he'd come here, to Charleston. Hadn't even been like that last year. Deacon had tried of course, but he couldn't completely overcome the shitty culture the ownership and coaching staff had created.

But this season everything was different. *And*, he reminded himself, *don't you want to give Deacon something special for his last season?*

A lump grew in his throat at just the thought of Deacon not being around anymore. He was like the big brother Carter had never been lucky enough to have—but had always wanted, so badly the lack had ached for years and years.

"Carter, do you think—"

In the end, it was a no-brainer.

"Yes," Carter said impatiently.

Riley shot him a look. "Do you even know what I was gonna say?"

"You want me to distract the defense at the beginning of every play so Nick or Landry can wiggle free of some of their coverage and you can throw to them for some serious yards."

"Yeah, uh, that was exactly what I was going to say."

Landry grinned at him. "Every time someone tries to tell me you're an idiot, I want to yell at them."

"Thanks," Carter said dryly.

In for a penny, in for a pound.

"Deacon showed me some film yesterday—it hasn't helped me yet, but it might help one of you." Carter proceeded to tell both Nick and Landry about the corner he'd seen hesitating on the line against the Raiders.

"He hasn't done it today so far, but it might still happen," Carter concluded.

Nick nodded. "I'll keep an eye on him."

"Might be able to use that hesitation against him if he's covering you, Carter," Landry pointed out.

"Oh yeah, totally," Carter agreed, and even though yeah, it *sucked* that he wasn't going to be the one winning this game, what he did was going to make it possible for Riley and the rest of the offense make some actual progress down field.

"Come on," Riley said, eyeing the field as Carter realized the defense had just shut the Saints down mid-field, Beck and Micah celebrating with Deacon as they stymied the Saints' third down play before it could even go anywhere.

They jogged onto the field after the Saints punted and the Condors downed the ball at the twenty-four yard line.

"You know what you're doing?" Riley asked as they jogged onto the field.

"Yep." Carter grinned at him. "Be the most Carter Maxwell I've ever been in my whole freaking life."

Riley nodded, smiling in return. "You got it." He turned to the rest of the huddle. "Fly, Condors, fly!" he yelled, and the rest of the players chanted after him and he clapped, breaking up the group.

Carter jogged to the right, lining up opposite one of the Saints' corners—and shot him one of his patented "Carter Maxwell is gonna score on you the next play" looks. Riley had told him to be his *most* Carter Maxwell, and he was gonna bring it.

"Make sure you can keep up," Carter tossed over the line.

The corner frowned. A second later, the safety dropped in, and Carter could see the other corner eyeing him with suspicion.

Was he that transparent normally?

He was gonna have to consider toning down his egotistical posturing if it was giving away how certain he was the ball was coming his direction.

Riley counted down the play, and the moment Cole, the center, snapped the call, Carter took off.

One of his favorite things to do was to study crazy patterns and routes. He took one of those now, leading the group trailing him in earnest on a wild-goose chase down the sideline.

Make it look good. Make it look legit.

He pushed harder and then took off in a curl, just in enough time to see Nick grab the ball out of the air and take it for another ten yards, for a total of almost twenty yards. Double what they'd needed for the first down.

The rest of the drive was much the same. Carter pushing hard, using the top range of his speed to keep the defenders on their toes. He went from being double-teamed to triple-teamed, but between the running game and a few throws Riley made to Nick and Landry, the Condors moved the ball down the field.

Then finally Riley kept the ball to himself, dodging around the remaining defense, which had struggled to hold him the whole game because he was just so much quicker and more agile than they were.

He broke right through the line and held the ball up, yelling in jubilation as they finally scored.

Carter was right there, too, in the thick of it, patting him on the back as Landry lifted him up.

"You," Riley said with a breathless laugh as they returned to the sideline, "totally tied them into knots. I've never seen such weird route running. But it *worked*."

"Not weird, Flynn. *Creative*," Carter reminded him.

And as they settled back on the bench, breaking down which plays had worked the best and which ones they could improve on, Carter realized he hadn't felt even the tiniest bit of envy or jealousy or frustration that the touchdown hadn't been his.

Carter was afraid he knew exactly what this new feeling was.

Freaking character development.

"You alright there, Carter?" Nick asked. "You look like you've just seen a ghost."

"Not a ghost. A better version of myself." Carter made a face.

Nick laughed and patted him on the back. "Don't hurt yourself, now," he said.

But that was the problem, wasn't it? It didn't hurt. In fact, it felt like the opposite of hurt.

On the field, the Saints' quarterback threw a dangerous pass across the middle, and Beck must've seen it coming, because he leapt up, going seriously airborne—he and Carter had worked together on the offseason on his vertical length—and came down with the ball. He took off, Carter and the rest of the sideline on their feet, yelling in support as Micah blocked one side and Deacon the other, Beck cruising into the end zone for an easy touchdown.

And just like that, they were up twenty to three, and for the rest of the game, they were able to cruise.

Carter played spoiler a few more times, and when the clock finally wound down, Deacon came up and slapped him on the back.

"What was that for?" Carter complained, but he was still smiling. This had been a good win. A different kind of win than he'd come to expect, but a W was a W, wasn't it? And it didn't even *feel* crappy. It felt good. In fact, it felt *great*. Like he'd contributed but the lack of having to carry the whole responsibility of scoring on his shoulders had alleviated some of the natural pressure he always felt.

The kind of pressure that usually led to a meltdown when it grew too intense.

"Don't think I didn't notice what you did," Deacon said. "That's the kind of shit that makes me crazy when offenses do it to us. But most of the time they can't, because you diva receiver types don't like to take a back seat."

"We don't, do we?" Carter pointed out.

Deacon nodded. Shot Carter a quiet look. "You're a good guy, Maxwell. Don't forget it, even when I'm not around to remind you, okay?"

Carter thought about it for a minute. "Yeah, I'll try." Maybe he didn't *need* Deacon around to remind him, but he still fucking wanted him to be.

God, it sucked that they were losing him.

The pain of it had been settling inside him, like a hard kernel buried in his chest that he couldn't quite escape. It didn't make him angry; instead, it just made him sad.

Deacon must've realized it, because he slung an arm around his shoulders and dragged Carter in, hugging him tight. "You're gonna be just fine," he promised. "Now, let's go find your boy."

"He's not my boy," Carter spluttered.

But even he noticed that he wasn't protesting calling Ian that these days.

CHAPTER 12

CARTER SHIFTED UNCOMFORTABLY IN his chair.

Just yesterday he'd thought to himself that he was changing—with purpose, of course, because he'd certainly been on board with all the lifestyle changes—but today's session with Moira had him questioning just how far he *had* come.

Probably because she was currently grilling him on his parents.

Who he never wanted to talk about.

That was almost definitely why they seemed to be the *only* thing she wanted to talk about these days.

"Can't we talk about something else? Something slightly less uncomfortable?" Carter tried joking, but he heard the painful earnestness in his voice. "Ian? The great game yesterday? Global warming? How Deacon leaving me feels like the end of the world?"

"Maybe we *should* talk about that last one," Moira observed. "But first, you've been ducking these questions about your parents for weeks now, and I don't want you to think you can just dangle some other appealing topic in front of my nose and I'll give up."

"Won't you?" Carter had meant to smile, but on the screen, he could see how it was more of a grimace than anything else.

"No," Moira said steadily. "Answer the question. Do you still talk to your parents?"

"When I have to," Carter finally said. He could've said, *way more than I ever want to, which is never.*

In a world where he hadn't become a wide receiver in the NFL, they probably would've left him on his own. Forgotten about him entirely. But he had become a receiver, a very good one, and that was when they'd decided he was worth their attention.

Worth being their son.

Only after he'd learned the hard way that he didn't want to be forgotten about or left behind or ignored any longer.

"Do they still contact you?"

"Sometimes." He could hear the anger simmering just under the surface of his calm voice. He wondered if Moira could hear it too—but who was he kidding? She was a professional, of course she could fucking hear it.

It wasn't the uncontrollable, searing fire of rage, but a slow burning, resentful kind of anger.

The kind that bubbled up every time he glanced down at his phone and saw that it was one of his parents calling.

"Carter," she said patiently.

"Okay, they call. Because...not because they fucking like me, understand? But because I'm Carter Maxwell. Because I make them look good now. Mostly, anyway. I never really felt like their son. But now I feel even less like their son. I'm just a famous person and they wanna be in my orbit. That's all."

"Have you ever told them how that makes you feel?"

"Of course not," Carter scoffed. "Why would I do something stupid like that?"

Moira's expression was unbearably gentle. He wanted to flinch from it, because *nobody* was going to feel sorry for him, but maybe she should. Maybe it was right that she did. "Because it's good and healthy to set boundaries. If they're not going to treat you like a son, then you don't have to treat them like your parents."

"You mean tell them to fuck off?" God, how long had he craved doing exactly that? In the middle of his most destructive meltdowns, that was always one thought that stood out from all the others. *I wanna make them regret it. All of it. Every single moment they rejected me and forgot about me. Every single time they took off for the weekend and left me on my own. Every time they worked late and never called. Every game they missed. Every school function. Graduation, when they didn't show. And then every moment they embraced me because I became famous and rich.*

"No," Moira said, but a corner of her mouth flickered like she wanted to smile. "No, not at all. Though I guess...*yes*, in a way. But not that way. I mean, set boundaries. Decide how far they're allowed into your life. You can either inform them of that line or not, it's your choice, though I always think communication is a good idea."

"You would," he muttered.

"What was that?"

"I said, *you would*," Carter said, because even talking about this made him feel shaky and slightly out of control. It was why he didn't normally even *think* about it. Not until he was too far gone to hold back the tide any longer.

"Why? What happens when you tell them the truth?"

"Nothing good," Carter said. He saw the brief flash of concern on Moira's face and hurried to correct her. "No, no, no, not like that. They never laid a hand on me. They weren't monsters."

"Physical abuse isn't the only kind of abuse, Carter," she said gently.

"I know." He did. It was just...*ugh*. He hated talking about this. "They didn't do anything bad to me. Just ignored me."

Moira raised an eyebrow.

"Forgot I existed, that's probably a better descriptor."

"And that's better?"

"No. No, it's not." It had never felt better. Not ever. Not since he'd been very young and realized just how little they cared about him.

When he was five, and he'd gotten sick at school, and the nurse had called them to come pick him up, and they just...had never come. Eventually, the school had called Enid, and she'd come, because she *always* gave a shit about him.

But when his grandmother died, everything that was terrible had gotten worse.

By then, he'd sort of learned to fend for himself.

That didn't mean it had been easier. Or hurt any less. Or he'd been less desperate to grab their attention by any means necessary.

"I didn't think so," Moira said reasonably. "You're *allowed* to be whatever you are by how they treated you, Carter. You realize, that right?"

Carter took a deep breath. "It's easier to just...deal with them when they come around if I don't push it. I don't need their victim-playing games. Or their passive aggressive guilt. If I deal with them, then they go away."

"But they always come back." Just like Moira kept returning, inexorably, to this point. Carter could understand why. But doing something about the concept she kept talking about was a totally different thing than just listening to it.

It would mean...it would mean actually tackling the problem of them. A problem he'd never managed to solve, but then before, he'd been entirely on his own.

Now he had Moira. Moira and Ian. And Alec. And all his friends.

He wasn't alone, anymore.

"Yeah, they do."

"Carter," Moira said after a long speculative silence, "you hold a lot of this in. I know you do. You can only hold all these feelings in for so long before you snap."

"I'm not acting out because they're assholes...I'm acting out because..." But suddenly Carter wasn't sure.

He scrubbed a hand across his face. Maybe he was.

"I think you wanted their attention, and at the beginning, when you were younger, you kept thinking, this time, if I do this, it'll get me what I crave, what I *deserve*. Their attention. It didn't matter that it was negative attention. It was still *attention*. You probably hoped that someday, the attention would change. They'd treat you like their son. But it never worked. Still, it became an unfortunate habit. A way to get attention, even if it was negative. Then, when you became older, you kept doing it, not just because it was a habit, but because it had a handy side effect of being an outlet for all this rage that was building in you."

"Oh."

"It's a lot to take in, I know," Moira said. "But that's why I want to talk about boundaries. If you can block your parents off, block them out, and no longer let them into your life, except on your terms, then you can truly begin to tackle the pain of their treatment and their behavior. Eventually—"

Carter finished her sentence. "I'm cured?" he said dryly.

"No, not *cured*," Moira said. "But...*better*. More controlled. Happier, I'd hope."

"Huh."

"I assume you'd *like* to be happy."

"I'm not really an *unhappy* person, doc."

Moira shot him a frank look. "I'm sure you want everyone to think that. You spend a lot of mental energy creating that false front that you're happy and carefree, without a single worry. But I bet that your friends don't really believe it. And you know what else? I think they'd want you to be happy too."

Suddenly, Carter *wasn't* sure. Did they see right through him?

Had he really done all that stuff, from such a young age, for attention? Was she right about everything?

He didn't know, but it seemed stupid to bet against her.

Because she was right, absolutely one hundred percent fucking right, about one thing: he wanted to be happy.

"Okay, doc, maybe you're right. What about these boundary things?"

She smiled at him.

Ian was slogging through a particularly thick and incomprehensible section of a contract—stopping every other sentence to look up a word or reference—when Carter came downstairs.

He'd known Carter had a therapy appointment this morning, and hadn't *exactly* been down here, on the couch, lying in wait for him, but after the last few sessions, they'd started discussing how Carter felt at the end of them.

But looking at Carter now, he didn't need to ask, because the blindsided look in his eyes told the whole story. Moira had obviously decided it was time to play hardball, and Carter had clearly not been expecting it.

"Hey, you alright?" Ian asked as he straightened. He'd been laid out on the couch, but any horizontal positioning near Carter was probably a mistake.

Okay. *More* of a mistake.

"I...I'm..." Carter flopped down next to him. Scrubbed a hand across his face. Looked sad and miserable and lost.

Ian didn't think, he just *reacted*.

Dropped his tablet to the cushion, and wrapped Carter up as best he could in his arms. Holding him tight. Not speaking. Not moving. Just reminding him in the best way he could that he was there for him.

"Wouldn't it just have been fucking easier for them to just...be *human*? Act like they were happy to be my parents?" Carter's voice was muffled in his shoulder, but Ian could still hear the pain in it.

"You'd think," Ian said quietly. "I know this sounds like a cliche, but it *is* their loss."

When Carter pulled back, there were tears glimmering in his eyes. "You really think so?"

Ian couldn't even believe Carter was questioning this. Did he not see the magic he brought to everyone around him: the humor and the lightness and the kindness and the plain fucking *sparkle*?

But words felt inadequate. Not nearly enough.

So Ian did the only thing that felt right. The only thing that had ever felt right.

He cupped Carter's scruff-covered cheek with one hand and leaned in, brushing a soft, gentle kiss across his mouth.

Carter jolted like he'd been shocked, his eyes widening like Ian had just grown a second head.

"I could tell you that you're an amazing friend. Or surprisingly sweet. Or that I wanted to be your friend—and *more*—since the first time you opened your mouth and promised you'd be hitting on me sooner or later. But—"

But I could only show you. The only way I knew how. By throwing away my professional parachute and proceeding to fling myself off a cliff.

But Ian didn't get the rest of that sentence out.

Instead, Carter kissed him back.

It wasn't as passionate as he'd expected. It was sweet like his. Careful. Gentle. Carter's mouth moving over his like he was precious and perfect. But that didn't make it any less consuming.

Of course they were always going to end up here. On Carter's couch. Kissing tentatively like they were both afraid they'd scare the other one away by how much they desperately wanted.

With how much they *felt*.

Because Ian knew now he hadn't thrown that parachute away, possibly rejecting Alec's career assistance, for nothing. Not even for something. But for *everything*.

He was falling head over heels for Carter Maxwell—and he was hoping it wasn't just him.

Carter's hand snaked its way around his waist and tugged him closer just as he tilted his head, slanting his mouth across Ian's, his tongue slipping alongside his own, and, like he'd just snapped his fingers, caution was a thing of the past.

The kiss turned wild and hungry, so good Ian was dizzy with it. Of course Carter Maxwell would be a good kisser, but it wasn't just Carter's skill blowing his mind apart. It was how many times he'd imagined this. How many times he'd wanted it to happen, even though he knew it shouldn't. How much he goddamn *liked* Carter and the stardust he trailed over everything and everyone—but also how Carter focused on him. Like he was the man he'd wanted to kiss above all others.

Ian broke the kiss, his harsh breaths loud in the silence.

"God," Carter groaned as his fingers tightened into Ian's side. "Let's do that again. Lots of times. All the times."

They shouldn't. But kissing had been like Pandora's box.

It was open now. There was no way to shove his feelings back inside and close the lid. Ian wasn't sure the box would even contain them anymore, not now that they'd finally touched each other.

"Don't say it," Carter said. *Begged*. Because there was no question at all that he was begging. "Don't you fucking say you regret it. Or that we're not gonna do it again."

Ian couldn't. Because both of those would be blatant lies.

He didn't regret it. And they sure as hell were going to do it again—and *more*.

"Actually," he said mildly, even though his heart was racing a thousand miles an hour, "I was gonna say what you didn't give me time to say. I could tell you all the ways that I think you're awesome and valuable and your parents are assholes. But I thought, wouldn't it be better if I just *showed* you?"

Carter frowned, like he'd just realized what Ian was possibly giving up by kissing him—but the last thing Ian wanted was to have that conversation right now.

His blood was already simmering from just that kiss, and if he wanted to finally know what it was like to have all that sensual attention of Carter's focused on him, who could blame him?

Leaning in, Ian captured Carter's mouth with his own.

This kiss got out of hand fast, their mouths devouring each other until Ian was practically half leaning on top of him, only vaguely aware of the uncomfortable nature of his position until one of Carter's hands slid down from his waist to the curve of his ass. He'd thought he was worked up before Carter had started touching him, but there was nothing else like the hedonistic way Carter's fingers skimmed over the curve, over and over again, like he was trying to memorize the way it felt.

Then a second later, that hand gripped him hard, Ian letting out a gasp of surprised pleasure, and Carter dragged him onto his lap, settling his back against the couch.

Ian dug his fingers into Carter's broad shoulders as he nestled his body right against Carter's. Felt his cock, already hard and aching with the need for release, press against Carter's. He wiggled against it, needing something more than the fleeting pressure.

Underneath him, Carter's eyes fluttered open. Pupils blown wide surrounded by hot, melted caramel. "You're incredible," Carter murmured reverently, like kissing Ian was like a religious experience.

It was a little ridiculous, considering how much experience Carter *did* have.

But before Ian could say that, or say something equally self-deprecating, Carter continued. "Never wanted anyone the way I want you," he said gruffly.

"Trust me, the feeling's mutual," Ian said. He leaned in, wanting to kiss again. Never wanting to do anything else, until he had no choice but to explode just from a few touches. Even then it would probably be the best orgasm he'd ever had.

Carter was experienced, yes. But it wasn't because of that. It was because Carter was *Carter*.

"No, *no*," Carter insisted and framed his chin with one of those big hands. "I didn't know it could feel like *this*."

"Like what?"

Ian knew what it felt like for him: like he was flying and drowning in the same breath.

"Like I can't even fucking *think*, like I just want to go caveman on you and…I don't know…rip your clothes off. Lose myself in you. But at the same time…make sure you know how special and perfect you are. Make sure I'm careful and sweet. How do I do that," Carter questioned, "if I can't even think?"

"Don't think," Ian said and closed the distance between them, nibbling at Carter's bottom lip with a ferocity that made it clear he didn't need to be treated like a piece of glass. Anything Carter wanted to throw at him, he'd take and he'd love.

They dove into each other, mouths devouring and hands everywhere, Carter stripping his shirt off and Ian doing the same for him.

Carter's chest was warm and wide and broad and he couldn't get enough of touching it, feeling the muscles tense and relax as he explored every inch with his fingertips.

Carter pushed him against him more insistently, his right hand never leaving the curve of his ass, and it felt completely natural to start rubbing against Carter's dick in his loose shorts more firmly.

It just felt good and Ian chased the pleasure, groaning into Carter's mouth as they kissed.

Then Carter slid a hand under the waist off Ian's shorts and it was his hand against his bare skin, not just touching it, but worshipping it. Murmuring into his mouth just how hot, just how insanely good it was between them.

How he couldn't get enough.

How he'd never be able to get enough.

How he was going to keep Ian in bed for a week. For a whole month.

For the rest of his fucking life.

Ian's brain went white-hot supernova at the thought, and his hips gave one last clumsy thrust as he exploded in what had to be the hottest orgasm of his whole life.

Carter gave a shocked gasp and a second later, his abs tensed under Ian's hands, and they were endlessly rutting and kissing, lost to the pleasure blooming between them.

Ian dropped his head on Carter's shoulder and tried to get his breath back, coming back down to earth slowly.

Wow, they had not just edged right up to the line, they'd obliterated it entirely.

And, like he'd told Carter just a few minutes ago, he couldn't regret it.

How could you regret something you wanted to do every day for the rest of your life?

Carter didn't say anything. Ian listened as his breath returned to normal.

They'd both made a huge mess in their shorts and it was entirely possible they'd practically destroyed Carter's couch while they were at it, but he didn't seem particularly bothered by that possibility, so Ian decided he wasn't either.

Maybe that was part of Carter's magic, too: when he was having sex with you, nothing else mattered.

Ian still hated the idea that it was like this with everyone else.

Despite how incredibly stupid and naive it felt to even think it, he wanted to be different. *Special.*

Sure, he'd most definitely caught feelings. But even though Carter had told him so many times Ian was different, he still wasn't *sure* it was the same.

Maybe it was just like this for Ian—but the thought felt ugly and wrong in his stomach, and those were the last things he wanted to feel right now.

He wanted to bask in the glow of some incredible sex. And *God*, they'd only been dry humping on the couch.

Ian lifted his head because he had to know.

Carter was staring at him, completely, utterly in awe. Not even trying to hide it. Staring at Ian like it was the very first time he'd ever seen him.

"That was great," Ian said cautiously, because *one*, he had to say something, and *two*, it was undeniably true. It had been great. And about several hundred more outrageous adjectives as well, but he could start with great. Nothing wrong with great.

Carter shook his head. Still looking blown apart. "That...wow...I knew you'd be a hot lay, but the way you just gave yourself up to it. To *me*. Like you couldn't do anything else, like you couldn't help it—*I* couldn't help but follow you."

Ian shot him a look. "Surely you've had sex with people who wanted you before. Who you wanted, too."

"Well, yeah, I thought so, but..." Carter wet his lips. "I'm not sure it was the same. I'm not sure I'd even call it the same thing. That was...*wow*." He paused. Grinned. "When can we do it again?"

"Easy, boy," Ian teased, digging his fingers into Carter's chest. "We gotta clean up first and uh..." Reality was slowly beginning to set in, and it wasn't going to be ignored much longer. "I need to call Alec."

Carter frowned. "So you can tell him what happened," he stated.

Ian nodded. "We...well, we broke a pretty important rule. The first one, in fact."

"And we're gonna do it again, right?" Carter looked at him hopefully, like somehow, in some universe, Ian wasn't going to be falling all over himself to do it again the very moment that was physically possible.

And maybe even sooner than that. Maybe they could just make out here on the couch for a while. Just kissing Carter was some of the best sex he'd ever had.

"I think that ship has sailed," Ian pointed out dryly. He didn't say that it was entirely possible Alec would fire him as soon as he confessed the truth and then sticking around here would mean he was no longer employed.

They would deal with that possible—and difficult—eventuality soon.

Ian had savings socked away, but he couldn't hang out in Carter's house indefinitely. Carter might not even want him to.

After all, it wasn't like before this he'd ever done a relationship.

He might not even want one with Ian.

Yep.

All the uncomfortable realities, crowding in on him now.

Ian gingerly pulled away, moving off Carter's lap.

"That doesn't answer the question," Carter said.

"If you want it to, it's happening again," Ian reassured him, leaning in and giving him a quick brush of his lips against his cheek. "Now, I'm gonna go clean up and call Alec."

"Shouldn't we call him together? We did *this* together."

"But I'm the one he hired to make sure the rules didn't get broken," Ian said. "It's my professional reputation on the line."

God, Alec was gonna have his head. Then there was the not-insignificant matter of how embarrassing this was. Ian didn't even let himself consider how humiliating it was going to be to have to call the man he'd hoped would be his boss and his mentor and confess that not only had he not been able to keep his dick away from Carter, he hadn't even lasted a whole month.

"Come on, don't be like this," Carter cajoled as he followed him up the stairs.

"Don't be like what?" Ian retorted. Was this going to be their first—and maybe their *only*—fight?

"I just...you weren't alone in there. Downstairs." Carter leaned against the doorjamb as Ian ducked into his room and then into the bathroom. He shed his shorts, grabbed a washcloth, cleaning up, and then, finding a new pair of underwear and another pair of pants, quickly changed.

When he came back to the doorway, Carter was still there, hovering uncertainly, but with an undeniable flare of determination in his eyes.

"No, but I'm the one who crossed the line," Ian said firmly. "If I hadn't done that, you wouldn't have."

"I—"

"No," Ian said, holding up a hand. "No, you'd never have done it. I *know* you, Carter. You'd never be physical with someone who didn't make it explicitly clear they wanted it."

Carter couldn't argue with that.

"Just...let me do this, okay?" Ian didn't say it was going to be hard enough to tell Alec without Carter hovering guiltily over his shoulder.

"Okay."

Ian shut the door, and took a quick, deep breath before grabbing his phone from the charger by the bed.

Alec answered on the second ring.

"Everything alright over there?" Alec said, sounding distracted on his end.

He wasn't going to be distracted soon.

Ian took another deep breath. "There's been some developments."

"*Some* developments?" Alec asked archly.

"Okay, *a* development." Ian could hear how heavy and resigned his voice was.

"One sec." Ian could hear movement and a few weird thumps over on Alec's end. "Let's go on video. This isn't a phone conversation." A moment later Alec's face popped up.

He was sitting in his office, but his tie was loosened and he wasn't wearing the vest he normally donned as part of his three-piece armor. His hair was mussed and there were tight lines around his light blue eyes.

"You slept with Carter," Alec stated before Ian could figure out a way to say the words out loud.

He nodded. Tried to look like he was owning it, not that he felt guilty about it, because he'd told Carter the truth: he *didn't* regret it. Not a single moment of it. And he wouldn't regret it when it hopefully happened again.

He was crazy about the guy.

He hadn't done it just because he'd had the most inconvenient boner in history—though that *also* happened to be true.

"Ian—" But Alec didn't get any more words out before the door flew open and there Carter was, striding in, hands on his hips, and the determination Ian had seen in his eyes before was nothing compared to the furor blazing there now.

"You don't get to do this alone," Carter said. He stopped next to Ian, gazed over at the phone. "Hi, Alec."

"Carter." Alec greeted him with a cautious tone.

But then Carter looked right at Ian. Like Alec wasn't even there.

"You don't get to do this," he repeated.

"You just said that," Ian reminded him.

"No, you don't get it. Not even close. So I'm gonna have to explain. *Again.*"

Ian opened his mouth to ask what *again* meant, but Carter had already started.

"I don't even need to tell you how I feel about the way you look, 'cause I already covered that, before. But God, Ian, you're like…freaking magic. You give a shit about people. You've spent the last few years doing something so hard I can't even imagine making that my career. But you didn't stop there. You said, *I'm not helping people enough,* and decided you wanted to do something to help them *more.* You're funny. You never take yourself too seriously. I always give a shit about what you say, and I can tell you, that doesn't happen. Not for me. But I care about you. And you care about me. You help me. You look out for me. And I've never been tempted to do it, not in any kind of real way, not before, but you *make* me want to be better. To act better. To think of you, not just about myself and what I'd like. You make me want to be a better man. Because a better man would deserve someone like you."

Ian's jaw had dropped a little.

Now he understood more what *again* had meant. Carter had told him weeks ago just how attractive he thought Ian was, but this was different. This wasn't just Carter liking the way he looked—this was Carter liking *him*.

Ian's gaze dropped to his mouth. He wanted that mouth on him *now*, more than before. More than ever. Maybe if...

"I see," Alec said, startling both of them.

Ian glanced guiltily back at his would-be boss.

"Do you?" Carter said.

Alec nodded. "To be clear, I'm not happy about this. But..." He sighed. "I guess I should have seen it coming."

Ian braced himself for the worst, which was surely about to drop.

"Are you gonna fire him? 'Cause if you do, I just want you to know, I'm gonna hire him," Carter said, his chin jutting out stubbornly.

"To do what?" Alec asked, confused. "You want to hire him to be your boyfriend? And to be clear, your *real* boyfriend?"

Ian froze. This conversation had started out in the top five most embarrassing conversations of his life and was rapidly moving into the top three. By the end, would any other moment even be left standing?

"Carter's not saying that," Ian said rapidly. Trying to cut that thought off before it even began.

"He's done shit for me, okay? He's made this whole thing easier, okay? If you're gonna freak out at him for something neither of us could prevent, then do it. But it's a mistake."

"I'm not freaking out. I'm just asking. What would you hire him to be?"

Ian wanted to drop through the floor, but instead of answering Alec, Carter turned to him. "I think he's asking me why I'd want you around. I thought I made that plenty clear, don't you?"

Ian could only nod wordlessly. He'd never question again whether Carter liked him for him. If he only wanted him because he'd been forbidden or because they'd been stuck together in this house.

"I'm not asking why you want him around. You *did* make that clear," Alec corrected gently. "I'm asking *how* you want him around."

"I don't see how that's any of your business."

"It is because I'm trying to make you live a more stable life. A more controlled life. And if Ian gives you that, then I don't want anything to change. But also, you wanting more than just sex with Ian means something in your emotional development, Carter. You don't need Moira to tell you that. You *know* that."

Ian wanted this conversation to end immediately. "We haven't even discussed that—" he tried to insert, but before he could, Carter interrupted him.

"Yes, I want him. For more than sex. For..." Carter glanced over at him, and uncertainty bloomed in his expression. Like he actually thought he might be alone in feeling this way, which was not even close to accurate. Ian *wanted,* more than was smart or sane. "For more. For everything."

Ian reached over and took his hand and squeezed it.

"I would ask you if that's true for you, too, but it's very apparent it is," Alec said dryly. "Congratulations are in order, I believe."

"So you're not going to fire him? You're still gonna train him to be an agent?" Carter asked.

"Ian's future is important to you, Carter?" Alec asked, and Carter nodded.

"Absolutely," he said. "I want him to have what he wants, and if he wants to be the mini-you, then he should be the mini-you. He'd be great at it. He's great at everything he does."

Ian wasn't surprised. How could he be, after everything Carter had said in the last five minutes? But it still floored him. He could *have* this. They could have this *together*, and it didn't have to end, not the way he'd dreaded it might.

They could stick together and be the person each other needed. He could give Carter the support he'd been lacking in his life and the belief that he was enough. Even if they never got naked again—though, God, he hoped they would. Very soon.

"Then nothing has to change," Alec confirmed. "I just want to say...I'm very proud of you, Carter."

"For breaking the first rule?" Carter looked adorably confused. "If that was the case, I'd have broken it ages ago."

"No," Alec corrected gently. "For waiting to break the rule until it was with someone you cared about. I'll let you two go. Remember, Ian, we've got that call tomorrow."

Ian nodded, and then Alec was gone, and it was just the two of them again.

The two of them plus all the elephants in the room.

The last thing Ian wanted to do was discount all the absolutely fucking incredible things Carter had confessed to feeling, but he had to ask. He had to be sure.

"Hey," Ian said, turning towards Carter.

Carter grinned. "Hey."

"I really appreciate what you said there. I can't say you saved my future job one hundred percent for sure, but I'm ninety-nine percent sure you did. But if you don't want to really be committed that way, the way Alec intended, it's okay. I think we can probably work something out. I know this isn't what you normally do."

Did it suck to be cautious? Yep, it did. Especially when all Ian wanted was to throw all his worries away with both hands and just embrace this new, glorious reality where he and Carter could be *together*.

But it was only going to be glorious if Carter hadn't said all that just to save Ian's professional future.

"You mean, do I not want to be your boyfriend?" Carter's face morphed into the fiercest smile. "I sure as fuck want to be your boyfriend. I'd want that even if Alec was an asshole and fired you. I'd want that no matter what."

"But you don't do boyfriends, not with your regular—"

"You keep assuming you're like everyone else." Carter's voice was firm, and he leaned in, voice rough velvet in Ian's ear. "I already told you. You're not like anyone else."

CHAPTER 13

CARTER OPENED HIS MOUTH to suggest something else and then realized that he had no fucking idea what it was he should say.

Ian was his *boyfriend* now. What on earth was he supposed to do with a *boyfriend*?

He still wanted it—he'd never imagined wanting to commit to anyone, but there was no question he wanted that with Ian—but God, he didn't have a fucking clue what to do or say next. Hadn't he said everything already that he could?

What even was there to say anymore?

Maybe they could *do* something next?

Carter—and Carter's dick—perked up.

"So," Ian said and there was an equally uncomfortable thread in his voice that matched Carter's own thoughts.

"So," Carter said, not bothering to hold back from his semi-leer. "You wanna?"

Ian shot him a hard look. "Wanna *what*?"

"Get naked?" Carter asked. Then added, "*I* didn't get a chance to clean up, not like you did, so I was thinking...shower. And it just makes sense to get naked together, you know?" He grinned. "Two birds, one stone. 'Cause I know you already wanted to get me naked. Probably for *ages.*"

"Did you really barge in here with come drying in your shorts?"

"Hell yeah, I did. If I waited…well, if I waited nothing good was gonna happen. So, you wanna get me all clean?" He waggled his eyebrows.

Ian rolled his eyes but he was smiling too. "Doesn't getting you clean only to get you dirty again kind of defeat the point?"

"Absolutely," Carter said. "Don't you want to defeat it right now, over and over again?"

Ian laughed. "Well, at the very least, we *can* get you clean."

"Clean-ish," Carter teased, nudging Ian's hip with his own. A little worried that he might freak the guy out with how much he already wanted him again.

God, what they'd done already had pretty much made his whole freaking life. He'd never imagined that dry humping with a guy on the couch would be so incredible or so satisfying. Which was crazy. He'd imagined he'd left that kind of basic, rudimentary activity behind ages ago, but instead, he'd had a better orgasm with Ian than he'd had in some of the more advanced and complicated group sex he'd had. Better and so much more satisfying. Because it was *Ian.*

"God forbid I assume it's totally clean, with you," Ian retorted lightly as he followed Carter out of his room and down the hall, towards Carter's own suite.

Was this the first time Ian had ever been in his room? Carter thought so. Though he'd certainly imagined about him enough in here.

In here and in the bathroom. Against the wall. In the shower. In the tub. On the fucking floor.

Carter flicked the bathroom light on and after opening the shower, turned the water on nice and hot.

A benefit of having a really excellent water heater installed, he didn't think they'd be running out of hot water for some time. Carter had *plans*, and those plans didn't include getting frozen out again anytime soon.

Ian had starred in so many fantasies and daydreams, he couldn't even count them all, and all *those* orgasms were going to pale in comparison to the next one he was gonna have. Carter was sure of it.

"Come on," Carter said, reaching for the hem of his T-shirt and tugging it over his head. Ian's eyes widened as he got naked.

Getting naked. Together. *Finally.*

Carter's blood heated up at just the thought of it, never mind how Ian's gaze was practically devouring him.

Next, when he began to slide his shorts down, he did it slower, more deliberate, grinning at Ian as he did it.

"You too," he reminded Ian. "I've waited a goddamn long time to see you without a stitch on."

"You've seen plenty of me already," Ian complained but he was already pulling his own shirt off, tossing it on the floor next to Carter's.

He didn't have the kind of muscle definition Carter did, but he was slender and perfect. More than enough tone in his arms and chest and stomach. And every inch of him was dusted with freckles. It had been too dark both times he'd caught him in the pool to see them properly. But today, he was going to see them all up close, in high definition—and he wasn't just going to be looking. He'd be *touching*. Carter's mouth watered.

"Trust me, not even close," Carter said, wiggling out of his shorts. Come had begun to dry uncomfortably. Gently, he peeled his briefs away from his skin, wincing as he did it.

"Sorry," Ian said and Carter realized he was staring.

And okay, he was a little aroused again.

A lot aroused.

"Are you actually apologizing?" Carter asked, as he finally eased his briefs off the rest of the way. To be honest, his erection was a lot more of a problem than a little fabric sticking to his skin.

Ian raised an eyebrow, the look he was giving him making Carter even harder.

"Well, if you are, you can always come over here and apologize *properly*," Carter teased. "Soothe me in all kinds of places."

"You'd like that, wouldn't you?" Ian said. He was toying with the laces on his shorts.

"I'd *love* that," Carter admitted.

He'd thought that was obvious.

"I mean, it was good, right? Before? Sort of...impromptu, I guess," Ian babbled.

Most of Carter's blood wasn't in his brain any longer so it took him a moment to realize that Ian was nervous. Or maybe worried would be a better adjective.

"It was good? It was fucking fantastic," Carter insisted.

"But you—"

Carter kissed him, not letting him get the words out, because he had a feeling he knew what Ian was about to say.

But you've had a lot of sex.

Yeah, he had, but it had never been with someone he cared about. With someone he just plain fucking *liked*.

With someone he'd taken his time getting to know.

He'd never imagined it would be all that different, but he felt like a virgin. Every touch of Ian's, every time he kissed him, just like now, felt brand-new.

The way Ian melted into him wasn't something he was ever going to get tired of, or the way he wanted to follow right along after him, losing himself when it had always felt, in every sexual encounter he'd had before this, as though a part of his brain had always held back, always watching and waiting. Hoping it would be enough.

But with Ian, there was never a question.

Ian was enough just sitting next to him on the couch, or sharing an ice cream cone, or hanging out on the sideline.

Ian groaned, his mouth opening wider as Carter's tongue brushed his own. They stumbled back towards the shower, Carter's fingers finding Ian's, helping him drop his shorts the rest of the way, and then Ian was completely naked against him.

It shouldn't have been a jolt. But electricity raced up his spine, anyway.

He opened the door to the shower and they were through it, Carter skirting them past the rain head, pressing Ian up against the shower wall.

"If I'd known it was like this," Ian gasped as Carter's mouth slid down to his neck, nibbling at the gloriousness of all those freckles scattered across his collarbone.

"Was it good?" Carter scoffed. "Good. *Good.* You are so fucking silly."

Ian laughed, the sound turning into more of a moan as Carter kept working his way downward.

Every inch of him was flawless, every inch of him was delicious and a thousand other superlative adjectives Carter couldn't even *think* because once the taste of Ian was in his mouth, it was like all other thoughts evaporated.

Anything other than: *more, yes, right now.*

"That feels amazing," Ian babbled above him as Carter swirled his tongue around his belly button and then lower still. He paused, his head right over Ian's cock.

It was flushed and red, and Carter took just a minute to *look.*

"Come on," Ian whined above him. "I'm not above begging."

"'Course you're not," Carter said. His hand pressed Ian back against the tiles, just holding him there. Because he wanted to *look*, damnit.

Carter had enough experience with dicks in his life but he'd never craved one the way he did Ian's. His mouth watered as he leaned in, smelling that distinctly Ian smell that he'd been chasing for weeks now, Ian's cock twitching as it brushed against his cheek.

"Shit," Ian ground out.

Carter could feel him trembling above him. Around him. And he wanted to reduce him to pure sensation. Every time Ian looked at him he wanted Ian to remember this moment—and a thousand other moments to come.

Bypassing Ian's cock, his lips found Ian's thigh, mesmerized by the flex of the muscles in their long, lean shape. Enjoyed Ian's squawk when he nibbled with a little more of a bite up to where his thigh met his pubic bone.

Ian's hands descended to his head, where they tangled in his hair. But instead of trying to push him, it felt like Ian was just trying to hold on.

Reaching up, Carter circled the base of Ian's cock with his fingertips and glanced up as another series of heated moans fell from his mouth.

God, he was unbearably hot like this. Curls damp and flattened by the steam, lips red and bitten from how good it all felt, a pink flush creeping up his chest.

He couldn't resist taking the tip of Ian's cock into his mouth any longer and he groaned a little as the taste hit his tongue.

Carter curled his tongue around the head and sucked hard, losing himself in the weight of it, and the increasingly desperate cries Ian kept making.

He took him right to the brink—nearly to the point of no return—but then instead of finishing Ian off with one last hard suck, he gripped his hip and turned him around.

Filled his hands with the generous curves of Ian's incredible ass.

Squeezed hard. Pulled the cheeks apart and feasted another way.

Teased with his tongue, until Ian was pushing back against the pointed tip of it, beyond desperate for more than just the velvet rough brush of it against his hole.

Carter knew he was good at this, and his skills in the bedroom had always been something he'd been proud of. He'd prided himself on never leaving any of his partners unsatisfied but there was something more deeply rewarding about making Ian fall apart with his hands and his mouth.

He slipped a finger wet from his mouth next to his tongue and pressed in just enough to make Ian gasp and mumble, "Yes, *yes*, God, *yes*."

But if Ian thought he was going to fuck him in this shower, he was mistaken, because while Carter definitely planned on doing that *at some point*, he wasn't going to waste *this* golden opportunity.

His finger sank in a little farther, and he used his other hand to turn Ian just enough that he could finally sink his whole mouth down onto Ian's cock.

Ian straight up yelled, and Carter had only gotten two really long strong sucks in before he was coming down his throat.

Carter swallowed and slowly got to his feet. Shower floors were somehow harder now than they'd been in his early twenties.

Ian was leaning with his full weight against the shower wall, his eyes fluttering open slowly, their soft green such a change from the frosty ice he'd greeted Carter with when they'd first met.

"Wow," Ian said slowly. "I think if you'd told me you could do that the first day, I wouldn't have had a chance in hell of resisting."

Carter grinned. "Oh, but, baby, you *did* know. Besides, I doubt that's true. You tried very hard to resist me."

"The hardest," Ian agreed, reaching down, his own lips curling into a knowing smile as he gave Carter's cock an experimental tug.

"Give me another minute. I'm convinced if I don't keep leaning against this wall, I'm just gonna float away."

"No hurry," Carter said, and it was true. He'd waited weeks for this. He wasn't quite to the point of saying he'd wait *forever*, but it was kind of terrifying how close to the truth that might actually be.

Ian stared at him. "You mean that."

"Well, *yeah*," Carter said, and he pulled away, Ian's hand dropping, as he ducked his head under the shower spray. He soaped up quick, hissing a little as his fingertips traced over the hardness of his dick.

But he didn't linger, because just as he'd wanted *all* of Ian, no holds barred, he wanted to give *all* of himself to Ian. No cheating.

"Come 'ere," Ian said in a low, rough voice. "God, just look at you."

"Yeah?" Carter said, and Ian had no compunction kissing him, because he reached for him, and to Carter's surprise, he manhandled *him* back against the shower wall.

"Ooph," Carter exclaimed as his back hit the wet tile. "Why didn't you tell me it was so goddamn cold?"

Ian smirked at him as he knelt at Carter's feet. "Use it to cool yourself down, baby, 'cause it's about to get hot in here."

"God, he's *perfect*," Carter exclaimed to the heavens as Ian's tongue touched his dick for the first time.

"And you don't even know about my oral fixation yet," Ian joked.

"Jesus fucking Christ," Carter groaned as Ian proved that wasn't just a quip, because it turned out the man could suck cock better than he'd ever dreamed—and Carter had some real good fantasies.

His tongue was agile and eager, swiping across the sensitive head, his mouth a hot wet cavern of pure fucking pleasure.

Carter could barely even glance at him, even though he'd learned long ago that sex was as much visual as it was physical. It was just too much, watching those curls bobbing up and down, hungrily sucking him like he'd never get another chance.

Well, as far as Carter was concerned, Ian was gonna get *all* the chances to blow him. Especially if it was this goddamn good. Though, he realized as he edged closer to losing control, maybe that didn't matter.

Maybe this was as good as it was because it was *Ian's* fingertips teasing his balls and *Ian's* mouth sucking his cock.

His orgasm hit him by surprise. But Ian didn't seem particularly perturbed about it, working him through it gently and carefully.

When it was finally over, Carter's eyes opened again to see Ian rocking back on his heels, a very smug smile across his face.

"A little better than *good*," Carter admitted, reaching down and helping Ian back to his feet. "Let's get clean. *Actually* clean. And then I'm *starving*."

"I thought you'd be more than satisfied," Ian joked, but he was already reaching for the soap.

"For now," Carter agreed. "*For now*."

"I kinda wish we weren't going to this," Carter said as they got out of their Uber in front of the Pirate's Booty.

"Isn't this some kind of tradition, though?" Ian asked as they walked up to the front door, security immediately waving them in.

"Well, *yeah*, Disco Night is my favorite night of the week."

"I thought that was 90s Night," Ian teased.

He was so soft and sweet and yet still charmingly prickly, tucked under Carter's arm like this.

"I do love 90s Night, but there's nothing like Disco Night. Even when we're not celebrating a win, it feels like...we can come together like a team. And it's hard to be depressed when disco is playing."

"Is that a scientific observation?"

Carter nodded. They'd had such a nice lazy afternoon. They'd had lunch. Ian had finished reviewing his contract, and then he'd jumped in the pool for his swim. And bless everything, Ian's tight swim briefs had finally made a reappearance. Carter had wanted to sit there on the patio and just watch him like some kind of creeper, but he'd ended up going for a nice run in his basement gym instead. When he'd finished, his legs had felt like rubber. And still, despite that and the two very exceptional orgasms he'd had already today, when Ian had come downstairs wearing these tight jeans that cupped his ass like Carter wanted to, and a tank top that showed off all his golden freckles, scattered across his skin like glitter, Carter's dick had gotten hard again.

He'd wanted nothing more than to just stay home. Make out on the couch. Take their time. Fuck Ian in his bed. Let Ian return the favor.

But instead, they'd headed out for Disco Night because Ian was right about that. Disco Night *was* a tradition.

Deacon had actually had to text *him* to ask if he was coming. Which…if Carter hadn't been so goddamn preoccupied today, he'd have been embarrassed he hadn't organized their weekly outing the way he normally did.

"Science and so much more," Carter insisted. "Come on, let's grab a drink."

Sure enough, there was Deacon at the bar, and even Carter was observant enough to realize he looked different. Lighter, maybe? Like a burden had been lifted.

Carter realized a second later what must have happened. Deacon had taken his advice—*his advice!!!!!*—and had finally told Jem that he'd be retiring at the end of the season.

"Hey," Carter said, slapping Deacon on the back and then Micah and Beck, casually slipping over next to them, dragging Ian right along with him, despite his protesting squawk.

"You're looking pretty cozy," Deacon observed.

Carter couldn't miss the panic that crossed Ian's face. Yeah, they'd told Alec, but they hadn't exactly discussed what they were going to tell everyone else.

He could brag. *Look at who I finally wore down. We spent half the day fucking and it was glorious.*

Old Carter wouldn't have hesitated to crow the loudest about what they'd done today.

"I'm just lucky he isn't sick of me yet," Carter said instead, squeezing Ian's shoulders, gazing down at him. Making it clear that this was undeniably true, but leaving the decision in Ian's court.

"Turns out, it's pretty hard to get sick of him," Ian said wryly. "Or to pretend you're not crazy about a guy even when you are."

"Aw," Beck said with a grin. "Carter, you're a real boy!"

Carter smacked him in the arm, pretending that he wasn't delighted even though it was pretty hopeless to deny that he was. His huge-ass grin was definitely giving him away.

"Who's real?" Landry asked as he and Riley approached, not touching but Carter could see now that they didn't even have to. They belonged to each other even when they were on opposite sides of the room.

Were he and Ian like that? Is that what everyone around them kept saying before?

"Carter," Ian spoke up before he could. His chin came up like he dared anyone to say a word.

"We're together now. Ian's my boyfriend." Carter was surprised at how easy it was to say, and how proud he sounded.

Beck seemed surprised and Micah downright shocked.

Even Riley and Landry looked a little shook.

"I thought..." Deacon squinted at him.

"I was just fucking him? No. *No.*" Carter should've guessed this wasn't going to be easy and everyone would just assume he'd pull an old Carter.

"Hey, it was an obvious assumption," Micah said mildly. "That is kinda your MO."

"Not anymore," Carter said firmly. "I can be...I can be different."

Okay sure. He wasn't *completely* different yet. But he was trying, wasn't he? He *wanted* to be different.

"Didn't you say once your soul would curl up and die if you had to fuck the same person every day? I think you did in fact say that to me, during our *bachelor party*," Micah said, chuckling under his breath.

"Or, how you wanted to decorate the whole bachelor party with black balloons and streamers because you said it was more like a funeral than a celebration?" Deacon asked, raising an eyebrow.

"Ouch," Beck said, laughing. "Or all those times you offered to have sex with us? I feel like we should've been keeping a tally sheet, so we could compare who's got the most tick marks."

"It was probably you," Micah muttered under his breath.

Carter should've expected that these guys would roast him over this.

After all, hadn't he roasted them somewhat relentlessly over their own nauseatingly happy endings?

Now *he* was the one who was nauseatingly happy.

At least you are right now, an insidious voice inserted into his brain, and that pointed thought was all that was needed to burst that happy bubble Carter had been existing in since Ian had leaned in on the couch and finally kissed him.

Though, really, it had existed before that. The bubble had been growing, slowly but surely, since the first moment Carter had ever laid eyes on him.

But what if it was *always* meant to burst? What if he couldn't hold up his end of the bargain? What if he broke down again? What if he exploded again? What if he couldn't control his temper or what he did when he lost it? What if he hurt Ian in the process?

What if he wasn't really that guy that Ian saw when he looked at him. What if he wasn't really New Carter at all, but just Old

Carter the whole time, with only a slight glow up that fooled Ian into thinking he might be worth taking on.

But what if he wasn't?

"Carter," Ian said in a soft voice, squeezing his hip. "Are you okay?"

"Yeah," Micah said. "You spaced out there for a moment. I'm sorry, we shouldn't have said all that."

"It was true," Beck said defensively, but he also looked concerned now.

"Am I what?" Carter heard the panic surging in his voice, echoing the panic accumulating in his thoughts.

Ian shot him a chiding look. "Okay? Are you okay? You got really quiet. You were smiling, too, and then all of a sudden, you weren't."

"I…"

God, was he okay?

What if he reverted right back to Old Carter. What if he did that and he *hurt* Ian?

If he did that, he wouldn't be okay. He wouldn't be okay at all.

Ian trusted him to be New Carter. And if he couldn't be…

Riley and Landry had shown up and were now cracking jokes right along with the rest of the guys. Comparing notes on all the bullshit Old Carter had said over the last few months. And because Old Carter had been kind of a selfish asshole, there was a lot of bullshit to break down.

God, what if Ian believed all of it? What if he heard all those stories and panicked, the way Carter was?

But no, he wasn't at all. Ian was staring at him still, like he wasn't angry, but worried.

"Carter?" Ian asked.

Maybe he didn't seem particularly worried about what Carter *had* done, but instead, he seemed worried about how Carter was doing right now.

Carter wanted to tell Ian what he should really be focusing on was what he was gonna do in the future.

Tomorrow, or next week, or a few months from now.

Because he could practically guarantee that Old Carter would appear again.

"I gotta get outta here," Carter said in a rush and before Ian could stop him, he took off, heading towards the corridor that led to the courtyard. It was still early and the dance floor was mostly empty.

Donna Summer was crooning about her last dance, and *God*, what if this was already theirs?

Carter dug his fingertips into the brick wall on the back end of the courtyard and tried to calm his breathing.

But panic was ugly and insidious and it didn't want to be placated.

"Talk to me."

Carter looked up and Ian was standing in front of him. Still undeniably worried—Carter couldn't have missed it in his eyes or in the downturn of his mouth—but he was *here*, wasn't he?

That's because it's his job.

But it wasn't, not entirely. He'd made it clear that he was still around because he gave a shit about Carter. More than he had about any of his other clients. He *liked* Carter.

He likes New Carter. Not so much Old Carter.

"I'm gonna fuck up again," Carter said in a rush. "I can guarantee it. I'm gonna do it."

"Yeah, you are," Ian said matter-of-factly. He leaned against the wall right next to Carter. Nudged him with his hip. "Is this what you're freaking out about? That you're going to have another anger problem and I'm going to get mad and walk away?"

"Yes." Carter wet his suddenly dry lips. He was *not* good talking about all of this. But maybe that was okay. As long as he *tried*. "And I'm gonna hurt you doing it. You see this guy that...I don't know...wouldn't even dream of decorating Micah and Beck's bachelor party exclusively in black. But I *did*. Deacon had to talk me out of it."

"I know," Ian said steadily. "I know everything you've done, Carter. Well, not everything, and there's no need to go into details of it now. But you don't think I've seen some pretty bad rock bottoms? I have. And trust me, none of them had balloons. You're gonna slip and you'll slide, and it's going to be fine. Because I know you, you're the most determined person I've ever known. You'll pick yourself right back up again and start fresh."

"You say I'm determined." That was *New* Carter, Carter was convinced of it. If Old Carter had been determined and stubborn in the way Ian described, he surely wouldn't have been wanting to change for so long but never managing to actually *do* it.

"Yeah, you are," Ian replied with a confident nod. "One of many things I like about you."

"But if I was so determined, like you say, surely I would've been able to do this before now. But..." God, this was hard to admit. And Ian knew it, he had to know it, but Carter still had to *say* it, out loud, and it was like stripping himself bare in a way totally different from nakedness. Naked was fine; vulnerable was something entirely different.

"Carter, this isn't easy," Ian reminded him. Reached out and took his hand. Squeezed it. "That's why we don't do it alone. And I was going to add, if you *do* slip, and let's just say you will, because everyone does and there is no shame in it whatsoever. But not only do you have your own iron will to pick yourself back up—you have *me*."

"But what if I don't?" The thought was pure fucking misery.

"Why wouldn't you have me? I've *promised* I'm gonna be there for you. No matter what." Ian's tone was gentle but inexorable.

"Not if I...not if I *ruin* this," Carter said through his suddenly tight throat. Because he could. So easily.

That was what he did, after all. Ruin things.

Ruin everything.

Old Carter had done it regularly, but what if New Carter was only Old Carter with a fresh coat of paint, obscuring not only all the cracks but every chip and scuff, too?

"Carter, you are *not* going to ruin this." Ian shifted in front of him, reaching up and putting his hands on his shoulders.

"But what if I..." God, he could not even imagine it. Wanting someone else who wasn't Ian. It just wasn't going to happen.

"You're not going to cheat on me. You don't even *want* to." Ian said this with such enviable confidence Carter wanted to feel it too.

"I don't *want* to," Carter agreed miserably. He didn't. He liked to think he wouldn't, but Old Carter had fucked around just because he could.

"Then you won't. I trust you. And don't you dare say that I shouldn't or that you're not worth trusting, because to both of those, I say, *bullshit*."

"Yeah?" It was hard not to believe Ian, because not only did Carter *want* to, but Ian looked like he meant every single word he was saying.

"Yeah," Ian said, and it felt so natural, even though they'd only been doing *this* for a few hours, to tip his head down and kiss Ian.

Let Ian's certainty become his own.

"God," Ian groaned into Carter's mouth, "we shouldn't have come."

"Because those guys wouldn't shut their mouths?" Carter asked, his arm snaking around Ian's middle so he wouldn't be tempted to escape. But Ian was resting his whole body against Carter's.

Like he had zero interest in being anywhere else.

Ian laughed. "No," he murmured, tucking his head into Carter's shoulder and his hands into the hair at the base of his neck. "Because we can't do anything I *want* to do here, not in public."

It was Carter's turn to moan in regret. "I *told* you we should've skipped Disco Night."

"I know," Ian said, grinning.

"But I guess..." Carter glanced behind Ian. Anita Ward was singing about someone ringing her bell. Honestly, all he wanted was for Ian to ring *his*—all night long. But this would be fun, too. "I guess we should take advantage since we *are* here?"

Ian raised an eyebrow.

"Come on, dance with me," Carter said, and led him onto the dance floor.

Landry and Riley were there already, and Micah and Beck—the latter flailing around, the former grinning like Beck's bad dancing was all he ever wanted to see in life—and it was so easy to join them.

Old Carter might have done this, but he'd never taken such pure enjoyment in just being close to Ian. He'd have always been looking for the other angle, someone to pick up to make practice tomorrow tolerable.

But he already knew it was going to be, because Ian was right. He was determined that it would be, and if it wasn't, then he had his friends—and he had Ian.

Chapter 14

"Mom," Ian said patiently, switching his phone from one ear to the other, "you need to calm down."

Moira Rogers was typically pretty calm. Ian couldn't remember the last time he'd had to tell her to calm down.

But apparently it wasn't every day that he told her that he'd started a new relationship and it was with Carter Maxwell.

He'd had to tell her today, because he knew Carter had a therapy appointment after practice, and there was no way she should find out from him.

He was going to be in serious shit anyway, but it would be worse if he didn't tell her himself. If he let Carter take that particular bullet alone.

Maybe Carter helped out with Alec—and that had actually gone better than he'd dreamed it would—but Moira was *his* mother, not just Carter's therapist, and he needed to tell her himself.

Of course, Ian had expected that it would go pretty much like this.

"Are you serious?" she asked, her voice edging closer to hysteria. "I *told you* to be careful and you *are* careful. You've always been so careful with clients."

"Carter isn't like any other client, Mom. You know that."

"Apparently," she retorted.

"It's not just because he's Carter. It's that he's Carter...*and* he's so much more than I imagined he was. So much more than I saw at first."

"It's not just because you were..." Moira cleared her throat. "Carter's told me some things I'm sure you know I didn't want to hear."

"Carter's an oversharer, for sure," Ian said, laughing, because it was kind of adorable how he'd told Moira everything even after he'd found out that she was Ian's mother.

"It's not just sex, then?" Moira forged on. Ian had to give her full points for saying the word *sex*. He thought the last time she had was during the one supremely uncomfortable convo they'd had when he was a teenager and they'd discussed how Ian needed to use protection.

"No," Ian said. He was not going to laugh. Because that would make it much worse. "We're...we're together."

"That's what you said, earlier." Moira's tone was still cautious. Calmer now, but still hesitant.

And yeah, he'd opened with that—*not* the sex bomb, because he was not an oversharer of Carter's caliber—also hoping that it would answer a lot of her questions up front.

"Yes," Ian confirmed. "We're committed."

"And Carter *wants* to do this?"

"You're his therapist," Ian retorted, "surely you know how well he's doing."

"A lot better, for sure, but he's still a work in progress."

"What do you like to tell me all the time, Mom? We're *all* works in progress?"

"True." She hesitated. "Do you think Carter would want to continue therapy with me or would he prefer to change to someone else? Normal professional boundaries would dictate—"

But Ian didn't let her get the rest of the sentence out, because he knew what was coming and he and Carter had already discussed this, when he'd told him that he'd be telling his mother the truth today.

"No," Ian said resolutely. "We know normal professional boundaries would mean you can't be his therapist anymore, but that's not what he wants. He feels comfortable with you. He feels like you're making progress, and the last thing he wants is to end up with someone new he doesn't feel as safe with."

Moira cleared her throat. "As long as he knows it's an option."

"He knows. Not that this'll be easy, but it'll be easier than starting over."

"I don't . . .disagree," she said cautiously.

"And, you can continue working with him, as long as he needs it, including on this new development," Ian continued, because he refused to let her doubts about Carter's ability color his own. He believed everything he'd said to Carter last night. Carter was fierce and filled with determination, and *together*, they'd pick him up each and every time he fell down. Until he didn't need to be picked up anymore. Until he just was who he was.

"What did Alec say?"

"He was actually pleased to see Carter making mature decisions about relationships." Okay, that was not *exactly* what Alec had said, but it was close enough.

"I am, too," Moira said. She hesitated. He practically heard her concerns rotating through her head as she tried to settle on which one she wanted to voice. "But I would prefer Carter wasn't trying this experiment with *my* son."

"Because of Carter's tendency to overshare?"

"Ian," Moira chastised. "*No*. Because I don't want you to get hurt, and I think you easily could. I can hear it in your voice. I have been for a while. You like him very much."

"And it's mutual, Mom." He believed that. More than he'd ever believed anything, ever.

"Of course he likes you, Ian." She didn't sound surprised. "You're a very likeable person, when you let people get to know you."

Ugh, he knew exactly what she meant. She'd been saying it for at least a year now, and if he was being honest, her admonitions about how he kept everyone he knew—clients, the few guys he'd dated, even friends and his family—behind a wall these days, were the beginning of why he'd decided to change careers.

If he kept working as a sober companion, he could only see the wall between him and the world growing taller and more impenetrable.

Carter had destroyed it. But it hadn't been just Carter. Carter had taken his hand and shown him how unnecessary the wall still was. Had supported him and stood by him as Ian took it down, brick by brick.

"You know that's why I came to Charleston in the first place," he reminded her. "Alec promised if I did this, he'd train me. Hire me to be an agent."

"And what about that?" she asked archly.

"He thinks I should stay here and keep helping Carter. That Carter wanting a relationship is a positive development."

"You don't need to convince me of that," Moira said testily. "I *know* that. I mean, what about when Carter's better and your time there ends, and you come back to Los Angeles to work for Alec?"

She had him there.

"I don't know," he confessed.

"You haven't talked about it," she guessed. Annoyingly. *Correctly*.

"No. Of course we haven't," Ian admitted. "We *just* decided to try this relationship thing. We're still figuring it out. And we will. I have money. He has *lots* of money. Plus he doesn't need to be here all year long. Maybe I don't need to be in LA all year long, either. In the scheme of everything else, some distance isn't something I'm concerned about."

"Not concerned about what Carter might do in your absence?"

"Jesus, Mom, we've been together officially less than a week, and you're already assuming he's gonna cheat on me. That's not okay."

"He's never done this before. In the past he's controlled his emotions and his temper with sex. If he doesn't have *you* for the sex, how does that work? Will he use his coping mechanisms or will he backslide into old habits?"

Ian didn't know what to say. "I trust him."

"I'm not saying you shouldn't." Moira had put on her therapist voice. Ian could hear it, clear as a fucking bell, even though she knew he hated it when she forgot she was his mother first. "I'm saying, it *could* happen. You have to be prepared for the worst."

This was where they'd always differed in their approach. "No, I don't," he said.

"But, Ian—"

"No, I'm *aware* of what *could* happen. I am. I'm realistic about our chances and realistic that I'm choosing to be with him because I care about him. But I'm not going to expect the worst. I'm going to expect something a hell of a lot better than that. I'm going to expect that Carter's going to continue working with me and with you and with Alec. That he's going to learn and grow and be the man I know he is, deep down. That *he* wants to be."

For a long moment, she didn't say anything.

"I hope for your sake that you're right here, and I'm wrong, and you know I don't say that lightly."

He knew she didn't, and it helped soothe the hurt she'd caused, at least a little bit. But he wouldn't forget it. Not right away.

"I am," Ian said. "I gotta run. Meet Carter for lunch."

"Okay. And, Ian?"

"What?" He couldn't help how testy he sounded. She'd actually *assumed* Carter would cheat on him. Didn't she know him at all? They'd been working together for over a month at this point. She should *know* he wasn't the cheating kind. That once he'd given his word and his loyalty, he wouldn't break it.

That he was the fiercest friend Ian had ever known.

"I'm glad you told me. I know it probably wasn't easy."

"No shit," Ian retorted.

"But you could've just let Carter deal with it."

"Yes, but I wouldn't care much about him if I did that, would I?"

She sighed. "I was afraid of that."

Ian had a feeling he knew exactly what she meant, and it wasn't the first time he'd thought it either.

He knew it was probably true.

Okay, scratch that.

He knew it was true.

He was falling in love with Carter Maxwell.

"Did everyone hear," Carter announced as the players and coaches were settling into the conference room for the first offense meeting of the week, "I have a *boyfriend*."

"I think everyone on earth knows you have a boyfriend," Nick grumbled as he took a seat. "Does this *boyfriend* know you're bragging about him every time you open your freaking trap?"

"Yes," Carter said, refusing to let Nick's disinterest stop him. He never had before, had he? "It's Ian, so he definitely knows. And he's the best so he actually *likes* it."

"I don't think anyone's surprised you wanted him, but maybe we're a little surprised *he* wanted *you*," Landry teased, elbowing him lightly in the side.

"Yeah, seriously," Riley added.

"Yeah, Carter, your crush was the worst kept secret on the team," Charlie, the backup quarterback, added.

"Way to take the wind out of my sails, guys," Carter complained, but he was still smiling. How could he not be? He and Ian had had a great time at Disco Night, after that initial hiccup. They'd danced the night away and then went back to his place and just hung out on the patio, Ian practically in his lap as they'd shared a chair and one last beer together, just talking until way too late.

Had Carter ever wanted to *just talk* to anyone else before?

No, he had not.

He hadn't even been disappointed that the night, great as it was, hadn't ended in sex, only in one achingly long kiss in front of Ian's bedroom door.

Then Ian had winked at him before informing Carter that he wasn't *that* easy, and he'd slipped into his bedroom and shut the door between them.

It had been adorable and a little frustrating, but only in a good way.

He'd fallen asleep with a smile on his face.

Believing, just the same as Ian did, that he could do this—but not just that. That he *wanted* to do this.

"Can we focus now?" Coach Oscar asked, tossing a smile in Carter's direction. "Not that we're not fascinated by your love life, Maxwell."

"Yeah, it was so freaking chaotic before, it was basically impossible to keep up," Nick said.

Ugh. Just when Carter was beginning to be willing to work with the guy, he had to be an ass.

"Better than it being full of nothing, like yours," Carter retorted.

Coach Oscar raised an eyebrow, and Carter knew that look so he shut up.

"We're playing the Chargers this week, and we know they can score, and we've gotta keep up. Do our part," Coach said.

"I've been watching some film of their defense," Riley said. "Well, Landry and I have. I think we can lean a little harder on their corners."

Coach Oscar frowned. "That could open you up to more pressure, Riley."

"I can take it," Riley said. "Worst-case scenario, I outrun their defense. Their defensive line isn't that young anymore. I can out-maneuver them."

"I don't like relying on you evading the defense," Coach said. "But I agree, I saw it on the tape. Their secondary *is* young and inexperienced. We can and we should exploit them."

"We can hold the line, Coach," Cole, the center, promised.

"Yeah," Boyd, the left tackle, echoed. "We got this."

"We'll see in practice this week," Coach Oscar said in what Carter had begun to recognize was a tentative voice. "I know Coach Kelley wanted to run you against the first team defense in an attempt to prepare you for the pressure. So if you can hold off Deacon, then I think you've proven yourself."

"It isn't the same without Jem," Riley argued. "They're not as strong without him."

"Are you actually *complaining* about that?" Nick wondered.

Riley shrugged. "Not complaining, just observing."

"They're getting better though. We got some rookies behind Jem, who are eager for the opportunity. They want to make their mark." Coach met their eyes, one at a time. "It's your job to make sure they don't—and that they're ready for Herbert and that explosive Chargers' offense."

Around the table there was a series of nods and "Yes, Coach" replies.

For the next hour, Coach went over film of the Chargers' defense and the beginnings of their game plan.

When they finally exited the conference room, Carter was fired up for practice this afternoon. If he could lengthen the field against the Condors' admittedly *much* better secondary, then Coach Oscar would be more willing to give in to what Riley wanted.

And what Riley wanted was what Carter wanted: an air attack punctuated by a few runs. The kind of game plan that would show off Riley's arm and give both of them lots of gaudy stats. The kind of game plan that would mean everyone looked at Carter and said, *yeah, we were wrong when we said he couldn't get it done. He can, just give him the ball.*

But at the same time, Carter could also admit that ultimately, they *all* wanted the same thing: to win this goddamn game.

This game and every game coming up for the rest of the season.

"I don't think I've ever seen you look this serious," Deacon said as they ran into each other in the hallway outside the cafeteria. "Ian dump you already?"

Carter made a face. "Seriously, that's the first thing you thought of? I *can* be serious about other things, you know. Like, I don't know, *my job.*"

"You got a job?" Deacon teased. But then relented. "Trust me, I already warned my guys you're gonna be pushing today. The Chargers' secondary is weak. You and Riley are gonna want to push the field."

Of course Deacon had looked at the tape and figured out the exact same goddamn thing.

"You bet your ass we will," Carter said.

Deacon grinned in that semi-devilish, totally charming way he had. "If Riley can get the ball out before I hit him."

"Only you'd be that excited about hitting someone."

"Hey, your job is to run real fast and catch the ball. Mine's to hit people," Deacon pointed out, as he pushed open the door to the cafeteria. "What's your boy's new job? To give you lots of orgasms so you don't feel like losing your shit?"

Carter shoved him, but Deacon was still laughing. "Be nice," he reminded him. "If you scare him off, I don't have to warn you how much you'll regret it."

Deacon wouldn't be the only one.

"No, seriously," Deacon said, slinging an arm around Carter's shoulders. "We love you, and he clearly loves *you*, or else he wouldn't have signed up for this. We're happy for you, really."

Carter shot his friend a disbelieving look. "He does not love me."

"Uh-huh," Deacon said, not sounding particularly convinced. "Sure he doesn't."

"I'm just saying...that's not. We're not. Uh..."

Ian spotted them from a table in the corner and waved, the bright smile emerging on his face proving Deacon's words more than disproving them.

"Words, Carter, *words*," Deacon teased.

"Well shit," Carter said.

"It's alright," Deacon said, patting him. "You're gonna be just fine."

He'd worried last night he could hurt Ian if he fucked this up. And that was before he'd even considered the possibility that Ian could *love* him.

If Ian loved him, *well*...

Hurting him seemed more like an inevitability.

"And," Deacon continued, like he hadn't just totally thrown Carter's whole brain—and his heart—into chaos, "it's not like you don't light up the exact same damn way."

"Are you saying that *I* love *him*?" Carter asked cautiously under his breath, as they approached the buffet line.

Deacon shot him a look. "Did you not think you did?"

"I don't know. I've never...nobody's ever..."

And wasn't that the goddamn truth? He'd been loved, sure, but by his grandmother, who'd been gone for ages. There'd been nobody since then. His parents surely didn't, or else they'd have treated him a whole lot better. He could see that now.

And as for loving anyone else, he loved his friends, sure, in a platonic sort of way, but he'd certainly never *loved*, not the way Deacon was describing.

"I told you, you're gonna be just fine. We all like him, you know? He's good for you."

"He thinks I'm good for him, too," Carter said stubbornly, sticking his chin out.

Deacon chuckled. "Isn't that the whole definition of love? Better together than apart?"

"Is it?" Carter didn't know how to even begin defining love.

"See? You're gonna be fine," Deacon said, grabbing a sandwich and a large bowl of salad, Carter trailing behind him.

He must've seen Carter's dubious expression, because he turned by the drink counter. "Listen," Deacon said under his breath, "do you care about him? Care about what happens to him?"

Carter nodded.

"Do you want to talk to him? Just sit next to him if he's busy and can't talk to you?"

Carter had to nod again. It was true. He was happy just being in Ian's orbit.

"I'm going to regret this," Deacon added with a lopsided grin, "but do you want him more than you've ever wanted anyone else? Like you'll die if you can't touch him? And you'd be *almost* satisfied with just touching him, even if that was all it was? Just a simple touch?"

Carter nodded slowly.

"Then, yeah, you're gonna be just fine. You're a good guy, Carter. And he knows it or else he wouldn't be here."

Carter was left staring after the defensive end as he headed back towards the cafeteria door.

Ian came up behind him, startling him a little with his greeting. "Hey," he said, "they have your favorite Asian chicken salad today, didn't you see it?" Ian gave a pointed glance to Carter's empty hands.

"Oh yeah," Carter said.

"What were you and Deacon talking about?" Ian said as he grabbed two of the salads. Apparently it had become Ian's favorite too.

"How he's gonna try to hit Riley today," Carter said. Which was *mostly* true. He grabbed them two Diet Cokes and two water bottles.

Ian raised an eyebrow as they headed back to their table with their lunch. "I bet Cole and Boyd and the rest of the offensive line had something to say about that. Never mind Landry."

Carter nodded absently. "The Chargers' secondary is weak. Riley and I wanna stretch the field. Get some deep balls in."

"Deep balls, huh?" Ian cracked up, and Carter thought back to what he'd said and couldn't help but laugh right along with him.

"But," Ian said, when they'd finally stopped chuckling about that double entendre, "that means he's gotta hold the ball longer. Thus, avoiding being creamed by Deacon and the linebackers."

"Exactly," Carter said, sitting down opposite Ian with a huff. "But it's gonna be fine."

"I didn't say it wasn't," Ian retorted lightly. "You guys know what you're doing. You're on fire these days. You got this."

"Thanks," Carter said, because he believed it too. He sure knew Riley did. He'd been confident enough on his first day as a Condor, but now? The way he took the field, the way he threw the ball, like he *knew* Carter was gonna catch it? The way he didn't get frustrated or down when they were losing or struggling, but just kept the faith that they'd figure out how to score?

It showed real development.

Carter would've rather died than admit it to Riley, but much of Riley's confident leadership of the offense reminded him of Riley's older brother, Aidan. Riley had mentioned that he and his brother were still talking, that they were working through some of Aidan's painfully overprotective instincts but that it was slow going.

It was hard to change, Riley had said, looking at Carter directly when he said it.

Carter could agree. It *was* hard, but it was also rewarding.

Without change, he wouldn't have Ian in his life. If he hadn't felt that intense need to be different, to be the man he *wanted* to be, he knew Ian never would've let down his walls and let him in. Carter never would've gotten to where he was, and that would've been a damn shame.

"So, practice is gonna be fun to watch this afternoon, huh?" Ian asked as he dug into his salad.

Carter made a face. "Are you not even gonna tell me if you talked to her?" They'd discussed Ian telling Moira on the way in to the practice facility this morning, and Ian had been unsure if her schedule was free enough to manage it.

"Yeah," Ian said. "We talked."

But he didn't say anything else, and didn't he realize Carter was sort of freaking out—about this, and also about what Deacon had theorized earlier?

Carter wasn't worried, exactly, about Moira's reaction. Because if she didn't like what he and Ian had, she could go fuck off. But at the same time, he couldn't tell her that, could he? He'd never been in a position with anyone else before where that was not a possibility. If Moira had only been his therapist, he'd have just found someone else. But Moira was also Ian's mother, and they were close. He cared what she thought. If she decided Carter wasn't good for her son, that would make everything awkward.

Goddamn it. No wonder he hadn't dated before this.

Dating kind of sucked.

Not the good parts. The talking all night parts. The sharing a chair parts. Or sharing a favorite salad parts. Or the effortless smile and the inevitable half a hard-on he got every time he so much got a glimpse of his guy. Or the parts where he felt like he could tell Ian anything and everything.

But everything else? All the uncomfortable, difficult parts? Absolutely.

He could leave those far behind and never miss them.

But should he just *ask*?

Carter debated with himself during what was undeniably a long, uncomfortable silence.

"She wasn't *happy*, but I think she really likes you," Ian finally said, casually, like he had no idea that Carter was panicking—or why.

"Yeah?" Carter's voice cracked. He shoveled a fork full of salad into his mouth, trying to cover it up. But Ian glanced up from his own lunch then.

"Were you really worried? You *were*." Ian answered his own question. "God, I'm sorry. Of course you were."

It seemed like a no-brainer to confess the truth—but that didn't mean it was easy.

"I've never done this before. I've never had a parent I wanted to impress. And she's already seen the worst of me...it wouldn't surprise me if she didn't want me anywhere near you."

"Carter," Ian chided.

"It's true," he insisted.

"Listen," Ian said, leaning in and dropping his voice, "it's not like that. I can promise you. Yeah, you've told her all your shit, I know you have. She's your goddamn therapist; you're *supposed* to. She wants you to. But that doesn't mean she judges you for it. She wouldn't. God knows, she can piss me off plenty, but it's never because she judges."

"I know *you* never did." But now Carter was forced to *really* consider this. Surely Ian would've had to learn that habit somewhere, right? Maybe he was right. Maybe even though Carter had apparently the worst luck on earth and his therapist also happened to be his new boyfriend's mother, it would be okay. Sure, he'd confessed pretty much every dark and sordid secret to his therapist—both because every time she looked absolutely shocked, it was so goddamn entertaining and *also* because just like Ian had reminded him, he was *supposed* to—but maybe his behavior wouldn't come back and bite him in the ass the way he was afraid it might.

"Well, she doesn't either," Ian retorted.

"You said she wasn't *happy* though," Carter reminded him.

"Like you, she's convinced I'm not an adult perfectly capable of making my own reasoned choices and you're going to break me into a million pieces," Ian said, not sounding even a tiny bit worried that might happen.

"Oh." Carter kind of hated that. But he understood it. His track record wasn't great. "What did she say about the whole continuing to be my therapist thing?:

"She said it was okay. It's your choice. But the moment you feel like it's too much, like you're uncomfortable, you need to say something, and we'll find you someone else, okay? We can even do a transitional period, if you want to."

"No," Carter said. He meant it. He wanted to stay with Moira. He was good at compartmentalizing. As long as Moira could continue to do it.

And, Carter supposed, he'd have to try a little harder not to overshare certain details.

Ian shot him a look. "Don't overreact, okay?"

"Do I overreact?" Carter could hear how high and squeaky and okay, *panicked*, he sounded.

"Babe, you've practically made a career out of overreacting, but remember—you're not doing that anymore, right?"

Carter nodded. "I'm trying."

"She's saying that as a mother, Carter. And as my mother, she's duty bound to assume that anyone I date is out to hurt her dear, helpless, innocent baby boy." Ian leveled a stare at Carter. "Do you think I'm helpless?" Ian licked his lips. "Or *innocent*?"

Fuck.

Half of Carter thought maybe he *should* be panicking right now. But the other half had gotten lost right when Ian had reminded him of just how innocent he wasn't.

How he'd leaned in just as Carter was heading to his meeting this morning and murmured into his ear, "Don't get too worn out today, 'cause I've got plans for you."

Innocent men did not say *plans* in that voice or stare at him with molten glass eyes, practically begging for additional debauching.

"No," Carter murmured. "You're not helpless, and thank God, you're not innocent."

"Exactly." Ian leaned back in his chair, regarding Carter with that same hot-as-fuck gaze from earlier. "Eat your lunch."

Because Carter was Carter and he couldn't just *behave*, he asked, "Why?"

Ian's stare grew somehow even hotter.

God, if he'd been like this weeks ago, Carter would have spontaneously orgasmed just being in the same goddamn room as him. It was unfair and uncool and totally fucking sexy.

Carter's fork started digging into his salad because apparently all Ian had to do was look at him and that was answer enough.

Between bites he asked, "Is this about the 'plans' you mentioned earlier?"

"No," Ian said.

Carter started to sweat but kept eating. Shoveling it in mechanically, barely even tasting the salad even though it was his favorite.

Scratch that. *Ian* was the thing he most wanted to put in his mouth, now.

"These are *different* plans," Ian added with a smirk.

Sweet baby Jesus, he was the perfect man. Ian had *more* plans? It was impossible for every part of Carter not to sit up and yowl.

"You gonna give me a hint?" Carter semi-begged.

Though really, he wanted to say to Ian, *don't tell me anything, just surprise me.*

Ian raised an eyebrow. "No."

Like he already knew. Like Carter didn't even have to tell him he might pretend that surprises were shit but that he not only loved a sexy surprise, they turned him on big-time.

Gah.

Carter finished cleaning his plate, gulped down the rest of his Diet Coke, not even *enjoying* it the way he liked to, normally, and stood—but not before using the cover of the table to slightly adjust his dick in his shorts.

Because yeah, when Ian was looking at him like that, his eyes full of *plans*—undeniably sexy plans—it was asking a whole fucking lot for him not to get hard.

"You're done?" Ian asked as he stood, just as slowly.

And yeah, *yeah*, he had tugged his polo shirt down, and once Carter really looked, he knew exactly why Ian had done that.

Carter wasn't the only one aroused by the conversation they'd just been having.

"What do *you* think?"

Ian smirked at him. "Okay, come on. You've got what...half an hour before practice?"

Carter glanced at his watch. "Twenty-three minutes. That enough time?"

"Oh yeah, plenty."

Carter had been playing here in Charleston for over a year now, and Ian hadn't even been here a month yet, but when they exited the cafeteria, Ian led them down the hall, seemingly confident in where he was going.

"Where are we going?" Carter asked, even though what he really meant was *God, please don't tell me. I wanna be surprised.*

"Worried?" Ian asked as he led them down a maze of hallways, deeper into the building, the people they passed growing more and more infrequent until they turned down another corridor and into a door marked as a bathroom.

"No. Should I be?" Carter asked, as Ian pushed the door open and they walked inside. It was clean—because when Mr. G had taken over the team, he'd made sure to root out not just all the corruption, but to do a full upgrade of the facilities, and that included a deep clean—but clearly not used.

Carter settled back against the door, very amused—and way more turned on than he had any right to be about an abandoned bathroom, but then this wasn't just any abandoned bathroom. It was an abandoned bathroom with Ian in it.

An Ian who had deliberately planned for them to end up here.

Every single goddamn part of his body thrilled with the idea—he'd known Ian wanted him, it was hard to miss it and hardly unusual—but he'd also never had someone desire him so desperately who hadn't *wanted* to.

Everyone had only wanted him because he was convenient and he was there and most of the time he was willing.

Ian had wanted him against all his better judgment. Until his judgment had changed. That made Carter feel like a million freaking bucks.

"Only if you're worried I was gonna do this," Ian said, coming closer and then leaning in, kissing him.

They'd kissed last night, *and* this morning, but it hadn't been quite like this. Like Ian wanted to not just take them off the leash but to burn the leash entirely.

Carter groaned into his mouth, his arm curling around Ian's waist and tugging him more firmly against him.

"I was thinking about this all morning," Ian panted as his hands slipped under Carter's T-shirt. They were cold against his skin, but he felt overheated already. Ready to burst, like he was thirteen again.

It was hard not to remember what Deacon had said to him earlier today.

Like you'll die if you can't touch him? And you'd be almost satisfied with just touching him, even if that was all it was? Just a simple touch?

If all he had was this, kissing like they were dying for each other, tongues slipping together, the little desperate gasps Ian kept making as Carter touched him, hands all over his chest, his arms and then lower, gripping his hips and dragging Ian against him, until his thigh was between Ian's, helplessly rubbing against each other—it would be enough.

It would be more than enough.

The painful bite of his denial might hurt for now, but in the end, they'd get what they both craved.

It hit him suddenly.

Because what he craved *was* this, but it was more, too.

It was a nice comfortable bed, Ian laid out before him like a feast.

It was not a quickie in a bathroom, hoping that they wouldn't get interrupted and nobody would come in.

Carter wanted to keep kissing Ian more than anything in the world—but then, he discovered that wasn't quite true either.

He pulled back, Ian blinking lazily up at him, like he'd just surfaced from a pool of lust so thick he couldn't quite get his bearings.

Carter got it. He felt the same.

But God, maybe he shouldn't have stopped them.

No. *No.*

Old Carter would've taken this and run with it.

But he didn't want to be Old Carter anymore. Old Carter could break Ian's heart—and there was no way that wouldn't break his own—and that was the last thing he wanted, especially if Deacon was right. And Carter was beginning to see that he might be.

"Are you okay?" Ian murmured. His fingers curled around Carter's neck.

It would be so easy to just lean back in. Get swept away by the arousal that was simmering so close to the surface of his skin.

He wasn't used to denying it. To denying anything he wanted.

He just took. Let everyone else around him take, too.

But in the last few weeks, he'd gotten more used to holding back.

Had even enjoyed it a few times. He'd hated it, too, at points, when he'd been thinking that he'd never get to have Ian this way, but now he knew he could.

There was no reason to rush.

No reason to take and take and *take*, just because he could.

"I'm fine," Carter said, pressing a light kiss against Ian's lips, just because he could, and also to test his own self-control. He didn't feel overwhelmed by it. He felt like he was controlling it, now, instead of it controlling him.

"Do you not want to?" Ian looked confused. A little hurt.

And that was absolutely unacceptable.

"I want you, desperately," Carter said and moved his body more firmly against Ian's. Let him feel how hard and ready he was to ride this to the finish line. "But not like this. Not like you're...disposable. Like you don't matter."

Ian frowned. "I don't think that. Not at all, I just..."

"Tonight," Carter said firmly. "You said you had plans."

"Yeah?" Ian's forehead crinkled. "I do."

"Old Carter would've done this, and not blinked," Carter said. Hoping Ian understood. "He'd have done it with anyone who lured him in here. But you're different and special and I..." He took a deep breath. He'd just been about to say *and I love you*, but he couldn't. Not yet. Not until he was a hundred percent sure.

"I get it." Ian's gaze was luminous. "Not only that, but it...it means so much. That it matters to *you* that it's different."

"It's amazing every time we're together. Every single fucking time. But I want more, you know? For me. And for you."

Ian nodded, and from his expression Carter was fairly certain he not only got it, but that he *appreciated* it.

"I can't wait to see what your plans are. Trust me, I'm literally *dying* to find out what they are but for now..." Carter kissed him again. "Do you wanna just make out until I have to go to practice?"

Ian gave a pointed glance to the line of Carter's hard dick in his shorts. "You gonna be okay doing that?" he asked skeptically.

"I'll be fine. I just want more of this," Carter said, framing Ian's face with his hands and drawing him in again. "If you want more, too..."

Ian flushed. "I think it's pretty obvious I can't get enough of you."

"Good, 'cause we have approximately twenty more minutes to make out," Carter said and leaned in.

CHAPTER 15

Ian leaned against the side of Carter's Range Rover and watched as he walked up, one of those irresistible—and catching—grins on his face.

"Good practice, huh?" Ian teased.

Carter unlocked the door.

"If," he replied, in a faux stern voice, "if you use that great fucking practice to subject me to blue balls for the rest of my life, I'm not gonna be very happy about it."

"Who are you kidding?" Ian refused to acknowledge how fast his heart began to race at the way Carter had said so casually, *for the rest of my life.* "You'll take it and you'll like it."

Carter laughed. Ian didn't have to know him as well as he was beginning to to see how good of a mood he was in. This was peak Carter, shining as bright as the stars that were just beginning to emerge across the dusk sky. "Like? *Like?* How about *love?*" he joked as he tossed his bag into the back seat and climbed into the driver's seat. He opened his arms towards Ian, still grinning. "Come 'ere, baby, and give me a kiss."

Ian rolled his eyes but did he go? He absolutely fucking did. He leaned into Carter's embrace like it was the most natural thing in the world.

The kiss started out a little bit of a joke, Carter smacking their lips together enthusiastically, but the moment their mouths met, Carter groaned into his mouth and it was game over.

Ian scrabbled over the center console, knee banging the edge of it, not even caring as pain blossomed through him, his lips attached to Carter's.

Carter broke the kiss, panting heavily as he leaned back against the door, like he was afraid if Ian got any closer, he'd crawl into his lap and he'd like it.

He'd *love* it.

Had he known it would be like this? Like they were dry tinder and the merest spark could set them alight? Ian had suspected it would be exactly like this.

"You should..." Ian gestured towards the parking lot exit and cleared his throat. His voice still sounded rough and desperate. "Uh, drive home?"

Carter chuckled and as he put his hands on the steering wheel after turning the car on, Ian noticed they were shaking a little.

How were they going to get home in one piece?

If Ian thought about what he wanted to do to Carter—what he wanted Carter to do to *him*—when they got back to his place, they were never going to get there.

"So, uh, practice, huh?" Ian said brightly as Carter maneuvered the car out of the lot. "And you talked to my mom. How was that?"

Carter shot him a look. "Changing the subject?"

"My mom seemed the safest subject I could think of," Ian said with a shrug. Talking about her meant he would *probably* not beg Carter to pull over to the side of the road and fuck him in the back seat.

"It was fine," Carter said. "Nothing unusual. I think she might've given me a slightly steelier look than normal when I logged on, but nothing else. We did talk about the new boundaries and the new normal. And I agreed, *again*, that if I ever think it's a bad idea for her to continue as my therapist, that I promise I'll be honest, and we'll transition to someone else. Actually it was a really good session."

He sounded surprised, but Ian wasn't really.

His mother was too much of a professional to take some of her *mom* worries out on a client. Nope, that would just be Ian getting the lion's share of those.

"Good," Ian said.

"And, *yeah*, what a practice. God, it was a fucking blast. I wish every practice could be like that."

Ian had watched it all from the sideline, because it had become very clear very quickly that the offense was running on a whole different level today. Riley's confidence had been growing, and he just kept throwing balls downfield, putting them up for Carter to leap up and catch.

Deacon had even gotten frustrated, yelling at Micah and Beck, who had been trying with the help of the other corner, to cover Carter.

But the thing was, when Carter was in video game mode like that, nobody *could* cover him.

Finally, as the practice had come to a close, Beck had gotten frustrated and, after exchanging a few clipped words with Deacon, came right off the line, not helping the new linebackers pressure Riley. But even double-teaming Carter with Micah, two of the best secondary defenders in the league on him, didn't seem to make a difference.

Carter had still caught the ball, coming down from a ridiculous leap, laughing like it had been the most fun he'd ever had in his whole life.

Ian knew a little of how tough some of his childhood had been. He'd had parents who hadn't really noticed him much, until they'd noticed him *too* much. To Ian, after all that, there was something extra special about how much joy Carter took from life.

Catching a football.

Laughing with his friends.

Meeting Ian's gaze from across the field, his stare full of promise.

Ian wasn't sure how much longer he could deny the very strong possibility he was falling for Carter Maxwell.

Or that the falling had already happened, and he was already in *deep*.

"Maybe I just need to tease the hell out of you before every single one," Ian suggested. Keeping things light. Not saying shit like, *I could watch you play like that, all day, every day. Just watch. You're beautiful, inside and out.*

"Don't you dare," Carter said, but he was smiling.

"That system's gonna work great, until Deacon figures out how to put more pressure on Riley."

"Then Riley will find a way out of it," Carter promised. "You've seen him. He's evasive as hell."

"Yeah, he is." But Ian had seen Deacon's face as he'd come off the field. There'd been a bone-deep determination there that even Riley Flynn's quickness might not be able to overcome, if he found a way to get through the offensive line and get to the quarterback.

"They're just struggling a little, without Jem," Carter said. His voice had gone more serious. Regretful.

"Yeah, it's not a surprise. Jem was the foundation of that defensive line."

"God, it sucks."

"You ever have an injury like that?" Ian asked. He could've just googled what he wanted to know, but it had become apparent very quickly, from almost the first moment they'd met, that he'd wanted *Carter* to tell him everything important about himself.

"Not serious like that. Not miss a whole season serious. Sprained an ankle in college once. Missed three, four games. That was tough enough." Carter shot Ian a grin. "Spent a lot of time on my back that month."

"And I bet you enjoyed that a whole hell of a lot."

In fact, he was *counting* on it.

"Oh, baby, you know I did," Carter teased, glancing over at him with a knowing look on his face. He didn't even need to say the rest, because Ian already knew what he meant. *But not as much as I'm gonna enjoy what we're about to do.*

Why the hell hadn't he just taken Carter up on his unspoken offer last night, after Disco Night? Why had he gone to bed alone?

He knew why. He'd been terrified he was getting in too deep. The day had been absolutely fucking perfect, and there was no way he wasn't falling hard for Carter.

It didn't feel like he was doing it alone, but there was always *some* risk in feeling this way.

Ian had told himself he needed to lie in his own bed, by himself, and try to get his bearings again, so he didn't lose himself in the tidal wave that wanted to sweep all his good intentions away.

But then, this morning, he'd woken up, alone, and thought of what he *could've* had, and there'd been a nearly irresistible urge to just *let* the wave take him.

Almost thirty, and he wasn't sure he'd ever allowed himself to be wildly, completely, insanely in love.

Maybe it was time.

Then again, maybe it wasn't so much the time as it was the man.

Carter made him want to throw away all his caution and concern, and just *wallow* in it.

"Oh, I know that look," Carter added with a quicksilver grin that lit Ian up from the inside out. "That have anything to do with your plan? You gonna pin me down and ride me, baby?"

"If anyone else called me *baby*, I'd have their balls for earrings," Ian said, changing the subject again.

Carter had clearly liked it earlier when he'd been deliberately mysterious about his plans for later—and now that they were so close to *later*, there was no way he was giving them away.

"Aw, seriously?" Carter sounded disappointed. "I'll stop, but..." He shrugged.

Probably with anyone else Ian would've suspected they were calling him *baby* because it was easier than remembering his name. Making him just another guy in an interchangeable lineup.

But when Carter talked to him, when Carter looked at him, there was no way he wasn't seeing and touching and being with *Ian*.

Ian had never been so sure of anything in his whole fucking life.

Maybe Carter had gotten around and had slept with a hell of a lot of people before him, but the only person Carter wanted now was him.

"No, I..." It was hard to be honest about this, when it demonstrated, so clearly, with neon flashing lights that Carter couldn't miss, just how deep he'd gotten. How much deeper he wanted to go. "No, I like it."

"Yeah?" Carter reached over and squeezed his knee. The touch rocketed through Ian like a blast of electricity.

"Yeah," Ian agreed. He pressed his lips together and tried to think of unsexy things.

Unfortunately he didn't get very far.

Finally, Carter turned down his long driveway and pulled up to the garage, hitting the button to raise the door. He pulled the car inside, turned it off, and neither of them moved.

Ian, because he was trying very hard not to say, *let's go to the bedroom and fuck right now*, and Carter, well who knew with Carter. It was unlikely he was trying to pretend he didn't want to get down and dirty—but then he *had* stopped them earlier today.

I want you desperately, Carter had said.

The feeling was most definitely mutual.

"Come on," Ian said gruffly, because he wasn't just going to sit here in the car and stare goofily and gooily at each other when they could be upstairs, in Carter's big bed, naked together, *finally*.

"No point in arguing," Carter said.

A minute later they were in the house, and the moment Carter put his bag down, he glanced up at him, heat in his eyes. "You gonna come here, or not?"

He opened his arms, and that was all the encouragement Ian needed.

He jumped into Carter's arms, and it was shocking how easily Carter caught him, laughing the whole time. Like he'd always do it, and never, ever drop him.

"See?" Carter murmured as Ian's hands tightened around his neck. "Isn't this better?"

"Yeah," Ian said, breathless. Then he leaned in and kissed Carter and everything else but the two of them fell away.

He was pretty sure Carter was taking him up the stairs, cradled securely and firmly in his big strong arms, the same arms that never lost his grip on a football, either, but he was too lost in Carter to know anything but his lips and his tongue and his body, hard and sure, against his own.

Ian had never assumed Carter would make him feel safe, but he did. Safe and valued and like this wasn't taking a chance at all, because how could it feel this way between them, if that was what he was doing?

"God," Carter groaned as he deposited Ian on the edge of the bed but didn't move from the circle of his arms and his legs. "I could kiss you all fucking day."

Like he felt the need to prove it, Carter dipped his head and kissed him again, his tongue slipping against Ian's.

Ian leaned back, breaking the kiss and tugged his shirt off. "You're good at it," he said. *The fucking understatement of the century.*

Carter's smile was quiet, intimate. "Never cared about it before and didn't really bother one way or the other. Not before you," he admitted.

"That's..." *Sad*. Ian kissed him again as his finger tugged on the hem of Carter's T-shirt. "Kind of depressing, actually."

He reached out for the waistband of Carter's shorts, more than ready to get them both naked and onto the next step of his big plan, but instead, Carter took a step back, right out of his reach.

"Not anymore, it isn't," Carter said. "I was gonna say, let's make up for lost time, but then, there's this big secret plan of yours, and I'm dying to know what it is."

Ian looked at him dead in the eye. It wasn't like he'd ever been ashamed of anything he'd wanted in bed. But somehow, it was still easier telling Carter, who he *knew* wouldn't ever judge.

"I want you to lie right here." Ian patted the bed behind him. "And I wanna ride you."

Carter's gaze heated up, singeing Ian wherever it fell—which was across every inch of his naked torso. Down lower, too, where his cock was hard and twitching against the zipper of his jeans.

"Anything else?" Carter asked, his voice rough.

Ian swallowed hard. Yeah, Carter made him feel safe. Reassured. And yet it *also* felt like he was about to let the beast off its leash.

"Yeah, that's...uh...about all I could come up with for now," Ian murmured.

Carter nodded and then he was gone and when he came back, he tossed the lube and a condom packet on the bed. "Come on, baby," he said, the need in his voice heating Ian up even more. "Maybe you're gonna ride me, but I'm gonna make sure you're ready for it."

"I can—"

But Ian didn't get the rest of the argument out before Carter was tugging him to the edge of the bed, then kneeling at his feet, like Ian was something he couldn't wait to worship, his fingers already deftly unbuttoning and unzipping his jeans. He leaned in and mouthed against Ian's cotton-covered dick, and Ian groaned deep in his throat.

"Yeah, baby," Carter murmured, "I know you want it. And I'm gonna give it to you so good."

"It should really not be so hot that you keep calling me that," Ian argued but it was obvious that he was so fucking weak for it.

Every time Carter did it, his knees felt wobbly and his cock somehow grew even harder.

Then Carter pulled his briefs down, and the look on his face as he licked his lips in anticipation nearly undid Ian the rest of the way. He had never been with *anyone* who was this eager for him. Who was so hungry, it destroyed all of Ian's own self-control.

He bit his lip. "If you don't get on with it," he warned, but that was all he could say, before Carter was pulling him down farther and lifting his legs, arranging him exactly the way he wanted him.

If Ian thought that meant Carter was going to be quick about it, though, he was wrong.

Completely fucking wrong.

He didn't tease—not exactly—but he was slow and deliberate, long, meandering licks along the underside of his cock as his thumb, wet with lube, circled his hole.

"Relax," Carter chided as he pressed in.

"It's..." Ian held back a groan as the thumb sank farther in, burning him up from the inside out. "It's hard to relax when you're this turned on."

Carter glanced up, his gaze smoldering as it met Ian's. "I've only dreamt about doing this for weeks. *Weeks.* So let me touch you, baby, *please.*"

Clearly, there was no hurrying him up, so Ian relinquished the rest of his control and let Carter play his body like it was his favorite instrument.

And goddamn, he was good at it. He seemed to know how just how Ian wanted to be touched, and how hard, and for how long. Giving him mind-blowing pleasure and taking him just up to the line where he shook on that edge of control, before backing him off again.

By the time Carter was three fingers deep, twisting them and pressing the pads of his fingers, rough with callouses that were driving him fucking mad, against his prostate, Ian felt like he'd already come a hundred times.

But his cock was still hard as a rock, flushed bright red, Carter leaning in and giving him a teasing lick or two just at the moment he pulled his fingers out, when Ian was worried he might just explode all over Carter's gorgeous face.

Ian dug his fingertips into the bedding. Unsure how much longer he could hold on.

"You okay, baby?" Carter crooned as he stood.

Ian kissed him, because he didn't think he had the words any longer. Carter had blown them right out of his brain.

Carter's own dick was hard and twitching, a mess of precome when Ian got his shorts off, so sensitive Carter gasped into his mouth as Ian fumbled with the condom, rolling it on.

"Don't worry," Carter panted after Ian finally broke the kiss and Carter slid back onto the bed, right where Ian had said he wanted him. "I got you, baby. I'm gonna make you feel so good."

Ian slicked Carter's cock with more lube and then tossed the tube to the side. His knees were shaky and every bone in his body already felt melted, but he'd wanted this, so fucking badly, and he was going to take it.

"*Baby*," Ian reminded him as he climbed on top of Carter's glorious body, positioning his cock at his hole, and circling it a little, the tip slipping inside. "You forget *I'm* gonna make *you* feel so good."

"Yeah, yeah," Carter echoed. "Goddamn, you're tight."

It *was* tight.

Ian didn't give Carter the satisfaction of telling him that was because his dick was *big*. Carter wasn't an idiot. He had an ego for a reason. But maybe other people had looked at him and only seen that, seen his dick and his money and that stupidly beautiful face and all that hair.

But Ian saw it all.

Loved it all.

The cock and the body it was attached to—and the way Carter smiled at him, the way he called him *baby*, and made Ian not only like it, but adore it. The unexpected but welcome sly sense of humor. His generous laughter and even more generous kindness.

He sank down another inch on Carter's cock and saw fucking stars.

"You okay, baby?" Carter asked, his hands settling on Ian's hips. Like he was going to stop him, and make Ian take *more* time. Even though it was obvious he was right on the edge himself, sweat beading on his forehead, five seconds away from just slamming Ian down and taking exactly what he wanted.

But Carter wouldn't ever. Ian knew he wouldn't.

He trusted him.

He *loved* him.

Ian squeezed his eyes shut, letting the emotion rocket through him just as he pushed farther down, letting himself relax into the stretch. He braced one hand on Carter's broad, muscular chest and wrapped the other around his cock.

"God, yes, touch yourself. That's so fucking sexy," Carter moaned.

Ian gave his cock a firm twist, as his ass finally settled onto Carter's thighs. He felt so fucking full, and he'd never loved it more than he did right now.

Never loved any other man the way he did Carter.

He began to fuck himself down on Carter's dick, Carter gripping his hips and moving him when his own body seemed to start shutting down, knees not working correctly as the pleasure overtook him and he hovered right there on the precipice of total fucking bliss.

"Come on," Carter panted harshly into the space between them, "kiss me."

Ian didn't need him to say it again. He leaned down and kissed Carter hard, bruising their lips as Carter set his feet and began really fucking into him.

His cock rubbed hard against Carter's abs, sliding in its own precome, and before he was ready for it to be over—because he wanted the pleasure to spin out longer and longer, until it felt like it became part of who he was—he was right there, hovering on the edge.

Carter pulled back, just for a second, eyes fluttering open, and the look in them—complete awe and a fierce, unrelenting affection—were what sent him over the edge, shuddering and pulsing between their bodies, his ass gripping Carter's cock.

Carter bellowed and then he was coming too, his fingertips digging hard into Ian's skin as they rode out their orgasms together.

Ian came down slowly, his head falling onto Carter's shoulder, Carter's arm pulling him in tight.

"That was..." Ian breathed out unsteadily.

"*Yeah*. Jesus. Let's do that every single day. Twice a day, even. Forever."

Ian's heart twinged. *Forever.*

There was nothing more he wanted than that. Even if all he was able to do was kiss Carter once a day, for every day he had left in his life, that would feel like enough.

"Yeah," Ian echoed, because he didn't trust himself to say anything else. They hadn't discussed the future—barring this moment, when Carter was still half out of his mind from what had to be an incredible orgasm, if it had been anything like Ian's—and Ian didn't know how to start. Or even if he should.

They'd only just gotten together. They'd known each other for just under a month.

It was a lot to assume that they were in this for the long haul, no matter how much Ian wanted to. No matter how much Ian wanted to tell him he loved him, that he'd thought he'd been in love before this, but it all paled in comparison to what he felt now.

"Let's get you cleaned up," Carter murmured and gently pulled out, depositing Ian on the bed like he was something precious as he groaned and hefted himself off the edge, heading to the bathroom.

He was back a minute later with a damp washcloth and after he helped Ian clean up, they both fell back onto the bed.

"I'm gonna have great practices for the rest of my life, if that's what's waiting for me after," Carter said, turning towards Ian.

Why did he keep saying this crap?

It made it almost impossible to keep a logical, level head.

"And maybe," Carter added, "we could switch it up next time."

"You...uh..."

Carter reached over and squeezed his hand, dragging it over his body until their intertwined fingers were lying on his chest—right over his heart. "Don't tell me some super smart, educated guy like you thinks that big, manly football players never want to take it up the ass. We got prostates too, you know," he teased. "And we *like* them."

"I know." Ian knew how flustered he sounded. "Trust me, I would not complain about exploring yours."

"Good." Carter's eyes fluttered close. "Next time, then."

"Is there..." Ian cleared his throat. He should not be bringing this up now, not when things were so goddamn good between them. "There's gonna be a next time, then?"

Carter's eyes opened. The brown was so warm and deep, Ian felt like he could drown in it. Wanted to drown in it, in fact, which could either be a problem or the best fucking thing in the whole world.

Depending on whether Carter really meant everything he was saying.

Whether he meant it now, and whether he meant it a month, six months, a year, *six* years from now.

"Do you think I let my boyfriends go that easily?" Carter said, and his voice was still light, but there was a crease forming between his brows.

"You haven't ever *had* a boyfriend," Ian retorted.

"Are you really worried about that? That I won't..." Carter cleared his throat. "That someday, I won't want you anymore?"

"This isn't going to be easy. It's not gonna be all great practices and unbelievable, mind-blowing sex," Ian said. He hated to say it, but it was the truth.

He'd been confident this morning, when he'd talked to his mom, and it wasn't like he was *less* confident now, but at the same time, pretending like there weren't possible problems—relationship destroying problems—seemed a certain way to guarantee they'd fuck it all up.

"I know that," Carter said, frowning.

"Like, I'm gonna have to go back to LA at some point," Ian said gently.

Carter tugged him closer. "I'm not stupid," he said.

"I never thought you—"

"I know," Carter interrupted him. "I know you don't think so. If you did, we wouldn't be here like this together. But a lot of people think I'm just some dumb football player who likes to party and fuck around."

"Then they're the stupid ones. Stupid *and* blind."

"Yeah, but I kinda make them think that," Carter admitted softly.

Ian knew that admission wasn't easy for him. "Maybe, but that doesn't mean you deserve it forever."

"You said Alec was gonna train you. I assumed he couldn't do that from here."

"Maybe some of it from here," Ian said. "He's already started. I've been doing lots of reading and sitting in on calls."

"The moment he doesn't worry about me, he's gonna summon you back," Carter said.

"And I might not be here *here*, but I'll be there for you all the same."

"Not as my chaperone, but as my boyfriend, right?" Carter's voice was hopeful.

"For someone without much relationship experience, you're sure fond of that word," Ian joked, nudging Carter with his shoulder.

"That's 'cause it means *you*," Carter said.

Ian squeezed his eyes shut for a moment, emotion swamping him.

"You're not making this easy, you know," Ian said when he could finally trust his voice again.

"No?"

"I'm gonna go back to LA, and you'll be out here on your own, technically."

"But I'll talk to you all the time. And we can have Zoom sex. That's a thing, right?" Carter actually sounded so excited about that possibility Ian couldn't help but laugh.

"I don't know, but we can make it a thing."

"And, it's not like this season will last forever. I have half the year off." Carter *didn't* sound worried. But maybe that was just another facet of his biggest problem: that Carter was fine until he was *not* fine.

"Right. We'd figure it out," Ian said. It was true. They would. He'd said it to his mother, and he'd *meant* it.

"This is pretty serious for pillow talk," Carter said thoughtfully, not complaining, just observing.

But Ian couldn't help feeling guilty anyway. "I'm sorry," he said, squirming.

"No, *no*," Carter said firmly and tugged him closer, until he was sprawled halfway across Carter's chest, which despite its undeniable firmness, was also surprisingly comfortable. "I didn't mean it like that. This is just new for me."

"In a lot of ways, it's new for me, too," Ian admitted.

"Really?" Carter sounded startled.

"I've never..." *God, don't say you've never been in love like this before, like you couldn't even help it, it just happened.* "I've never wanted so much with someone so fast," was what Ian *did* say. Which was enough. Not everything. But enough.

"Yeah?" Carter's gaze on him was so affectionate and fond. "I'm honored."

Ian knew he meant it—which was exactly why he'd ended up here, in love with Carter even though he wasn't ever supposed to touch him.

He'd probably been half-in-love before he ever had, honestly.

They were so fucking inevitable.

"Me too," Ian teased. "Your first boyfriend. I should get a medal or a trophy or something."

"You deserve it," Carter said earnestly.

"So we're doing this, really doing this?" Ian asked, even though he already knew the answer.

"I kinda thought we already were," Carter said. His hand slipped down Ian's back, stroking him, and then he said, hopefully, "We could always do it again, if you needed more convincing that it's definitely happening."

Ian laughed.

That was the thing about Carter. Even when he was frustrated or lost or struggling, every single bit of him was *joy*.

Ian had never laughed so much in his whole life with another person, and he didn't think that was something that would ever change. Maybe there would be hard times, but as long as they could have *this* right here, he knew deep down they would be alright.

"In case that wasn't clear," Carter added with a smirk, "I *am* offering."

"Give me another ten minutes, and maybe I can move again," Ian said. But his cock was already stirring, half-hard on his thigh, and the idea of Carter doing all the work this time, just pounding him into the mattress until he nearly cried with how good it was, had a lot of appeal.

A *lot* of appeal.

"And this time, *I'm* doing all the work," Carter promised, the heat in his gaze telling Ian he'd been thinking the exact same thing.

Ian turned his head and met Carter's eyes. "Then what are you waiting for?"

Chapter 16

"If you're trying to persuade anyone you're not madly in love, you're doing a shit job of it," Landry told Carter as they headed towards the practice field.

"Who says I'm trying to pretend I'm not?" Carter retorted. And yeah, Landry was not wrong. He was currently and undeniably staring sappily over at Ian, sitting on the far end of one of the benches lining the practice field, typing away at something on his laptop. He'd never expected sex with someone he loved—and *yeah*, he was pretty goddamn sure Deacon had been right about that, just like Landry was right now—would be so fucking amazing.

But each time with Ian was better than the last, and it wasn't just the sex either. Yesterday after practice, they'd swum in the pool, laughing and teasing each other, Carter doing everything he could to splash Ian. They'd only had sex later, in the shower, a pair of quick, hot and heavy hand jobs, and it turned out that it didn't matter what they did. As long as Ian was dick-adjacent, Carter was going to come his brains out.

Even better, after their shower, Ian hadn't protested as Carter had led him to his bed. As far as Carter was concerned, it was now *their* bed.

"I think it's awesome you embraced this, embraced him," Landry said.

"What, you thought I'd just be fucking around with him?" Carter felt annoyed but kept his voice even.

It wasn't Landry's fault he'd believed that. Carter hadn't exactly given anyone the impression before this that he was interested in settling down. But then, before Ian, he hadn't wanted to.

He knew Ian worried, in the back of his mind, that Carter wasn't in this for the long haul. That he'd get tired of the boyfriend thing. But he didn't know how to say any clearer that as much fun as his lifestyle had been before, nothing had ever felt as good as what he shared with Ian.

"No, not exactly, but that you might get tired of it," Landry said honestly. "I guess you might still."

"Not likely." How could anyone get tired of feeling like *this*? Of loving and being loved in return?

Because while Ian might not have said the words, Carter had seen them, in his eyes. And Carter knew Ian never would've risked his future for anything less than serious feelings.

"I don't think so either," Landry agreed.

Carter was surprised. "You really believe that?"

"Were you gonna argue with me?"

"No, I just thought...I don't know, that I'd *have* to. That I'd need to prove myself, I guess."

"Carter," Landry said, patting him on the shoulder, "we *always* knew you were a good guy. That you had an enormous capacity for love, if you decided you wanted to tap into it. If you ever met someone who insisted that you had to."

Maybe someone else might be insulted at Landry's words, but Carter wasn't. And he wasn't insulted on Ian's behalf either.

He was worth everything, and Carter would've worked a hell of a lot harder—*would* work a hell of a lot harder—to have him in his life.

"Well, thanks," Carter said.

"And," Landry added with a smirk, "the way you look at him *does* sorta give it away."

Carter rolled his eyes, but he had a feeling he knew what the look was. He'd seen it on Landry's face enough times.

At the beginning of the season, when it had started appearing, always when Riley was around, Carter had actually felt *sorry* for him. Now, he understood exactly why Landry had looked that way, and why he'd been so fucking happy about it, too.

"Yeah, yeah," Carter said.

"Come on," Riley said, jogging up to the pair of them. "Get warmed up. I wanna run some of those long routes again today."

"Don't you think we've demoralized the defense enough?" Landry wondered, after he glanced around first, to make sure none of the defense was in hearing range.

Riley shook his head. "I don't expect them to take any of this lying down. And what we're doing, it's helping them too. They gotta get ready for the Chargers and Justin Herbert."

"What kind of quarterback would you be if you were built like Herbert?" Carter wondered as they began their warmup.

Riley shot him a look. "A damn good one."

"But not as good as you are now," Landry insisted loyally.

"Agreed," Carter said after really considering his own question. "You had to fight for everything you got, every single chance. And you can run way better than he can. Lower center of gravity."

Landry looked unamused but Riley looked the exact opposite.

"Stop sucking up to Flynn," Nick said, as he joined them. "He throws the ball your way enough."

"That's 'cause I fucking catch it," Carter retorted without heat. That was just a fact as much as Nick hated it.

Though, if he was being honest, Nick *had* been doing a lot better.

Ian's voice echoed in his head. *That's 'cause you put your ego aside and decided the team mattered more, and all he needed was someone to give some pointers. To believe in him.*

"Children," Riley said firmly, even though he was the youngest in the entire group.

"We're behavin', I fucking swear," Carter said, throwing his hands up as Coach Oscar came over, tapping his clipboard with a pen.

"Y'all ready to run some plays?" Coach asked.

"Yes, Coach," they all chorused back.

Carter would later wonder if they'd just become complacent, after two killer practices in two days. Scoring at will, without any real challenge from a defense still figuring out its identity after losing Jem Knight to a season-ending injury.

The first inkling something was different was the new formation the defense took opposite them.

"What's this?" Cole barked out, a little uncertainty coloring his voice as he bent over the ball.

"It's fine," Riley said, still sounding composed himself, but Carter could hear a thread of concern in his, too. "We're keeping the play."

"What the hell you doin'?" Landry called out.

But Beck just grinned at them with an expression that resembled a shark about to feed.

But there's no blood in the water, Carter reminded himself.

Cole snapped the ball, he and Landry took off, running downfield, Micah tracking him across the field, but he was still a good foot or two off from doing jack shit to stop him from catching the ball.

But then a cry went up, and Carter turned, slowing down, realizing that the ball wouldn't be coming his way because Riley's ass was currently on the ground, Deacon and another of the linebackers hovering over him.

"Shit," Carter exclaimed and turned back.

"What happened?" Landry asked as they were nearly back to the line. He was frowning. A boyfriend's prerogative, Carter decided. He didn't like seeing Riley on the ground, except if *he* put him there.

"Don't know," Carter said, frowning.

"All-out blitz," was all Riley would say as they joined the huddle. He met Cole's and Boyd's gazes, then the rest of the offensive line. He didn't look worried. "We got this, still."

But they didn't.

The next play, Riley ended up scrambling to the left, where Beck ended up containing him for a loss.

And the next and then the next, all the same goddamn story.

Coach Oscar called a break, and Carter stomped over to the bench. Riley was behind him, consulting with their offensive coordinator, trying to find a way out of the new scheme the defense had put together.

"Shit," Landry said, grabbing his Gatorade bottle. "That was a rough series."

"We're gonna be just fine," Carter said stubbornly, even though a rising fear, like heartburn creeping up his throat, kept insisting that they were not even remotely fine.

After all, they weren't going to be playing the Condors' defense on Sunday. The Chargers weren't going to deploy any scheme like this. They'd be totally solid.

"Maybe we shouldn't be living on the long ball so much," Carter heard Riley say to Coach, and he frowned.

"We could always add Carter in for some extra blocks," Coach Oscar suggested.

"I can't block worth a shit," Carter announced. Which was true. Coach should give that job to Landry, who could block like crazy because he was a tight end. Carter was a *receiver*. He rarely blocked, even on running plays.

"But maybe you should be," Coach said, frowning.

Well, shit.

"We're really gonna just give in to this pressure?" Carter argued.

"We're dying out there," Cole retorted, and Boyd nodded along with him.

"Then don't get beat," Carter said snidely. Which was not his best move, okay, but that temper was boiling inside him, he could *feel* it, and if they gave in, if they resigned him to blocking poorly on the line, instead of *doing* something, he wasn't sure how he'd contain it.

He breathed deeply, in and out, and it did help, a little, but it didn't extinguish the fire, either.

"Landry," Coach barked out. "Let's try a few plays with you blocking on the line."

"Sure, Coach," Landry said, not complaining because *one*, that was his job, not Carter's, and *two*, because he loved Riley and had a vested interest in him staying upright.

So do you, and not because you're in love with him, but because he's your teammate and your friend.

It was funny, because those breathing exercises hadn't helped his rising temper much, but the voice inside that sounded suspiciously like Ian, calmed him right down.

The reminder that he gave a shit about Riley, and about this team, was all he'd needed.

"I can block too, Coach," Carter spoke up.

Coach Oscar glanced over at him, a surprised expression on his face. Like the last thing he'd expected was for Carter to either be willing to block or to *volunteer* to block.

"We'll see, Maxwell," Coach said. Patted him on the back.

"You block? Has hell frozen over?" Landry teased as they returned to the field for the next play.

Carter made a face. "I *can*, it just seems silly to waste my talents when I could be doing something I'm actually good at."

"But you'd do it, if it meant this team winning." Landry sounded distressingly serious. Carter wanted to shake him and tell him to cut it out because if he didn't, he was going to spiral again.

"Yeah," Carter said.

"The Carter I met at the beginning of the season might not have cared about that," Landry said, his voice careful.

"Well, you said it yourself," Carter retorted. "There was a good guy, buried under all that crap. Just had to find him."

Landry stopped him just before they reached the huddle with a hand on his arm, his grip firm. "Carter."

"Come on," Carter said, because he didn't want to have this very earnest conversation. He didn't need to *care more* than he already did.

He already felt turned inside out by how much he fucking cared.

"Carter," Landry repeated patiently, never loosening his grip. And wow, yeah, that man had a *grip*. Not surprising, considering all those muscles Riley got to climb every night. Kind of unfair, that he'd never managed to sleep with the last Banks brother.

Or maybe the best thing that had ever happened to him.

Because if he had, who knew if he'd have ever connected with Ian. Felt *worthy* of Ian's love and affection. Maybe he'd just have descended into another one of his "fuck everything that moved" spirals.

"What?" Carter asked, finally.

"I know it's not easy, doing this, but I wanna say...we all respect the hell out of you for doing it," Landry said. There was all that earnestness in his gaze again.

Carter shook his hand free. "Yeah, yeah, so everyone keeps saying. Let's win this game, and then a meltdown won't even be on my radar."

But it was, anyway. Carter could feel it simmering away inside of him.

Even if this play worked.

Even if Landry blocked.

Even if he caught the pass.

Even if he scored.

Moira had told him that football was always a convenient excuse to let his temper boil over, but he had never really believed her, not until now.

It annoyed him that she might be right. It also scared the hell out of him.

"Sounds good." Landry grinned at him like it was just that fucking easy.

It's not. It's not at all.

It took the offense a bunch more plays—and almost the rest of practice—to work out the new wrinkles that the defense had introduced, and even then, Riley was scrambling, barely able to toss the ball out to Darius, the running back, or even Carter coming around the other side.

"Well, that sucked," Nick said, flopping down next to Carter on the bench in front of his locker.

"Speak for yourself. I think Riley spent half that practice with his ass on the turf," Carter grumbled.

He had not lost his temper. But that felt like a hollow victory, because it was still simmering away inside him. Reduced, perhaps, but not gone.

Ian had texted him that he'd be waiting at the car, ready to go home, and he hadn't been quite ready to face him yet.

Didn't know how to say, *I almost lost it today, over some fucking practice reps.*

How long would Ian want to stay with him if that was all it took? If he lost control that easily, that quickly? If he continued to struggle?

"Seriously, though, are you okay, man?" Nick asked, lowering his voice.

Carter looked over at the guy. The player he'd dismissed from the moment he'd arrived in Charleston as a mere WR2 or WR3, barely hanging on to his spot and his relevancy. Nothing like Carter.

He was an average looking guy—light brown skin, decent enough features, perceptive brown eyes. And a mouth that never failed to give Carter shit.

Carter couldn't even remember if he'd ever hit on him. Maybe he had, half-heartedly, and Nick, no doubt, had given him a look of bafflement and turned his ass right down.

It wasn't like that didn't happen on a regular basis. It did. Of course, there was always someone else, always another distraction, always another person not only willing, but falling all over themselves for a chance at the great Carter Maxwell.

But he and Nick had never been close, probably because Carter had been an asshole.

Okay. There was no *probably* about it.

And here Nick was anyway, not exactly extending an olive branch, but trying to be there for Carter, and that meant something too. The anger simmering inside him died down a little.

"I'm okay," Carter said slowly.

"You looked pretty unhappy out there earlier."

"I don't think any of us were *happy*," Carter said, "except maybe Deacon and Beck, who had a pretty damn good practice."

"And that new backup linebacker. I guess the new *starting* linebacker," Nick pointed out.

"Yeah," Carter agreed.

"I give you shit, but you gotta know," Nick said, "we're better with you on the field. On the field, catching those ridiculous balls Riley throws your way, not melting down on the sideline."

"Thanks," Carter said dryly. What was it today with all this fucking earnestness? Was all his worry showing? He'd need to get ahold of that before he met up with Ian.

"You don't need me to say it, you already know it." Nick's voice was wry. "But maybe you did need a reminder."

"Yeah," Carter agreed. Because he had.

The team needed him.

His team.

"You got anyone you can talk to? Maybe that redheaded kid who keeps trailing around after you?" Nick asked.

Carter rolled his eyes. Imagine someone reducing Ian to *that redheaded kid*. No wonder he didn't always like Nick. Maybe Carter could be an asshole, but Nick could definitely match him. "Not him," Carter said. Though he *could* talk to Ian. That much was true.

"Then someone. Your agent, maybe?"

"It's annoying how you keep redeeming yourself," Carter retorted, but Nick just grinned and stood.

"You're welcome," Nick said, and Carter nearly said he hadn't *thanked* him, but then he was walking away, and yeah, maybe he should have.

He could call Alec.

No, scratch that. He *would* call Alec.

First, he sent Ian a text telling him he'd be a little bit, and Ian replied immediately telling him to take his time, he was gonna go grab some takeout and he'd meet him back in the parking lot.

Carter was already dressed, and so was most everyone else, because the locker room was nearly empty by this point, but he still ducked down a little-used hallway before he dialed Alec's number.

"Hey," Alec said, answering almost immediately. "You okay?"

"I'm…" Carter moistened his lips. "I'm doing alright. Had a hard practice."

"Not all of them can be extraordinary, right?" Alec said lightly. Carter had texted him about the last few, about how he'd felt like he was really finding a new gear with Riley passing him the ball.

"Right," Carter agreed. But it was more than that. "I'm afraid it's all gonna fall apart, because I can't keep it down. I'm gonna fucking mess it up." The words came out in a rush.

"Carter," Alec said in a sympathetic voice. "You aren't going to mess up anything. Have you talked to Moira? To Ian?"

"Yes and sort of." Carter hesitated. "This is a very good thing for me, so don't start thinking because I tell you this that it's not. I…I want Moira to like me."

"She *does* like you, probably more than she should," Alec said.

"Yeah, but not just as my therapist, but as Ian's mother," Carter said. It was crazy to him that just a month ago, he had found out and barely blinked. It certainly hadn't changed how he'd behaved or what he'd said to her.

Now he didn't want to tell her the truth, because what if it meant she thought less of him? Thought he didn't deserve Ian?

Maybe he should think about switching...but then he thought about what that would mean. That he'd have to adjust to someone *new*. Someone he didn't trust. And that was even worse.

"You need to talk to her about this," Alec said firmly. "And if you really feel you can't talk to her, Carter, which would be disappointing, because I know you've developed a real rapport with her, then we'll find you someone else. I know that's the agreement you made with her."

"You don't think I should break up with Ian?"

Alec chuckled under his breath. "Would you do that even if I told you to?"

"No," Carter said. Then with more confidence. "No, no, I wouldn't."

"Exactly."

"I just...how do I ever feel like I *deserve* him caring about me like this?" These words, too, escaped out of Carter's mouth before he could snatch them back. He'd never worried, not once, about what he deserved. But now he was, and it was not fun to consider the possibility that he could be found lacking.

When Alec didn't say anything immediately, Carter pressed on. "How did you feel like you deserved Spencer?"

Alec laughed then. "Who says I ever felt like I did?"

"I mean, you *must* have, because you're not just together, you're *married*. You're all happy and shit. Well-adjusted and everything. What I want to be with Ian."

"You've just started dating Ian," Alec reminded him gently. "You don't have to do all this now, not suddenly. It's okay to go about this cautiously. Take your time."

Carter leaned against the hallway wall and squeezed his eyes shut. "I can't stop feeling this way. Like I don't deserve him to care about me. To love me. The way I love him."

"Aw, Carter," Alec said softly, "we never feel like we *ever* truly deserve that kind of love. It always feels like we need to work hard to deserve it, even when we don't. Because love isn't something you can earn, it's something that Ian's going to give you freely, without expectations and without strings."

"Argh, that *sucks*," Carter said vehemently.

"Yeah, it kinda does." Alec sounded amused. "But I think actually...yeah, I do. I think you need to talk to someone else. Someone who just happens to be right here, with me."

"Who is it?" Carter was immediately suspicious.

"Hi, Carter," a deep voice said into his ear. "It's Spencer. Spencer Evans. You know, the guy who's gonna hand your ass to you if you don't stop stressing out my husband."

"I haven't stressed Alec out, not for a while now," Carter argued.

Spencer laughed. "Okay, fair. But still, warning's a warning. Alec just doesn't need to lose any more sleep than he already does."

"Agreed." Carter felt the same. He did not want anyone else losing sleep over him, that was for fucking sure.

"So what's the problem?" Spencer asked.

"I...I'm not sure." It was one thing to tell Alec, who had become a friend over the last few months, and it was entirely another to tell Spencer Evans, one of the biggest, toughest badass defensive linemen in the NFL.

"Come on now," Spencer said, and there was that edge of danger in his voice Carter recognized all too well.

While Spencer had come out his senior year of college, Carter knew he hadn't always been comfortable embracing who he was. Part of that had been the team he'd played for, who'd never wanted a queer player in their locker room. Carter didn't know what the rest of the reason was, but he suspected it might be because Spencer too didn't feel like he *deserved* good things.

Things like his relationship with Alec.

Alec had said a few offhand things during the last few months of conversations he'd shared with Carter. Like how he and Spencer had known each other for a long time, *liked* each other for a long time, before they'd finally started dating.

It sounded like maybe part of that reluctance had been on Alec's end, but considering how Alec had handed the phone over to Spencer when the subject came up, Carter had a feeling the problems had been more on Spencer's side.

"Okay," Carter grumbled. "I...I don't do this relationship thing often."

"Or ever?" Spencer corrected.

"Fine, *ever*," Carter conceded.

"I didn't do relationships either," Spencer said, surprising Carter. "Not until Alec. Didn't think anyone would ever take me on, with all my shit baggage. And of course, having a boyfriend probably meant he'd eventually want everyone to know, and I couldn't have that."

"Not playing for the Stars," Carter said, nodding in understanding.

"Exactly. So I didn't. But actually, who I really wanted was Alec." Spencer sighed. "Don't be like me, Carter, and take ages to get out of your own way. But then I hear that's not really your issue."

"Not so much," Carter said wryly. "I got the guy. I just...how do I keep him?"

Carter thought Spencer would need a minute to really consider this difficult question. But instead, Spencer answered almost immediately, like it was the easiest thing in the world to address. "By *worrying* about keeping him. By never taking him for granted."

"Oh."

"Thought it would be tougher, yeah?" Spencer teased.

"Well, *yeah*. I don't know, I thought this whole thing would be harder. Would feel harder. Would make me feel hemmed in and out of choices and out of chances..."

"But instead it's a whole new universe? Yeah, I get that."

"Everyone told me, but I didn't believe them," Carter said. "I was having so much fun, how could it possibly be *more* fun to do all of that with just one person? But when it's the right person..."

"Surprise, surprise," Spencer said dryly. "But yeah, if you didn't angst a little over whether you deserved him or not, then yeah, maybe you *should* be worried. Maybe you would start to take him for granted. But it seems you really care about the guy and want things to be right between you. That effort makes all the difference."

"Even if I get it wrong? Even if I fuck it up?"

"You gonna be too much of a big man to apologize?" Spencer asked archly.

"Hell no. I fuck up, I know it. It's not that hard, usually."

"There you go," Spencer said. "You got this."

"Do I?"

"I think so. And talk to your therapist. Sure, she's Ian's mom, but she's also a damn good listener. Helped me a bunch."

"Yeah?" Carter hadn't realized that Spencer had gone to Moira too, but then that made sense. There was a reason she'd come so highly recommended from Alec. And Alec would hardly let his husband, the man he *loved*, go to anyone who was less than spectacular at her job.

He would talk to Moira. Tell her his concerns. If she still thought he wasn't worth Ian's time, then, well, they'd deal with that. But he hoped that she wouldn't.

"You're gonna be good," Spencer said. "Off the field, anyway."

"On the field, too," Carter said stubbornly.

Spencer laughed. "You just keep hopin' that, Maxwell."

He would, though, and it was funny how hope seemed to extinguish the worst of his temper, cooling down the worst of its heat.

But it wasn't just hope. It was Landry, telling him he was a good guy. It was Nick worrying about him. Spencer telling him he had this.

Alec's quiet confidence.

But also, it was Ian's belief in him.

He *could* do this.

"Thanks, Spencer. Really," Carter said.

"You feel better?"

"Yeah, actually."

"There you go," Spencer said. "Now, remember what I said, don't cost my husband any more sleep, alright?"

"You got it."

But what Carter really believed was that *he'd* gotten it.

"You're quiet tonight," Ian asked as he drifted along the edge of the pool.

He'd just finished his workout, Carter not joining in physically, but in spirit, lazing around on one of the lounge chairs, feet up, barely even making innuendos about Ian's tight swimsuit.

At first, Ian had just worried that it was the difficult practice getting to Carter, but when he'd asked on the way home, Carter had insisted that *no*, he was actually better than he'd expected. "I even called up and talked to Alec," Carter said.

Ian had been happy to hear it. "Good, you can't just talk to me," he'd said.

But after they'd gotten home, and Carter had drifted off towards the living room, the TV on, but toying with his phone, Ian had announced he was going to take a swim.

Space, he'd thought, could be a very good thing.

Then, to his surprise, Carter had eventually come outside, not saying anything but settling down on the lounger.

Ian had finished his workout, but instead of getting out, continued to swish casually through the water.

Waiting for Carter to tell him something, because he'd guessed that was what this was about: Carter wanted to tell him something but didn't know how.

He'd just needed to give him time—but at this rate, he was going to be totally wrinkled all over, so he'd finally taken a risk and straight up *asked*.

"Am I that obvious?" Carter asked with a resigned sigh.

Ian shrugged. He still wanted Carter to *talk* to him. Yeah, talking to Alec was great. Talking to his mom was good, too.

But Carter was *his*. They belonged to each other in a whole different way.

"Is it weird for you, that your mom is a therapist?"

"You mean, has she tried her best to therapy me my whole goddamn life? Or is it weird for me that she's *your* therapist?"

"Well, both?"

There was the honest truth Ian was finally hearing.

"You're feeling weird that you're telling her your problems," Ian guessed, "but you also want her to like you, 'cause she's my mom."

"Yeah," Carter confessed. "What do you think I should do?"

Ian shook his head. "I can't tell you what the right thing is for you to do. Only that if you're concerned, we can transition you to a new person."

"I don't want a new person," Carter said stubbornly. "What I want is to stop feeling like I'm not enough. I'm trying to feel worthy of you. Trying to *be* worthy. It's not easy."

Ian swam over to the side, put his arms onto the concrete edge, and set his chin on them. Gazed over at Carter. "You ever think that I worry about that too?"

"Me deserving you?" Carter laughed, but it was tinged with a self-consciousness Ian absolutely fucking hated.

A self-consciousness that wasn't Carter. Had *never* been Carter.

"No," Ian corrected gently. "*Me* deserving *you.*"

"Oh. *Oh.*"

"Yeah," Ian said.

"Huh." Carter considered this for a long time. "Actually, never. I...you're such a good person, Ian. Kind and giving. Your whole fucking thing, it's giving to other people."

"Trust me, I was well paid for it, too," Ian inserted dryly. "I wouldn't have done it for free."

"Yeah, but *still.*"

"Doesn't matter," Ian said. He wasn't going to let Carter get away with this. "I bet you everyone who meets you falls half in love with you. Me being crazy about you—that's *not* new."

"I guess." Carter looked dubious.

"Don't tell me some of those people you slept with didn't text you and call you and practically fucking stalk you after?"

"'Cause I'm Carter Maxwell. They think I'm rich and famous. Well, I *am* rich and famous. But they think they can use me. And then the sex..." Carter shrugged, still in that self-conscious mode Ian hated.

"Yeah, because you're *Carter Maxwell.* And I don't mean because you're rich or you're famous or you're notorious or because you're hot or good in bed. You're all those things, yeah," Ian said and watched Carter grin. He rolled his eyes. "Yeah, yeah, your ego doesn't need stroking, I know. But you're so much more than the sum of your parts, Carter. If you were just those things, I wouldn't have been anything else than your friend."

"Huh."

"I mean it. So yeah, is a part of me afraid you're going to get tired of a normal guy like me? Sure. But I'm not going to let you go just because of a little fear. And you know what else? I know Moira sees it too—what you bring to the table that isn't all that other crap she doesn't give a shit about. She sees your capacity for love, your loyalty, the friendships you've built on the team. The way you're *wanting* to change, to be better. All of those things make her like you plenty. No matter how much you struggle."

"You make me seem pretty dang awesome." Carter waggled his eyebrows. "You wanna come over here and show me just how awesome I really am?"

Ian laughed. "I'm gonna take a shower first. I'm all chlorinated." He shot Carter a speculative look. "You wanna join me?"

"After. Just want to do this first."

Even though Ian was a *little* disappointed Carter didn't join him in the shower—Carter wet was a sight to behold, and never failed to get his dick hard—he was also proud that the guy was beginning to prioritize other things as more important than sex.

He lifted himself out of the pool and *yeah*, there was that very important character development and then there was the way Carter's eyes followed his ass, briefs clinging to it damply, after he dried off and headed towards the patio door.

"Keep it warm for me, baby," Carter called out just as the door shut behind him.

Ian laughed all the way up the stairs, was still chuckling to himself as he collapsed, clean and dry but still naked, onto his bed after his shower.

Not even five minutes later, he glanced up and saw Carter leaning against the doorjamb, eyes roving over every single inch of his body.

He'd already taken his own clothes off—Ian would probably find them later, scattered up the stairs, like Carter couldn't even wait to undress—and his cock was hard and curved, brushing against his chiseled lower abs.

Ian's mouth went dry.

"Hey, baby," Carter teased. But he didn't move.

"It's amazing how much I still hate that nickname," Ian said.

"And amazing how much it turns you on still," Carter said, pushing off from the door and prowling into the room. "I can see it."

"Not gonna complain if you look a little harder. You can even touch." Ian didn't let himself even think of all the gorgeous people Carter had slept with. Or how flawless and perfect Carter himself was.

Ian knew his ass and his thighs jiggled. He didn't have ridiculously cut abs. And then there were all his freckles.

But Carter never seemed to notice—and Ian wasn't going to remind him. Or obsess over all his very obvious flaws.

"Don't mind if I do," Carter said, leaning over and giving Ian a long, slow, sweet kiss, and then his lips drifted lower and then lower still, detouring across his hip, until they finally crossed over to where his dick twitched against his stomach.

When Carter finally slid it into his hot, sweet mouth, Ian swore, gritting his teeth against the sudden, overwhelming pleasure.

But even a fairly simple, straightforward blowjob with Carter was still a whole fucking experience. He teased and he cajoled, easing more ecstasy out of Ian than he'd ever imagined feeling before.

Carter, even with his mouth full of cock, couldn't shut up either. He was full of *baby, give me more*, and *yeah, baby, let me hear you*, and *God, fuck my mouth. Yeah,* he moaned around Ian's dick, like it was the greatest thing he'd ever tasted in his whole life, *give it to me, baby.*

And Ian did, because Carter's mouth was so fucking perfect it was impossible not to just chase what felt so goddamn good.

Then, right as he was about to explode, Carter pulled back, grinning like he loved it so much, he didn't want it to end just yet.

Finally, after the third time teasing him, Ian, still teetering right on the edge, lost control and thrust hard. Carter groaned in approval, and just took it as Ian fucked his mouth and throat and came in an explosion he wouldn't forget anytime soon.

"Fuck, I'm sorry," Ian mumbled, but Carter didn't look sorry at all as he wiped the back of his hand over his mouth and stood.

"Don't you dare apologize for a thing," Carter said, and Ian realized he'd been touching himself while sucking him off. And he was still doing it, working his own dick with tight, slow strokes as he stared at Ian.

Like all he was going to need to orgasm was the taste of Ian's come in his mouth, and the sight of his naked body sprawled across the bed.

And God, wasn't that the hottest thing in the world? Carter teased him about stroking *his* ego, but having Carter look at him like that, like he was everything he'd ever wanted, wrapped into one irresistible package, made Ian hot enough that he wished he could get hard again right now.

"Come on me," Ian said, and Carter moaned, his hand moving faster.

"Yeah, just like that. Paint me with it, *baby*," Ian crooned, and that was all it took before Carter froze and then began to do just as he'd asked, stripes of come landing all over his chest and thighs.

"Shit," Carter said, collapsing onto him, like he didn't care how much he was smearing his own come around. "That was so good."

"No kidding," Ian said, unable to keep the awe out of his voice. He'd never had orgasms like the ones he was regularly sharing with Carter. They were addictive, but then that wasn't very surprising, considering the man giving them.

He was more than addicted to Carter. He was obsessed, in so deep, he didn't even care that he was drowning in him.

Crazy, madly, illogically in love.

"I texted your mom before I came up here," Carter said. Apparently he'd lost his concern, and had no worries about bringing up Ian's mother and his own therapist while Carter's come was still drying, sticky and tacky, between their two naked bodies.

Ian smiled anyway. Now *this* was his Carter. No weird self-consciousness and refusing to doubt himself.

"Yeah?" he asked.

"You were right." Carter flushed. "She said the same thing you did. That she's happy for us. Happy for *me*. And you know what? She's happy for you, too."

"I told you that she said that to me when we talked," Ian reminded him.

"Yeah, but...I thought maybe it was different for you than for me."

"And it's not." Ian knew it was true.

"It's not," Carter said wryly. "But she did say we still need to work on boundaries. And not just mine with my parents, but with her and our relationship."

Ian laughed. "Yeah, I bet she did."

"Maybe I shouldn't have told her thanks, I'm gonna go make you scream now," Carter teased.

Ian shuddered, but he was happy, anyway.

Like he couldn't possibly get happier.

CHAPTER 17

"You know, I meant it." Carter turned to Riley as they finished warming up before the Chargers game.

Riley shot him a look. "Meant what?"

"I'd take you over Justin Herbert. Or Pat Mahomes. Sam Crawford. Pax Kelly. Any of those guys."

It had been bothering Carter for several days now that Riley might actually believe that he'd rather have someone else throwing him touchdown passes. And the thing was, six months ago, he wouldn't have thought twice about it.

Maybe it was just like Moira said and progress was slow but as long as it happened, change inevitably followed. He was not the same man he'd been when he joined the Condors—or even the same man he'd been when *Riley* had signed here.

"How about Tom Brady?" Riley said, serious, focused expression still plastered across his features.

"Oh, come on, you're not playing fair," Carter complained, catching a little pass Riley tossed him.

Riley grinned. "Hey, but Brady didn't throw the deep ball much, especially later on, right before he retired, when he was *old*," he pointed out.

"True," Carter admitted. "But yeah, I'd take you over any of those guys. Even Tom Brady."

"Aw, Carter, that's sweet. It must be true love."

"Completely platonic quarterback-receiver love," Carter reminded.

"It must be pretty damn platonic," Riley said. "It's been awhile since you tried to grab my ass."

"You know you like it when I do it, and that it turns Landry on to remind you that you're with *him*. It's practically a public service, grabbing your ass. But unfortunately, that's off the table now, 'cause I'm betting Ian wouldn't like it."

Riley grinned. "Probably not. But we all know why —you got another ass you want to grab."

"Guilty as charged." There was no point in even trying to deny it.

"We're happy for you, Carter, really," Riley said sincerely.

"I'm happy too," Carter said, and he really meant it. "Now, let's go kick some ass."

"Fly, Condors, fly!" Riley teased, but there was a thread of determination that Carter recognized now because he felt the same.

What happened to this team mattered to him more than it ever had.

It was great—and it was also terrifying, because what if this game didn't work out? What if this season didn't work out? He didn't know what he'd do.

Was this why he'd spent so many of his seasons not giving a shit?

He didn't want to think so, but maybe it was. Maybe he'd been protecting himself this whole time. Maybe not caring was just another shitty coping mechanism he'd used throughout his life.

Panic rose inside him, but Carter resolutely pushed it down.

They were gonna be fine.

Sure, they'd had a few tough practices, and Deacon and that new rookie linebacker, along with the secondary, had made them work hard.

Hopefully that hard work would pay off today.

Carter returned to the bench, to get ready for the anthem. Landry was there, and they hugged briefly.

"Where's Ian?" Landry asked, after looking around.

"He didn't want to be a distraction, so he decided to watch from one of the boxes," Carter said. "I think Mr. G invited him to his, actually."

"Oh sweet," Landry said.

"It was nice of him," Carter agreed.

And there was that pressure again, building away inside him even as he tried to pretend it didn't exist. If they lost today, if he didn't do the job he was being paid—really fucking well, he might add—to do, then he wouldn't just be letting himself and his teammates down.

He'd be letting down the owner of this team, who'd stepped in to buy it when it had been teetering on the edge of disaster. Grant Green had pulled it back from the brink. Fixed everything that was wrong. All with his own neck and fortune on the line.

Carter didn't want all his sacrifice to be in vain.

Didn't want anyone to begin speculating that a tech genius who didn't know jack shit about football shouldn't've bought an NFL team.

"He's a great guy," Landry agreed.

Carter made a face.

It was undeniably true, but it was another reminded he didn't need.

"You okay, man?" Landry asked, glancing over at him as they took their places for the anthem.

"I'm fine," Carter said shortly, but he wasn't sure it was true.

The game started, Ethan kicking off and the Condors defense taking the field first.

But immediately it became clear that the defense had their hands more than full with Herbert and the Chargers' offense. They had too many weapons, and Herbert might not've had Riley's mobility as a quarterback, but they went right down the field, scoring a touchdown with only a few minutes of play time.

"Guys," Riley said, as they watched Herbert run in the touchdown himself, "come on, let's get prepared."

Carter joined the group on the sideline—Cole and the rest of the offensive line was there, and Landry and Nick, Darius and him—and they watched the defense jog off the field, determination still flaring in their eyes, but it was dimmer than it had been before the game started.

"We knew they could score," Landry reminded everyone as he met each and every player's eyes. "And so can we."

It should've been just that easy, but from the beginning, from the first play of their first drive, it was like the Chargers' defense had somehow known exactly how to penetrate even their most inventive blocking plays.

Riley spent more time on the ground in the first quarter than he had in the last few months.

And forget about throwing downfield. It wasn't going to happen. Quick, short throws were all he could get out before being pummeled into the turf by a relentless defensive line.

Carter was left pathetically attempting to block—not his strength—or running down the sidelines even though there wasn't going to be a throw in his direction—something he was unbelievably worse at than blocking.

Five drives and one field goal later, Riley sat gingerly on the bench. Halftime was only a few minutes away, but they were down by fourteen points, and it didn't seem particularly likely they were going to make up the difference.

Not if they could barely move the ball and the only points they'd put up were courtesy of a key roughing the quarterback penalty right when they'd been about to punt.

Carter's temper had long passed the simmer stage and was now roiling at a full boil.

"Goddamn it," Carter bellowed as Riley winced. He'd been beaten up some, for sure. There was no question that under the flak jacket he wore to protect his midsection, his ribs were black and blue.

A hurt Riley, even a hurt Riley who could continue to play, wasn't going to be nearly as effective, and they all knew it. He wouldn't be able to run for first downs or be nearly as evasive as he was when he was at one hundred percent.

"It's alright, Carter, we got this," Landry said.

"No, *no*, we do not. Riley's getting his ass handed to him out there," Carter argued.

"And bitching about it is gonna change that?" Landry challenged.

No, it did not. But it at least gave some outlet to the black hole of pain and frustration that was threatening to swallow him whole.

"Carter, you gotta hold it together, man," Nick said.

Rage spiraled and Carter flexed his hand into a fist. Would've loved nothing better than to plow it right into Nick's patronizing expression.

"He's right," Riley said, and that was all that saved Nick. Well, that *and* Carter knowing, deep down, in a place that could still think clearly, that if he did it, if he punched someone on the Condors' sideline, he'd be out of the game and maybe out for the next one too. Mr. G wouldn't tolerate it.

And that possibility—that he could let his teammates down even more than he already was—felt worse than just taking Nick's bullshit.

Except, Carter knew, in a place that even the anger couldn't touch, that it wasn't bullshit. He *did* need to keep it together.

His fingers bit into his palms and he breathed out once and then twice. Again. And then again.

It didn't help, and it certainly didn't stop the Chargers from inexorably marching back down the field again, only a last-minute pass deflection by Micah preventing another touchdown and forcing the Chargers to settle for only three points.

"Okay," Carter said, trying for chill optimism and landing somewhere else, more like frustration and fury, "so we're only down by seventeen now. *Fuck.*"

"Carter, you're either with us or you're against us. It's your choice," Riley said with steel in his tone.

Somehow, misery and guilt heaped on top of everything else didn't do anything to make him feel better.

He felt *worse*, in fact, but the reminders that it wasn't just him he'd be letting down did help to rein in the worst of his temper.

He could do this.

In fact, he *had* to do this.

"Extra blocking on the line," Riley said as they made their way back out onto the field for one last drive before halftime. "Carter, you got this?"

Carter could not block worth a shit. But he *had* to, so he would.

"I might be able to pull a double-team still, if we could keep you upright long enough to make them think you might actually throw," Carter suggested.

But Riley shook his head. "We're going short," he said. "You're blocking."

It sort of worked, enough that they'd actually made it into Chargers' territory when they just plain ran out of time and were forced to kick another field goal.

The score heading into halftime was seventeen to six.

"Could've been a bloodbath," Deacon said, tugging his helmet off as they jogged back into the locker room.

That did not make anything better.

Truthfully, everyone knew if the Condors could play the game they wanted to, if they could just get around the defense's relentless blitzes, they might actually have a chance at still winning the game. And somehow that actually made Carter feel *worse*.

Because he didn't know how they could do it.

Landry was already doing everything he could to block.

The secondary defense against Carter was tepid at best, but it hadn't mattered, because he couldn't catch a ball that Riley didn't have a chance to throw to him.

Their normally high octane offense was being totally fucking smothered by the pressure.

You're either with us or against us. Carter reminded himself of Riley's words as he settled down onto the bench to listen to Coach K try to motivate them to do something even he no longer believed they could do: win this game.

"That could've gone better."

Ian was impressed at how casual Grant Green's words were, when the last few minutes of the game against the Chargers ticked down.

The Condors were down by eighteen.

The defense, led by Deacon and bolstered by Micah and Beck, had managed to hold the Chargers to only one touchdown in the second half, but it hadn't been enough, because the offense still hadn't been able to move the ball enough to score points and close the gap.

Ian was acutely aware of the tension on the sideline, even though he was up higher, far out of hearing distance, only able to see as Carter paced back and forth in front of the bench, like if he kept moving, if he kept pushing himself, he might be able to contain what Ian had guessed had to be a supernova of a meltdown.

It was exactly what Carter hadn't needed, if he was looking to prove himself.

And also, it was *exactly* what Carter needed.

Progress wasn't progress until it was battle-tested and Carter was certainly under siege today.

Moira had already texted him three times. **Watching the game**, the first text had read. The second text had been, **Guess it's not going so well.** And the third? **If he needs me, I'm here.**

She'd obviously seen the same thing he had, even if she was over three thousand miles away from the stadium and watching the game on TV.

Carter was only a moment away from losing it completely.

But Ian had to give him credit. It had been a frustrating game from the first series. The Condors had never gotten their feet under them. The defense had barely broken under a stellar Chargers' offense, but it hadn't been enough because the Condors just couldn't figure out how to score. How to keep Riley in the game.

Still, Carter had not totally lost it.

He was still playing.

Still pacing.

Still talking to his teammates, though Ian could see the increasing strain on his face every time he returned to the sideline.

He knew they were going to lose, and Ian was just praying that knowledge wasn't enough to push him over the top.

"You've got a good team here, sir, but they *are* still figuring their shit out," Ian told the owner.

Mr. G just shrugged. "Yeah. They'll learn from this. They'll learn, and they'll get better."

"Still in the playoff hunt, too," Ian reminded him, but Mr. G's smile told Ian he hadn't forgotten.

"You worried?" Mr. G asked, not specifying what Ian would be worried about because no doubt it was blatantly obvious.

"We've got this, sir," Ian said firmly.

It was not technically a lie. Ian—and therefore, Carter—had a lot of resources at his disposal. In fact, he'd dealt with lots of worse situations with his prior clients. Plus, Ian also had his mother and Alec on speed dial. Along with Ian himself, they'd do anything to help Carter, making sure he didn't fling himself into the deep end.

Ian might've been a little *more* honest though, if he hadn't realized just how much being on this team meant to Carter. The last thing he wanted to do was jeopardize that. Convince Mr. G that even though Carter could bring enormous upside to a football team, his baggage made him too difficult to deal with—and he'd trade Carter away again or let him go to a different team.

"It's hard not to root for him," Mr. G said calmly. "He's a charismatic guy."

Maybe if he'd only been charismatic, or only hot. Or only funny, in a completely unexpected way. Or kind and loyal and generous to a fault. Maybe if he'd been just one of those parts, instead of the sum of them, Ian wouldn't have fallen so hard for the guy.

But he was all those parts, and the sum, and so much fucking more.

"Yeah," Ian agreed.

"And," Mr. G added, shooting Ian a knowing look, "he seems very happy. With you."

It was easy to believe this calm, affable exterior was all the Condors' owner was, but then that cutthroat edge to him emerged, unexpectedly, and it was impossible to forget that the guy had made a couple billion dollars in less than ten years.

"Yeah," Ian agreed, because he couldn't exactly deny it. They *were* happy together. Happier than Ian had ever dreamt he could be with someone else. Of course, that happiness was tempered with the inevitable concern he had for Carter and his own journey. Moments like today, when he wished he could wave a magic wand and make all of Carter's baggage vanish. But then, if Carter didn't have his baggage, was he still the Carter that Ian knew and loved?

"Personally, I think it's a very good thing," Mr. G said.

Ian hadn't been sure the Condors' owner had heard the news, but now, it was clear he had.

From Deacon, maybe? Carter had told him once that the defensive captain and long-time Condors player and the new owner were, to use his word, "tight."

Ian hadn't been sure then what that meant and he still wasn't exactly sure—but it was clear Mr. G was getting his info from somewhere.

"No arguments here. But I am sorry for the loss," Ian said regretfully.

"It's going to happen. We can't win them all, no matter how much I'd like us to," Mr. G said with a resigned sigh. "As long as we don't let this loss get to us. We gotta start fresh next week."

Ian got another one of those probing looks, and he knew what it meant.

Make sure Carter doesn't spiral—and if he does, figure out how to pull him back.

Or maybe he was selling Grant Green short and what he really meant, Ian considered, as he headed down to the elevator that would take him to the bowels of the stadium and the locker room, was, *help Carter so he can figure out how to get ahold of himself. Help Carter so he doesn't have to go through this every goddamn time we lose.*

If that was what Mr. G meant, then Ian could get behind that one thousand percent, because that was all he wanted for Carter—for him to live his best, happiest life.

Ian waited outside the hall. Carter had to shower, change, talk to the media—if he was willing—and then they would tackle his frame of mind.

While he waited, Ian worked his way through all his hard-won knowledge and the considerable experience he'd gained while working as a sober companion over the last five years, carefully compiling anything and everything that might help Carter right now.

Slowly, players began to emerge, heading for their cars and home. A lot of them were quiet, dejected even. Ian glanced up every time the locker room door opened, and greeted the players he'd met before with a quick nod. None of them seemed particularly in the mood for talking. But Carter didn't show up.

Then Deacon appeared. He was frowning but didn't look discouraged like so many of his teammates. Instead, he looked fired up, like the loss, while frustrating him, had also lit a fervor inside him that still burned bright and hot.

"Tough game," Ian said, speaking out for the first time since he'd taken this spot. He'd have left Deacon alone, especially after that kind of loss, but it was possible he might know something about Carter, having spent the game sharing the sideline with him.

"Yeah," Deacon agreed. "He's in there. I..."

But Deacon didn't finish his sentence.

"What? Is he okay?" Ian asked. The worry, already a sick feeling in the base of his stomach, grew exponentially.

Deacon didn't answer immediately. "He's—he's got ahold of himself. I think." He shook his head then. "Never seen him like this. Like he's...I don't know. You'll see soon. I think he didn't want to leave the locker room til Riley finished with the media."

Ian almost asked why that was, but Deacon was already heading down the hallway.

When Ian glanced back, he saw that the person Deacon had spotted was Mr. G, also loitering a few dozen feet farther down the hallway.

He was lying in wait, just the same as Ian was, he realized. Just not for Carter. Or Riley. Or any of the coaching staff.

It was clear from his expression he was waiting for Deacon.

But before Ian could parse what exactly *that* meant, the door opened and Riley and Landry walked out, holding hands.

Riley looked tired and Landry looked worried—and Ian couldn't blame either of them.

"He's still in there, but he told me he'd be ready in a moment," Landry said, gesturing back towards the locker room.

"You okay?" Ian asked, directly his question towards Riley, who'd spent most of the game getting his ass kicked.

"Sorta," Riley said honestly, "but I will be."

"I've got him," Landry said, sounding like a man in love. "Just like you've got Carter."

Riley rolled his eyes, but the way he gazed up at his boyfriend made it clear none of his exasperation was genuine. He clearly loved Landry's concern and care, just like he loved the man himself.

God, Ian wanted that too. To support Carter the same way. But Carter had to let him do that. To stop carrying all his burdens on his own.

"Yeah, I do," Ian said. "If he doesn't—"

But Ian didn't get the rest of his question out. The door swung open and there Carter was, framed in the doorway. He was wearing a slim cut black suit, with a thin black T-shirt underneath, scooped low enough Ian could see the ridiculous curve of his collarbones.

His hair glowed gold and brown and almost red against all that black. But his eyes weren't their usual molten honey brown. Today, Carter's gaze was flat. Furious. Frustrated.

"Hey," Ian said stupidly. Didn't reach out and touch him or embrace him, because normally, PDA at the stadium felt wrong, but what felt even more wrong was doing it when Carter looked like that.

"Hey," Carter said, his voice as flat as his eyes.

Ian had a lot of experience in these situations. But usually his clients left him a way in. Carter felt like a solid, slippery wall and he couldn't even get a grip on him, never mind wiggle his way inside.

But he would.

He had to.

Not just that; he *wanted* to. He'd be here helping Carter, no matter what he was paid or not paid. He *loved* Carter.

But it was still tough to reconcile this tall, beautifully dressed, remote being to the soft, warm, gorgeous creature he'd fallen for so goddamn easily.

"You ready to go home?" Ian asked stupidly.

Landry and Riley were still watching them. Both of them, Ian realized. Wondering what they were going to do.

Ian gave them a little nod that meant *I got this*, even though he wasn't sure that was entirely the truth.

You'll make it the truth.

"Yes," Carter said, voice clipped.

Ian had never heard him so contained, all those emotions sheared off and buried deep behind the wall of his composure.

This was one way to handle it, and truthfully, Ian knew there were a hundred ways out there, but Ian felt confident enough to say this was not the *right* way. Not for the Carter he'd begun to know so well.

"Great," Ian said. He'd play along til he got Carter alone. And then surely some of this shiny hard exterior would crack.

But they walked out of the facility, to the parking lot, and then drove the entire way in relative silence.

Ian had tried a few times to break in. "How are you doing?" was his first attempt.

"Fine," Carter said.

A minute later, he made a second. "If you'd had another quarter, I think you'd have found a way to wiggle out of that coverage," Ian said, and meant it. They'd been getting there, slowly, but surely, but the loss had happened because they just didn't have enough time to figure it out on the field.

"Sure," Carter replied flippantly.

Which wasn't the Carter Ian knew.

The Carter Ian knew cared deeply. So deeply, it was partially why he'd struggled so much with his temper.

Caring made him want things, things for himself and things for other people, and not getting them triggered the cascade of emotion that generally resulted in a breakdown.

That was what this was. An instinctual response to pretend that if the internal chaos didn't show, then it didn't exist.

But it did. Ian could fucking *feel* it, boiling under Carter's steely exterior.

So he tried again, as Carter pulled his SUV into the garage.

"How about a swim?" he suggested as they walked into the house. "That would be a great way to properly process—

But that was all he got out before Carter turned to him, and a moment later, Ian was backed up against the kitchen wall by Carter's big body.

Then his mouth was descending on Ian's, and his kiss was ravenous. So hungry that for a second, Ian couldn't process what was happening. Definitely not *why* it was happening.

Not why Carter's hands were cradling his ass or why they were boosting him up against the wall.

Or why he was moaning helplessly, riding the hard muscular ridge of Carter's thigh like he was born to do it.

His brain went that fuzzy that fast.

He went from concerned to aroused in only the time it took for Carter to turn to him.

Carter's tongue was insistent in his mouth, stroking his own, and Ian let himself get lost in it, lost in the sensation of Carter's hands delving under his clothes, tugging his polo shirt out of his jeans, palms rough and warm on his skin.

"Gonna fuck you right here, against this wall." Carter's voice was rough, guttural, a slur of words Ian barely comprehended because then he was palming the hard line of his cock through his jeans, and that was all he wanted, too.

Touch me more, he nearly begged.

Why didn't he?

There was something not quite right. A persistent feeling of wrongness wound its way through his uncooperative, mostly shut-off brain.

Then it hit him.

Shit.

He elbowed Carter hard in the stomach and Carter flinched, stepping back. Ian's feet hit the ground again and he wobbled, his knees not quite steady.

That was how fucking good it was with Carter.

It was so incredible, their sexual chemistry so off the freaking charts that Ian had actually *forgotten* how Carter normally worked off his temper.

With sex.

And he'd just been about to do it with Ian. Who'd been totally willing to let him do whatever he wanted.

"We can't do this," Ian mumbled, hating every syllable he was saying.

Because he really wanted to. So fucking badly.

But if he did let Carter use him, even if Carter cared about him, even if Carter and he were in an accepted relationship and they normally had no issues enjoying themselves in bed—or against a convenient wall—then Carter would be reverting to the same bad habits that had always hurt him before.

Ian couldn't let him do that, no matter how desperately he wanted to just say *fuck it* and let Carter do exactly what they both craved.

"What?" Carter said. He sounded just as hazy as Ian. Like he didn't even comprehend Ian saying no. Not that he wouldn't respect it. Ian didn't worry about that for a second. Carter had never forced himself on someone unwilling, and in some ways, Ian was *very* willing, the most goddamn willing. Carter just didn't understand why Ian was stopping them.

Ian took a deep breath, hoping the oxygen would clear his brain.

At least return his brain to his head. Because it seemed like most of it was currently residing in his cock.

"We can't do this," Ian repeated again, slower this time. "This is what you *do*, Carter."

"So?" Carter's chin jutted out stubbornly. "It's with *you*. Someone I give a shit about. It's not like I went and picked up some random person at a club—or let them pick me up. It's *you*."

God, this was going to be even worse than Ian had imagined.

"It doesn't matter." Ian was going to have to force himself to be ruthless, even if he didn't want to be.

"It...doesn't...*matter*?"

Ian nodded.

Carter shoved his hand through his hair and began to pace in front of Ian. So much for that impenetrable surface. It was crumbling by the second.

Ian never would've imagined his refusal to have sex would be the key, but it was undeniable.

"Are you fucking kidding me?" Carter's expression was full of agonized disbelief. "But, God, Ian, I *need* you. I need this. I need…"

"What you *need* is to deal with this loss and your struggle to contain your temper with better coping mechanisms. Not with sex. Let's talk about some of the ones Moira's worked on with you. I know she has. And if you can't recall any right now, we can call her up." Ian whipped his phone out of his pocket. It would be slightly humiliating to have to tell his mother what had just happened, but to help Carter, he'd do it. In a heartbeat. No questions asked.

"You want to call her *right now*? When I…when *we*…" Carter sounded incredulous. He gave a short, unamused laugh. "Can't we just go to my room? Your room? Go back to the wall? I know you were enjoying that, the way I was enjoying it. God, the noises you make when you're turned on. When *I* turn you on."

Carter looked like the angel *and* the devil. He was every form of temptation Ian had ever experienced and more.

But Ian knew what he had to do.

If he loved Carter less, he couldn't have done it.

"No," he said firmly. "No, and please know, I really want to. I love having sex with you. It's…it's the best I've ever had. And the next time you want to, when I know you're not using it—using *me*—to stave off a meltdown, I'll willingly do it anywhere you want. But not now, not like this."

Carter just stared at him.

Ian prepared himself to explain again. To reject Carter *again*.

But instead, Carter turned and stormed off, heading back into the garage.

A minute later, he was driving off. Ian could hear the engine roar as he gunned it, gravel spraying as he hit the turn.

He swallowed hard, facing the decision he had to make.

He could let Carter go do whatever it was he was going to do—and that was a very short list. Or he could do something about it. He could show Carter that no matter what, he was with him. It didn't matter if he was the angel, or the devil. Ian just wanted the man underneath.

In the end, it wasn't really a decision at all.

CHAPTER 18

Carter threw back another tequila shot, the lime sour against his tongue as he sucked on it, and tried not to crawl out of his fucking skin.

The Pirate's Booty was busy tonight, and as he'd prowled in, every eye in the place had swiveled in his direction.

Exactly the way he liked it.

Or, at least, the way he *used* to like it.

Now, the attention made him squirm and for all the wrong reasons.

Now, he knew what it was like to be wanted for more than just his body or his job. For more than just his hands and his mouth and his dick.

Ian had changed him, in a hundred tiny ways and in a few very large ones.

When he'd first driven away, he'd not really thought through coming here. Certainly hadn't really *intended* to come here and pick someone up and break his promises to Ian. Even after walking in and sitting down at the bar, he hadn't gotten that far.

He'd just needed *something*, and this familiar place, with its all-too familiar vices, had felt like the best choice.

Or the least bad choice, anyway.

A guy sauntered up to where Carter was holding court at the end of the bar. Kieran glanced over. Didn't come back over to see if Carter needed another shot—or to see if the guy would be staying long enough to need a drink of his own.

Ugh, it was annoying how well the guy knew him.

How well the guy knew *everyone*.

"Hi, handsome," the guy trilled as he approached.

Carter just stared at him.

"You here alone?" he asked, clearly not getting the memo.

Carter still didn't say anything.

But then he didn't need to.

Because another voice was speaking up behind this average-looking twink.

"No, he's not."

Someone not average looking. Someone whose voice made Carter's heart soar, even though he'd been so fucking sure he was furious with him only five minutes ago.

Someone he'd been positive he wouldn't be forgiving anytime soon.

But love was funny that way.

His anger evaporated, extinguished in a blast of chilly air.

"Ian," Carter said gratefully.

Ian raised a reddish-brown eyebrow. God, he was so gorgeous. So gorgeous and so *here*, and all Carter's, even though Carter had been a complete ass.

He was here *anyway*.

Maybe because he's paid to be, an uncomfortable voice inside Carter wondered.

But Carter dismissed it, because he knew the truth.

The look in Ian's eyes as his gaze swept over Carter, head to toe, like he owned him—and he *did*, that much was clear—made it obvious that Ian wasn't here because he was supposed to be.

He was here because his place was right next to Carter, and Carter had been stupid enough to doubt it for a second.

But he wasn't doubting it any longer.

"Do you two know each other or something?" Unassuming Twink asked.

"Know each other? Don't be ridiculous. This is my boyfriend."

Ian shot Unassuming Twink a look that made Carter hard as a fucking rock. Without saying a word, like he'd known without being told Carter wouldn't have ever touched this guy, even if he hadn't been unassuming. Even if he'd been the hottest guy or girl he'd ever seen. But then, that crown was already taken, and it was resting right on Ian's gorgeous curls.

That faith, that unshakeable loyalty, it was something so completely precious Carter didn't know how he'd lived his whole fucking life without it.

"Is he really?" Unassuming Twink looked annoyed, but not like he truly understood what was happening.

Which was ridiculous, because to Carter, it was so obvious who he belonged to.

That they belonged to *each other*.

"Yes." Ian said it before Carter could.

Carter wanted to touch him. To wrap a hand around his waist and drag him over. Kiss him until they couldn't breathe.

Until Unassuming Twink *knew* without a single doubt that he was not wanted or needed.

But the sting of Ian turning him down earlier still hurt, and Carter wasn't going to do anything Ian didn't want. Even if this desire had nothing to do with his temper and everything to do with Ian being *Ian*.

It was hard not to reach for him, but Carter had begun to realize that good things were worth waiting for. He'd wait until Ian was sure that the Carter touching him was a Carter who was in control of himself.

But to Carter's surprise, he didn't wait. Or else he was even more sure than Carter was. Because Ian came over, and tucked himself into Carter's side, turning his face up towards Carter's own.

Ian didn't kiss him, but he might as well have. The look in his eyes felt like a brand, pressing right into Carter's skin. It burned, and Carter fucking loved it. His dick throbbed in his slacks.

He'd had a lot of sex in his life, but nothing had ever been hotter than Ian claiming him like this.

"You okay?" Ian asked softly. Soft enough Carter knew, he'd asked the question for Carter and Carter only.

"Yeah." *I am now.*

He wanted to say, *I wouldn't have cheated on you, even if Unassuming Twink hadn't been unassuming.* He wanted to say, *I'm not sure I'm good, but I know I will be, eventually.*

"Good." Ian nodded once, in approval. "You ready to go home?"

In Carter's periphery, he saw Unassuming Twink make a face and then turn and walk away. Good riddance.

Carter knew the question he was meant to be answering, but "How did you find me?" popped out instead.

Ian just chuckled. "It was obvious where you'd go. But also I texted Kieran, and he confirmed you were holding court at his bar."

"I wouldn't have—"

But Ian didn't let him get the rest out. "Of course not," he said, with bone-deep certainty.

"You're all I want. All I've ever wanted, it turns out," Carter said, because apparently they were being that kind of honest tonight.

Ian curled a hand around his neck and tugged Carter down towards him. "Ditto." Then Ian kissed him, and all the other confessions, all the other promises seemed to fade away because this was all that really mattered.

"Come on, let's go," Ian murmured when he finally broke the kiss.

And Carter was happy to be led by him outside, until they reached Ian's car and suddenly he remembered he'd driven here too.

"Shit," he said, stopping in his tracks.

"What's wrong?" Ian asked.

"I drove here, too," Carter reminded him. "Remember?"

"Oh yeah. *Duh*. Well—" Ian hesitated. Then grinned. "I guess just think about me on the way home, huh?"

"Scratch that," Carter said. Then he jogged back inside, had a quick conversation with Kieran, tossed the guy the keys to his Range Rover and then headed back to where Ian stood in the parking lot, his bright hair shining under a streetlight.

"Took care of it," Carter told him.

Ian shot him a dubious look. "What did you take care of?" he asked, as he unlocked the car and slid inside.

Carter sat in the passenger side and shut the door behind him.

"I'll send someone to take the car back to the house tomorrow," he said. "Left the keys with Kieran."

Ian rolled his eyes, but he still shot a fond look in Carter's direction. "Still throwing your influence around?"

"Hey, I'll pay the guy to detail it and for the delivery," Carter insisted. He knew just the one he could convince to do it too—a guy he could easily bribe with Condors tickets, and a signed jersey, for his five-year-old son.

"So, throwing your *cash* around, then?" Ian teased.

"To go home with you? It's worth it."

Ian shot him a look. Hot and speculative, under those long auburn lashes. Carter didn't think he could get more aroused, but then practically everything Ian did turned him on.

"What did you think was gonna happen on this drive home? Did you think I was planning on seducing you in the back seat?" Ian asked archly.

"No," Carter mumbled.

A guy can dream, can't he?

"Well, I actually wanted to talk to you," Ian said.

"Talking? Oh." Carter attempted to not sound horribly disappointed.

Talking was good too. He liked talking. Especially talking with Ian.

Just...not when he was craving something a little more...*involved*...than talking.

"Yeah, *oh*," Ian said. "I wanna talk through what happened earlier."

"You mean me being an asshole and running off?" Carter didn't really want to remind Ian of the facts of the situation but pretending it hadn't happened wasn't going to get him anywhere either.

"Sure, yeah, I guess." Ian reached over and gripped his knee, his fingers warm through the fabric of Carter's pants. "For the record, you weren't an asshole. But yes, you did run away. I just wish you'd stayed. We would've talked through it. Gotten Moira on the phone. She could've helped."

Ian paused as he pulled to a stop at a red light. "I just don't want you to think there's nothing that can help you. There's always new things to try, Carter."

The sincerity and belief in Ian's voice were undeniable.

"I thought I could just...you know. Hold it in. And it would...dissipate?" Carter shook his head because now, only a few hours later, he could see how stupid that was. How asinine and doomed to fail he'd been. "If I could just hold it in and get to you, I could let it out. But that didn't work."

"No," Ian said gently.

"I just felt...I don't know...*dumb*. A big dumb football player, repeating his feelings out loud."

"But it helps."

Carter hadn't tried it so he couldn't say. And that was the whole problem, wasn't it? He'd been afraid to try it. Afraid it wouldn't work. Afraid he'd lose it, right there on the sideline, and doom his team to another loss, when they'd been doomed all along.

It was an ugly, vicious cycle, and one he didn't know how to break.

"This week, I think you and Moira should work on a specific plan for when things go south," Ian suggested gently. "I know she'd be on board with that. You've talked through a number of coping mechanisms with her, but maybe what you really need is a solid plan. Something you can always turn to, no matter what."

Carter considered that. And yeah, in the moment, his brain did feel too slippery to decide on one specific way to deal with it. Maybe what he really did need was a plan. Maybe he wouldn't go into that panic spiral of *what-if* if he knew exactly what he was doing.

"That's a good suggestion," Carter finally said.

"Good." Ian nodded. "Now, let's talk about what happened."

"Are you telling me we're not going to have sex any time soon?" Carter felt almost ashamed asking the question, but if sex was going to be off the table again, he needed to know. Plus, he was going to need to stretch out his right hand, because it was about to get a lot of action.

But if that was what Ian thought they needed to do, he'd deal with it, because he could live without sex, but losing Ian was not an option.

"No," Ian said, shooting him a grin so wide it popped one of his dimples.

"Oh, thank God," Carter said, sinking back into the seat with relief.

Ian laughed. "You're calm now. You wouldn't be using sex as a stress or anger release valve. We'd just be having sex."

"Please say *sex* again," Carter begged.

Ian kept laughing, and it was the best sound in the whole world.

"I know," Carter said. "I'm adorable, right? Completely, totally irresistible. You want to pull this car over right now and—"

Ian gripped Carter's knee harder. "No," he said. "I want to get home and then let you push me back against that wall again."

Carter groaned. "You're freaking killing me."

Ian pulled down the driveway that led to the house. "Somehow," he said, "I think you're gonna survive the next two minutes."

"I don't know," Carter threatened.

"Well, you're gonna have to. Because I want to say this first, before we get inside." Ian pulled into the garage and turned the car off but didn't move a muscle.

"Fine, *fine*," Carter said. "As long as we get to go inside and—"

"I promise," Ian said, the corners of his lips quirking into a smile. "I stopped us earlier not because I don't want you, because I do, or because I don't care about you, because I think you know I do."

"You did it because it's not supposed to be that way between us," Carter said, before Ian could.

Somehow it was more palatable acknowledging his own error than having Ian call it out.

Moira would probably tell him that was character development.

"Right, it's not." Ian was still smiling over at him.

The way Ian looked at him made him feel a million feet tall and like he could in fact, *do* this.

"Can I..." Carter cleared his throat, suddenly more emotional than he could remember being in well...*ever*. "Can I show you how it's supposed to be?"

Ian nodded.

Carter slipped out of the car and was around to Ian's side before he could climb out. He bent down and kissed Ian more gently than he'd ever imagined he would. Before, he'd thought that every time they came together there would be fireworks and shooting stars and the kind of explosive passion that meant they'd already waited too long for each other.

But it didn't feel that way tonight.

Yeah, he wanted Ian. He *always* wanted Ian.

But this was softer, quieter. Less painfully desperate.

Ian's mouth opened under his, and their tongues brushed.

They kissed like that for a long time, Carter leaning into the car, Ian straining up to meet him. Then Carter finally reached down and flicked his seat belt off and scooped him right up.

"What are you doing?" Ian asked, but he said it softly, with stars in his eyes as Carter carried him into the house. "You shouldn't...you played today..."

"Like you weigh anything," Carter grumbled right back.

Ian smacked him lightly in the arm, but he was smiling. "I weigh *enough*, okay?"

"You're perfect. Absolutely fucking perfect."

"You say that like you're not the most gorgeous person anyone has ever seen, like *ever*," Ian retorted, his hands roaming Carter's back and then dipping lower. Carter nearly stumbled as Ian's fingertips dug into his ass.

"When you say that, I *almost* believe it," Carter said, his breath coming a little short as he made it to the top of the stairs. Ian wasn't heavy, not exactly, but the closer they got to the bedroom, the more distracted and the more aroused he got.

"Let me show you," Ian said, and the moment they crossed over the threshold into his bedroom, Ian slipped from his grip like it was nothing, and knelt at his feet, reaching up to tug open his belt and his pants.

Carter gasped as Ian made short work of his clothes, tugging down his tight briefs, his hard cock bobbing out of the fabric.

Jesus, how many fantasies had he had like this?

But he'd *said*—but not only that, he'd *thought*...

"Wait," Carter croaked out as Ian's tongue teasingly circled the tip of his cock. God, he wanted to be in his mouth more than he wanted his next breath. But he'd had a *plan*.

"You don't want this?" Ian's mouth was so hot and wet as it moved around him.

Carter groaned. "No, no, I do. I really fucking do. But I said—"

"I kinda thought what you meant," Ian said casually, like he wasn't blowing Carter's mind and Carter's dick between every word, "was that we'd give each other pleasure. That's the way it's supposed to be between us. Just you and me, making each other feel good."

"Yeah, *that*," Carter croaked as Ian took him deeper, tongue caressing the sensitive underside, his fingers stroking his balls in just the way he liked.

God, Ian's mouth was everything he'd ever dreamt of, and so much more.

Carter's hands drifted down, and he tangled them in Ian's hair, not pushing him, not even guiding him, just wanting to feel him as much as he could. Grounding himself in the reminder that this was *Ian*, the man he was completely fucking crazy about.

He'd love him even if he wasn't this good at sucking cock.

But bonus points to Carter, he was *amazing* at it. And extra super duper brownie points, he seemed to love it just as much as Carter did, his mouth working over him eagerly, as he reached down to stroke himself, like he couldn't handle how good it made *him* feel.

"That good, baby?" Carter crooned, barely able to form the words.

Ian groaned around his dick, and God, didn't that make him even harder?

How could he have thought sex was good before this?

Nothing had ever been as unbelievable as this slow, intimate blowjob.

Then Ian pulled off, lips red and wet, panting a little, and somehow that was now the hottest thing Carter had ever seen.

He didn't know how Ian kept managing to top himself, but Carter certainly wasn't going to argue with it.

"Bed. *Now*," Ian directed.

"I like this bossy you," Carter said, as he shuffled backward, his knees hitting the edge of the mattress. "It's hot."

He liked it even more when Ian detoured to the drawer for the lube and came back with determination and lust shining in his eyes.

That look was all for Carter; he'd eat it all up and then ask—no, *beg*—for seconds.

"You said you wanted to," Ian said cautiously, as he slid his lube-slick fingers across Carter's balls again, making him groan. "You still want me to fuck you?"

"Yes," Carter said emphatically. "*Yes*. Finger me open while you suck my dick, baby."

Ian didn't need any more directions. His touch was confident as his fingertips circled Carter's hole, tongue just brushing the tip of his cock, and he slid a finger in just as Ian took him deep into his mouth again.

"Fuck," Carter cried out. He loved doing this—but he didn't do it with just anyone. There was a basic level of trust he needed to let someone into his body.

But Ian was already there; had been there ages ago.

In his body. In his mind. In his *heart*.

So deep Carter couldn't imagine him not being there.

When Ian was two fingers deep inside him, thrusting in and out at a slightly different pace than his sucks, a difference that put him deliciously off-balance, never sure where the pleasure was going to come from, Carter mumbled, "Can you...*now?*"

Ian glanced up at him, pupils blown, but obvious concern on his face.

"But—" Ian said.

"I wanna feel it. Wanna feel you," Carter slurred. He was pretty far gone, and while coming down Ian's throat was a pretty fantastic way to end this, he wanted *more*.

"Anything you want, baby." Ian's voice was hushed and for the first time, when he used the nickname, it didn't have that sly slant to it, but it felt *real*.

Carter dug his fingers into the bedding as he scooted farther up onto the bed, watching as Ian shed his clothes. How had he gotten this lucky? This gorgeous guy and all his kindness and humor and light was *his*.

And he was going to fuck him, and Carter already knew it would be amazing, because already this was the best sex of his life.

"Wanna feel you all around me," Carter said quietly, as Ian finished putting the condom on and crawled onto the bed.

"Anything," Ian repeated softly and leaned down, kissing him firmly.

Ian's cock was gorgeous, just like the rest of him, perfectly proportional, which meant it was slightly smaller than Carter's—but it still felt huge as Ian pressed against his hole, and it slowly gave way.

Whenever Carter did this, which was not very often, he liked to feel it the next day. Liked it to burn a little. He loved how the sharp bite of pain offset and complemented all that pleasure. And it was sliding through him now, as Ian pushed inside.

"Fuck, you feel amazing," Ian murmured under his breath.

Carter's eyes fluttered open and he watched as Ian reached down, hand pressing against his chest. Grounding both of them. He reached up and gripped it.

He'd known he could always count on Ian to be there.

But today? Today had proven it.

"Love you," he said, and meant it.

Ian's eyes widened, but he didn't stop. Kept pushing in, until he was breathing hard from the control he was exerting to not just fuck Carter like his life depended on it.

"I'm good," Carter murmured as he reached up, stroking Ian's arms, his chest, his neck. Anywhere he could reach.

Nothing had ever felt as good as Ian inside him—finally physically as well as mentally, emotionally.

"Touch yourself," Ian gasped out as he began to move faster.

Carter didn't let go of Ian—instead, he reached down, and with his other hand circled his cock. His back bowed with the pleasure sizzling in a hard jagged line up his spine.

Ian moved his hips in a sinuous pattern, somehow thrusting into Carter both hard enough he'd feel it tomorrow and gentle enough he felt like something unbearably precious, his cock hitting that spot inside him over and over again, until Carter felt like one raw nerve. He hadn't been wrong—Ian knew how to fuck. Knew how to fuck *him*. How to make him want to beg for it, crawl for it, but Carter knew he never would. Knew this would always, *always*, be freely given and taken between them.

All it would take was a few more strokes to come, and he wanted to do it, so fucking badly, but he also wanted to wait for Ian.

"Come on," Carter panted. "*Harder.*"

Gripped his cock at the same time as Ian let loose, fucking into him with purpose, sending Carter right over the edge into ecstasy.

"*Yes*, baby," Ian cried out as Carter clenched around him, pulling him right along with him.

Carter gasped out as he came again and again, stripes of come splattering up his chest, hitting their hands as they clasped together firmly.

Like they weren't ever letting each other go.

Ian half-collapsed onto him, breathing hard.

"Wow," he said after a long moment of silence, wide green eyes blinking open slowly, meeting Carter's gaze.

"Yeah," Carter agreed.

He knew what he'd said.

Maybe Ian would think he didn't really mean it, since he'd said it during sex. Sex so good it felt life-changing.

But he'd meant it then, and he meant it now.

"I gotta clean up," Ian stuttered out as he slowly pulled out.

"Quick. Then come back to bed," Carter ordered.

Ian didn't need his encouragement to do that, though. He was back in a flash, minus the condom, and with a damp washcloth he used to carefully clean Carter.

Then he collapsed onto the bed next to him, and cuddled into his chest, Carter putting an arm around him and tugging him in even closer.

For a few long minutes, neither of them said anything.

Carter wondered if he *should* clarify that *yes*, he'd meant it.

But then he hesitated, because maybe clarifying it took something away from the moment. He'd said it, of course he fucking meant it. Surely Ian had to know that.

Before he could decide one way or the other, if he should say *yes, I meant it* or something else totally meaningless, Ian spoke first.

"I love you, too," Ian said.

Carter twisted so he could look Ian in the eyes. See his face when he said those words. So many people wanted him, thought they cared about him, but who, other than his beloved late grandmother, had ever *loved* him?

Nobody, as far as Carter could figure out.

Ian was smiling, soft and fond.

"Yeah?" Carter asked, breathlessly.

Worried, almost, that Ian would take it back, but he knew, deep down, that he wouldn't. That he meant it, same as Carter did.

That somehow he also knew, even from that first meeting, when Carter had wished Alec had sent someone way less hot, and way less cold, that they'd end up here.

"Yeah," Ian said.

Carter settled back down, but tugged Ian even closer until he was half-sprawled against his chest. "Imagine that," he said softly.

"I certainly never did," Ian said, "but it feels sort of inevitable, doesn't it? I was the worst person in the world for you to fall for. And here I was, supposed to keep you *from* having sex. Not convince you it was the best idea in the world to have it with me."

"But it was," Carter said. "The very best idea in the world."

Ian laughed, which Carter took to mean he definitely agreed.

"I think," Carter said softly, "that my grandmother would've loved you."

Ian didn't say anything right away, just squeezed Carter's arm extra tight. "I bet," he finally said, "I would've loved her too. Just like I love her grandson."

Carter didn't mention his parents, though, because there was no need to bring their imperfectness into such a beautifully perfect moment.

Ian would have to meet them eventually—but Carter kept hoping it would be later, rather than sooner.

Boundaries, Moira kept echoing in his head, and Carter decided that was enough of a good reason to push them right back out of his head again. Where they belonged. On the outside.

Instead, he wanted to welcome in everyone who'd taken their place. Who'd become his *real* family.

"Let's host everyone tomorrow, here," Carter said sleepily.

"What?" Ian, however, did not sound sleepy. Not after Carter had just made that suggestion.

"I mean it," Carter said, stroking his back, trying to get him to relax again. "I want to gather everyone here. We gotta stick together."

Ian smiled at him. "Are you sure you're Carter Maxwell?"

"Pretty damn sure," Carter said, "and also pretty damn sure I love you."

"Then I suppose we'd better have everyone over," Ian said.

"Give me five minutes, then I'll send some texts," Carter said, closing his eyes.

But less than five minutes later, Carter's phone started beeping away. Once, then twice, and then again.

"What is that?" Ian asked, sitting up.

"One sec," Carter said, groaning as he shifted out of bed.

He found his phone in the pocket of his discarded slacks and scrolled through the messages, sitting down on the edge of the bed when it turned out there were even more than he'd realized.

"Everything okay?" Ian asked, coming up behind him, and hooking his chin over Carter's shoulder. Carter could feel the warmth of him all along his back and even though it felt like he'd just come his brains out, he already wanted him all over again.

"Micah and Beck are hosting a get together at their place tomorrow." Carter didn't want to whine about it, but at the same time he sort of *did.* That was what he'd been about to do, and Micah and Beck had beaten him to the punch.

"Okay, so that's cool," Ian said.

When Carter didn't say anything, Ian poked him in the side. "It *is* cool," he repeated.

"Yeah, I guess," Carter said.

"You wanted to do it, instead."

He'd be lying if he said he didn't—and yet admitting to something ugly and painful inside him if he said he *still* did. That he wished he'd gotten *his* text sent before Micah had sent one.

What kind of person did that make him? And while Ian said he loved him, would he continue to feel the same way about him if he knew how just how petty he could be?

"It's okay to admit it," Ian said softly when Carter didn't answer.

"Is it though?" Carter said, running a hand through his hair.

"Yes." Ian tucked an arm around Carter's waist. Hugged him close.

"It feels shitty to admit it though. The last time I held something here, I didn't know it would feel so good when everyone pulled up and they saw this house. Like they were finally seeing the real me, behind all the stupid crap. And I thought they'd see it again, and see *us* together, if we hosted."

"And they won't see us together if we go to Micah and Beck's house?" Ian didn't sound judgmental, but Carter had to wonder all the same.

"Of course they might," he grumped.

"But you wanted it," Ian said. He nuzzled into Carter's back. "I get it. But you know...not everything is about you."

"Ouch," Carter said, laughing weakly. Hoping desperately that Ian didn't think he believed everything was. He could be generous, couldn't he? He thought about other people! He was just about to panic that maybe Ian actually thought otherwise, but then he slipped from his back and moved next to him.

"You mentioned awhile back that Micah and Beck had a lot of shit to sort through, yeah? Before *and* after they got married?" Ian asked.

Carter nodded but still tried to look away. Not meet Ian's eyes.

What if he saw the truth of him? What if he saw the truth *and* didn't like what it was?

"Then, there you go," Ian said. "They need this, maybe, more than you. To show their united front. We can go with our own, and maybe later in the season, we'll have something else here."

"How are you so smart and reasonable?" Carter grumbled, but already he was smiling again. Less worried than he'd been only a moment ago.

"I had to be," Ian said wryly. "First, because if I didn't, Moira would therapy me, and second because if I didn't, then my clients might be in jeopardy. And I couldn't face that, if I was even partially responsible for them not staying sober."

"She therapy you a lot when you were growing up?" Carter asked.

Ian chuckled. "All the freaking time."

"I knew she was good, 'cause she *has* helped me a lot," Carter said seriously, "but if she helped you turn into the guy you are today, then she's even better than I imagined."

Ian looked very pleased at this. "Yeah?"

"Yeah, you're amazing," Carter said, and pulled him into a tight embrace. "And," Carter continued, as he let go of him, finally, "you're especially cute when you blush."

"Text Micah and tell him we'll both be there," Ian ordered, but it was undeniable, he *was* blushing, and it was absolutely adorable.

Chapter 19

When Ian and Carter arrived at Micah and Beck's house, Ian didn't know what to expect, or if any of this was even a good idea—though he hoped it was.

He remembered, all too clearly, some of the disgruntled and disappointed faces from yesterday after the game.

But the moment Riley arrived, coming out onto the wide patio behind Beck and Micah's house, a wide smile on his face when he spotted Carter, Ian knew he'd been stupid to worry.

Carter had been right; this *was* exactly what everyone needed.

"Hey, man, how you feelin'?" Carter asked as Riley and Landry approached. "Ribs okay?"

"They're a little sore," Riley admitted, but he was still smiling. "Not sore enough that I can't give you a hug, though."

"Good." Carter beamed, reaching down and pulling Riley gently into his embrace.

"I'm not sure whether I'm relieved or disappointed you stopped trying to grope him when you do that," Landry observed.

"Come on, you miss being a little bit jealous," Carter teased. "I bet your sex life isn't even as good as it used to be, now that I've stopped."

Riley shot Carter an unimpressed look, then his gaze moved to Ian. "Do you think it would hurt his feelings if I told him he had absolutely *zero* impact on our sex life?"

"What?" Carter exclaimed. "Zero!"

"None, nada, nothing," Landry chimed in.

"That's..." Carter spluttered, looking comically outraged.

Ian grinned. "Don't worry, I think he'll live."

Carter tucked an arm around Ian and tugged him tightly against his side. "Only 'cause I've got you," he murmured, gazing down at him.

"Exactly," Riley said, nodding approvingly.

"Hey, Riley," Beck said as he and Micah walked over to them. "I didn't realize you and Landry had gotten here."

"We snuck in," Riley said, a mischievous smile on his face.

"Beck's very proud of his grass, so make sure to admire it," Micah teased.

Not for the first time, Ian was surprised at how comfortable and familiar he and Beck were with each other. Considering Carter had told him only a few months ago that Beck had been furious Micah had been traded to the Condors. That he hadn't wanted him there at all.

And now they were not only happy and together, they were *married*.

That was a pretty big adjustment. But then hadn't he and Carter gotten very familiar and easy with each other? Didn't it feel like they'd always been together even though he'd been here in Charleston for only a month?

Riley and Landry took off with Beck to check out the extensive grounds surrounding the house, while Micah headed towards the front to greet Cole and Nick, who'd just walked in.

Ian turned to Carter. "Babe, you're just going to have to get used to the idea you're no longer impacting everyone else's sex life."

Carter made a face. "Can I keep impacting yours?"

"I sure hope you do."

"Then, you got it right earlier. I'll live." Carter grinned. Dipped his head low. Brushed a kiss across Ian's mouth. It still felt amazing every time Ian got to be close to him. To see his handsome face tucked so close to his own. To know that Carter was *his*.

It was unbelievable that Carter actually worried Ian would find out something about him that he didn't like. Didn't Carter see that to Ian, he was basically an open book? And all the things that made him human—that made him *real*, and not just a famous guy Ian might see on TV or on a billboard—only made him more attractive? Meanwhile, Ian couldn't help but think sometimes that he was just some ordinary guy, and one day Carter was going to wake up and realize that.

"You know, of all the guys I pictured looking *that* happy to be with someone, you weren't even adjacent to the list."

Ian glanced over and Deacon was standing there, smiling, a beer in one hand.

"I'll give you that," Carter agreed, straightening. Carter let go of him, but then hesitated, and Ian didn't know if it was because of what Deacon had said, or because of yesterday.

Surely Carter was not still feeling responsible?

It had been a bad matchup, one the Condors' defense had even discovered during practice that week. Eventually, Ian knew the coaching staff would find a way around the problem, but of course, that didn't mean it felt *good* to have lost.

"You here alone?" Ian asked, trying to smooth things over.

Deacon shot him a look. "Who else would I have come with? Jem? He's already back home for the holidays. Going to be some big shot in this parade thing. Like riding right at the front, on a float and everything. He's even going before Santa."

"You know who he means," Carter said, "and it's *not* Jem. He's your best friend. Mr. G is...well, what exactly *is* Mr. G?"

"The owner of this football team," Deacon said firmly, but even Ian could see that something else flickered in his eyes at the mention of Mr. G.

"*And?*" Carter prompted. "Are you really trying to claim there's just business between you two?"

"What else could there be?" Deacon retorted lightly.

"But you're *retiring*," Carter murmured under his breath. "You could—"

"No," Deacon said firmly. "Just don't go there."

"Are you really trying to claim you don't know him?" Carter pressed.

"I never said that," Deacon said and then looked closer at Carter. "Whatever you think you know—"

Carter pounced on that. "What do *you* think I know?"

Deacon threw up his hands and turned to Ian. "Officially, you're a saint for agreeing to put up with this one."

"It's definitely never been boring," Ian said.

But there was something about the way Deacon had changed the subject when Carter had specifically said, *are you really trying to claim you don't know him*, that bothered him.

But it was impossible to say what it was exactly that had made Deacon recoil.

Ian decided he would probably never know.

An hour later, the tacos and burritos Micah and Beck had ordered in were demolished, and a big group of them were lounging around on the patio, the sun setting behind the house as they all shared one final beer before heading home, discussing the upcoming week, which happened to be Thanksgiving.

"So, where's your family going this year for the holidays?" Beck asked Landry. "They coming here?"

"Yep," Landry said. "Technically it was supposed to be Levi's year, but my dad claimed Seattle in November was miserable—and he's not wrong, there—but I think what really changed their mind was how much they wanted to meet Riley."

Riley made a face. "No pressure or anything. Just your beloved parents and your twin sister. That's all."

"Oh, they're gonna *love* you," Micah teased. "They've practically adopted Dylan, so I think you're golden."

"Who's Dylan?" Beck asked.

"Oh, that's his brother Logan's boyfriend. He's the kicker for the Piranhas," Micah said, nudging his husband. "I *told* you about him."

"Oh, yeah, that's right," Beck said.

"Ugh," Riley whined. "Like I said, *all that pressure.*"

"You cooking the dinner?" Carter wanted to know.

"No, he's definitely not going to be cooking because he's going to be *quarterbacking*," Landry said. "We'll order it catered. Have our big meal after the game."

Ian realized earlier that *yes*, it was Thanksgiving. Not only was the game this week early, falling on Thursday, it also happened to be a Thanksgiving Day game.

No wonder his mom had texted him and asked what he was doing this week.

He'd thought it had just been a way for her reach out and check on Carter without specifically asking about Carter, but no, she'd been asking something else entirely.

Like what he was doing for Thanksgiving.

"Micah's mom and my family are flying in," Beck said, his arm flung casually around Micah's back. They exchanged a soft private smile.

"You're all getting along these days?" Carter asked.

Micah nodded. "It's slow going, trusting her again, but we're getting there. Her coming here for Thanksgiving, with Beck's family, is a big deal."

"Our first blended family holiday," Beck said, sounding excited about it.

Ian wondered then if he should have *one*, realized earlier that this week was actually a holiday, and *two*, invited his mother out, at least once he and Carter had made their relationship official.

But then, that might've been very weird, as neither of them were quite used to the fact Moira was both Carter's therapist *and* his boyfriend's mother.

"What about your parents, Carter?" Landry asked. "Are they coming?"

"No," Carter said, with finality, and his expression shuttered.

Ian knew he wasn't close to them, and from the little Carter had said about them that he'd had problems with them growing up. From the session notes Moira sent to both him and Alec, he knew she'd advocated for Carter to establish boundaries with them, but he hadn't ever read any closer into the details, because he'd always wanted *Carter* to tell him. Not to read about it in his mother's impersonal files.

It sounded like maybe that conversation was going to be tougher than Ian had expected it would be.

"I know if anyone's at a loose end, Grant said he'd be hosting a dinner at the stadium after the game," Deacon said.

Carter shot him a look, but Deacon didn't engage, just glanced away.

"And," Deacon continued, standing, setting his empty beer bottle on the coffee table in front of him, "I wanted to say a few things before we break up for the night. It's been such a fucking privilege to play here with you this year. I know last year was a dumpster fire—a lot of us got to experience that firsthand, and the rest of you have heard plenty of stories—but this year, this year has been so great."

"A breath of fresh air," Beck agreed, lifting his beer bottle in mock salute.

"Anyway, I just wanted to say, no matter what happens with the Condors this year," Deacon said, "it's been an honor. Absolutely my honor. I didn't want to come back if it didn't mean something, and you've made it mean something. Every single one of you. So for that, thanks. For making my very last year mean something."

There was a round of gasps.

"Yeah," Deacon added wryly, "you heard me right. This is my last year. Gonna be hanging it up after this, but I didn't want to go out like last season was. Instead, we've made some damn good memories together. Ones I'll never forget." He grabbed his bottle and raised it. "Fly, Condors, fly!"

And around the patio, hand after hand went up, full of beers and glasses and water bottles, every single player there, more than half the team saluting their defensive captain and the guy who had defended them, through thick and thin, through the worst of the old regime.

Who'd stood by them when nobody believed in their redemption.

When only one man had believed, and now he was telling them that he was calling it quits.

"We're gonna make it a good one, I promise," Riley said, standing up and embracing Deacon. "I *promise*."

"You know what?" Deacon said to Riley. "You already have."

Half an hour later, they were driving home when Ian turned to Carter, his brain still working at what Carter had said—or *not* said—about his parents coming for the holiday.

"What do *you* want to do for Thanksgiving?" Ian asked. "Besides play in the game and kick the Cowboys' ass, of course."

"I sort of expected that we'd spend it just the two of us," Carter said after a long, awkward silence. "Or, we could go to the dinner thing Mr. G's throwing together. Might be fun. Might be a good opportunity to tease the hell out of Deacon." He was silent again for a long moment. "Not that many chances left to do that."

"It's not like you'll never see him again. No way he's not involved in some form with the Condors next year. Maybe Coach K will hire him to be an assistant coach. Or Mr. G will make him a scout."

Carter waggled his eyebrows. "Or maybe Mr. G will just make him a husband."

"Be serious." Ian had noticed the vibes between Deacon and the Condors' owner too—it was kind of hard to miss them once you spotted them—but that was a lot to assume, even for Carter.

"I am! He's not gonna be Deacon's boss anymore. He's got no control over him after he retires. Frankly he's got no control over him right now, if he's planning on calling it quits. If they like each other, why not do something about it?"

Ian shot Carter a knowing look. "You know why. Shit's complicated, sometimes. Don't interfere."

"Even when I'm so good at interfering?" Carter grinned.

"Even then. *Especially* then," Ian said and he was chuckling now, because he just couldn't help it.

"I helped you know, with Beck and Micah. If I hadn't offered to have sex with Beck—"

"You were *not* going to have sex with Beck," Ian interrupted, feeling very sure that he was right.

"Well, *no*, though I guess if he had said yes, I wouldn't have exactly complained..." Carter trailed off, the corner of his mouth tilting up.

The way Carter was teasing him wasn't cute at all. Nope. Not at all.

He had not, even in the slightest, charmed Ian's pants right off. Except...

"Don't worry, baby," Carter continued to tease. "It's you I really want."

Ian rolled his eyes, but yep, he was charmed. He was almost surprised to find that when he glanced down, his pants were, in fact, *still* on.

"So how did you offering to have sex with Beck somehow convince him and Micah to settle their differences?" Ian asked.

"Micah got jealous, of course," Carter said, like *duh*, that was exactly why.

"Well, I sort of thought they got together because they'd always had a thing for each other," Ian joked, "but if you really made Micah *that* jealous, you should definitely take all the credit."

Carter smiled and pulled the car into the garage. "Glad you can finally see it," he said with the cutest smirk. "So, you good going to the team thing for Thanksgiving?"

"Yeah, whatever you want," Ian said. Hesitated. "I guess I could have asked my mom to come out here. But that might've been a lot to deal with. Especially since we're just sort of figuring this relationship stuff out."

Carter was still smiling. "You mean, *I'm* still figuring this relationship stuff out."

Ian reached over and grabbed his hand. Squeezed it. "Yeah," he said.

"It's alright." Carter shrugged. "It's just Thanksgiving."

"Is that why your parents aren't coming?" Ian regretted asking the question the moment it was out of his mouth, because Carter's expression froze.

"No."

The one word Carter uttered sounded final, but Ian waited because he'd gotten to know Carter well enough by now to know there was going to be another shoe and it was going to drop. He just had to wait.

Sure enough, a minute later Carter said, "Really, they're not coming because they're self-centered, smug, obnoxious assholes who've only wanted me to be a different person my whole fucking life. Who, for longer stretches of time than anyone can imagine, literally forgot I existed. Until I became rich and famous, and now they can't get enough of me."

Ian had known a revelation like this was coming, but hearing the words and seeing the look on Carter's face as he said them—the bleak acceptance, like he knew it wouldn't ever be different, as much as he'd always hoped otherwise—hit hard.

"God, baby," Ian said and unbuckled his seat belt, sliding over as far as he could, wrapping his arms around Carter's neck and hugging him tightly.

"I kinda thought you knew," Carter mumbled into his shoulder.

"I knew they were an issue, but I didn't know all of it," Ian said, pulling back a little so he could meet Carter's gaze. "I didn't want to learn from Moira's notes. I wanted *you* to tell me, when you were ready."

"Even when you weren't my boyfriend?"

"Carter," Ian said seriously, "even when I wasn't your boyfriend, I still wanted to be. More than anything."

"You really mean that, even when I'm..." Carter gestured at himself. "My fucked-up self?"

Ian gently smacked him on the side of the head. "You're not fucked-up. Don't say that. You're perfect—and even more than that, you're perfect for me. Don't forget that, okay?"

Carter nodded. "Got it."

"I know you don't want to, but we *do* need to talk about the boundaries again," Moira said firmly, her expression on Carter's laptop never wavering.

"Do we have to?" Carter complained. They'd already spent the last forty minutes putting together a very specific crisis plan, with several detailed steps, for the next time he found himself in a difficult situation.

When he'd first logged on to their call—ducking into an empty meeting room while most of the team and staff were eating lunch before practice—she'd been surprisingly sympathetic about what had happened during the game and after.

"You're going to have bumps in the road," she'd insisted.

"But what I did to Ian," Carter had insisted, for the first time not wanting to go into details with Moira, even though she should probably hear all of them. Not because he was ashamed of the sex they shared, but what if she judged him as Ian's mother?

No, he reminded himself. *You're choosing this. She doesn't feel like you're hopeless. The only person who feels like you're hopeless is you.*

"Ian is a grown man," Moira said, and he heard the words she wasn't saying, *and he knows what he's doing. What he wants. And clearly, what he wants is you.*

In the end, she proved both of them right. First, Carter for sticking with her even though everyone had told him to find someone new. And her, for steering him away from a shame spiral. Instead of self-recrimination, they'd spent the session focusing on the positive and developing a real plan for when he went off the rails, again.

"Because it's inevitable," she reminded him. "And nothing to be ashamed of, if you do."

It had been a surprisingly good session. Productive in a way Carter hadn't expected. And then she'd thrown the *b* word in again.

Boundaries.

"I didn't have a meltdown because of *them*," Carter continued. Even though he knew it was probably pointless to argue with her.

"I didn't think you did, but we've talked about why they impact what you're doing now, even if your parents aren't directly involved," Moira said firmly.

Carter considered this again. The problem was he *hated* thinking about his parents. Even though, *yes*, she was probably right. So much of what he'd been, what he'd created of himself, was in direct response to their bullshit.

Or complete lack of bullshit.

Sometimes, he'd just wanted nothing more than for them to fucking *look* his way, but all he'd ever gotten was their apathy.

Was it any wonder he'd done anything he could to draw their attention, even if it was entirely negative?

"It's funny," Carter said slowly, "I hate them. I hate thinking about them. But even still...I can see so much of who I am comes from them." He paused. "God, I hate that."

For a split second, he wanted nothing more than to just throw everything he was out with the trash. But it couldn't all be bad, right? If it was, Ian wouldn't look at him in that approving way. He wouldn't have the friends he had now, in his teammates. The Condors wouldn't have traded for him.

There was *value* in him, even if the way he'd gone about grabbing it was all wrong.

Moira's gaze softened. "Maybe who you are was shaped by them, yes, but that doesn't mean who you are is wrong, Carter. I look at you and I see a man who's built a very successful life. Who's liked wherever he goes. Who's carved out a position where he's valued and appreciated. Who found someone to care about, who cares about you in return. You could have just settled, but instead you're taking steps to better yourself. To become the best version of yourself. That's not something your parents created. That's something *you* made."

Carter wanted to believe it was true. "I don't know…" he said, hesitating.

"Don't give them too much credit, or yourself not enough," she retorted sternly. "They're not around. I'm assuming, not for some time."

"They like to pop back up just when I think I've finally shed them for good," Carter complained. "It's nice for them to have a son who's Carter Maxwell."

"Then let's really talk about the nitty-gritty of you establishing those boundaries," Moira insisted. "For when they *do* pop up, because you just admitted they might."

"They might," Carter hedged, and goddamn, he hated to even *think* about the possibility, never mind talk about it, but maybe Moira was right.

She'd been so right about so many other things.

Which…

"Thank you," Carter said in a rush before he could overthink it.

She raised an eyebrow. "You're welcome?"

"For everything," Carter said, more confidently now. "You didn't judge. You listened. You…you made me *make sense*, for the first time ever."

"Carter," Moira said softly, "you've always made sense. But you're very welcome. I'm glad…I'm glad you deciding to be with Ian didn't change anything about our relationship."

"I guess I should be thanking *you* for that, too," Carter said wryly.

She smiled. "It's not been easy for me, either, but I saw how much value you were getting out of our time together, and just like I want the best for him, I want the best for you, too." She paused. "Which are these boundaries."

Carter couldn't help it; he threw his head back and laughed. "You know," he said, when he could finally stop chuckling, "you and Ian are *very* alike. Both sneaky. And *very* stubborn."

"I've heard that," Moira said, sounding amused.

"So, boundaries. That means I tell them to get the fuck out, right? I never talk to them again? I hang up whenever they call? Block their number?"

If that was true, Carter thought that sounded fucking fantastic. Of course, there was *doing* it, which was always his sticking point. He'd craved their attention and their care for so long, and gone without it for all that time, that there was always the hope, buried under all the certainty they sucked, that they might finally give him what he wanted, after all.

And even when they never did, it didn't make it any easier the next time they came around.

He was still tempted to give in to that voice that claimed it might be different *this* time.

"No, that's not what boundaries are. Ignoring them and not making sure they know the limits of your relationship is not the solution." Moira paused. "Think about this. When you picture them in your life, where are they at? Not how they are right now, or how they *have* been in your life, but where they'd be in your ideal life?"

Carter closed his eyes and thought of that life.

It was so easy to see it.

Ian might be a recent addition to it, but he was right there, in the center, right next to Carter. Loving him. Supporting him. Letting Carter love and support him right back. Being his most brilliant, intelligent, funny, and beautiful self.

His teammates and friends were there, surrounding them in a circle.

And where were his parents?

Way out on the edge. Maybe they were technically present, close enough he could keep tabs on them, but so far away they couldn't touch him, and he *liked* that.

He didn't desperately crave their attention anymore, because he didn't need it. He got everything he needed from the man next to him and their friends. The love in the circle was enough.

He was enough.

Carter opened his eyes. "Wow," he said softly. "I do see it. They're there, right, because they don't just go away. But...they don't impact me. And I'm not only okay with it, I made that happen. I put them there and kept them where they couldn't affect me anymore."

"Exactly. So let's talk about exactly how we make that happen. I know you like specifics, so we're going to go into specifics. A *plan*."

"I like a plan," Carter said and discovered that was actually true. He did. Never had before, but now he could see the advantages of having one in place.

It felt reassuring in a way he hadn't even realized he needed.

But Ian had known.

God, he loved that man.

How much had he been missing out by not loving anyone before this, when it felt so goddamn good? So freaking satisfying?

But then, Carter realized, it wouldn't feel that way with anyone else. It had to be Ian; it would *only* feel that way with him.

"How do you feel about that plan?" Moira said after they'd finished discussing it.

"I feel..." Carter considered it, really took his time deciding. "I feel good about it. I feel like I can do it. Might take some time to really come to terms with *wanting* to do it."

"That's the key," Moira said.

"I'm gonna get there though," Carter said.

"If you can see it in your head, then just remember that, every time you're worried or tempted to let your guard down and think things might be different. Just think of that vision in your head."

"I will," Carter said, nodding. He hesitated, wondering how much he should say. It wasn't just him and Ian navigating their new coupledom, Moira was there, too, in some strange amalgamation of therapist *and* boyfriend's mother, but it felt right to tell her, so he did. "He's there, you know?"

"Ian?" Moira looked pleased, her smile wide.

"Yeah. Yeah, he's there. Not just there, but right next to me. Right in the center of the circle. And...I love him, you know? A whole hell of a lot, it turns out."

Moira actually looked startled. Not unpleasantly, like he'd told her something she didn't want to hear, but actually, the opposite. Like he'd just given her an unexpected gift that she hadn't even realized she wanted.

"That's..." And even more suddenly, she was wiping a tear from her cheek. "That's really beautiful, Carter. I'm so happy for you. For both of you."

"I'm glad," Carter said and meant it.

And if he had to clear his throat a few times after their session ended, well, the only witnesses to it were a few empty chairs and the four walls of the room.

CHAPTER 20

"Practice went better today, then?" Ian asked as Carter walked into the kitchen.

Carter had only walked in the door a minute ago, and hadn't had time to say anything, but he assumed the smile he was wearing was enough for Ian to correctly assess the situation.

Ian leaned down and pulled a pan out from the oven, setting it on top of the stove.

"Aw, baby, you cooked dinner," Carter cooed, and wasted no time circling around the kitchen island to give Ian a nice long kiss.

Ian pulled back after a moment and gave Carter a look. "I threw some salmon in the oven and chopped up some veggies for a salad, if we're going to call that cooking."

"I *definitely* call that cooking, though it would be even better if you were wearing an apron," Carter said, leaning back and giving Ian's body—currently clad in a loose tank and shorts—an assessing look. "*Only* an apron, maybe."

Ian rolled his eyes, but he looked very charmed. Exactly where Carter always wanted him. Fond and affectionate and just plain fucking gooey with it. "Come on, let me get this dished up, and then you can tell me all about what's put you in such a good mood."

"Well, *first*, I scored on Micah today, had a really A plus move that'll probably keep him up half the night," Carter said. He wasn't sure if it would be too mean to do a fist pump at just the thought of how glorious it had been, but then Micah wasn't here, was he?

He fist pumped anyway.

And even better, Ian laughed.

"I'm sorry I missed it," Ian said, as he rummaged around in a drawer for a spatula.

"Hey, you had a meeting. How was that, by the way?" Carter leaned against the counter. He hadn't realized how much he liked the look of Ian making himself at home in Carter's kitchen, but he *did*.

Maybe it was that, maybe it had been that touchdown he scored in practice, but Carter really wanted to score something else right now.

Screw waiting for dinner.

He was ready for dessert.

"It was really good," Ian said, looking up from scooping the salmon onto two plates he'd already piled with salad. He frowned. "Why are you looking at me like that?"

"Like what?" But Carter already knew how he was looking at Ian.

Like he wanted to eat him alive.

Adrenaline was still rushing through him from the fantastic practice, and nothing made him want to get naked—and get *Ian* naked—more than killing it on the football field.

He didn't think it would matter how long they'd been together like this, it would still be true.

"Don't even start. I made dinner, we're eating it. And *now*, not in an hour, after it's cold," Ian said firmly, but he was smiling as he took the two plates to the table.

"Dang it," Carter said, disappointed, but also not at all. Because even if he couldn't get Ian naked, he'd still get to enjoy sitting with him at his kitchen table, eating food that he'd prepared for them with his own two hands.

It was funny, because a few months ago, he'd have scoffed at spending a quiet evening at home.

But a few months ago, it would've been just him, alone with his thoughts, and even if he and Ian didn't talk at all, Carter knew he wasn't alone anymore.

He was *loved*.

Even now, just sitting here at the table, eating dinner, Ian glancing up at him every other bite, the look in his green eyes fond and affectionate, Carter could feel the warmth of Ian's heart.

It turned out, heat wasn't always necessary. Sometimes just warmth was enough.

"So what else happened that was great at practice? Besides you scoring on Micah and probably fist pumping about it?" Ian asked, as he leaned back in his chair, pushing his can of Diet Coke around in a circle.

"Hey, give me a little credit. I didn't fist pump *then*, 'cause he's still a friend, and I wouldn't disrespect him like that," Carter said.

Ian shot him a look, and this wasn't just warm, it was downright steamy.

Okay then.

Carter shoveled salmon and salad into his mouth faster.

The sooner he finished eating, the sooner he could convince Ian to take all his clothes off.

"You going to tell me?" Ian asked, raising an eyebrow.

Oh yeah. He was supposed to be talking about his great practice.

"We scored every drive we had, against the first team," Carter said. "Landry got in twice. Once on a freaking gorgeous slant pattern. I nearly dropped to my knees right then and there and begged him to…"

That reddish-brown eyebrow raised again. "Begged him to?" Ian questioned.

Carter laughed. "Oh, baby, you know I'm not serious."

"Oh, I *know* that, but I can still be curious."

"If you really wanna know…" Carter leaned forward. So did Ian, his gaze intent and mesmerized. *Oh yeah, baby, I got you right where I want you.*

Ian licked his lips. "Yeah, I wanna know. What did you want him to do to you?"

Carter opened his mouth, but before he could say anything, the doorbell rang.

"Fuck," Carter exclaimed.

"You wanted him to fuck you?" Ian teased.

"No, *no*," Carter clarified. "This is why I live all the way out here, I hate it when people just show up at my house." He grabbed his phone, which he'd dropped on the table, and found the security app he'd had installed when he moved in.

There was a webcam set to broadcast whenever anyone showed up at the front door. After Carter clicked on it, he stared at the screen in disbelief, sure that he had to be imagining things.

This had to be a dream.

Or a nightmare.

Had all the talk of them today conjured them in front of his door in some kind of reverse fantasy?

"What is it?" Ian must have recognized that it was nothing good from the look on his face, because he was already out of his chair and moving towards Carter. He put a hand on his shoulder and leaned down. "Who are they?"

Carter looked up at him. Met his concerned eyes. "My parents."

"They just *showed up* here?"

"They don't live that far, though clearly it isn't *far enough*," Carter retorted.

"I thought..." Ian hesitated. "I thought you weren't close."

"We're not." Carter could hear how hard his voice was. "We're *not*."

"Then what are they doing here?"

Carter shrugged. "Every so often they remember they have a son and that he's famous and maybe they should spend holidays together, because everyone else on the fucking planet Earth expects that."

"You think that's why they're here? It's Thanksgiving in two days?"

"If I had to guess," Carter said.

Ian stared at him. "Are you going to..." He gestured towards the front door as the doorbell rang again.

It couldn't sound any different, but somehow, still, Carter could *hear* the impatience in the tone.

"I don't want to," Carter said, even though that was probably really freaking obvious.

"Carter," Ian said carefully, reaching down and taking his hands and squeezing them, "you can't leave them out there."

Why not, Carter wanted to scream. *In my vision, they're not here. They're not in this house, not with me. Definitely not with you. They're far away, where they're supposed to be, and there's a wall between us. A hundred walls and I put up every single fucking one of them.*

"Moira said I needed boundaries. Isn't this just boundaries, leaving them out there?"

Ian chuckled. "No," he said.

"Ugh," Carter groaned. "I don't want to deal with them. I just want them to fucking go away. Forget they have a son again."

Ian leaned in. Touched his forehead against Carter's. Squeezed his hands. "I want you to remember that they can only touch you if you let them, okay?"

Carter didn't say anything.

The doorbell chimed again.

"You'll stay, right?" Carter asked, even though of course he would. Even if Ian wasn't here as Carter's boyfriend, he was here to be Carter's support system—and Carter knew he'd never needed it more than he did right now.

"Even if I wasn't supposed to, I would," Ian promised, like he knew exactly where Carter's mind had gone. "And we can tell them whatever you want about me. Everything. Or nothing. It's up to you."

There was part of him that very desperately wanted to brag—*look who loves me, more than you ever could, more than you ever wanted to*—but there was another, louder part, who was terrified of letting his parents' fuckedupness even touch Ian.

Sure, Ian was more than capable of handling it. But because Carter knew how much they could hurt, he *needed* to protect Ian from them.

"Okay," Carter finally said. Reluctantly, he stood.

When he opened the door, dread flooded him.

His mom smiled brightly at him, like they'd been expected.

"Carter!" she exclaimed. "I thought maybe you weren't home, but your father said you would be."

"'Course, you like to go out, but you're not stupid. You're always careful around games," Ted Maxwell said, as Carter opened the screen door, but didn't move out of the way so they could come in.

They'd been in this house exactly once, and it had been a terrible experience. After they'd left, he'd very nearly considered calling in the local hedgewitch to smoke out all the bad vibes they'd brought in.

"Carter!" Elaine exclaimed. "Come on, let us in." She looked over at where Ian was standing. "And who's this?"

But Ian didn't say anything. He was waiting on Carter.

God, he *hated* this.

"Why are you here?" he finally said.

"*Carter*," his mother repeated. "It's Thanksgiving! I sent you an email, didn't you read it? I said we were coming."

"I told you to *text*," Ted hissed over at his wife. "And God, Carter, leaving us out here on the front porch like we're some kind of door-to-door salesmen. We're your *parents*."

"We have a game this week. On Thursday. Thanksgiving." Carter knew he was delaying. Sure, he hadn't let them in. But he hadn't told them to fuck off either.

Why not?

It was just like he'd told Moira yesterday. It was hard to kill that tiny, struggling bit of hope that wanted to believe they'd come for *him*. Really, for him, this time. There was a part of him, still holding out, that still didn't want to close the door on them, literally and figuratively.

"Carter," Elaine chastised. "We're your *family*. It doesn't matter if you have a game or not."

"Though we wouldn't say no to tickets," Ted added with a fake jovial smile that made Carter vaguely nauseated.

He could still hear Moira in his head telling him to *stick to the plan.*

Yesterday, she'd told him in times of crisis, he didn't have to think, he only had to fall back to the plan.

So today, he did just that.

Opened the door, even though his hand shook a little.

"Sure, yeah, come in," Carter said.

They weren't huggers—hadn't ever been, so it was no wonder, Carter realized, that he'd been searching for physical comfort his whole fucking life—so they just walked in with their bags and stood awkwardly in the foyer, both of them still staring at Ian.

"This is Ian," Carter said, more reluctant to go *there* than to even let them into his house.

"You know better than to let some...random guy...come here to your home," Elaine said firmly. She turned to Ian. "It's nice to meet you, but I think you should go."

"Ian's not random and he's not some guy." God, he did not want to do this. He didn't want to give them even a tiny sliver of his life, but they were here, and they were not going to stand there and insult

Ian that way. Not when he was everything. "He's my boyfriend. We're together."

"I mean, we heard the rumors," Elaine said. "But I didn't think they were true. I didn't think you *did* that kind of thing."

"It's not usually like that with you," Tad said, laughing and slapping Carter on the shoulder, like he was actually proud of Carter's reputation.

"It is now," Carter said firmly.

"Nice to meet you," Ian said, and he was scrupulously polite, offering his hand to both his mother and his father to shake, but it was obvious to Carter, under the act, that Ian actually meant the opposite.

"And what do you do?" Elaine asked, because that was, of course, the most important thing. *Who are you? And how much money do you have? If this is actually serious, what can you bring to me long term?*

But she didn't even have to say any of that, because Carter already knew the way her mind worked. He was long familiar with it.

Too familiar.

"I was a sober companion, but I'm actually training to be a sports agent," Ian said.

Ted's expression brightened. *Going to be working with rich and famous people, check.*

"That's...interesting." Elaine was less impressed. Probably because she'd gotten hung up on the "sober companion" part.

Carter had been telling himself for the last five minutes to stick to the plan, and he had, but now that the moment really came, he found himself easing right into the idea of it, not dreading it and not putting it off.

It was just another step in making sure that he preserved that vision he wanted so goddamn badly.

"I'm sorry, but you can't stay here," Carter said, and he tried to copy Ian's *polite but very firm* tone.

"Excuse me?" Ted retorted.

"You can't stay here. I have a game on Thursday and I need my rest and my space to prepare."

Both of them looked shocked. "You catch a ball for a living, Carter," his mother retorted. "It's not like that's very mentally taxing."

"No joke." Ted chuckled. "It's like you're still a kid on a playground."

"You have no idea how difficult it is to do what Carter does on a weekly basis, and be as good at it as he is," Ian said softly.

"And you haven't ever tried. You only came around when it was convenient to you," Carter added. "You can't stay here. You can't show up without talking to me first."

"But I sent an email," Elaine whined.

"And the *tickets*," Ted said.

It was the moment of truth.

You're going to establish the boundary, Moira had said to him just yesterday, *and then they're going to push back. The hard part isn't setting it, the hard part is keeping it there, even under duress. It would be easier to give in. Far less painful. But you won't.*

Except Carter wasn't sure he believed that was true anymore. How could anything be worse than this? He *wanted* that vision, he fucking craved it, with every molecule in his body.

He and Ian at peace, loving and in love, surrounded by people who actually cared about them. His parents, somewhere else, anyplace they couldn't get to him anymore.

In order to preserve that vision, it was so easy to just say, "No." So he said it.

"No," Carter said. "No tickets. No free place to stay. Nothing. I didn't ask you to come. I don't want you to be here. Right now is not a good time for me, and if you cared about that, or me, at all, you'd respect that. But I know you don't, on either count, so I'm going to ask you to leave."

Elaine's jaw dropped. "Carter, we're your parents. We don't have to be *invited*."

"Yes, you do," Carter said firmly. "This is my house, that I paid for, with my very successful career. That I freaking rock at, no matter how silly or stupid you think it is. And if it was really that silly or stupid, you wouldn't even be here, trying to pretend that you're still relevant to me."

"I can't believe your disrespect," Ted said angrily. "How dare you talk to me and your mother this way? You were always a problem child. Always getting into things you shouldn't. Always pushing. Always questioning. And we were there for you, anyway."

"That's not true," Carter said softly. "You pushed me away every day of my life. I was never what you wanted. But you can't do that anymore."

"I think," Ian said in a voice full of steel, "that Carter asked you to leave."

"And, what, *you're* going to kick us out?" Ted laughed, like it was all just a joke. Or a misunderstanding.

But they didn't know Ian like Carter knew Ian.

Didn't know that hidden spine of steel.

Ian whipped out his phone. "No, but I can get the police here in ten minutes, and *they* can kick you out."

Carter smiled. If he looked in the mirror right now, he'd see someone fierce. Someone in control. Someone who wasn't going to be pushed around or dominated or questioned any longer.

Someone who believed in his own worth and was willing to fight to protect it.

"Yep, that is definitely something he can do," Carter agreed. "And none of us want that, so please just go."

"Carter, we are your *parents*," Elaine screeched.

"I'm not saying we won't ever see each other again." Carter paused. "But," he warned, "not like this anymore. Not ever again. Not on your terms. On *mine*."

"Fine, if that's how you're going to be," Ted said. He turned to his wife. "Let's go. He was always this way. Disobedient and respectful. We should've known this was coming."

They didn't look back as they marched to the door and slammed it behind them. Carter enjoyed nothing more than reaching over and locking it behind them.

"Well," Ian said, smiling up at him. "You did it."

"Yeah. *Yeah*," Carter said. And he fist pumped again, for the second time today.

"How did it feel?"

"Good, and well...well, and bad. Because I wanted them to give a shit about me and they don't. I don't have to let that control me anymore, but it doesn't mean it doesn't suck. It doesn't mean it doesn't hurt." Because it did. He still felt a pang. It was less violent, but it still existed.

It would probably always exist, no matter what, but at least now he had ways to deal with it.

And someone who loved him, whom he loved, who'd help him every step of the way.

"You wanna tell me about it?" Ian asked.

"Yeah, yeah, I think I do," Carter said.

For the next hour, they sat on the couch and Carter talked and Ian listened. He hadn't been sure at first how much Carter would be willing to share, but to Ian's surprise, once Carter started telling him about how he'd grown up, with parents who hadn't ever really wanted him, or liked who he was, he hadn't been able to stop.

He'd told him about starting to act out, and how he liked it, at first, because it got him some of the attention he'd always craved. But then, how it had always turned ugly, in the end, because it was never how he wanted it.

He told Ian about his grandmother, and how when she'd died, it had felt like the last thread holding him in place had snapped.

"I'm sure you've heard all of this before, from your mom," Carter said once in an apologetic voice, and Ian had shaken his head emphatically.

"No, I mean, she did mention some things in the notes, but I never read in-depth. I wanted...I wanted you to tell me, someday, when it felt like you were ready to share."

Carter had stared at him, then, like he was too good to be true.

Ian had always felt, nearly from the beginning, that lots of people knew and liked Carter Maxwell. But it was clear very few people had ever gotten close enough to him to really *know* him. And never close enough to love him the way he deserved to be loved.

When Ian said that, Carter looked at him, and said, "You're the only one."

There was a part of Ian that ached for the old Carter, the bright but lonely guy who'd had a thousand friends, but nobody who really gave a shit about him. And another part that was fiercely glad that he could be there for him now.

That he could love him today, and Carter would not only let him, but welcome it, and love him in return.

"I love you," was all Ian could say when Carter finally stopped, his voice falling silent for the first time in nearly an hour. "I love you. I'm proud of you. You survived."

Carter was quiet. Just wrapped an arm around Ian and pulled him tightly against him, and it felt so right to just curl into his touch.

"Yeah, I did. Glad I did, because of now. Didn't think I'd ever say that, but there it is. I'm..." Carter hesitated, like he was feeling out the words. "I'm happy. I'm so fucking happy."

"Me too." It made perfect sense for Ian to show him just how much, so he leaned in and kissed him.

He'd intended to keep it short and sweet, just a reassuring sort of peck. But then Carter swooped in, cupping the back of his neck with a warm, calloused palm and pressed their lips together more firmly. Ian groaned in the back of his throat, and before he could stop himself, he was sliding onto Carter's lap, and they were kissing, open-mouthed and desperate.

"God," Carter said, his voice rough and guttural, as his hips thrust into Ian's, "I want you so goddamn bad."

"Yeah?" Ian considered this and then thrust back, rubbing his hardening cock right against Carter's big muscular thigh. *Jesus, that feels good.* So he did it again. And again.

"Fuck," Carter exclaimed, moving right along with him.

The first time they'd ever kissed, they'd done this, just exactly this, in precisely this spot, and it felt right to do it again.

Back then, Ian had been pretty sure he was falling in love. He wouldn't have broken Alec's rules otherwise. He hadn't been so sure of Carter then, but he should've been.

And now?

He'd never been so sure of anyone else in his whole life.

Carter's hand around his neck gripped him firmer and then his other dropped down to his dick and the perfect pressure of his hand coupled with the feel of Carter's thigh under him had Ian throwing his head back and moaning at how good it was.

"Yeah, baby," Carter murmured to him, his lips dropping down to Ian's throat and he was kissing and sucking there, the pleasure fizzing up until he couldn't do anything else but let go and ride it out.

Carter worked him through it, lips still on his skin, like he didn't want to stop—like he couldn't ever stop, until finally, he shuddered and dropped his head onto Carter's shoulder.

"Good?" Carter murmured into his ear, pressing a tender kiss right under it.

Ian nodded wordlessly.

He could still feel Carter's cock, hard and twitching against his body, and he wanted to make him feel just as good as Carter always made him feel.

So he slid down, kneeling in the V of Carter's legs, and tugged his shorts down. Wrapped his hand around the base of Carter's cock and groaned a little at the first taste of it against his tongue.

"Your mouth is so fucking good," Carter mumbled, hand reaching down and tangling in Ian's hair. Not pushing him, just feeling him. Like all he wanted was just to connect to him as Ian sucked his cock.

Ian worked him deeper, stroking him and reveling in the noises Carter made. Every moan, every half-bitten off word, every gasped *fuck* made him feel bigger and better and more amazing.

He could give Carter this. Give him the comfort of his touch and pleasure enough to white his brain out to forget for a little while what he'd just done.

Carter knew a lot about sex. So much about the nitty-gritty act. But that didn't mean he necessarily knew about loving sex. Ian hoped he was teaching him, a little bit, every single day.

Ian licked up the underside of his cock, teasing him a little before taking him deep again, feeling Carter's cock twitch against his tongue. He knew he was close.

"Shit, yes," Carter breathed out unsteadily, and Ian went for it, squeezing hard as he sucked. Carter tensed and then pulsed down his throat, his body shaking in ecstasy.

"Goddamn," Carter murmured as his dick slipped out of Ian's mouth. "That was so good, baby, thank you."

Ian rested his cheek against Carter's thigh, feeling his fingers tighten in his hair.

"Yeah," he agreed. "I love you."

Carter sighed. "After that, I think I love you even more."

Chapter 21

"There's nothing quite like playing on Thanksgiving Day," Riley said to Carter at halftime.

"That's because you've spent half the game in the giant Salvation Army barrel," Landry teased, referring to the giant prop the charity put on the sideline of every Thanksgiving game. A few years back the Cowboys had started incorporating it into their celebrations, but now it was a tradition. "What do you have now? Three touchdowns?"

The whole team was in a good mood. It had been a short week after a difficult game and they'd worked hard—but practice every day had gone better than Carter could have expected. The team was coming together, driven by determination and also a little, he thought, by Deacon's announcement of his retirement.

Now that they knew their beloved captain wasn't going to be playing after this year, it added another layer of pressure and conviction to what everyone in the building was doing—players and coaches and staff.

The Condors had come out of the tunnel on fire and hadn't stopped once. Five drives in the first half had resulted in four touchdowns, three of which Riley had been directly responsible for.

One he'd run in, one he'd tossed to Landry, and the last one before the end of the half, to Carter—a gorgeous long pass Carter had caught on the run, taking it in for the score after ditching his defender with an instinctual cut.

"Yeah, I'm probably going to get fined for that," Riley said, referring to the barrel-hopping but he was still grinning and didn't sound like he would regret any of the fines. "Maybe I'll donate a matching amount to charity."

He could, now, because Carter had heard a rumor when he'd come into the building Wednesday before the game that the Condors were already negotiating to sign a long-term deal with Riley.

Nobody, Carter decided, deserved it more.

Not even him.

Before this year, he might have had at least a moment's worth of jealousy and envy, because he'd *love* for the Condors to start making noise about extending his own time here in Charleston, but now, he couldn't even dredge up a split second of anything but joy for his friend.

Your time will come, Carter promised himself. It wasn't necessarily easier to sit back and *wait* than it ever had been, and yet, he felt a lot more relaxed about it.

Somehow, he knew the Condors weren't going to be sending him off to another team, a problem that had to be dealt with, rather than a promising player to be embraced.

"Game keeps goin' this way," Coach Oscar said, addressing the loose group of offensive players in the locker room, "don't expect to play much in the fourth quarter."

"Aw," Carter said. "What if we *want* to play?"

Coach Oscar shot him a look. "You having a good time out there, Maxwell?"

"Actually, yeah." What a difference from the week before. Of course, being ahead by three touchdowns really helped his general attitude, but it was more than that too.

Putting together that specific plan with Moira had given him confidence.

And executing another one, when his parents had shown up, had solidified it.

He could do this.

No matter how frustrating or infuriating the game was, Carter felt sure he could handle himself—and once he felt that way, it was amazing just how much he could relax and actually *enjoy* playing again.

"Well, you look good out there. *Real* good," Coach said gruffly, patting him on the shoulder pad. "Best you've looked all year."

"He's sure puttin' on a clinic for us," Landry said, giving Carter an approving nod.

"Thanks," Carter said.

"Well, I'll take it under consideration, but I'm also not gonna run up the score. No team deserves that," Coach said.

"Agreed," Riley said, nodding.

"But before they pull us..." Carter shot Riley a grin. "Let's have some fun, right?"

"You just want to show off for Ian," Nick complained. "I saw him down on the sideline."

"Sure, why wouldn't I?" Carter shrugged.

Riley laughed. "Even more fun than we're already having? Sure. Let's do that."

And okay, *some* of Carter's motivation was definitely to show off for Ian, who looked like he was having at least half as much fun as Carter was as he tore up the field.

Before they'd gone into the locker room, Ian had cornered him and with a wide grin on his face had tugged him close and murmured to him, *a hundred yards and a touchdown? Think you can double that?*

Carter knew he sure as hell wanted to—if he got the opportunity.

Ten minutes later, they jogged onto the field.

"Call another long one," Carter teased as Riley leaned into the huddle.

Riley's glare in his direction contained almost no heat at all. "You score and they're gonna pull us *now*," he reminded him. "We're gonna run the ball, with Darius, and you're gonna block."

"Or at least he's gonna try," Nick chimed in.

Carter smiled. "Joke's on you, 'cause I'm getting better."

"Long way to go, but you'll get there," Landry said, giving Carter an approving nod.

Sure enough, Riley called the running play on first down, and also on second down. Darius, Carter was sure, appreciated getting the ball and some really good work.

Riley ran for a first down on the next set.

But by then they were at mid-field, and while Carter was *willing* to block all the way down the field, that wasn't the kind of action he craved.

"Come on," he asked Riley again. "A fifteen yarder, that's all I want. Just to stretch my legs a bit."

Riley shook his head, but he was grinning.

"First down run. If Darius doesn't get it," he said, glancing over Darius' way, "I'll consider it."

"Fine, fine," Carter grumbled good-naturedly.

It was actually more fun than he'd realized, though, watching Darius, who didn't get as much play time in such a pass heavy offense, get the ball and do something with it.

He tore off runs of ten yards and then another one of seventeen, the last one Carter making the block that set him free to go down-field.

"Thanks, man," Darius said, as he returned to the huddle, smacking him lightly on the ass. "Great block."

"See!" Carter exclaimed. "I can do that, too!"

"Yes, darling, the sun shines right out of your ass," Nick retorted.

Riley glanced down at his wristband and called a play that they'd gone over a few times in practice that Carter had absolutely loved.

It was a straight shot down the sideline, Carter running at full speed, then unexpectedly crossing over deep in the end zone.

It was high risk, high reward.

Carter met Riley's eyes and nodded. If he fucked it up, there was a chance the safety could intercept Riley's pass, but he wasn't going to let that happen.

He lined up opposite the corner who'd gotten bored and complacent over the last two quarters, not expecting Carter to go deep, because he'd spent all these plays hanging back, helping Landry and the offensive line block for Darius' runs.

The bored expression on the corner's face was just going to make this so much more fucking amazing, Carter decided.

Carter dug his cleat into the turf, Cole snapped the ball to Riley, and then he took off, finding his stride almost immediately, as his legs were still so fresh. The corner lost a step at first, but caught up, and they were sprinting down the sideline together, the lights and colors of the Condors' stadium a blur across Carter's vision.

Timing was everything on this play. He glanced back once, saw Riley was not quite ready, and risked a second glance.

If the safety saw him looking back, he might guess that Carter was going to come his direction and he could possibly cross in front.

But Carter wasn't going to let that happen.

Beck never would've let him get away with it, but Beck was a way better safety than this dude.

On the second glance, Riley was pulling back, getting ready to throw. Carter met his eyes and then abruptly, suddenly, changed direction, ditching the corner and crossing right into the end zone—right into the path of the safety.

The safety responded faster than Carter had ever anticipated he might. Maybe he was Beck-caliber. But in any case, Carter knew he had to make this play now, because there was no way he was going to mar Riley's perfect game by letting his pass get intercepted.

Riley unloaded the ball, and Carter watched as it soared over the field. He had one advantage over the safety, who was now breathing down his neck, jostling his position—he caught passes from Riley in practice every day of the week, and he knew exactly how to time the catch.

Riley's pass dropped down, and right when it was at the very edge of his vertical, Carter launched himself up, pushing with every bit of his strength, stretching out his full body, and his fingertips just brushed the edge of the kidskin, before he grabbed the ball, pulling it tightly into his body as he came back down to the turf.

He hit hard, but he never let go of the ball.

The safety landed on top of him and Carter gave a loud *ooph* as the full weight of him drove him down.

But still, he didn't let go.

A second later, the safety finally begrudgingly moved and Carter leapt up waving the ball in his hands as the refs ran in, their arms up.

Touchdown.

Carter had a split second to decide. He could head over to the bright red cauldron that Riley had spent so much time in the first half or...or he could do something else.

In the end, it wasn't a decision at all.

He jogged over the Condors' sideline, right to where Ian was standing, at the far end of one of the long benches.

Ian's expression was full of excitement—and surprise.

He hadn't expected Carter to come over here.

Well, that made two of them.

Carter hadn't expected to come over here.

Carter hadn't expected him *at all*.

But there he was. The only man he'd ever loved—and Carter knew the only one he'd *ever* love.

He dropped to his knee in front of Ian and held out the football.

Surprise turned to shock turned to pure pleasure on Ian's face.

He took the football from Carter's hands and pressed it to his heart, the biggest smile on his face.

Yeah, Carter knew he couldn't have designed it any fucking better than that as he stood.

Ian smacked him lightly on the butt. "Still got a few yards to go," he pointed out, still smiling that big, wide, *I'm-charmed-and-I-never-wanted-to-be-but-that-ship-has-totally-fucking-sailed* smile.

Carter hoped he never stopped seeing it.

"Got it, baby," he said, giving Ian a mock salute.

"Well, you didn't *quite* get there," Ian teased as he and Carter stood together in the cafeteria.

It was decorated with streamers and balloons, all in Condors' red and yellow, and there was a massive papier mâché turkey at one end, right by the long buffet table, groaning with food that Ian hoped tasted as good as it smelled.

"Hey, I got damn close," Carter retorted, wrapping an arm around Ian's waist and pulling him in close. "I think I still get whatever it was you planned. No question. Wasn't that second touchdown worth it?"

Worth it? *Worth it?*

Ian had never imagined Carter giving him his touchdown ball. Or so publicly declaring himself to him, but it turned out it was basically every fantasy and every daydream wrapped up into one glorious package.

He hadn't let go of the ball for the rest of the game, afraid he'd lose it—even though the memory of it would last long after it deflated.

"It was everything," Ian said, "which you were definitely counting on. And which you *expected*."

Carter laughed.

"Come on, baby," Carter cooed, "I *know* you. You fucking loved it."

Yeah, he had.

Before the game, they still hadn't decided where they were going for the rest of the day. Ian had almost thought they might head home, pick up takeout on the way, and spend the rest of the evening cuddled on the couch—then the bed.

But after the game, it had felt right to come here.

To finish celebrating such an incredible win with the rest of the team.

Carter had suggested it when they'd met up outside the locker room after the game, and Ian hadn't hesitated for a moment. Because he'd already known they wouldn't be heading home after all. And honestly, it wasn't a hardship to celebrate with Carter's teammates—because they'd become Ian's friends, too.

"That was quite a display," Deacon said, wandering over to them, a beer bottle in his hand. He sounded amused. "Were you proposing eternal love with a...football instead of a ring? Are we gonna have another bachelor party on our hands soon?"

"Someday," Carter said, and Ian's heart hiccupped.

He hadn't really expected *that* was what Carter had meant. But it seemed Carter was serious.

"We're just taking our time, you know, *enjoying* each other," Carter said, shooting Ian a fierce smile. Then he turned back to Deacon. "Like you could be doing."

"Oh, not this again," Deacon complained. "Who would've guessed you'd become the world's most determined matchmaker after spending your entire life avoiding relationships?"

Ian considered himself a fairly observant person, and he didn't miss the hint of uncertainty and pain lingering in the back of Deacon's eyes. The *envy*.

Oh, Deacon might talk a big game, but he wanted it, too. What Riley and Landry had found. What Beck and Micah had re-ignited. What Carter and he had accidentally stumbled into and then held on to with both hands.

"It's pretty simple," Carter said. "You meet the right person, and you don't let them walk away. That's all."

"Oh, that's all," Deacon retorted sarcastically. "Not sure there *is* a right person, but I do know there's a turkey leg over there on the buffet, calling my name."

When he was gone, Carter turned to Ian. "He's in some serious denial."

"Yes, and no," Ian admitted.

Carter raised an eyebrow.

"I mean, he *knows*, so it's not really denial," Ian explained. "I understand a little of how he feels. Like he's caught between a rock and a hard place. I was there too, so I get it. You want what you want, even when you shouldn't. So sometimes...I don't know...you pretend."

"How did *you* pretend?" Carter asked.

Ian laughed. A little hysterically. Why had he brought this up? And *here*? Was he crazy? Maybe a little. Love did that to you. "You don't want to know."

"Trust me, I *do*," Carter insisted. He tugged his arm and drew him away from the majority of the crowd. "Come on, talk to me."

"I..." Ian rubbed the back of his neck with his hand and tried very hard not to flush bright red. Especially not in front of all these people. Carter's teammates. Professional acquaintances. Men and women that Ian might be negotiating with himself in a few short years.

"Tell me, baby," Carter repeated, and he didn't even need to deploy that particularly persuasive voice, because it wasn't like Ian was any good at denying him anything he wanted.

Anything they *both* wanted.

"I used to pretend that...well, that you'd hit on me and I'd say yes, and we'd..." Ian trailed off as Carter's brown eyes lit up with delight.

"You fantasized about saying yes when I hit on you? How? What? When? Tell me *everything*."

"I'd just...you know, imagine what it was like. What it could be like, between us. If I said yes." Ian shifted uncomfortably from one foot to the other. His khakis were not as loose as they'd been only a few moments ago.

Carter dipped his head lower, even closer to Ian's. Close enough to kiss. He murmured right into Ian's ear, his breath warm against Ian's skin. "I want to hear every detail. I want you to tell me every single thing you fantasized about, when you believed we weren't going to have sex."

"Later, when we get home," Ian practically begged. Or else, he was going to beg for something else, and they were *not* doing that here.

"Yeah," Carter agreed, nodding, the corner of his mouth tilting into a smirk. "You're going to be naked, in our bed."

"Our bed, huh?" But Ian had already started to think of it that way, too.

"Baby, it's always been yours. I've been keeping that spot warm, just for you. Didn't know it, at the time, but it's the truth," Carter said. "It's all yours."

"Just like you?" Ian questioned lightly, but he knew how serious he was.

Carter must've too, because just as his lips found Ian's, his fingers brushed against Ian's own, circling a certain finger. Not a proposal, necessarily, but Ian understood. It was a promise. An oath. An unbreakable vow.

"Just like me," Carter said.

Don't miss *The Play*, the final book of the Condors series and Deacon and Grant's book – coming in 2024.

And if you're too excited to wait, make sure to download the bonus scene, and learn: *1) how Deacon told Jem he was retiring* and *2) How Deacon and Grant met.*

Interested in reading more about Alec and Spencer? Check out *The Red Zone* on Amazon & Kindle Unlimited.

INTERESTED IN READING MORE OF
BETH'S BOOKS?

CHECK OUT A FULL LIST OF TILES
BY SCANNING THE QR CODE
OR VISITING HER WEBSITE

WWW.BETHBOLDEN.COM/BOOKLIST

WANT TO FOLLOW BETH?

MAKE SURE YOU NEVER
MISS A RELEASE?

SCAN THE QR CODE BELOW
OR VISIT HER WEBSITE
FOR A SOCIAL MEDIA LIST,
NEWSLETTER SIGNUP,
AND SO MUCH MORE!

WWW.BETHBOLDEN.COM/ABOUT

www.ingramcontent.com/pod-product-compliance
Lightning Source LLC
Chambersburg PA
CBHW060424310726
48977CB00001B/44